FIRST LIGHT

A NOVEL

S. ELLIOTT LAWRENCE

2

Stephen E Lawrence

"1-6"

3

*This book is dedicated to
my family, all of them, past
and present, who loved
the person who came back
and the person who tried to
tell a story for years.*

*It is also dedicated to
Keith Tucker, who gave me
strength to believe in myself
when there was every reason
not to; to Robert Kuta and
John Nagorka who let me learn
without making me look bad
and Ralph Dahl who showed
me how to be a leader.*

Preface

FIRST LIGHT is a novel, based on a real year in Vietnam and on events experienced as an infantry platoon leader with the 1st Air Cavalry Division for six and a half months and as Division Protocol Officer for the remainder of my time in country.

The attempt was to portray, as realistically as possible, what it feels like to learn about war first hand and the real struggle to rationalize a soldier's participation in such a war. Most soldiers feel they are the only one having such feelings of fear and grief and they are afraid to show it at the time.

Characters are often based on real people but there was no attempt to portray what those people actually did, only the kind of person they were. Fiction is fiction. Memories are not accurate. Any similarity to actual events is purely coincidental.

S. Elliott Lawrence, 2013

Contents

FIRST LIGHT

CHAPTER ONE - THE VOLUNTEER
MARCH 10, 1968

"Get the hell out of here!" First Sergeant Wiggins yelled at a recruit who was sweeping the linoleum floor within earshot. Second Lieutenant Kenneth McKenzie watched the soldier scoot out the front door of the orderly room, then turned back. Top Wiggins was smiling, his feet on the wooden desk, sipping a cup of "drill sergeant coffee" made by taking a hand full of coffee grounds and throwing them into a pan of boiling water. Two stars sitting on top of Top Wiggin's Combat Infantry man's Badge, sewn above his left shirt pocket, was a strong reminder of implied authority. His face resembled a shriveled orange peel topped with short, white hair, sparse on top. The acrid coffee smell permeated everything.

The first day McKenzie reported for duty, three months earlier, "Top" had invited him into the back room, shut the door and threatened him. He'd done it all in one breath.

"Sir, you can call me Top if you like but I will tell you one thing now and this is between you and me. I got thirty years in this man's army and you got less than one and I don't like smart ass second lieutenants just out of OCS, too dumb and wet behind the ears to know it and I don't care what you do with your career and I'll try like hell to help you in any way that I can but I promise you one thing. If you mess with me in any way, I'll have your butt in Vietnam inside of sixty days. We got a deal, sir?"

The First Sergeant's green fatigue uniform was starched crisp that first day and the toes on his airborne boots shined like glass. He looked exactly the same every day. McKenzie stepped a little closer to the desk.

"Top? You remember that first day when I reported in and you threatened me?"

"Yes, sir. I threaten them all. It's good for 'em."

"Was that just bluff or can you do me a favor? I've decided to volunteer early to go to Vietnam so I can pick my unit. I want you to get me orders to the First Air Cavalry Division."

"Oh, you do, do you?" Top Wiggins took his boots off the desk and stood up.

"You think I was shitting you, don't you young lieutenant?" The old soldier reached down and put his hand on the phone. "You sure about this? Cause if you are, I can call the Pentagon right now."

McKenzie nodded and swallowed hard against a pit of uncertainty. Before he could blink, Top picked up the phone and called.

"Major Rose? This is First Sergeant Wiggins down here at Fort Benning. I got me a young shave tail who tells me he wants to go to Vietnam." Top Wiggins paused and looked up, then said, "...early. He wants to go to the First Cav. Let me put him on the phone."

Major Rose told McKenzie his orders would be there in two weeks.

McKenzie had walked into the Officer's Club on Harmony Church Road earlier that week. He needed a drink to wash the red Georgia dust out of his throat. The walls were lined with cheap plywood paneling with a sort of rubbed in walnut stain. A dozen tables, arranged in a half circle around a square parquet dance floor, were nothing more than round cuts of three quarter inch plywood with metal rings around the edge, similar to hoops that hold barrel staves in place. Each table was supported by a single metal pedestal. Johnny Mathis was singing Misty in the background. Two couples sat together eating dinner.

McKenzie approached a captain who was sitting at the bar nursing a drink.

"Good afternoon, sir. Kenneth McKenzie. Mind if I have a seat?"

"Nope. Steve Morton. Glad to meet you, lieutenant." The officer reached out and shook McKenzie's offered hand. On his right shoulder was a First Air Cavalry patch and above his left shirt pocket was a Combat Infantry Man's Badge, which meant he'd been in combat more than 30 days.

"How long you been back from Nam, sir?" McKenzie asked.

"About six months. You going?"

"Not yet, sir. I applied for helicopter flight school when I was in OCS and I'm waiting for my orders. In the mean time, they got me training troops over on Sand Hill."

Captain Morton was a big, stocky man with a very short crew cut and dark eyes focused squarely on McKenzie. He reached

up, stroked a thin mustache and leaned sideways against the edge
of the bar.

"The best advice I can give you is don't go to flight
school. Particularly, not helicopter flight school. Go to the Cav.
You're an infantry officer." He tapped the crossed rifles on
McKenzie's lapels. "That's what you were trained to do. There are
enough crazy warrant officers willing to fly helicopters anywhere,
anytime in Vietnam. One way or another, you will be going to
Vietnam but you're needed on the ground, in the Cav," he said,
picking up his drink.

"Sir? I was told the life expectancy of an infantry officer
was damn short."

Captain Morton raised his eyebrows. "It can be but it's a
damned site shorter for helicopter pilots. There are men out there
that need you, McKenzie and the Cav is the best place for you to
do what the US Army trained you to do."

McKenzie stayed for a couple more hours talking to
Captain Morton about the Cav and how they operated. Morton's
tour had been as a platoon leader and he told McKenzie there were
some important things he would need to remember. The first was
obviously to pick the right unit and the second was, "You don't
know everything. Learn from your men." The third was given with
strong emphasis, "Take care of your men and they will take care of
you. The chain of command won't."

JUNE 17, 1968

"So what was officer candidate school like, Lieutenant?"
the soldier asked.

McKenzie was sitting next to the plane's emergency door, fighting a weird compulsion to open it and get sucked out into the clear, blue sky. He might fly like an eagle for a while but the end would be ugly. He was wondering if that was like going to Vietnam when the question brought him back inside the plane.

Private First Class Wright was sitting in the aisle seat, no one between them. His khaki shirt was stretched tight on either side of his buttons. McKenzie, 190 pounds of muscle, could do a hundred push-ups nonstop. In OCS, he was Pugil Stick champion easily taking care of Candidate Hardy, the biggest guy in the company. Guys like Wright scared him. Maybe they were the real threat. If they couldn't move, how could they do their job?

"Why do you ask?" McKenzie said, turning to look at Wright.

"Oh, I thought about going to OCS once but after basic training, I decided I didn't need any more harassment."

McKenzie gritted his teeth. The plane ride was taking too long. He reached up and turned the cool air to high.

"You better hope that kind of harassment saves your butt, soldier. It's meant to weed out the weak hearts and to make sure you get an officer who won't break under fire. You're infantry. You ought to know that."

"So what unit do you think you will be going to Lieutenant?" Wright said the word, "lieutenant", slowly, as if he didn't like to say it.

"I don't have to guess. I know. It's the First Air Cavalry Division, the one with all the helicopters. You have heard of them, right?"

"Yea, I heard of them but I thought everyone wanted to go to an airborne unit like the 82nd or the 101st or maybe even the Big Red One."

McKenzie leaned on the armrest in Wright's direction. "You really don't know much about Vietnam, do you? The Cav's got more helicopters than the 82nd and the 101st put together. That means gun ships, medical evacuation birds, resupply and troop carriers, large cranes and Chinooks that can carry any artillery piece you can name. You're damned right I know where I'm going. I specifically asked for the First Cav. You better hope you get the Cav and not some unit like the Ninth Infantry down in the swamps or maybe even the Americal Division which hardly has any helicopters." McKenzie knew he was lecturing, so he stopped.

Wright's face got red. "Excuse me, sir." His eyes narrowed to an angry slit. "Officers might get those kinds of choices but nobody asked me. They drafted my butt, shoved me through basic and advanced infantry training and put me on this here plane to Vietnam."

Wright picked up a Newsweek magazine and began flipping through the pages. McKenzie looked back out the window to see if he could spot land.

June 18, 1968

When McKenzie stepped out onto the plane's stairway after landing in Cam Ranh Bay, Vietnam, the air made him gasp. It felt like a sauna turned up as high as it would go. Not even the hottest summer along the Columbia River in Oregon, where McKenzie grew up, compared to this. He walked down the stairs and crossed the runway toward a receiving door marked, "Incoming Officers Report Here". In his right hand, was his duffel bag stuffed with every military possession he owned and a few civies, his left hand held the orders.

Private Wright yelled good luck to him. McKenzie yelled the same back, suddenly worried about him. He stood for a moment and watched Wright join a line in front of the "Incoming Enlisted Report Here" sign.

A helicopter drifted slowly between them, hovering above the shimmering hot runway. Heat waves distorted the image but McKenzie saw it - a First Air Cavalry patch painted on the helicopter's nose. McKenzie felt like yelling but he didn't know what to yell.

He walked into a typical military building, resembling a metal warehouse more than anything else. The gray concrete floor held four metal tables at the far wall and behind each sat an Army clerk. There was a hum of conversation echoing off the walls. A line of officers stood in front of each table. He looked around. Some officers were laughing or talking as if they were going to the movies while others stood mute, looking pensive. McKenzie headed for the end of the line in front of a table with initials I through R on a sign hung on the metal wall above. Twenty minutes later, he stepped forward and handed his orders assigning him to the First Air Cavalry Division, to Specialist Fourth Class Brown, who read through them, noisily flipping the pages.

"Sir, I'm sorry but these orders don't mean nothin' over here," Brown said, looking up. "We just filled our quota for the Cav yesterday. Right now, all new officers are going to the

Americal Division. You need to report over to the officer's billets. Here's a map of the compound. You're looking for building six. Don't get too comfy though, your plane leaves in about four hours."

"Look, Specialist. Obviously you don't understand." McKenzie bent over slightly so he could talk in a low voice. "I don't give a rat's ass about quotas. I volunteered to come to Vietnam six months early so I could pick my unit. That unit is the First Cav and its been guaranteed to me by the Pentagon. I had my First Sergeant arrange it, so you just tell me where to go to get there."

He straightened back up. McKenzie's heart was banging inside his chest. He was revved up. His adrenaline was pumping and he felt scared. He didn't know what to do. He didn't want to make a scene but he wanted to go to the Cav.

"Sir, I'm sorry. These kinds of orders aren't any good here. We got a war that tells us where we send replacement officers. Right now the Americal has fifty percent casualties on officers. They need replacements. I'll have someone bring your new orders when they're cut. Meanwhile, I'd suggest you go relax. It may be the last rest you get for a while."

"Damn it, Specialist." McKenzie leaned over and put his hand on the desk so he could get closer. "You listen to me. You can tell whoever gives you your quotas that this officer isn't going anywhere but the First Cav or he ain't goin'. You can tell whoever stamps those things or throws the dice in the air that if they don't send me to the Cav, they might as well sweep out a cell in the stockade because I'm not going to any other unit, especially the American Division."

McKenzie ripped the orders out of Specialist Brown's hand, threw his duffel bag over his shoulders and walked out the door. He was almost running. The First Cav had become his security blanket. He had seized onto the idea that if he did this, if he had faith in the Cav, it would bring him back home to the banks of the Columbia River. That's how you get through tough situations. You grab a straw of cheat grass and you bite down on it.

He wasn't sweating any more. He felt cold. His stomach was knotted up and his legs felt like rubber. It reminded him of his first fist fight when one of the kids at school had called him a dirty Indian. His parents could look the other way but McKenzie had fought.

When he found Building Six and went inside, there were rows of Army bunks, each with a sheet and a green Army blanket folded up under a white pillow, on both sides. Three duffel bags lay alone on three of the beds. McKenzie threw his onto the nearest empty one and walked out the opposite end to go look for a beer. If he was going to jail, he wasn't going sober.

"Hey Lieutenant!"

McKenzie turned to see Spec Four Brown running toward him.

"Here," the Specialist said, thrusting a piece of paper forward. "Take this boarding pass over to gate 32 and give them a copy of your orders." He pointed toward a chain link fence with a gate. On the other side was a C-130 transport plane being loaded with huge crates.

"I got to thinkin'," Brown said, breathing heavily from the run. "That cargo plane is going north to An Khe where the First Cav is. I figure if you get up there with your orders, they'll find a place for you. But sir, this ain't official. You're on your own." Brown smiled.

McKenzie ran back to the building, grabbed his duffel bag off the bunk and ran toward gate 32 as hard as he could.

CHAPTER TWO - IN COUNTRY
(JUNE 18, 1968 - 364 DAYS LEFT)

AN KHE

The big cargo plane descended clumsily out of the clouds toward An Khe. McKenzie looked down at the golf course, the Cav's affectionate name for a large, square of green grass with two landing strips. Dozens of helicopters sat on individual pads of concrete. Two light helicopters lifted up and floated over the hill to his left. From his right, six UH-1 troop helicopters full of soldiers, came over the trees in a straight line like a flock of geese, spread out and landed on the golf course.

An air traffic control tower sat to the North next to a small metal airport building with a large painted sign at least twenty feet tall and forty feet long, which read, "Home of the First Air Cavalry Division." It was painted in the distinctive black and yellow colors of the Cav. McKenzie had read how those colors were chosen by Mom Dorsey, wife of an earlier commander, who was asked to design a patch that could be seen easily. He liked the way it looked.

No one inside the small airport building was expecting new personnel and no one offered him a ride. After thirty minutes of nosing around, he caught a ride to the orderly room with Captain Roth, the pilot who had flown the C-130 up. During the flight, Captain Roth quizzed McKenzie.

"So, how come you couldn't find a desk job that would keep your ass out of the jungle, Lieutenant? I've already carried a bunch of you guys out of Cam Ranh Bay so far and I still haven't got a straight answer."

"I guess I don't have one either, sir."

"You know much about the First Cav, Lieutenant?" Captain Roth had leaned back and turned to look at McKenzie for an answer.

"Well, I guess I know as much as I could without being here, sir. I've read everything I could get my hands on including how they began as the Eleventh Air Assault Group back in 1965."

"No. I mean do you know what the Cav's been up to lately in I Corps? It ain't been pretty."

McKenzie shook his head and started to say something but was suddenly thrown out of his seat backwards into the cargo bay hitting his head on the plane's fuselage as the plane banked away from green tracers rising from the ground. McKenzie crawled back into the navigator's seat after the plane was put back to level and secured the seat belt he had previously neglected. His head was bleeding where he'd hit the fuselage. He held his handkerchief hard against his forehead and leaned over to look out the window.

Craters stitched the earth in long, staggered rows, disrupting the unreal congruence of endless square rice paddies. Bomb craters, the pilot told him. "Grunts often bath in them if they hit fresh water," he explained. What a sight, McKenzie thought. Soldiers, dirty and tired, diving into a crater of clear, blue water. Naked, half-brown boys from Clearwater, Kansas or Boonesville, Mississippi, screaming off the lip to splash into other soldiers already floating amid soap suds generated by serious bathers. The soul brother, the Jew, the southern rebel, the Mexican, and the American Indian, all sharing the same water. More sharing than a hippie festival. At least, he hoped it would be like that. He remembered hot summer days on the basalt cliffs bordering the Columbia River where he and his native friends would dive into the cold, blue water and be dried off after by the warm wind. He pressed the handkerchief harder against his head.

McKenzie was assigned a bunk by the night orderly. A Spec Four checked his orders the next morning and told him to board a bus parked outside. The driver said to bring his duffel bag. He and a dozen other new arrivals were driven down a long, dusty road filled with so many pot holes the driver only avoided them by making spasmodic jerks on the steering wheel. Eventually, the bus crossed a small bridge and pulled into an area containing one wooden structure, one large tent and one small tent.

Orientation was held in the smaller tent full of metal chairs. It began with an indoctrination speech given by a thin, First Lieutenant, wearing coke bottle glasses who handed each soldier one form for notifying their next of kin in case they were wounded or killed and another for naming insurance beneficiaries.

"Pack all your state side military and civilian shit into your duffel bag," the officer said. "You won't be needing anything you got in there. Grab your dop kit, one book and your stationary. Everything else you leave behind. Take it up the hill and check it, then go down to supply and pick up your new gear." It was a speech delivered in a monotone from too many orientations.

McKenzie and the others walked up a hill toward several long, dismal looking wooden buildings filled with storage spaces separated by chicken wire. There were four levels of wooden shelves inside holding row after row of duffel bags, each tagged with a soldier's name, military number and next of kin. A layer of dust several inches deep covered everything. McKenzie threw his bag where he was told, causing a mushroom cloud of dust to explode around it and got the hell out of there.

He'd held back his journal, a few pictures, toiletries and Hemingway's memoir, "A Movable Feast", a love story about when the writer and his first wife, Hadley spent their early years in Paris in the 20's. He wanted it for times when he would be lonely for the one he loved back home, for memories of pure love and for things that were true. Returning to the officer's billets, it was time for a nap.

"I'll be back around nineteen hundred hours and take you over to the officer's club," the driver shouted as he shut the bus door with a bang.

It seemed like only minutes before the driver was honking him awake from outside. In the bus, he was greeted by Captain Roth, who was still waiting for his next flight, two infantry lieutenants, O'Kusky and Kingman, and a Major Sparkman, who said he was returning for his second tour. The bus hurried across the compound in the direction of green hills outside the perimeter and stopped before a building that might have been a sharecropper's shack in southern Texas.

The dirty brown, wooden officer's club, well ventilated with wire windows, was scabbed together with very little protection. There were no sand bags along the walls, no protective roofing and it felt too close to the concertina wire outside. Two sergeants were pouring generous drinks behind a rough looking hand made bar. The place was full of dirty and weathered officers, all dressed in bleached jungle fatigues.

McKenzie looked around for officers with a CIB patch sewn above their left shirt pocket. It wasn't long before the FNGs or "fucking new guys," which included McKenzie, were being regaled by stories from the veterans of killing "gooks," springing ambushes and fire fights. Some of the stories were grotesque and he felt uneasy listening, so after an hour, he wandered outside to wait for the bus. That was not the kind of conversation he was looking for.

The club closed and the other officers he'd come with wandered outside to find no bus waiting. McKenzie was sitting on a large rock. Several officers stood off to his right smoking and talking loudly. He had spent his time outside staring up at the sky looking for familiar constellations and listened to night sounds that were strange and unfamiliar to him. A hint of breeze cooled the air. Maybe he would get a good night's sleep.

His thoughts were interrupted by the roar of a loud engine followed by the sight of a jeep careening around the corner of the club with Major Sparkman at the wheel. He slid the jeep to a stop and stood up with his hands gripping the top of a dirty windshield.

"It's an old Army tradition, boys. It's called midnight requisition. Jump in." McKenzie and the rest clambered aboard and hung on as the Major managed to hit every bump and pot hole he could find. McKenzie staggered into his barracks, crawled onto his bunk and listened to the disappearing sound of the jeep as Major Sparkman headed off to stash the evidence. He closed his eyes to the sound of distant artillery firing into the night.

CAMP EVANS

JUNE 20, 1968

McKenzie and the other FNGs were driven out to the airfield the next morning for their flight north to Camp Evans where they would receive in-country training. Major Sparkman was already waiting inside the small building.

"Hey! Good luck to all you short rounds. I'm gonna pass on the basic training. Been there, done that," he said. He was a large man with a pock marked face from teenage acne and his shirt was already sweat soaked even though the morning air was still cool. He picked up his pack and walked out to a waiting helicopter.

"Rank has its privilege," McKenzie said, sitting down on a white, plastic chair next to Lieutenant O'Kusky, who was slightly overweight for an infantry officer. Then again, everyone there looked out of place with their new jungle fatigues, boots, steel pot and backpacks. Ammunition, canteens and other essentials would come from their company's supply. O'Kusky, who had not been very talkative, told McKenzie he hoped they would make it back there in a year without getting too many others killed. They agreed to drink a beer over the deal in a year as a C-130 Caraboo lumbered down the runway toward them. Its propellers slowed to a stop, making a whirring sound like the playing cards McKenzie used to attach to his bicycle frame to slap against the wheel spokes.

It was a short trip. At An Khe, they climbed into an open two and a half ton truck, which drove them under a sign that read, "First Air Cavalry Training Center" and into a compound that was nothing more than a bald patch of compacted red clay, very similar to the dirt at Fort Benning. It had been ground into a fine powder, inches thick, which floated everywhere. There was literally no appreciable vegetation anywhere.

An officer dressed in full Cavalry hat and boots greeted them as they climbed down off the truck.

"The next couple of days will include basic information on the mission of the First Air Cavalry Division, some physical training, exposure to CS gas and demonstrations of air mobile tactics. Officers' tents are to your left, enlisted to the right. Find a bunk, gentlemen. We'll see you back here at oh eight hundred tomorrow." The officer sounded as if he never tired of saying the same thing over and over.

Tents were lined up along straight lines with sharply cut rain trenches all around. McKenzie shouldered his pack and headed for the officer's tent area, entering the first one that appeared to have empty bunks. Hot, humid air hung inside in a vaporous profusion of body and canvas smells. A familiar shoulder holster lay on the bunk next to the front door. It belonged to Major Sparkman who apparently had not escaped the training. McKenzie had mentally nicknamed him the "True Believer" after listening to his speeches about the war.

An hour later Major Sparkman walked into the tent without explanation, and assumed command.

"Most of you new officers probably do not have green underwear, so here," he said triumphantly, reaching into a bag and throwing several pair on each bunk as he walked toward the back.

"McKenzie, I understand you're going to First of the Fifth," he said.

"How do you know that, sir?"

"I make it my business to know. Lieutenant Colonel Fishmuth, who's running that outfit, is a loose cannon. I met him several years ago in the states. He bragged about what he would do when he finally got to Vietnam and had his own battalion to command. I probably shouldn't say anything but I thought you deserved fair warning. Somebody once did me that favor and I'm just passing it on. This war is all about field grade officers making their careers and don't you believe otherwise. You just worry about your ass and your men."

McKenzie thanked the major and rolled up his new, green underwear, placing it into a plastic bag to go inside the plastic liner inside his new backpack. He considered the information about Colonel Fishmuth to be idle gossip but he would judge for himself. Everyone had told him underwear was useless. Most soldiers went without any to prevent crotch rot and restriction. He decided to cut these into strips for weapon cleaning.

The following several days involved bleacher sitting, watching demonstrations of air-mobile tactics, soldiers rappelling out of helicopters and a brief course on how to call in artillery. Instructors talked a lot about Custer's Seventh Cavalry. The heat was thick and there was no escape from the weight of it. McKenzie and the others sat sweating and perched on hard, wooden bleachers for hours trying to concentrate. How could anyone walk the jungle trails or fight, let alone carry a weapon and a full pack plus ammunition in such heat? Salt tablets were supposed to protect the soldier from loss of water but after the first couple bounced back and exited his stomach, he had stopped taking them. He was drinking a ton of water and yet, never had to pee - sweating everything out.

Official orders were handed out on the third day of training. Sparkman was right. McKenzie was going to Delta Company, First of the Fifth, commanded by Captain Moore. Kingman, an ROTC helicopter pilot, and O'Kusky were both going to First of the Ninth, a helicopter scout unit. Lieutenant Kregor, who had come in on another flight and joined their group, was going to First of the Seventh.

"Hey, Kregor," Major Sparkman said walking over to where he was laying on his bunk reading his orders. "I think you're just what the Seventh Cav needs. Airborne, ranger, West Point, gung ho, ready to go. Just don't get your ass shot up with all that enthusiasm. Now, McKenzie here, he's the one we're gonna have to worry about: a Second Lieutenant, who volunteered to come early with no air borne or ranger patches and no jungle training. What's his company commander gonna do with him? Maybe you ought to pass some of your special training on to him, so he'll survive the year," Sparkman said, turning around.

"By the way, McKenzie, you part Indian?"

"Mostly Irish but I got some WyAm Indian in me, why?"

"Well, there you go. You think you know something we don't cause you're part Indian?" Major Sparkman laughed as if inviting others to join in.

Kregor looked over the top of his orders. "McKenzie's on his own. I don't know what he's up to but I got enough to worry about and I get the feeling he doesn't want anyone thinkin' they have to nursemaid him anyway. That right, McKenzie?"

"I think I'll be all right but I do appreciate Major Sparkman's concern. Like Kregor said, you boys worry about yourself and I'll be OK after I get all this fine First Cav training."

Kregor grunted a hoorah. "You tell 'em, McKenzie."

There were brief goodbyes on the fourth morning at Camp Evans. It was you go your way and I'll go mine and hopefully, we'll all meet up in a year. McKenzie was directed to climb aboard a UH-1 troop carrier headed for Landing Zone Jane, up near the village of Quang Tri in I Corps. He knew from looking at a map he'd been given that to the West was the A Shau Valley and to the North, the city of Hue and Khe Sanh, where the Marines had been besieged for so many days. He did not watch any of the others board or fly away.

He tried to imagine what the next year would be like as the helicopter lifted up slowly, then dipped its nose and slid over the ground, reminding him of a pelican skimming a lake for fish. His head was full of rumors, in-country training, war stories and his own heritage and beliefs, all mixed together. He was being pulled north toward men who he hoped wanted and needed a new platoon leader.

LZ JANE

The pilot flew north along the coast, over white beaches and the blue water of the South China Sea and then banked hard left. LZ Jane, a reddish, brown mound of dirt at the end of a thin, dirt road, bordered by a rice patty to the East and a long expanse of mountains to the West, eventually came into view. It was ringed by huge bunkers covered with brown sand bags lining the perimeter of a compound approximately five hundred meters across. Inside the perimeter were dirty, brown tents in rows here and there. One large bunker sat at the highest point, in the center, with four tall antennas sticking out the top.

The compound also contained four, 105 Howitzer artillery guns, two, 155 Howitzers and one eight inch gun, all pointed in different directions. The big, eight inch, which was pointed straight at the mountain range, fired a gigantic two hundred pound high explosive round and was deadly accurate. Concertina wire rimmed the outer line of bunkers. There were also five one hundred gallon cans, containing foo gas, a liquid jell made of gasoline and napalm, which he had learned about at An Khe. They had been strategically placed behind the wire. When ignited, the foo gas would spread a burning, hot hell on anyone in front of it for a range of one hundred meters. It was there as a last resort if the LZ was about to be overrun.

One of four replacement privates also riding in the helicopter yelled over the din of engine noise, "Hey, Lieutenant. I hear First of the Fifth has had a lot of casualties in the last few months. You know anything about Charlie Company? That's where we're goin'."

"Nope. I'm headed for Delta," he shouted back. "I'm as new as you guys. If I was you, I'd wait and find out. No use guessing about it."

McKenzie had been listening to them speculate about combat the entire trip. He wished them all good luck as he climbed out. A First Sergeant Kauffman was waiting to greet him.

COLONEL FISHMUTH

"Welcome to Jane, sir. Our battalion CO, Colonel Fishmuth, wants to see you first thing. Give me your pack and weapon. He's inside that big bunker, top of the hill. I'll walk you up there and then you can find me afterwards at our company tent over there." He pointed to a row of tents.

McKenzie could see Kauffman was giving him the once over. The sergeant smelled of alcohol and spoke like he was protecting loose dentures. His short hair was pepper gray, his skin rough and full of worry lines. "You still a butter bar, sir? How the hell did you get over here so fast?" he said.

"I volunteered to come early, Sarge, so I could come to the First Cav."

"Who told you the Cav was so special, sir?"

"Friends at Fort Benning who had already been with the Cav. You disagree, Top?"

"No sir. I just never seen a Second Lieutenant show up over here with no ranger training or nothing. You better keep your ass down when you get out in the field or you ain't gonna make it, that's all. Sergeant Koop has run First Platoon for the last several months cause the last guy didn't know what he was doin' or how to take care of his men and that's where you're goin'."

McKenzie stopped walking. "What does that mean?" He got no answer. Sergeant Kauffman walked ahead and disappeared into the command bunker. When he came out, he was followed by a Sergeant Major Butner, who offered a sloppy salute and told McKenzie to follow him. He gave no other greeting. Kauffman walked away.

Inside the bunker were four radios manned by enlisted personnel. One overhead bulb shrouded the inside with dim light. Along the sides were several bunks with sleeping bags. A Lieutenant Colonel sat ramrod straight behind a small, olive green, portable table, perched on ammo boxes. He was smoking a cigarette in a silver holder stuck in the corner of his mouth like FDR used to do and looking at a map. He had no visible upper lip but his lower lip was full. Before McKenzie could stop, the officer asked crisply, without looking up, "You Lieutenant McKenzie?"

"Yes, sir. Lieutenant McKenzie reporting for duty, sir."

"Well, that's good Lieutenant. I'm Lieutenant Colonel Fishmuth. I need officers," he said, looking up for the first time. He wore thick, black military glasses and nervously twitched his nose like a rabbit. He studied McKenzie for a minute and then removed his glasses. His mouth slowly dropped open and his eyes got bigger. He had no eyebrows to speak of.

"Jesus Christ, man. You're a goddamned second lieutenant. How the hell did I get you? Sergeant Major? Did you know I was getting a second lieutenant?"

He didn't wait for an answer. He stood up and walked around the desk hitting his knee on the edge, which caused him to limp toward McKenzie.

"Let me see your orders," he said, rubbing his right knee. McKenzie unfolded the copy he had put into his leg pocket and handed it over. After reading the orders through several times, flipping the pages back and forth, the Colonel's eyes narrowed to a squint. He stepped back and looked McKenzie up and down, from his boots to his hair.

"Just when the hell did you graduate from OCS?" he said.

"November 22, 1967, sir."

"Well, no shit. Do you think I didn't know it had to be 1967? You're so God damned new you smell like baby powder. What's your experience in this man's Army, if any?"

"I was a training officer on Sand Hill at Fort Benning for two training cycles."

"So, how did you get here so soon?"

" I volunteered for Vietnam early so I could request the First Cav, sir."

"Oh, you did, huh? Did you request ranger training, Lieutenant?"

"No, sir."

"Airborne?"

"No, sir."

"Jungle training?"

"No, sir."

"Why in the hell not? I need fully trained officers in my unit." The Colonel's voice was getting louder with each question.

His neck was turning a blotchy pink and he was now practically standing on top of McKenzie, having advanced with each question. His breath smelled like tobacco and he looked angry. McKenzie stood his ground, took a deep breath and tried to sound calm.

"I made a conscious decision, sir. I wanted to come early so I could request the First Cav and I did not want to be brainwashed before coming over here. I believe I have good common sense and I did not want to lose my ability to exercise it."

The Colonel stepped back and turned toward his small table, still limping. "Well, I'll be damned. Sergeant Major, did you hear this shit?" He sat down, put his glasses back on and looked up at McKenzie.

"I think you, Second Lieutenant McKenzie, and I are going to have a problem. You are going to go out into the field and take over Delta Company's First Platoon and you will not fuck up on my watch. You hear me, Lieutenant? You do everything Captain Moore tells you to do and if you do not, I will have you up on courts martial so fast it will make your arrogant head spin, that is, if you haven't already gone home in a body bag. Are we clear?"

"Yes, sir."

"Now, you get the hell out of my command bunker and tell Sergeant Kauffman to put you on the first available helicopter out to the field."

McKenzie saluted but Colonel Fishmuth looked away and began yelling at his Sergeant Major. McKenzie walked back toward the entrance and stood there for a minute waiting for his eyes to adjust to the bright sun light, listening to his new battalion commander yell something about no more God damned second lieutenants.

DELTA COMPANY

McKenzie searched a row of dirt-laden tents until he found one with a wooden sign that said, Delta Company and went in. One of the clerks jumped up and started issuing him ammo and grenades. He added a couple of canteens, c-rations and two long-range, freeze dried meals. The company radio was monitoring Delta's transmissions in the background, so McKenzie sat down to listen. Sergeant Kauffman said there were no helicopters available to pick him up. They were all out supporting the battalion.

"The whole battalion's been sent in to help Second of the Eighth corner an NVA regiment in the village of Bien An. Our executive officer, Lieutenant Gill, is running Delta because Captain Moore is in Danang. Normally, the exec would brief you or I would, but today, I'm kinda busy. You'll just have to pick it up as you go and I'll try to fill you in when I can." Sergeant Kauffman turned back to the radio.

That was it. The next morning was the same. Sergeant Bush, the lead clerk, a laconic faced kid with red hair and freckles, issued McKenzie cleaning solution, mosquito repellant, several large gauge bandages, a thin camouflaged blanket called a poncho liner, a poncho half, which was only half a tent, an inflatable rubber mattress, a plastic pouch to cover his map and a roster of everyone in Delta Company. Several names had been crossed off. On the north side of the tent stood a grease board with all the company names on it with those same names crossed off.

Around ten, the Exec called. "Double Time Five, this is Double Time Four, has the new oscar arrived? Over."

Sergeant Kauffman picked up the black hand set hanging on the side of the PRC-25 radio. "Double Time Four, that's affirmative. Over."

"Roger that, Five. His ride is inbound. Pick up at eleven hundred hours. You copy? Over."

"Roger that, Four. Can he get in at your location? Over." Kauffman looked at McKenzie.

"Maybe. I got two more kilo india alphas. You ready to copy? Over."

"Roger that, go." The First Sergeant stretched out the radio cord so he could reach the grease board and drew a line through the names of two soldiers. The other clerk, a Spec Four named Murray, got up from a table where he'd been writing a letter and walked over to the other end of the board and wrote the same names below a list with the heading, KIA, which stood for 'killed in action.' He looked back at McKenzie without expression, then moved to the other end where Kauffman had been and wrote, 'Lt. McKenzie' at the top of the roster for First Platoon.

On his way back, Murray stopped at a filing cabinet, pulled out some forms, returned to his table, pushed the letter aside and began filling the forms out. McKenzie went over to see if his roster matched what was on the board. Murray looked up. He had a sad look that told McKenzie these weren't the first names he'd had to deal with.

"You want me to show you what's going on out there now, sir?" Kauffman said, as he brought over a large map and spread it out on the ground. The smell of hot, tent canvas seemed thicker near the ground.

"You're gonna like Sergeant Koop. He's twenty-two and he's an E-six shake and bake. A good man. He's been runnin' the platoon since Lieutenant Evans got wounded. Kind of a freak accident. A grenade in his bunker one night."

McKenzie looked into Kauffman's face. His forehead was squeezed into a million wrinkles but his eyes said nothing. "Anyway, you go out there and listen to Sergeant Koop and you'll be OK. Now let me show you on this here map."

While he was pointing out how the battle at Bien An had developed, Kauffman informed McKenzie that the exec was not at all happy about being back in the field. He had less than thirty days left in country and was very eager to leave the 'Nam. He ended with, "If you know what I mean." Then he got up and walked toward the tent door. "Let me show you where that whirly bird's comin' in, sir. You might want to grab your gear."

The two men walked slowly over to the helicopter pad, which was no more than a hard patch of baked dirt reserved for such, marked for the pilots by a circle of chalk. McKenzie looked up at a whitish blue sky, the colors so vivid they reminded him of an early colorized movie. Kauffman said, "You sit tight and I'll be back with the mail."

McKenzie's bowels suddenly felt weak and loose. He had fifteen minutes to contemplate what was about to happen to him. He headed for the crapper.

"Grab your socks, sir. That bird's inbound," Kauffman said, pounding on the latrine door. McKenzie sprinted out of the commode toward his equipment, which was already engulfed in a cloud of dust from a small helicopter that had just landed. He grabbed his backpack and rifle before backing away.

ONE SIX

The pilot, small and very young looking, pointed to the passenger door. McKenzie approached bent over under the whirling blades and climbed into the open, glass bubble cockpit, stowing his gear behind the seat. He put on the radio headset and microphone handed to him and buckled in. Kauffman threw the mailbag onto his lap. The helicopter was nothing but Plexiglass, top to bottom, and only enough floor to accommodate pedals. The pilot looked at McKenzie, "Warrant Officer Bowman at your service. Welcome to the Nam."

Sergeant Kauffman stood back grinning like a mother bear watching one of her cubs and waved. The helicopter lifted, wobbled a little, then shot over the concertina wire and went careening into a small gully before finally beginning to gain altitude.

"What unit you going to, Lieutenant?"

It was a question shouted over the din of rotor and engine noise, which came to McKenzie as a far away voice in his earphones. Bowman was making that small helicopter dance through the trees, flying below tree top level, tipping sideways to pass at the last second, the blades more vertical to the ground than horizontal. A tree limb slapped the bottom of the glass bubble. McKenzie thought he was going to hyperventilate. He sucked in as much air as he could get.

"I'm taking over First Platoon, Delta Company, First of the Fifth," he said.

"Oh, yea, I know them. We've been supporting them at Bien An where you're goin'. You meet Captain Moore yet? He's one of the best. They need a new One Six. One five is just a young kid but he's damn good."

McKenzie stopped looking at the blur of trees going by and looked at Bowman.

"One six?"

"That's your radio call sign, Lieutenant. That's going to be your name for the next six months. Every platoon leader is a Six and since you're gonna be with First Platoon, you're One Six. Company Commander's are just Six. Don't worry. You'll get the hang of it and I'll be around to help when you run into the shit." Bowman smiled at McKenzie as if he hadn't told everything he knew.

McKenzie remembered hearing call signs on the company radio but he hadn't paid too much attention. He'd been more interested in what was being said.

BIEN AN

They flew toward the South China Sea. There were few trees. White sand ran toward the water where scrub brush ended. Bowman tipped his helicopter to the left, flew up the coastline for about ten minutes and began losing elevation. He called ahead and asked where he could drop his "cargo."

"We're goin' in Lieutenant. It's been hot down there so you get your ass off my bird when I touch down 'cause I ain't stayin' long."

Bowman was screaming over the sound of the popping rotor blades as he descended. He dropped in fast toward sand dunes and a row of coastal trees that seemed to appear out of nowhere. Smoke spiraled up from several areas on the beach. Up ahead was a cloud of yellow smoke spreading just on the other side of the trees. Bowman identified the color over his radio and feathered in for a soft landing.

McKenzie scrambled out with the mailbag and his rifle. Bowman kicked his backpack out the door and reached to close the passenger door. Two men appeared through the yellow smoke. One picked up McKenzie's pack and grabbed the mailbag. The other stuck out his hand. His hair was matted and dirty brown and his face was hollow cheeked supporting a thin, wispy beard here and there, in patches. An olive green tee shirt with several holes in it and cut off jungle fatigues hung from a frail, thin body. His boots were worn badly.

SERGEANT KOOP

This couldn't be Sergeant Koop. Not the same man McKenzie had listened to on the radio, who seemed to be everywhere, calm when an enemy mortar crew had begun to walk round after round toward his position. McKenzie had listened intently as Koop called in map coordinates to the artillery command center. His speech pattern had been calm and deliberate. It was the kind of voice used by preachers to soothe a troubled parishioner. He had tried to imagine the man. Two Cav soldiers were killed before artillery fire quieted the mortar,

A combat infantry platoon was supposed to contain 44 men with a platoon sergeant and a platoon leader. First Platoon had only 19 men, not counting himself and Koop. McKenzie had heard at Camp Evans that First of the Fifth had lost over 800 men during the previous six months.

Kauffman told him the company had gone into Khe Sanh to replace the Marines, into Dong Ha to confront a crack North Vietnamese regiment, into Hue during the Tet Offensive and into the A Shau Valley where the landings were a disaster. He said that McKenzie was going to find a few members of First Platoon, young kids by age, who were old timers by combat, weathered and hard. He wondered how they would react to him.

A sudden, large explosion sent shock waves knocking McKenzie down against the hot sand.

"You tryin' to make a grand entrance, LT?" said the thin soldier lying next to him.

McKenzie looked into the gaunt face. Blue, crystalline eyes looked back from deep sockets while a slow smile, full of bright, white teeth erupted.

"Just tryin' to save your ass, LT. I'm Sergeant Koop. You can call me One Five. This here's Sergeant Doll, Second Squad Leader. Let's go find your platoon. They been waiting to meet ya." His accent was Midwestern drawl, definitely not southern or eastern. Maybe Kansas or North Carolina.

"Glad to meet you, Sergeant. I been listening to you on the radio. You sure you need my help?"

"Yes, sir. I didn't ask for this job. It's all yours. Keep your head down as we go over this sand berm. We're headed toward that next couple of trees."

FIRST PLATOON

Both Koop and Doll were already dog trotting away by the time McKenzie picked up his pack and rifle. He felt vulnerable as he followed. First Platoon was spread out among the trees. Koop's introduction resulted in a series of grunts from soldiers sitting and laying around on the sand. A few said, "Hi" and a few said, "Welcome." No one seemed very enthusiastic. McKenzie felt grossly out of place in his new, crisp jungle fatigues and boots. His face was sun burned, not tan like the others.

Koop told him company headquarters "is just over a short rise toward the sea, Second and Third platoons are on the other side." Looking around, the world seemed made of only two colors - sand brown or faded army fatigue green. That is, except for McKenzie, who's new, green fatigues made him stand out like a Christmas tree ornament.

When he looked around he saw eyes dark as pencil lead blinking at him from brown, dirty faces adorned by adolescent beards and matted hair. He moved among the men, wanting to meet each one until Koop tapped him on the shoulder.

"Let's go meet the Exec. The old man's in Danang."

"Yea, Top told me, Sergeant."

"You can call me One Five, sir." Koop stopped as he said it and scratched something out of his hair.

"I hear you're gonna call me One Six, is that right?"

"You got it, One Six."

They walked on, passing a group of soldiers watching two others dig sand away from the entrance to a collapsed hut. The sun was a very bright, white light and heat radiated off sand crystals as they walked through the loose drifts.

The XO was sitting talking into the receiver of a PRC-25 radio, still attached to the backpack carried by his radio operator. He was looking at a plastic terrain map, similar to the one Top had given McKenzie.

"Four, this is your new officer," Koop said. His voice was soft. It sounded like an apology. The XO looked up angrily and continued to listen to the receiver as he stared at McKenzie. He looked down and shouted into the mouth piece.

"Well, we need some more support here. See if you can't get us more gun ships, so we can blast those bastards off the beach, will ya? We got em shoved up against the water but they're dug in pretty damned good. Over."

After listening awhile, again looking up at McKenzie, he said even louder, "What? Waddya mean Six isn't gonna be here before we leave for the mountains? I got at least two days clean up here before we leave. You let me know by tomorrow cause I gotta get the hell out of here soon. I'm too short for this shit. My tour's almost up. I know you know. Just tell Six to hurry up. Out."

He handed the radio hand set to a private nearby and stood up. Lieutenant Gill was probably no more than twenty-one or twenty-two. His long face was unshaven. He had dark hair and wore a new Army green tee shirt with faded pants. When they shook hands, McKenzie estimated him to be around six feet, two inches tall. Nice target.

"Well, Lieutenant, I hear you been in the rear for almost a week. It's about time you showed yourself. How long you been in country?" Gill bent over to pick up a canteen.

"Ten days, sir. I came out as soon as they would put me on a bird. I was only at LZ Jane for two days. If you can brief me, I'd like to get back to my platoon so I can get better acquainted."

The air hung hot. McKenzie wanted to remove his fatigue shirt. Gill took a long pull on his canteen, a larger than average Adams apple bouncing up and down on a thin neck as he drank.

"Well, I'm not even supposed to be out here. I did my six months in the field but the old man's on some command junket down in DaNang and here I am," Gill said, slowly screwing the cap onto his canteen. " You're gonna take over First Platoon. Sergeant Koop can show you what to do. He knows. I don't have the time right now. Besides, I don't intend to be out here more than a couple more days and I don't lead platoons into combat any more. Be back here in one hour and bring One Five."

SQUAD LEADERS

Sergeant Koop was gone when McKenzie turned around. Great. He had to study the area carefully before determining the return route. He found Koop talking to three soldiers, all E-five buck sergeants, one of whom he recognized.

"You're kidding me," McKenzie said as he reached out to shake the man's hand. "Sergeant Casey here was in my first basic training company at Fort Benning. How the hell did you make buck sergeant so fast, Casey?"

"Welcome, sir. Out here it happens fast. Hey, Doll. You remember me tellin' you about the asshole training officer I had in basic? That was the XO and it was our new One Six who called bullshit on him. I'm sure glad to see you, sir."

Koop next introduced Sergeant Kemper, First Squad leader, who wore an earring in his left ear and was even thinner than Koop.

"Well," Kemper said, as he broke eye contact and looked at the ground. "I just hope you're on our side out here. You know how the last One Six left, don't you?" He said it with a chuckle as he looked up.

McKenzie glanced over at Koop who looked back with those big, blue unblinking eyes. Neither said anything.

"He was an asshole and somebody fragged him. We don't know who it was but it was some bad shit," Kemper continued glancing over at Koop as if to invite comment.

"No, Sergeant Kemper, I never heard that," McKenzie said slowly. "If someone takes a shot at me, however, or throws a grenade in my bunker, they damn shore better get me fast or they will be very sorry. I thought we were gonna be in this together? You know, I take care of you, you take care of me. You don't know a thing about me but I guarantee you one thing, the next One Six will be a bigger prick than I ever thought of being. My goal is to bring back as many of you as I can and to learn from you. Anything else you have to say right now?"

"No, LT. I guess we'll have to see about that." Kemper looked around again for support but got none. He lit a cigarette and tried to look bored. Koop had told McKenzie that Kemper was one of the old ones with jungle smarts beyond his nineteen years of age.

Second Squad was led by Sergeant Doll, whom McKenzie had met earlier. He was a California surfer with thick, brown hair, the big, quiet type with an easy grin. Casey had Third Squad. Koop sent them away with resupply and security orders and showed McKenzie the platoon command post, nothing more than a spot in the sand.

The other two platoon leaders and their 5s were already with Gill when they returned. Two Six was Lieutenant Jankowsky, from New Jersey, with a noticeable accent. Three Six was Lieutenant Rudor, from Pennsylvania, big and Swedish looking. A linebacker at Notre Dame maybe. They were both cordial and welcomed McKenzie. At the end of the meeting Lieutenant Gill looked at McKenzie.

"You won't have much time to learn the job as you go, so you better get your shit together fast. Any questions, One Six?"

McKenzie shook his head.

"By the way, what the hell is a second lieutenant doing in Vietnam?" When he said it, Gill reached out and tapped the gold, embroidered bar on McKenzie's lapel. "You better cut this off or some gook's gonna do it for you," he said.

"I just decided to come and get it over with. That OK with you, sir?" McKenzie was beginning to feel hostile about having to explain himself all the time.

Lieutenant Gill didn't answer. He stared at McKenzie for a couple of moments, then bent over and picked up his map from the ground.

"OK. Meetings over," he said. "One Six, you got any questions, you come see me. You got that?"

McKenzie and Koop walked back to the platoon in silence. Koop took a knife out of his pocket and cut the strings holding the embroidered gold bars off his new 1-6's shirt lapels, then sat down and pulled two tins from his pack - one crackers, the other peanut butter. McKenzie sat down.

SERGEANT CASEY

"Hey, One Six, you got any chow?" McKenzie looked up at Casey, who stood before him holding two boxes of C-rations.

"I just can't get used to being called One Six, Casey."

"Well, that's your call sign LT and that's your name out here, whether you like it or not." Casey sat down crossed legged and handed him a box.

"You were in that group that graduated in February, weren't you Casey."

"Yep. When I left Benning, I went to Fort Leavenworth for AIT and after that, they gave me 30 days leave and sent me here. I been here since May."

"So how did you make squad leader so fast?"

"Simple. You promoted me to PFC in basic, I came out of AIT a Spec Four and when I got here, they had no first squad leader and no one wanted it. This company has been through some shit. Hasn't anybody told you?"

"Yea, Top gave me a brief run down but it was a little hard to digest. Tell me one thing, Casey, how many platoon leaders have come through here in the past six months?"

Casey looked at Koop and stirred a can of ham and lima beans he'd just opened. "You are the third in the last six months, LT but I told the guys you were OK. Don't worry about them. They would love to have an LT who had his shit together and would stick around for a while."

Koop stood up. "I'll see you two later," he said

They ate their chow together and laughed about basic training. It was obvious McKenzie had a friend in Casey. He got the run down on most of the men, who would fight and who seemed the most afraid.

There was Whitcom, a black soldier from Kentucky. He was their sniper and willing to walk point with his M-14 scope mounted rifle. Several of the men were crack shots with their M-79 grenade launchers and Mack, who carried Second Squad's M-60 machine gun, was a big, gutsy kid who had raced dirt track before being drafted. He was always good for some serious lead in a fire fight, Casey said.

There were also a few guys who had been through all the shit over the last six months and who went sort of crazy in a fire fight. The "old ones," he called them. Koop had used the same name. They were very hard to control once the shooting started. He told McKenzie not to worry about Kemper or Doll. They were squad leaders because they were the best. Kemper, especially, had a sixth sense of knowing when the enemy was near and Doll was absolutely unflappable, like Koop. Casey's descriptions made McKenzie feel good about the men.

NAVORSKI

"The best man in the platoon is Navorski, here." Casey patted McKenzie's radio man, who had begun following him around with the PRC-25 radio, on the shoulder. "First, he's a Pollack from Pennsylvania, which is gotta be good and second, he can put red leg in your hip pocket. Right Navorski?" Navorski smiled and shrugged his shoulders. He was a stout five foot five with curly black hair and quiet.

That evening, Navorski told McKenzie about the other lieutenants who had come and gone. One had been picked off by a sniper. He also told of a Second Platoon leader, before Jankowski, who was killed in an ambush.

"The NVA will concentrate most of their fire power on the radio antenna, cause they know that's where the officers are." He was talking as he showed McKenzie how to put their two poncho halves together for a tent.

"Third Platoon once had an LT who got up during an ambush and charged. Everyone else just lay there watching him run forward. Bam! He was shot before he got ten feet. Died on the trail where no one could get to him until it was all over. The guys are hoping you will hang around for a while, huh One Six?" Navorski grinned. He showed McKenzie how to calibrate the radio, talked about its strength and how long the battery would last. It would be their only way to communicate with the company commander, other platoons and the higher chain of command, call in artillery, gun ships or resupply.

That night, McKenzie lay inside the make shift tent evaluating his circumstances. He had trust in himself. He had grown up in the Northwest, along Oregon's Columbia River, where fathers raised boys with lessons of common sense, like not peeing on electric fences and where Indian grandfathers teach lessons of inner strength and talk about ancient warriors.

The military had trained him to assume that senior officers had more experience and training, had made mistakes or seen mistakes and had learned from them. Still, he was not willing to follow blindly. He wanted a chance to survive and to help his men survive. That would mean he might have to limit the control of others but he also knew the very nature of war, the enemy, the weapons and the chain of command would have something to say about that.

NIGHT

Delta had orders to sweep a set of bunkers close to the beach the next day and either kill who ever they found or take prisoners. If nothing else, they would push the NVA into the water and Charlie Company would come in from the North, straight down the beach with Bravo Company set up as a blocking force to the South.

McKenzie looked out of the tent opening and stared up into the black night, full of billions of twinkling stars. Back in The Dalles, his Irish father would get up in the morning and go to the high school where he taught wood shop and mechanical drawing.

He would have no idea it was McKenzie's first day in combat. His Mother, who was half Wy-Am Indian and half white, would make biscuits or bread and walk the house in moccasins, still her favorite kind of shoe. There were probably friends in college who didn't know why he'd left school after running out of money or where he was tonight.

Bien An had been under siege for about a week. As the night imposed itself, artillery shells landed here and there and parachute flares popped overhead swinging back and forth producing eerie shadows. Helicopters flew overhead either firing at something or kicking supplies out. It was a science fiction highway in the sky. There was no sleeping for a new guy.

Watch was set for two hour intervals. Around two, during his first watch, McKenzie walked away from the tent. Koop had warned him that NVA sappers had tried to sneak in the night before and throw satchel charges into tents. McKenzie could see his own shadow lengthen and shorten from a flare floating down as he moved toward the perimeter. He tried to walk only when it was dark. He didn't know if he was scared, if he should be scared or if he just didn't know enough to be scared. He thought he smelled the sweet odor of marijuana riding along a slight breeze up to him from one of the sand bunkers.

The bunker was dug like a slit trench and it appeared no one was in it. McKenzie got down on his stomach and when the next flare lit up, he looked down into the hole. A soldier was sitting in the bottom against the end wall, his chin on his chest, a half smoked joint burning slowly between his right thumb and fore finger, his hand resting on his right knee.

McKenzie swung his legs down into the trench and hit the man in the face hard with an open hand. The soldier scrambled to his feet, blood trickling from his nose. He grabbed for his M-16, which was lying out of the trench across a sand bag but McKenzie had already put his hand on it. They looked at each other. It was Spec. Four Brahmin from Second Squad.

"Brahmin, you're either trying to get killed or you're trying to get me killed. Either way, that pisses me off," McKenzie said. He left the bunker without saying anything more. Later in the morning, Koop asked him about it but McKenzie said it was between him and Brahmin.

BLOCKING FORCE

Delta's mission changed the next morning. They would be the blocking force. "If the NVA make a run for it, they're gonna be coming straight at us. Recheck your fields of fire," Gill told the platoon leaders. "I want them all interlocking. That's all," he said, picking up his radio receiver to talk to battalion.

McKenzie walked back and sat down to think about fields of fire. "Navorski, call One Five and ask him to come over here."

"I'm right here, One Six." Koop was standing behind him.

McKenzie swiveled around and looked up. "Call the squad leaders together so we can discuss this operation."

"I set the squads in earlier, One Six. The claymores are in and they're marking fields of fire right now. My RTO has all the coordinates and call signs for artillery and air support. I understand the Navy is standing by. Is there something else you want me to do?" Koop said it all in a voice so low, it was hard to hear.

"Jesus, One Five. Where did you get your orders?"

"Listened in on the battalion command radio frequency about an hour ago. I figured you'd want me to get started."

"Right, Sarge. I'll be over to look in a minute. Thanks." He looked at Navorski, who just smiled. When Koop left, Navorski said, "That's just the way it is, LT. Don't worry about it."

"How the hell am I going to show that I know what I'm doing at this rate?" McKenzie said. Navorski just shrugged.

When he went out to look, it was clear Koop had set the positions in perfect locations. It looked like an instructor's diagram at OCS. First Platoon was still under strength but now had 22 able bodied soldiers for three squads after three men returned from R & R that morning. Koop had placed two M-60 machine guns on the South end and one on the North, with crossing lines of fire to cover the entire area in front. Extra hand grenades were laid out on sand bags with extra ammo bandoliers and ammo clips pre-loaded.

Later, when he and Koop sat down to go over things, Koop pulled out coffee and hot chocolate from his pack.

"You boil a canteen cup full of water, throw in large quantities of hot chocolate, one pack of coffee and three packs of dry cream. One package of sugar if you like it extra sweet. You want some, LT?"

"Sure, One Five."

"There's a bunch a things like this, LT, including recipes for C rations and LRRP meals that you will learn in time. Fields of fire ain't nothin more than watchin' and usin' your instinct but if you can't fix your own food or forget to take your malaria pills or put purification tablets in your water, you're not gonna make it anyway."

McKenzie looked up to present his cup and saw Koop had been talking with his canteen cup raised toward his mouth, looking over the top at him. McKenzie decided the drawl was either North or South Carolina and that One Five was about the raggiest noncommissioned officer he had ever seen. His hair was thick with a dusting of red and brown dirt, sticking straight out in four or five directions. A flimsy mustache and wispy beard framed a mouth without distinction except that it was there. The beard was not uniform, growing heavier on his neck where it seemed to collect as much dirt as possible. Yet, his face was clean and healthy looking and his eyes were quick and intelligent.

After coffee, McKenzie followed Koop back toward the line of firing positions. His platoon sergeant looked like a walking cadaver, gaunt and tattered in the pale blue of the morning. There were no sounds of battle, only the distant roll of the surf. It was as if the war had been suspended. Wars over. Everybody go home. Palm trees rustled softly from a cool ocean breeze blowing inland.

AK - 47

Koop dropped into a fox hole, disappearing before McKenzie's eyes. From three sides, McKenzie heard a cracking sound like distant fire crackers popping in the air. "What the hell is that?" he said. Koop grabbed his left leg and dumped him on the ground before pulling him into the fox hole. Time felt like a slow walk across a busy intersection in LA. Things began to happen fast but his mind saw things in slow motion. By the time McKenzie got to his feet inside the fox hole, the world was full of machine guns and M-16s firing and people shouting. The cracking sounds got louder and sand jumped to his left.

"One Six! Ain't you ever heard an AK before? You're not gonna live long standing up there like some big assed bird."

The person yelling at him was a small, blond headed kid in the fox hole who he recognized from First Squad. His name was "Trigger" and Koop said he had a hard time being any kind of a leader. He'd turned down squad leader when asked. All he wanted to do was fight.

McKenzie ducked down and put his hand on Trigger's shoulder and yelled, "You're right and I would like to live a little while longer."

The fire fight went on for several more minutes then slowly began to die down. McKenzie tried to see the fight but it wasn't visible. It was obvious Koop had positioned the platoon impeccably. Most of the enemy fire came from a tree line on the right and the M-60s were able to stop it immediately. He had yet to feel any fear. The strange cracking of the AKs seemed distant and non-threatening.

As morning progressed, there was little contact. A few NVA in sandy colored uniforms and pith helmets tried to sneak through but they were easily captured or gunned down. Most of the enemy was killed on the beach by gun ships. Others were dug out or blown up where they hid in tunnels along the beach edge.

"One Six, you want to go see a tunnel complex?"

Navorski held up the radio hand set toward him as he stood up and began to walk away.

"Four has a tunnel complex about two hundred meters to the Southwest and he wants one of our squads to come over and check it out. He thinks its empty but wants it fragged anyway just to be sure. One Five's got Second Squad headed over there now."

McKenzie took the hand set tethered to the PRC-25, which Navorski thrust at him. "One Five's on the horn, LT," Navorski said. Trying to keep up, McKenzie pressed the handset bar.

"This is One Six, over."

"One Six, this is One Five. I've got Second Squad coming to my location. Spread out the other two squads to cover our area and come over here about two hundred meters to your sierra whiskey. We've got an old victor charlie complex we need to check out. You might find it interesting. Over."

"Roger that, One Five. Out." McKenzie handed the hand set back to Navorski. "Why Second Squad?"

Navorski stopped. "That's Sergeant Doll's squad. He's the best tunnel rat in the company. Takes things nice and slow. By the way, I already called in our coordinates for red leg in case we need some help."

A few minutes later, after making sure the platoon's position was covered, they found Doll and Second Squad, spread out and moving slow.

"Don't you think we can move a little faster, Sarge? We have to cover two hundred meters in a short time. One Five is waiting." McKenzie said as he moved along side.

"No disrespect, LT but we always move laterally in an open area. That column stuff they teach is Charlie's favorite.

Sometimes we have to do that in the jungle but its ugly." Doll's response was made as he kept moving.

Out of the corner of his right eye, McKenzie saw someone hop to his left, jump back and begin firing a machine gun into the sand sideways so it moved in a straight line. McKenzie went down on one knee. No one else hit the dirt. Two squad members ran over and pulled a body out of the blood soaked sand, some of it caked on the face of a dead NVA soldier.

"Nice trick, huh, LT? This guy had a reed in his mouth and I saw it. He was gonna let us walk over his ass and open up on us." It was Mack and his adrenaline was in full flow.

McKenzie looked around. The squad had gathered around Mack to congratulate him.

"OK, break it up Sergeant Doll. One mortar would kill us all," McKenzie said.

"You got it, One Six. Move out."

Sergeant Doll looked proudly at his men and hand motioned the squad to spread out and move. The rest of the day was spent looking into empty bunkers. Whatever was going on up and down the beach, First Platoon was not a part of it. Occasionally, they heard automatic fire or a grenade thud.

Around seventeen hundred, McKenzie and Koop were called back to the company CP.

ORDERS

"Orders are, we're gonna CA (combat assault) out tomorrow morning into the mountains for a God damned search and destroy. Six is flyin' in around nine. Secure your area for tonight and check supplies. Any questions?" Gill looked around, pulled a pipe from his shirt pocket and began to open a tobacco pouch.

"Order of movement for the CA?" Jankowski asked.

"I haven't got that yet. I'm hopin' Six will be here. If not, I'll let you all know in the morning." Gill was busy with his pipe.

Before he could get his bearings around sand dunes and coastal trees, McKenzie was being moved to the jungle. He walked back with Koop. The sun had begun to drop slowly over the edge of the distant mountain range. In Vietnam, the sun rose out of the ocean, just the opposite of the Oregon coast where McKenzie had spent so many evenings with his family watching the sun turn red and sink into the Pacific. Here, everything was backwards. Navorski sat cross legged mixing a LRRP ration with hot sauce.

"How'd you get saddled carrying the radio, Navorski?"

"I volunteered, LT. I figured that way I would know what was happening."

"How long you been with Delta?" McKenzie asked.

"I got here 10th of March. Nine months to go. Seems like a long time."

"Well, you could be me with three hundred fifty-four and a wake up." They both laughed.

"Just remember, One Six. If you live, you get out of the field after six months. Enlisted grunts get to stay out in this paradise for a full year unless we get lucky and pull a rear job cause we got shot too many times. That ain't about to happen to me. Six is already talking about taking me for his command RTO. Guess I'll be out here after you're long gone."

"What? You mean I might not have you for long? That's a pile. I'm just beginning to catch on to what you do. So tell me about Six."

SIX

"He's a West Pointer and proud of it. A ring knocker and a hard charger. Real tough. Doesn't take any shit off his platoon leaders. He'll expect you to know your job first day. Just act like you know what you're doin and me and One Five will cover your ass. My advice? Try to keep from talking too much. Our last one six was always letting his mouth overload his ass. Six has a very sensitive bullshit detector."

"So, he's gung ho in the field under fire?"

"What you really need to know, One Six, is the old man does not get along with Black Knight, the battalion commander. You'll hear that for yourself the first time he's on the radio with him and you happen to be standing by. Its a wonder he gets away with some of the things he says but then Black Knight doesn't give a shit about us anyway. The way I see it, Six is just trying to do what he knows is best to keep as many of us alive as he can. You wanna try some mucky moo? That's what I call jelly mixed with peanut butter on these dry c-ration crackers to make them taste a little less like cardboard."

"Sure." McKenzie ate what he was given while they talked about what would happen in the field.

Navorski continued, "Black Knight wants strict company size operations but Six has other ideas. The jungle's not made for walking the whole company up and down trails waiting to hit the shit. Your lead squad usually gets hit that way and by the time anybody can react, the shootin's over and somebody is either KIA or WIA. Six likes to move platoons separately. Cover a broader area and out Charlie, Charlie, as he always says. He's big on ambushes and moving when the other guy don't expect it. My guess is, Six is down in DaNang gettin' a little face to face ass chewin'. We'll see when he gets back."

While he was listening, McKenzie was asking himself, 'Why was this happening?' The officers and NCOs who trained incoming soldiers at Camp Evans were first class. At the same time, McKenzie recalled what Major Sparkman had said.

CHAPTER THREE - THE FIELD
(JULY 3, 1968 - 350 DAYS LEFT)

COMBAT ASSAULT (CA)

Delta lifted out of Bien An the next morning without Captain Moore. Huey troop carriers came in at ten hundred hours with First Platoon in the lead. Koop was on the first bird, having set the order of loading before McKenzie returned from meeting with the XO. Powerful rotor blades sucked sand off the ground and stung the faces of bent over soldiers as they walked toward the helicopters.

These were experienced soldiers loading as if they were climbing into a New York taxi. Bent low, in orderly lines, half went to each side and with one foot on the landing skid, they climbed in easily. McKenzie boarded the third bird as Koop had suggested. He looked for a seat but the webbed seating had been strapped up against the bulk head. Soldiers sat against the inside walls of the chopper or on the edge with their legs dangling loosely over the side. McKenzie flopped down square in the middle, half way between the doors.

The bird wobbled and started to lift. McKenzie felt his butt slide toward the left door. He tried to stop but the hard soles on his new boots were slippery and he kept sliding until someone grabbed his backpack and pulled him back against the bulk head. The ground was already dropping out from under them. Wind buffeted away any conversation. There was nothing to say anyway.

They flew toward the mountains, away from the coast. Vegetation began to change from coastal trees and sand dunes, to rice fields and heavy scrub brush. Pilots lined up their aircraft and flew in a straight line, one behind another. The crew chief handed McKenzie a headset. He put it on and listened as the pilots discussed whether the landing zone was going to be hot, meaning did command expect enemy resistance.

"Platoon leader? What can you tell us?" the pilot said over the intercom.

"S-2 doesn't really know," McKenzie shouted over the engine noise. "All I know is we're going into the mountains to look for bad guys."

"Roger that. Well, we got ARA going in right now so hopefully Charlie's got his head down. We'll try not to drop you right into his lap."

"That would be appreciated," McKenzie said. He felt light headed and spacey. The helicopters were carrying Delta Company toward the mountains and he had no idea what to expect.

LEARNING

Rumor had circulated they were going back into the A Shau Valley or close to it. Delta had been there in February and March when the First Cav tried to penetrate deep into the upper northern part. Kemper had sat cross legged the night before and told of those difficult times as if relating stories of Vikings centuries ago. He was a natural story teller. McKenzie stood off to the side, in the shadows, and listened. Kemper was picturesque with his silver stud earring in his left ear lobe and a red bandana worn Indian style, rolled across his forehead and tied in back. It wasn't surprising to see the others, especially the new guys, gathered around.

Was this how they learned what to do? Was this how the pecking order was established and reinforced or was this simply a reality check, a teaching by Kemper? He described in vivid detail the dense, dark, menacing forests of the A Shau Valley. Located in Thua Tien Province near the Laotian border, west of the coastal Imperial City of Hue, it held the Rao Loa River, which provided water for the North Vietnamese soldiers making their way south. He imparted these facts as if he were a student of Vietnam.

"You couldn't see shit, man. Point was either hackin' at the brush with a machete or else we'd be walking up those big, highway trails. Bad karma. Even the landing was some bad shit. Daisy cutters knocked over so many trees, I mean big trees, they were laying all cross ways like pick up sticks. We had to jump into that mess. Guys were getting hurt and the gooks were waiting with heavy anti-air craft guns. I saw birds get hit and guys spilling out of them.

On the ground, we were scattered all over hell. If you got lost without a radio, it was real spooky. We were there three weeks. Delta had six KIAs and twenty-three WIAs. Two KIAs and six WIA from First Platoon alone. It felt like we were never gonna get outa that place. One of the Chinooks that came in to pull us out, drifted too close to a tree with its rear blade and bam, its ass end spun around right on top of guys who were waitin' to get the hell out of there. Me and Hardaway, who was killed later, were able to pull a few of them guys out from under it. Thank God it didn't blow. I sure as hell hope we're not going into that thick shit again."

"OK. That's enough for tonight," Koop said as he stepped from the shadows. "Make sure your gear is ready for the morning." He had interrupted Kemper with his softest voice. "We're not going anywhere near the A Shau, Kemper. I got the word from Top. We're just going into the highlands this side of the mountains."

He never looked directly at Kemper. He squatted down on his heels and began drawing something in the sand as he said it. McKenzie walked over to look. It was a First Cav patch. Koop scratched it away. Without looking up, he told the squad leaders to meet him in thirty minutes. Then he said, "Get your perimeters secure and bring me your resupply needs. We got a mail bird coming in tomorrow afternoon. If you need ammo, claymores or batteries, tell me now so Top can get them on that bird. Otherwise, its just mail, c-rations, water and the Captain." He looked up and surveyed the group.

It seemed as if Koop kept the whole war in his head. So far, McKenzie hadn't seen him write anything down. They both carried the same little green Army notebook and McKenzie had been furiously writing in his - lessons learned, orders from battalion, artillery coordinates, names of soldiers with their critical information, like when they were due to go home. He reached up and touched the hard backed notebook in his left breast pocket as the helicopters carried Delta company across grassy highlands toward the mountains.

STANDING ORDERS

He thought about what he had learned. What should he believe? They were going toward the mountains. Should he use specific rules of combat and leadership learned during the past year or should he make decisions by the seat of his pants, according to the situation?

In OCS, each candidate was given a two sided copy of "Standing Orders, Rogers Rangers." Incredibly, Major Robert Rogers had organized America's first version of Special Forces, Long Range Recon and Army Rangers, all rolled into one unit in 1759 to fight in the War for Independence against England. These were his rules. They were still good today and there were nineteen of them.

McKenzie carried the card inside his pack, inside his journal. The first rule was, "Don't forget nothing." How could he forget what he didn't know? As they flew toward the landing, he tried to go through the list mentally. Did they translate from 1759 to 1968? Number five weighed in with a thud. "Don't never take a chance you don't have to." That's where the real battle was going to be.

"Hey, Lieutenant, this is your pilot. We're about five minutes out and Yellow One spotted a couple of bad guys near the tree line, so you be careful. The gun ships are going in now to light up that area but this one might be a little hot."

"Roger that. Thanks for the ride," McKenzie said. He took off the ear phones and handed them back to the crew chief.

The pilot's words had caused a sudden, pressure in his chest that made it hard to speak. He motioned for others on board to lock and load as the line of ships dropped down at a steep angle, snaking one after the other, their noses pointing toward the ground. Door gunners on both sides began to fire their machine guns, which hung free by tethers from the door frames.

Time slowed down. McKenzie's heart felt like it was growing larger and louder until it filled his chest and threatened to move into his throat. He swallowed hard to keep from choking. It was beating so loud he couldn't think. They were floating toward earth, lower and lower but the helicopters did not land. They stopped and hung suspended above tall grass. As they rocked from side to side, soldiers jumped from the skids, hitting hard.

McKenzie got to one knee just as the pilot decided to drop a little lower. The sudden movement caused him to lose balance and fall back on the deck of the helicopter. He slid all the way to the opposite side where the weight of his pack pulled him backwards out the door. He fell upside down holding onto his weapon with both hands while watching the helicopter rise away until he hit on his backpack, like a turtle on its shell, knocking the wind out of him.

Someone grabbed his pack strap, pulled him to his feet and pushed him toward the tree line. He ran, mouth open for air, hoping that someone knew something he did not. Don't never take a chance you don't have to, he thought.

He found Navorski down on one knee next to a tree line. "Red broke his ankle in the jump and Koop has called back one of the helicopters to pick him up," Navorski said. Red was one of the 'old ones' from First Squad.

MOVEMENT

There was no enemy contact, so after 'Red' was picked up, they moved away from the tree line toward the mountains. Cool morning air allowed the company to move easily. Second Platoon took the lead. McKenzie walked behind his lead squad, where Koop had told him most platoon leaders walked. It was close enough to move up if needed but far enough back that he and Navorski would not be the first target in an ambush.

"Charlie loves to go after that antenna and anyone who looks like he's the platoon leader," Koop told him for the third time.

The sky was true blue against the distant mountains. McKenzie tried to guess how far away they were. One of his assignments in OCS was to walk a hundred meters and count his steps. His count was one hundred and eighteen. This was done over and over until each candidate knew for sure what his count was. All maps in Vietnam were measured in thousand meters or "clicks." Candidates were told they would have to constantly count their steps as they walked. Otherwise, they would have no way of truly knowing whether their map was accurate or not.

McKenzie walked along counting his steps, trying, at the same time, to be aware of his surroundings, keep pace, carry his weapon at the ready and occasionally, look at the plasticized map he'd pulled from his leg pocket. He'd marked what he thought was the point of destination on the map with a black grease pencil and he was trying to calculate the distance of march when he ran into Navorski's radio. The column had stopped.

"Second Platoon probably found a trail, LT," Navorski said at the same time listening intently to his radio hand set. "They got Ho Chi Mien sandal tracks," he said, looking up.

The soldiers ahead were fanned out on each side of the trail and down on one knee looking outward from the column. Behind McKenzie, everyone was also spread out and down. He was still standing, so he quickly knelt down. Soon the column was up and moving again.

By fourteen hundred, Delta occupied a knoll about two clicks from where they had landed. Gill had been looking for a night position where Captain Moore could come in. The knoll was covered with rocks and light, brown dirt with bunch grass on the slopes. Each platoon was given a sector of the perimeter, about seventy-five meters away from the company CP, which was right in the center. It was First Platoon's turn to put out the night ambush and McKenzie let Doll know he would be going out with them.

FIRST AMBUSH

Second Squad gathered to leave. McKenzie and Doll examined the map to see if they could spot a natural terrain feature for the ambush. Koop went over each man's equipment, eliminating anything that could make noise or reflect the moonlight and taping down loose hanging smoke grenades.

Private Suski, a small freckled face kid from Chicago, stepped up to Doll and began drawing streaks of camouflage paint diagonally across his squad leader's face. First, olive green then dark gray. Doll looked up from his map to make it easier but he never stopped talking.

"We don't know what's down there, so we gotta move slow. Charlie may have already spotted us," he told the squad.

Suski moved over to McKenzie, who got a similar paint job. The sun had dropped below the horizon and dusk was in full movement toward dark.

"Shouldn't we get moving, Sarge?" McKenzie said.

"Yea. It's time. Hey, Carson. Take us out of here," Doll said without looking to find the soldier. One of the soldiers, apparently Carson, moved away from the group, carefully stepped over a trip wire and began to move down the trail.

If there was to be a moon, it would show itself soon. Fourth in line, McKenzie looked down into a valley already as black as obsidian. The column seemed to be moving too slow. They would be moving into a virtual black out in ten or fifteen minutes. He walked up to the front and passed Carson.

"Carson, you keep watching up front. We need to get into position while we can still see," he said.

McKenzie stepped forward on the red clay trail. He was unsure if he would even know what to do if he met an NVA soldier but he needed to take charge. The night became dreamy and he floated in a state of hyper ventilation as he moved. Buckets of adrenalin were being dumped into his nervous system. He heard a faint noise up ahead and stopped. The darkness closed in around him. Suddenly, he was jerked backwards. They still had about three hundred meters to go to reach the ambush site and he was agitated. He twisted around to see that it was Doll who had grabbed him by the collar.

Getting close to his face, Doll said in a whisper, "Sir. You only got six months in the field and then they send you back to some rear job. We have to be out here twelve months unless we die or get wounded. If you want to live, I would suggest you not walk point." His eyes were unblinking. McKenzie could see there was a knowledge too unfamiliar for him to challenge. As if to further make his point, Doll said a little louder, "Do not walk point at night when you don't know what the fuck you're doing, sir. Comprende?"

Everything felt suspended in time. There was no war, no earth, no night. There was only Sergeant Doll's face and his words.

"Ok, Sarge. Let's get this ambush into position," McKenzie said in a low voice.

Doll nodded and moved around him to take point. As it turned out, the night was quiet, which gave McKenzie time to think. This was his platoon to lead. It was a group of soldiers, some experienced and some not, which would live and die under his leadership or lack of it. After he received his orders to Vietnam, his company commander at Fort Benning, began to talk to him about being a platoon leader. "Take care of your men and they will gratefully and willingly take care of you." McKenzie needed to make that his first rule.

A cool breeze came in from the South China Sea, pushing the mist out of the valley as they headed back in the morning. There had been no real reason for McKenzie to be on the ambush except he wanted to feel like their leader. He wasn't yet.

HEAVY ROLLERS

The rest of the morning was spent with the company in place, waiting for Captain Moore to arrive until battalion called and said there were no birds available until the afternoon. Gill decided the company needed to stay put. It was an opportunity to write letters or do whatever. He showed up at 1st platoon around noon and told McKenzie to recon to the East and see where the trail led.

After shedding most of their gear, except weapons, ammunition and canteens, the platoon left the perimeter and retraced the ambush route. Soon, they were walking down a long slope where the trail turned gently to the right toward several small hills. The sun felt extra hot and the column moved cautiously up over the hills.

PFC Hampton was on point. It was Third Squad's turn. Hampton, nicknamed Hambone, was known for his quick reactions and ability to spot Charlie before they spotted him. McKenzie watched how cautiously he checked for booby traps or trip wires. There was no sound from the walking.

Sweat rolled out of the men. McKenzie couldn't taste any salt in his sweat, just clear warm water. He had tried taking the salt pills again but they bounced back causing him to throw up. There seemed to be no smells out there on the barren ground. His mouth had no taste. The hot air hugged him as they moved down the other side of the second hill, toward a thick tree line. He shifted his M-16 and placed his thumb on the safety lever. Was it on? Did he know how to find it if he needed to in a hurry? The black color of the M-16 stock distracted him from counting steps and trying to interpret terrain features on his map. Why was it black? He needed camo tape on it.

At one click out, it had become obvious the map was wrong. The hills they'd just come over were unaccounted for on his map. Ahead was the beginning of a combination triple canopy jungle and mountain forest. Koop moved up to third position and motioned for Hampton to move into the trees. He had McKenzie move back behind the next squad.

Koop had said Hambone was a gun fighter who preferred to walk point. "He's quick on the trigger and accurate as hell," was the description. The column slowed down. McKenzie moved back up where he could get a better look. About two hundred meters inside the tree line the trail started to climb, turning to the right up a gentle slope full of broad leaf jungle plants scattered among trees. Suddenly, there was a blinding flash of whiteness. McKenzie heard Hambone's weapon before his conscious mind accepted it. The point man emptied a full magazine at the slope.

Electricity fired into McKenzie's blood stream causing a flash behind his eyes and his legs to weaken. He dropped to the ground. More firing. Cracking sounds flew around him. The machine gun from Second Squad answered back. None of this occurred at his command. People moved around him. Koop was talking to him on the radio hand set that Navorski shoved in his face.

"One Six, this is One Five. We just walked into an ambush about to happen. Point shot the first two and we got more up here. No friendly casualties. Can you bring First Squad to our echo so we don't get flanked? I'm going to see what else we got."

"Huh, this is One Six. Roger that." McKenzie thought he sounded dumb. Navorski took the hand set and yelled at Kemper to move up. More shots were fired. They sounded far away. One Five was at work.

"Kemper! One Five needs protection on his left flank and it's ......" McKenzie said, yelling as Kemper ran by, followed by four soldiers, one with an M-79 grenade launcher. Three other soldiers moved up and formed a perimeter around McKenzie. He could hear Kemper's fire team open up with full automatic fire. Rounds from the M-79 whumped into the ground somewhere off to the left. Cracking sounds came back in return.

McKenzie looked at Navorski, who said, "AKs. Lots of em, LT." The radio came alive. "Roger that, One Five." Navorski said. "Sarge says he needs heavy rollers so they're gonna pull back." Navorski got to his feet.

"He needs what?"

"He's gonna call in a couple of F-4 phantom jets off that carrier sitting out there in the ocean." The radio crackled. Navorski listened. "Roger that," he said into the handset. "One five says he's got em coming. We need to move outside the tree line. Come on, One Six."

McKenzie dropped his head. A layer of fine red dirt covered his new boots. He looked at the three soldiers around him. His heart was racing. They didn't seem to notice. One was smoking, another drinking from his canteen. He got up, followed Navorski away from the tree line, into the open. There was still firing from an M-60 and choppy M-16 bursts coming from inside the trees. Then Koop appeared, holding his M-16 by the pistol grip on his shoulder and dragging his radio man at the other end of the cord while he talked to someone on the radio.

Kemper's squad and Hampton followed a few minutes later. Hampton had been hit in the right elbow and was in pain. Koop smiled at McKenzie as he walked up and sat down. He was calling for red leg. One marking round sailed over head and Koop began placing artillery rounds from LZ Jane into the forest. After a few minutes, he cancelled the fire mission and turned to look at McKenzie.

"We got two heavy rollers on the way. We got lucky. They were already in the air. I want to see if I can catch Charlie with his pants down. They tried to flank us but Kemper killed two more and now they're on the run. It looks like we got more than a hasty ambush, One Six. Those guys were look outs and I'm sure there's more in there. My guess is a bunker complex or a hospital. Anyway, get down. Here they come."

Koop lay back with his legs crossed and the radio hand set up to his ear. McKenzie tried to absorb everything he was seeing and hearing while feeling embarrassed he wasn't the one controlling this. He didn't dare look around to see if others were watching him, so he lay on his back next to Koop and looked up.

"That's a roger, Sky Rider. We got bad guys just inside the tree line. Cover as much area into the trees and sideways as you can. Kemper, pop yellow smoke." From behind, a smoke grenade canister flew toward the tree line. "Your target is south of that smoke about three hundred meters." Koop was now screaming to be heard.

Two jets came straight overhead from behind and released huge, oblong bombs, which spun end over end just beyond the tree line. The impact was deafening. Air became wind as it blew out of the forest full of dirt, carrying tree fragments and shrapnel whizzing through the air at the platoon. McKenzie heard a piece drop in front of him and sat up to look. A six inch piece of twisted steel lay in the dirt between his legs, about eight inches from his crotch.

"Those are five hundred pounders, One Six. Nice, huh?" Koop did not look over when he said it. The two jets made a wide circle as Koop spoke into the radio. "That was great. Now, could you put the other two one hundred meters further in the same direction? Roger that, Sky Rider and thanks." Koop's voice was calm. He could have been in a delicatessen ordering a smoked turkey sandwich.

McKenzie lay back and closed his eyes. He saw a delicatessen with a clean linoleum floor, Koop standing in front of a glassed enclosure which holds hams and turkeys, brie cheese and roast beef slices, perfect for a French dip sandwich and a clerk, who's greatest care in the world is whether the hairnet looks as bad as she thinks it does.

The jet's second run filled the air with more noise and intense air pressure. More shrapnel came whistling overhead and around. The whole thing was over in minutes. When they flew away, McKenzie sat back up and reached for the shrapnel between his legs. It was gray metal, jagged and sharp. He put it into his pocket.

First Platoon moved inside the tree line to assess the damage. They found vegetation shredded and trees splintered from flying shrapnel but no dead enemy. The trail was a perfect ambush site with steep banks and thick foliage close to the sides. It turned back to the left and continued down into a gully, which would make anyone walking there a perfect target. McKenzie studied everything. The darkness increased as they walked deeper, the trees becoming more frightening and oppressive. He had felt the fear in the men who came back from the fire fight.

Hampton was as jacked up as a brahma bull even though his pain was dulled by morphine. The only person who did not seem to react was Koop. He was an enigma. McKenzie wrote in his notebook to recommend Hampton for an Army Commendation Medal with "V" for valor. By the time their assessment was over, it was fifteen hundred and Hampton was hurting. He needed Medivac.

THE CAPTAIN

The afternoon sun was taking a toll. Many of the men had consumed all their water and there was not enough among those who had any left to make a difference. Gill called for a status report and Navorski gave him their coordinates.

"We're about two clicks to your sierra. One Six has been checking out the damage. He wanted to see if there was a hospital in there," Navorski said.

McKenzie could hear Gill shouting. Navorski held the hand set away at arm's length so they could both hear. "Six is on his way and he wants One Six back here when he gets in, you copy?" Gill said.

"Copy that, Four. He hears you. We got some men with heat problems so we're taking a break. Out."

"What the hell was that all about, Navorski?" McKenzie said.

"You can bet Four has been listening all day. You don't need to talk to him unless you really want to. Six wouldn't have us strung out here this far on some recon lark and he knows it. Screw him!"

It was the first time Navorski had showed any enmity toward the XO and it was uncharacteristic. Just as McKenzie started to ask why, Kemper came back and kneeled down.

"I got two men in trouble, One Six. Heat. I can't give em salt now cause they'll just puke it up and we haven't got enough water to cool a hummingbird."

"I know. How much water do you have?"

"Mine's gone. I already gave the rest to Allen but he's down. There's really no water. We're gonna have to send them in on Hambone's Medivac and get some water fast."

McKenzie got reports from the other two squad leaders. Four men were in serious trouble, a few others on the verge. The rest were probably OK. Watson, the platoon medic, felt they should send four back to LZ Jane.

"After they get enough water in them to recover, their next twelve hours will probably be in the beer tent but that's OK, LT," he said. " Better to send them in with heat exhaustion than to have to deal with heat stroke and explain it to Six." Koop came back wearing the first worried look McKenzie had seen on him.

"You and me screwed up, One Six. This map's one hill shy. We're more than two clicks out and there's at least half a dozen men with heat problems. We need to send some in with Hampton." His right hand was scratching his head. It was a way of acting, looking and moving that McKenzie was beginning to realize meant symbolic deference to his rank whenever Koop was telling him what to do.

"Yea, I know. OK, let's do it," McKenzie said.

Koop grabbed his radio and stood up to walk away. McKenzie followed him. Heat waves fluttered in the air making the world look like a prism. Most of the men were down on one knee. Two were holding a dirty towel over Allen to provide shade.

"Roger that, Four. We got one WIA and four heat casualties and we're low on water. Either we get a bird with some H2O who can take a couple of casualties out of here or we're going back in and look for water. No two ways about it."

The response was again loud enough that Koop held the hand set away from his ear. He looked at McKenzie and handed over the phone.

"This is One Six. You got our coordinates. I need water and a Medivac now. You copy?"

"One Six, that's a negative. Six is inbound your location. Out."

Navorski leaned down and turned on the speaker. They listened quietly as Six had his XO explain why One Six was out so far, how they had managed to run out of water and why it took him so long to get help.

Six was about fifteen minutes out so Koop had Doll get ready with smoke and move the men back down the hill into the shade. When the helicopter approached, Doll stood up, red smoke swirling around him with both arms in the air for landing direction. The pilot feathered the bird's nose up and gently placed the skids on the ground.

Captain Moore came striding out through smoke and dust carrying three canteens over his right shoulder and a water can in his left hand. He was short and stocky, maybe a hundred sixty-five pounds and five foot, nine. He had short blond hair, a blond mustache and walked with authority. The pilot sat looking out at this unscheduled landing while his door gunners nervously scanned the tree line and fingered the chain linked rows of ammunition fed into their M-60s.

"Well, Lieutenant McKenzie, I'm Captain Moore. Welcome to the Cav. Sort of got yourself strung out here a little?"

"Yes, sir. My mistake, sir. Sergeant Koop's got the men with heat problems down the trail closer to the trees where they can get some shade. Let me carry the water can."

"LT!" Navorski said loudly. "Let First Squad take the water. Hey, Pete. Get over here."

The four men, who were too dehydrated to stay, were given water and loaded up, their packs and weapons piled into the center of the helicopter. Captain Moore helped Hampton climb aboard, pulled his own gear off and gave the pilot one thumb in the air. Dirt swirled in an upward spiral as the top rotor blade began to accelerate and raise the skids. At about ten feet, he dropped the nose and slid down the hill like a skier on a winter slope, then gently rose up toward the sky.

Captain Moore motioned McKenzie over to the side. "You know, One Six. I heard Colonel Fishmuth gave you a hard time about being a second lieutenant. I'm not any too thrilled about it either but I've been listening and your guys did good today. That doesn't mean I'm not suspect. This water problem is bullshit. You ask questions if you're unsure what to do. We clear?"

"Yes, sir."

The late, afternoon sun was a hot spotlight in front of the platoon's direction of march and applied its heat without sympathy. Dust jumped off the trail in large clouds as they shuffled along single file back the way they had come. Captain Moore walked only three men from the point. The platoon was inside the company perimeter by seventeen thirty. McKenzie was wrung out and exhausted. A resupply bird had already brought more water.

Second and Third Platoons had spent the afternoon strengthening established fields of fire in front of each foxhole, including First Platoon's. McKenzie was told to report to the CP at nineteen hundred hours. He thanked the other platoon leaders for preparing his area and sat down in the dirt. He opened one of his LRRP meals - beef stew, contained in a dark brown, thick plastic pouch, designed to be eaten directly from the pouch by adding hot water. He was beginning to prefer them because they were light to carry and contained rice or dried vegetables. He sure didn't like c-rations except for the crackers and peanut butter and jam. All coffee and cocoa went to Navorski for his magic brew.

WARNINGS

Several men gathered at the platoon CP to discuss events inside the tree line. Private Andrews described excitedly how Hambone had dropped the first NVA soldier before he could raise his weapon and nailed the second guy as he stood up to fire.

"Even though he was hit, Hambone sprayed the area with enough lead to keep anyone else's head down. This was damn sure an ambush. It was no look out. We found blood trails but no NVA. I sure as hell wish we could have gotten to that first guy cause he looked like he was wearing a Chinese pistol. Maybe we'll find him under a bush tomorrow. If he's got a pistol, it's mine. We can leave a Cav patch on the guy so Charlie will know who he's messin' with."

McKenzie looked up. Andrews was not one of the old ones. "What good does a Cav patch do, Andrews?"

"Hell, LT, it lets em know we're not gonna be messed with by those mothers. It let's em know we been through the shit and if they live, they better be afraid of what we might do to them."

There was laughter from the group and a few comments from others who agreed with Andrews.

"Hey, LT. You know what happened to the last one six we had?" Andrews said.

"Why don't you tell me Beetle Bailey," McKenzie said.

"Who's Beetle Bailey?"

"Never mind, Andrews." McKenzie was feeling impatient.

"He got his ass fragged one night in his bunker. No one knows who did it but it sure as hell wasn't Charlie. He was regular army. Whatever Black Knight came up with, he was all over it. He even tried to tell Six what to do. Lucky he wasn't killed. He just got his legs blown all to hell and went home. That's how come we didn't have an LT for a while. One Five's been running this platoon just fine for us."

"So what's your point, Andrews? That's the third time I've heard that story. Is that some kind of warning?" McKenzie said it in a low voice, as menacing as he could make it. He knew his ears were probably getting red, which happened when he got mad. He also thought this was probably a test and he did not want to fail it. Before Andrews could answer, he stood up quickly and walked over to where he could stand face to face with Andrews.

"I just got here," McKenzie said. "There's a bunch a things I don't know but I can tell you one thing. If I see anyone mistreating a prisoner or mutilating a body, they will answer directly to me and I don't give a shit how much action they've seen. As for the rest of it, I'm depending on you and everyone else here to tell me if they don't like what's going on and we'll figure it out." He looked around at the rest of the group. "The only way I can learn what to do is from guys like you who have been through it. Right now, why don't you all go clean your weapons or something."

Andrews started to say something but Koop interrupted him. "Andrews, you go double check all fields of fire for the entire platoon and the rest of you guys go clean weapons like One Six says." He used his soft voice.

ONE THUMB

McKenzie sat back down to finish his LRRP meal. When he was finished, he picked up his own M-16 and reached into his pack for cleaning materials. The strips of green underwear had been working great.

A shot fired behind him. He rolled over onto his side with his M-16 in both hands, waiting for more shots. Koop came running by. There was shouting near the perimeter. By the time he got down to Second Squad's area, Doc Watson was trying to get Private Wells to show him his left hand.

"He shot his thumb off, the stupid bastard," Doll said angrily. "He didn't want to go back into the mountains. He told me yesterday, he wants to go home. I never thought he would do this. You, son-of-a-bitch!" McKenzie put his hand on Doll's shoulder to calm him down.

Doc Watson bandaged Well's hand and gave him a shot of morphine. Doll gathered up his pack and weapon to wait for the incoming helicopter that Six India had called. After Wells left, Navorski found McKenzie.

"Six wants to see you up at the CP, right away, One Six." Navorski was looking apprehensive. "I think he's mad about what Wells did."

When McKenzie got up on top, the other platoon leaders were already there. They were standing off from Captain Moore who was pacing and kicking at the dirt. He stopped and looked from one officer to the other.

"All right. Listen up," he said, standing with his feet apart and his hands on his hips looking right at McKenzie. "One of First Platoon's men just shot his thumb off so he could go home. I'm not going to lose men to that kind of crap. You got anyone who's having trouble, let's get him some help before any more of this goes on." He walked closer to McKenzie.

"One Six, you haven't had enough field time to learn who might be having trouble and who's OK but I expect you to get to know each man inside and out and you talk to Koop and you get those squad leaders of yours to pull their heads out of their asses. You understand me? That man's squad leader should have been on top of this. This should never have happened.

We're operating at less than two-thirds strength now and who knows what we're gonna run into in the next few days. Delta Company has been the best company in this battalion for some time and by God, I don't want anyone to let up now. Black Knight wants a big push tomorrow. I just got off the radio with him and he's got Alpha and Charlie Companies coming in from the Southwest.

S-2 thinks there might be a big NVA movement, so this operation is growing. One Six? Since you're new here, I want you to take third position tomorrow. Third Platoon will lead out with Second following. First Platoon's got security ambushes tonight. Any questions?"

When McKenzie found Koop, he was cleaning his own weapon.

"We been in these mountains before, LT," he said. "The problem will be if Six lets Black Knight order him to operate with bigger units than he wants to."

McKenzie took a deep breath and let the air out noisily. "Well, I figure I'm being tested anyway by my own men, by Six and who ever the hell else wants to see how a second lieutenant's gonna survive." Koop didn't look up. "We got night ambush again and this time I'm gonna go out with Kemper so I can see how he operates. I don't want any bitching about it. Navorski, you're going too."

"No problem, One Six," Navorski said. He was busy cleaning his radio.

"One Five, how come Doll didn't say anything to you about Wells?"

Koop looked up. "I've taken care of it. It won't happen again." He stood up. "I'll get Kemper's ambush put together," he said as he walked away.

SECOND AMBUSH

They went out the opposite direction as Doll had gone the night before. Their movement was even quieter and slower. A bright moon threw out gaunt shadows from the six moving soldiers, starting at their feet. McKenzie felt absolutely naked. They walked until they found a wide trail intersecting their own, which Kemper said he'd checked out earlier when they first walked through the area.

The trail traveled out of the mountains, directly toward the coast. There were signs it was being well used. By the time Kemper put each man into position to form a linear ambush, McKenzie was sure the enemy was sitting in the dark all around them, watching and waiting. It seemed to take a long time for the ambush to get set up in grass just down from the intersection.

Three men would sleep and three would stay awake with rotation every two hours. Kemper had given a short reeducation on noise and movement discipline at camp before they moved out. Violating either could get you killed, he had said angrily. McKenzie suffered a cramp in his right foot during his second shift around two in the morning. He was thinking about shifting position when he heard the faint sound of someone talking in sing song Vietnamese. He could not immediately tell what direction it was coming from. He stopped breathing.

The smell of his own sweat seemed to permeate the night air. He was certain the moon had decided to get brighter at that very moment, making the ambush visible. He could feel his own fear so hard his hair tingled. His eyes began to burn as he strained to look for the origin of that voice.

A warped image slowly entered the intersection from his left. Then another and another - they were moving shadows. North Vietnamese soldiers in full uniform, rifles slung over shoulders, moved in an easy manner as if they owned the night, apparently unaware anyone else was near. A cricket rubbed its legs together making a distinctive clicking sound. Off in the distance, a gecko screamed.

What McKenzie could not hear was the sound of feet upon the ground or weapons rattling. There were no canteens bouncing against ammunition. The noise discipline of this large group of enemy soldiers was so good, they seemed to float along the trail like specters out of an Edger Allen Poe story. Fifty-three NVA regulars passed so close, there was no reason they should not have sensed the Americans and yet they did not. He could smell the strong odor of their spicy food. As the last soldier disappeared off to the right where the trail dropped away, Navorski rolled over next to McKenzie and squeezed his radio handset three times, the squelch signal to the FOB they had enemy in the area.

"That was unbelievable, One Six," he said in a whisper. McKenzie's left leg was completely asleep. Navorski's radio gave back a low squelch. He brought the handset up and listened.

"That's a roger, Six. We got fifty-three, november victor charlies moving away to the East. That last guy's probably 50 mikes away by now and they're spread out." Navorski had his free hand over the mouth piece to muffle his voice. "Roger, we preset our coordinates. We can adjust off them."

McKenzie's mind felt like Jell-O. Retracing those agonizing minutes of watching the NVA, he wasn't sure he had breathed once. What would he have done if they had been discovered? He knew he would have fired his full magazine but then he didn't know if he would have been able to reload fast enough. He began to shake. Sweat rolled off his forehead into his eyes. Navorski was still talking low into the radio.

McKenzie's mind slowly drifted away. He was standing on steps behind the family house in Oregon. A light fall rain fell on his head. With it, temperatures would cool and give a signal to the deciduous trees it was time to change color and abandon the chlorophyll of summer and the hope of last spring. It was almost autumn. Very soon, winter would come.

He looked over the dying vegetable garden and then up at the honking Canadian geese flying south. How do they always know where to go? He watched as each goose took his turn in the lead, flying from the back along the line of geese until reaching the apex. It was a choreographed dance in the sky. It was the part of fall that always brought him faith and joy.

A white phosphorous spotting round exploded in the air to the West. He had been in Oregon only a few seconds but it had been so real.

"Adjust 100 mikes to the sierra and fire for effect," Navorski said calmly.

Whistling projectiles in the air were still novel and unnerving to McKenzie and he jumped when the night suddenly filled with rounds traveling like freight trains toward the enemy. He could hear them explode in rapid succession and knew that somewhere in the darkness, fifty-three human beings were down on the ground or running to get away. Some might die immediately, others would have wounds that would kill them if not treated soon enough and some would walk away.

What a disjointed war. No battle lines, no staged confrontations. Everything he had experienced so far had occurred more as a furtive dance of happenstance. Nothing was really planned. They walked down a trail until they ran into the NVA or they sat off the trail and waited to see if someone would walk by.

How could he strengthen his convictions for being there if he had no opportunity to forge them into steely resolve by participating in the crucible of a prolonged and desperate armed battle? Isn't that what Black Knight wanted? Instead, they were anonymously killing the enemy long distance.

CHAPTER FOUR - COMBAT

(JULY 7, 1968 - 346 DAYS LEFT)

PRIVATE WRIGHT

The big operation never happened. Alpha and Charlie Companies left after two days. Captain Moore immediately split up his platoons to operate separately. McKenzie was glad because he had started to believe he might be getting combat legs.

On July, seventh, Delta Company was brought together and picked up. A recon pilot had spotted heavy enemy activity and taken ground fire. Their assault helicopters dropped toward a plush meadow, full of wavy waist high grass, which sat at the foot of a small valley. Standard preparatory artillery fire exploded on the ground, producing eruptions of dirt, as they flew into the area. Now that the company was back together, First Platoon was told to walk last again. Black Knight had insisted on a full company operation during a heated discussion with Captain Moore on the radio. Double Time Six was so mad his face turned bright red, looking almost crimson under his blond hair.

They moved out with Third Platoon in the lead. The smell of cordite from exploding artillery was tangy and irritated the nose. Around fifteen hundred, word came back that point had run into bunkers and spider holes. Captain Moore pulled the company back, called in red leg and blasted the hell out of everything. That was the day.

The next morning Second Platoon took the lead as they walked back toward the valley, which narrowed into a trickling creek bed. It was eleven hundred hours when they finally reached the foot of the valley. Six and Black Knight had agreed Delta would move up the creek bed which ran down a hill on the back side of the bunker complex. Intelligence suspected this was an NVA staging area for attacks on the coast.

The valley was bordered by forest that hung progressively darker as they moved forward along the creek bed, which came out of the trees at the far end. Delta made its way along the South side. Ribbons of sunlight ran across the hill to the North. A thin trickle of water snaked through and around a jumble of round, worn rocks reminiscent of streams back in Oregon.

Second Platoon entered the area cautiously. Two Six described the creek over the radio as splitting off in two directions mid way to the top. Captain Moore started to answer but two Chinese machine guns interrupted in short bursts and then increased to continuous firing. McKenzie heard the now familiar high pitched crack of AKs and the sound of men screaming over Navorski's radio. They ran forward.

Moving around the corner of the trail, they saw water, mud, rocks and white hot air flying from the creek bed as enemy bullets churned the ground. Two members of Second Platoon lay in the water face down. Several others were wounded and pinned down behind small rocks. Two soldiers moved forward to help. One of the rescuers raised up to look just before he was shot through the head. An M-60 machine gun fired back across the hillside. M-79 rounds exploded in the trees above where the NVA were dug in. Blue trickling creek water turned pink around the dead men.

"Six, this is One Six. I'm ready to move some men anytime you want. Over."

"Negative, One Six. I want you to secure a pickup zone for Medivac. We got at least three KIAs, maybe more. Let me know when you get an area. Over."

Captain Moore's voice rose and fell with heavy gulping breaths. He directed Third Platoon to flank the enemy and get a firing line to shut them down. Within minutes, the eruption of combat had stopped. Silence grew louder as McKenzie moved First Platoon back and they began to clear the edge of a small meadow, chopping with machetes at underbrush and bamboo.

When Medivac called inbound, McKenzie pointed to an area on the East side of the clearing, next to several large ant hills.

"One-five, get two men over behind those for security."

From up the trail came the sounds of men grunting under heavy loads.

"One Six, we got two KIAs and one more comin. We got four WIAs that need Medivac."

Sergeant Morris, from Second Platoon, was yelling over the sounds of combat still in his head as he put his end of a hastily made rain poncho litter on the ground. Koop leaned down and rolled a bloody shoulder over to get dog tags. There was not much left of the neck or hairline. There was no person there. Only a pasty body, already the color of wet canvas. The hole was full of dirt and flesh.

McKenzie took a step back. It was Private Wright, the overweight, newly married military novice he had sat next to for six thousand miles from McCord Air Force Base to Cam Rahn Bay.

After watching Wright walk across the tarmac, McKenzie had seen him again at Bien An filling sand bags. He was very surprised to see Wright in the First Cav, let alone in Delta Company. Wright had looked up from digging in the sand as if he'd just seen his oldest friend and grinned ear to ear.

"I heard you were going to be the new one six. What took you so long? I've been here almost a week."

McKenzie had only answered, "Hi, good to see ya" and moved on. Since then, he had not had any occasion to speak to Wright, who was a member of Second Platoon. Now he wanted to say something. His throat was constricted and dried up as he stood there wanting to reclaim lost moments.

"How the hell you doin?", he should have said. "I didn't know you were coming to the Cav. When did that happen? I never saw you at An Khe or Camp Evans when I went through. How's your wife? Get any mail yet? Come on over to First Platoon when you're done and I'll buy you a cup of canteen coffee. You can tell me about Delta and how you and me are gonna get through this year. I want you on that plane next to me when we leave this dump, OK?" He had said none of it.

Dry red dirt, turned to bloody mud, was caked along Wright's collar and shoulder. His steel helmet lay next to his feet in the poncho. What used to be tan skin was waxy, grey green. McKenzie wanted to turn him over but he could not bring himself to do it. How were they ever going to fix him up for his family? He was standing there trying to remember Wright's face when Koop knocked him to the ground as a mortar round exploded about twenty-five meters away. A gun ship, now on station, was directed to the enemy mortar position and began firing rockets over the crest of the hill.

The Medivac chopper came in out of the bright sky, blades popping. It was not Wright they laid out across the chopper floor. McKenzie had sealed off that memory. Three hundred and forty-four days left and whatever he had felt was so politically important about the war had suddenly vanished. He had lost it. He looked up at another UH-1 slick hovering to the side as the Medivac bird lifted away.

CHAIN OF COMMAND

Purple smoke swirled into the rotor blades of the second helicopter, which had a big, yellow Cav patch on its nose. It flared back hard and landed softly on the grass. Captain Moore came from behind McKenzie and went stomping over as the copilot's door opened and Black Knight stepped out. His jungle fatigues were starched and creased, his flight helmet polished as bright as his boots.

Captain Moore and Colonel Fishmuth exchanged angry words immediately and it continued as they walked back toward the sight of the ambush. First Platoon had begun to relax, some smoking, some looking for something to eat. Private Jones, from Third Squad was brewing a cup of hot chocolate, his canteen cup sitting on top of a C-ration cooker when the two officers walked by. Neither noticed the soldier and he didn't look up. The gun ship continued to fire its rockets and mini-guns at something over the hill.

Jungle noises began to return as if nothing had happened. A few birds began to regain their voice. McKenzie moved inside the tree line and listened to see if he could distinguish how jungle voices in the day were different from those at night. Sounds seemed muffled or captured by the ubiquitous, wide, green tropical plants. Overhead, triple canopy jungle consisting of three or more layers of tree limbs, closed off the sky, bouncing all noise back toward the ground. Wet, dripping sounds from the rain forest filled the empty spaces threatening to drown out any other sounds. In between spaces were occupied by the echoing sounds of bugs near by and the songs of far away birds, their talk traveling until they met other sounds.

Smells also rode rough shod over the air dominated by a pungent smell of decay. Flowers blew off sweet fragrance everywhere. Only when those smells were dealt with and separated would McKenzie be able to detect the cooking rice or the nuk mam made of rotting fish heads favored by the NVA or VC. It worried him.

He'd started to smoke. McKenzie slid down next to a tree and tried to fix into his memory what had just happened. He sucked hard on a newly lit Salem cigarette. Delta Company had walked up a terrain feature that formed a perfect Y, the basic ambush configuration described over and over in OCS small unit tactics class.

Captain Kneeland, with two tours in Vietnam, was the OCS Instructor who lectured at them those first summer classes. The Georgia heat was sweltering inside the class room at Fort Benning, Georgia with no air conditioning, forcing the candidates to put handkerchiefs beneath their writing hand to keep from soaking their notebook paper as they listened.

"Never, never walk up a creek bed unless you have to. Never walk into a Y terrain feature and for God sakes, never walk up a creek bed that ends in a Y! Never approach a hill with two descending cuts in the ground, made by rain draining into a creek, even if it's dry. It's a perfect ambush. Unless you are the one sitting in the cat bird seat, ready to spring your own ambush, you are in the wrong place and you and your men will likely come home in body bags. That's not acceptable, Candidates! Those young soldiers will be depending on you to make good decisions." It was a mantra Captain Kneeland chanted over and over.

McKenzie suddenly remembered that was where he had first heard the most important lesson: "Take care of your men and they will take care of you." Captain Kneeland, ram rod straight with a CIB on his chest and a First Cav patch on his right shoulder, was adamant. He cited, more than once, an official pamphlet titled, "Vietnam Primer (Lessons learned), published April 21, 1967, which was a critique of US Army tactics and command practices in small combat units, gleaned from interviews of soldiers following operations from May, 1966 to February, 1967.

It had been prepared by Brigadier General S.L.A. Marshall and Lieutenant Colonel David H. Hackworth, two esteemed infantry experts. There were fourteen lessons to be learned in the pamphlet. Number nine was, "Ruses, Decoys and Ambushes." The pamphlet was another one of those things McKenzie had brought with him to Vietnam. He had not looked at it since he first entered the country. He needed to pull it out and review all fourteen.

Captain Moore stalked the men like an angry tiger after Black Knight had left, walking back and forth along the trail and jumping people at random for the slightest thing. He told his platoon leaders that night that he would not operate any more according to what Black Knight wanted. Platoons would go back to operating as single units, unless he decided otherwise.

"We are going to out Charlie, Charlie," he growled through clenched teeth. Later that night, Six sat alone and wrote three letters to three waiting families.

"Six has got his balls back," Koop said.

BUNKERS

The next two days were spent looking for an elusive enemy unwilling to fight. Delta found little in the bunker complex except signs that rice had been cooked recently. On the third day, Black Knight informed Delta they would be a blocking force for Bravo Company, who would sweep the area and try to drive the enemy toward them. Instead, Bravo walked into a large ambush, losing three killed and eleven wounded. McKenzie sat and listened to the radio as frantic calls for air support, artillery and rocket gun ships were made. Finally, disengagement by the enemy allowed Medivac to come in. There was no time for Delta to move in close enough to help. The fierce moments were over quickly.

Black Knight's response was to bring in as much artillery and air strikes as were available. It appeared he was trying to pulverize the enemy. Delta's platoons continued to operate separately, setting up ambushes and catching small groups of NVA as they moved. McKenzie was learning.

A recon helicopter spotted more bunkers to the Northwest as the operation moved into its fifth day. They were described as huge, twenty by ten feet. A few appeared to have two stories. The pilot said it looked like a hospital area but it sounded more like a death trap to McKenzie. Delta was told they were going in for a look in the morning. Captain Moore brought the platoons back together. This was going to be a company operation.

McKenzie was too tired to eat that night. First Platoon had been on ambush every night. While Koop checked night positions, looked for infections, made sure malaria pills were taken and settled a couple of inter-squad issues, McKenzie walked the perimeter. He was no longer the new guy and these members of his platoon were not only familiar but his comrade in arms. They were all different. Some guys built deep fox holes with pocket ledges down inside for cooking without casting a light. Others merely cleared a depression in the ground where they could roll into if the company received incoming or were attacked. He found Sergeant Kemper alone, cleaning his weapon.

"Hey, One Six, whaddaya think of the bush so far? Fucked up, ain't it."

"I don't know, Sarge. Seems like things happen quick out here."

108

"Yea and ya don't want to listen to that little voice in your head too much or you will go crazy. Ya know what I mean, LT?"

"I don't yet but I'm gonna need that little voice if I hang around you for too long. What do you think?"

Kemper laughed but McKenzie thought about the voice in his head, which had been chattering a lot. When he got back, Navorski and Koop were sharing a cup of Mojo.

"We're going to have to keep an eye on the infections. I saw several that are getting out of hand," Koop reported.

It was the kind of statement that needed no response. It was advisory only. If a soldier got scratched during the day by a wait a minute vine, medics had to treat it that night to prevent the scratch from becoming a major issue. This meant literally going through the entire company and checking every man, every night.

McKenzie lay down on his poncho liner without eating. Since coming to the field, McKenzie had instructed Navorski to wake him around two-thirty and just before day break. He, Navorski and Doc Watson rotated radio shifts. Koop had his own schedule. When it was McKenzie's turn, he always walked the line and he wanted his second shift at first light. He had learned that was the most important time - the most dangerous time. Charlie liked to come in just as day was breaking, when soldiers were often lax and prone to fall asleep. McKenzie felt he was starting to identify the real dangers, the ones that could fool you and the ones that could kill you. He was so tired, he fell asleep before finishing the thought.

As usual, Navorski woke McKenzie for his first watch. The night was quiet except for the irritating taunt of the "fuck you" lizard. When McKenzie first heard it, Kemper explained that the sound came from a gecko, who's call, repeated over and over, sounded just like "fuck you." Soldiers had been known to break night silence with a burst from their M-16 or M-60 and scream back into the night, "FUCK YOU!" He listened to it awhile and chuckled. It really was maddening.

ARC LIGHT

Night hung black and heavy with ebony and tar colored ribbons. So little variation. Waiting for his eyes to adjust was useless. Sight recognition ended about ten feet on a moonless night like this. Yet, when there was a full moon, it seemed to turn night into day. Sitting there on guard duty, with no moon at all, McKenzie felt even more exposed and vulnerable.

He was concentrating on training his eyes to get stronger when off in the distance he heard a low rumbling. It grew louder and sounded like thunder. He looked in the direction of the sound and saw the horizon light up with flashes. The rolling thunder and flashes moved toward him and the earth began to quiver. He reached over and shook Navorski. "What the hell is that?" Navorski sat up.

"Arc light, One Six. Its not even close." He lay back down and pulled his camouflage poncho liner over his head.

McKenzie felt the shaking increase. "What the hell's an arc light?", he said pushing Navorski's shoulder.

"B-fifty two bombers, LT. They love to catch Mr. Charles walking around at night. No big deal."

"Bullshit! They're coming our way." McKenzie heard his voice get higher. He stood up. The ground was shaking hard enough to move under him. He reached for the radio. Navorski sat up and grabbed his right wrist.

"Sir. I know this is your first arc light but who you gonna call?"

"I'm gonna call this thing off. It's too close. Those guys up there may not know we're here."

"LT. Those bombs are at least two clicks away. It may even get louder. Sit down. Believe me, they aren't going to come close."

McKenzie sat down and re-holstered the radio hand set. Doc was up on his elbow looking at him. The growing thunder was causing the ground to roll under him. Doc lay back down. No one else around him moved. The rumbling grew louder and the ground seemed to swell. Then it stopped. McKenzie realized he was holding his breath again.

Within minutes, the southern sky lit up off in the distance but he felt no more movement. Another arc light farther away. It looked like an electrical converter blowing up. Balling his hands into fists, he placed both on the ground, knuckles down and closed his eyes. What in God's name was happening to the poor souls on top of who those bombs were being dropped? There were so many explosions - the bombs had to be huge. It sounded like a jack hammer.

McKenzie looked at Navorski who was beginning to snore and realized he was not going to get back to sleep so he took all the rest of the watches, preferring to let his team get some rest.

Finally, first light came, the morning sun slitting open the darkness to rise in the East. Time to make coffee. This was becoming his favorite time. He was the protector of these men and it was his responsibility to get them through danger zones like first light.

ENEMY SOLDIER

It was a typical morning, with each soldier mixing personal needs with military preparation. Shit, shower and shave didn't quite cover the subject but if you had to relieve yourself, you had to decide where. Most people wanted a little privacy but not too much. Many a soldier took home the story of that one time when an NVA or VC walked up on them when they were squatting with their pants down around their ankles. The ones who lived to tell the story were those where the enemy, just as shocked to see them, simply turned and ran.

McKenzie already had his own story. During his first days at Bien An, he had risen just after first light and moved over a sand berm for a little such privacy. His new diet of field rations was not sitting well and his bowels were growling loudly. It felt like a good case of the runs coming on. He moved fast without taking his weapon. Early morning shadows from coastal palm trees ran inland across the dusty looking sand as he moved into them.

After he dropped into a full squatting position to take his relief, the black tree to his right moved slightly. He froze as the shadow slowly took the shape of a soldier in full uniform and pith helmet, his AK pointed to the right in the direction he was moving. McKenzie saw the man's head slowly turn left to look at him. With the morning sun on the rise behind the soldier, there was only black where he looked for a face. Sun rays streaked past the NVA soldier like a spotlight in a dark theatre, blinding McKenzie. He closed his eyes and waited for the shots that would end his short career.

"LT. What the hell? You're too far away without your weapon. Better finish your business and get out of there." It was Sergeant Doll off to his left whispering at him. McKenzie looked back but there was no longer a soldier in the trees.

LESSONS

Captain Moore called his platoon leaders together around 0700. He had been going over the map, trying to figure a way not to get fooled by having to charge up another valley into what may be a bunker complex or a major hospital area.

"There's a small, stream bed off to the Northeast here. If this is a hospital, guards or personnel are gonna draw water from that stream. It doesn't take much to guess the NVA are not gonna be wandering about midmorning," he told them.

"We're gonna use a lead element, a scout squad with three of our best point men. Their job will be to spot any guards and help fashion our approach. First Platoon will pull up the rear. Third Platoon will follow the scout team and I'll be with Second Platoon. Any questions?"

The morning felt hotter as if the upper atmosphere was letting in more heat than usual. First Platoon waited and watched the long line of Delta Company descend toward low, rolling hills, then move across an open grassy field to the forest. Soldiers resembled, from that distance, a line of ants marching toward a dropped piece of fruit. Far ahead, the scout team entered the edge of the forest. For the next thirty minutes, sixty-seven soldiers stepped into the tree line one at a time. Radio chatter was eliminated except for the occasional squelch.

McKenzie wrapped the sling on his M-16 around his elbow so the weapon was tight in his grip, his left hand on the barrel guard, right thumb on the safety. He had taped his grenades down and now carried extra ammo clips in an NVA shoulder pouch liberated off one of their ambush victims. On his hip rode a two quart plastic canteen, next to two smoke grenades. Eventually First Platoon entered the forest and McKenzie began assessing the terrain on both sides of the trail. He had just inventoried a new plant with large, bright yellow striped leaves when all hell broke loose. Chaotic firing came from up front, increasing sharply and dramatically. The radio crackled.

"Third Platoon's got two KIA and two WIA and our scout unit is pinned down by a machine gun on one side. They walked right into a V shaped ambush."

Navorski reported all this in an excited voice. "Six is moving a squad from Second Platoon to the left flank and bringing the other two just far enough to lay down suppressing fire," he said. Chinese rockets slammed into the ground somewhere up front. McKenzie grabbed the radio and listened.

"This is Two Six, I got incoming from my whiskey. I need help over here." McKenzie hand signaled First Platoon to move toward the firing. Doll and Casey ran by McKenzie so fast it startled him. Two others ran with them and crossed the open creek up the hill to a small ridge and over, coming down on two NVA who jumped up and fired. Doll shot them both and moved his group above Second Platoon on the opposite flank of the ambush. One grenade silenced a Chinese machine gun. Captain Moore yelled, "Cease fire! Cease fire!". It was over in about ten minutes.

First Platoon moved back and began cutting an area for Medivac. Third Platoon come down the trail with its KIAs and WIAs. Doll brought Private Crowley back with a serious wound in his shoulder. Another Medivac to end another operation. McKenzie walked forward. The trail turned left and ran up a short incline where the scout team had spotted movement and opened up. Two were dead. Three NVA were step-ons. The world had grown hollow with no emotions roaming around in his head any more. What he saw was just information.

CHOAGIES

Search of the area the next day resulted in no more contact, only discovery of a staging area but no hospital. Days turned into weeks with little contact. Battalion seemed to change orders daily and Delta continued to operate in small groups. Around ten, one morning, Kemper's point man was following a well worn trail up the side of a narrow draw. It began to turn more sharply toward the ridge line. Doll stopped movement with a hand signal and came back to where McKenzie was kneeling next to Navorski.

"Kemper hasn't seen anything but says he smells gooks."

Lesson Nine in the Vietnam Primer; "If the US unit commander is to keep his guard up against ruses and ambushes, he must be receptive to the counsel of his subordinates and draw on the total of information concerning the immediate presence of the enemy that has been collected by his people. (page 31) The average US soldier today, in Vietnam, has a sharper scouting sense and is more alert to signs of the enemy than the man in Korea or WW II. The environment has whetted that keenness and quickened his appreciation of any indication that people other than his own are somewhere close by, either in the wilderness or in an apparently deserted string of hamlets."

McKenzie made his way up to where Kemper was kneeling down just back from where the trail turned around a bush.

"What have you got, Kemper?"

"Point man heard equipment up on the ridge and I smell gooks," he said.

Kemper slipped past the point man, whose eyes were as big as sewer lids with small pupils from being alert and on point, then turned and motioned McKenzie forward. They peeked around a bush. There it was. A line of NVA soldiers moving from left to right, single file, in full uniform with battle equipment and "choagies" carrying supplies.

If they spotted First Platoon down the hill, they would not only possess the high ground but they would be able to attack off the ridge quickly. It would be a disaster. McKenzie scooted back and waved Navorski forward. Six was working with Second Platoon about a click away. McKenzie called him and described the situation.

"Six, it looks like an entire company with choagies carrying all their equipment and lots of it. Over," he whispered.

"Roger that, One Six. Get red leg on the horn and see if they can do a tango oscar tango. Give them your coordinates. Over."

McKenzie repeated the message to Navorski who got his code book out. Operations quickly approved the idea. Navorski spoke with a hushed voice, "This is Delta One Six India, lima tango says give us the tango oscar tango. One willie peter with one adjustment. Victor Charlie in the open."

Tango oscar tango meant time on target, a request for as many artillery pieces as could be put together, all firing at one time at one specific target. The only warning Charlie would get would be a white phosphorous marking round that would burst in the air somewhere near them. McKenzie would only have time to make one adjustment and OK the shot. Within seconds, rounds would start dropping in Charlie's pocket.

McKenzie crawled back for another look at the ridge line. What he had failed to see earlier came as a shock. This was a company of NVA women, in full battle gear, carrying AKs and rocket launchers. There were no men except the choagies. Kemper, who was beside McKenzie, turned to say something just as a white phosphorous round popped high over the column. The NVA turned to their left and disappeared off the ridge line. Their discipline and reaction was amazing. McKenzie adjusted one hundred meters in the direction he guessed they were heading and said, "Fire for effect." Everyone got down and lay flat against the hill.

The next few seconds seemed forever, hanging in a shroud of silence until they heard the whistling sounds of incoming rounds come over their heads and begin to crash exactly where they wanted them. Shrapnel came careening over the ridge and small pieces of metal landed around the platoon as rounds hit the ground in multiples.

McKenzie tried not to think about what he had done, although a picture of the imagined chaos and panic flashed before his closed eyes. He was killing women. He did not count the rounds. Instead, he lived in his head during the long time it took until the radio announced, "Fire mission complete." Red leg asked if they wanted more. Navorski said negative and thanked them

"OK, Kemper. Let's go have a look." McKenzie said

They cautiously topped the ridge where they found a wide, heavily traveled trail, running up from the left, out of a narrow valley. It continued to the right for another fifty meters and then turned left, dropping down into a clearing that sloped gently toward a low draw. A heavy stand of trees lined the bottom of the clearing, its sparse foliage similar to scrub oak. Many were blown apart.

Abandoned equipment lay everywhere. Koop moved past the lead group and quickly established a perimeter with fire teams near the bottom. Kemper moved down the trail with a squad to see if they could spot blood trails and to establish a hasty ambush for any attempt by the enemy to recover their equipment or to counter attack.

"Jesus Christ, One Six. You cannot let these guys walk into an open area like big dumb ass geese and start pawing through equipment without any security." Koop had come back and walked over close to McKenzie. He spoke low so only the two of them could hear. Soldiers had scattered around the clearing to grab equipment or look for souvenirs

"This is a perfect set up for Charlie to catch whoever put the hurt on them," Koop said.

Navorski walked up and held the radio hand set out toward McKenzie. "Six is on the phone," he said.

"This is One Six, over."

"This is Six. Give me a sit rep. Over."

"Roger that, Six. We got beau coup equipment but no bodies. Over."

"One Six, see if you can find something for S-2. That was too many people not to come up with any KIAs, over."

"Roger that, Six. It was a company full of females with choagies, over." McKenzie said.

After a long pause, Captain Moore answered, "Set up security and stay put. I'm coming over to work with you for a while. Over"

BACKPACK

Searching found nothing significant. Navorski radioed in what information they had, while others stacked equipment to go back to battalion intelligence. There were a few blood trails and drag marks, a couple of weapons and some ammo in ammo pouches. The platoon rested and waited for Six. McKenzie sat down to look at his map. Kemper came up and dropped two empty backpacks in front of him. NVA backpacks were prized by GIs as being larger and better suited to the jungle than their own Army issue.

"One Six. Take your pick. I figure you got a little salt on you now," Kemper said. Not waiting for an answer, he handed the best one to McKenzie. The other two squad leaders stood behind him with big grins looking like they'd just robbed Fort Knox. Koop was off to the side like he wasn't a part of it but McKenzie saw him watching. He got up. "Thanks, guys. At least now I'll look like the rest of you hard cases." Kemper got everyone out of an awkward moment by reporting he had discovered a rest station with signs of more blood and bandages but no bodies. Further on was a much larger and well traveled trail, he said. It came straight up out of a dry creek bed and circled around the rest area.

He also confirmed what the map showed. They were sitting on a small knoll. Six showed up with Second Platoon around 1700 and agreed with McKenzie they needed to set up an ambush on the down hill side to pick up anyone coming out of the creek bed. Second platoon moved away to the South for a separate night position.

AMBUSH SPRUNG

The sky darkened. A late, afternoon rain began as a drizzle, then increased, soaking everyone. McKenzie set a linear ambush perpendicular to the trail at the top of a small clearing closer to the creek bed. Everyone would have a shot at whoever came into the kill zone. He also sent a small defensive squad back up the trail in case there were more travelers coming from the same direction. The night began wet and miserable.

Around midnight, sounds of something moving through foliage came from the under growth at the bottom of the clearing.

McKenzie looked hard into the darkness and quietly moved his safety to full automatic. As if in answer, a low growl let him know a tiger had winded them. Was he stalking? How many others were awake?

The big cat moved from left front to the middle of the tree line, still out of sight, still growling low as it came closer. It sounded agitated. A second low growl grew to a loud roar. Up and down the line safeties clicked to full automatic. People were awake.

Captain Moore had brought a Chu Hoi with him to act as their scout. He was a VC who had defected. The man sat up, looked around boringly, shook his head and lay back down. McKenzie listened so hard for the tiger's next movement, his head hurt. Finally, the tiger moved off to the right and over the hill. He suspected no one else was going back to sleep except the Chu Hoi.

Hours passed and McKenzie thought about John Steinbeck's Cannary Row, a book he had read in college. In it, early morning was described as "the hour of the pearl," the interval between night and day, when time stops and examines itself. McKenzie sat waiting for that glimmer of first light and wishing he was back in college. A faint glow finally crept in from the East and dawn turned night to a milky gray as cold rain drizzled down the back of his neck. Fog became visible, drifting lazily out of the creek bed below and overhead clouds spread apart becoming thinner. A few hopeful strands of light wiggled through the treetops.

~~

As McKenzie sits musing about the possibility of a warmer, dryer morning, he sees the fog move; A North Vietnamese soldier silently and gingerly steps into the bottom of the clearing. Their ambush has become visible in the morning light, yet the soldier does not react to what is in front of him. He takes two more steps into the clearing followed by two others, then stops short causing number two, who is looking at the ground, to run into him. Number one appears not to believe what he sees. He stands and looks without any sign of expression as time gets hung up in the tree vines.

In a flicker of movement, the lead soldier says something in Vietnamese and starts to raise his weapon. First Platoon opens up, M-16s, M-79s and M-60s, all firing at once. So much firing the area becomes cloudy with smoke. M-79 rounds thump and explode as bullets and red tracers fly through the air. McKenzie screams ceasefire several times before the roar quiets. His ears are ringing. The Chu Hoi jumps up and charges toward two bodies laying on the trail.

"I got you," he yells in broken English. He dances around the bodies in a frenzied celebration. Captain Moore explained to McKenzie how the man had defected after other Viet Cong killed his parents. He is obviously happy at this revenge. Three small puddles of blood pool in the dirt, two beneath the bodies and a third where the last man had been but now is gone. The Chu Hoi runs to the edge of the clearing looking for the wounded NVA.

~~

AN EAR

Koop found a set of orders on one of the dead soldiers, which the Chu Hoi interpreted. It directed an NVA unit to move in small groups toward the border and join a larger group. Captain Moore reasoned there were no others behind these three because there had been no return fire. If they were moving in small groups, this area was going to be an ambusher's paradise. The company of NVA women apparently kept on moving.

"Did you find anything else, Koop?" McKenzie asked.

"No. That was it, One Six." McKenzie walked over to where the two soldiers had fallen. Large pools of blood on the trail was smeared into the dirt but there were no bodies. He could see drag marks off to the right. He turned around and looked at Koop.

"What did you do with the bodies?"

"Whaddaya mean? We leave em. Let Charlie take care of them. One of the guys took an ear but that's all."

"Who the hell did that?" McKenzie said.

"Carter. He sort of collects them."

"Wait a minute, One Five. Not in my platoon he doesn't. You go get Carter and tell him to come over here. Now!"

McKenzie said it loud enough so everyone could hear him. He looked over at Six who shrugged his shoulders and walked away. Around him others stopped what they were doing.

Carter was from Tennessee. One of the "old ones." He'd been in the field a long time and had been through it all. He had been the platoon sniper for a while but without the aide of a scope. He used Kentucky windage, a technique that allowed him to hit targets at incredible distances. McKenzie knew Carter was near the end of his tour. He was considered a gray beard among the others and when he walked up, it was clear he had no idea what the problem was.

"Where's the ear you took off that man?" As he said it, McKenzie saw the bloody ear dangling from a piece of leather around Carter's neck. He reached out and grabbed it with his right hand, slowly undid the snap holding his Buck knife with his left hand and cut the leather.

"You listen to me, Carter. I don't give a shit what went on before I got here but you will not cut off ears, stick First Cav patches or the ace of spades or whatever on dead bodies and you will do what I say. Are we clear?"

Carter stood glaring at McKenzie but did not answer. His eyes were cold and his expression flaccid. He turned to walk away but McKenzie grabbed the back of his shirt collar with two fingers of his right hand, still clutching the ear. He leaned up to Carter's left ear and said, "Are we clear?" McKenzie held on tight and waited. No one moved. Flies buzzed in and out of the dark, thickening blood on the ground.

"Yea, LT. We're clear." It was an answer given through clenched teeth but he had acquiesced. Men like Carter put bounties on officer's heads if mad enough but McKenzie didn't care. He walked off the trail and threw the ear into the trees before walking away from the killing. Navorski came over to him.

"Don't worry about it, LT. Everyone knows Carter's a little psycho. He's still a good soldier. The last LT was a suck up and a gutless wonder. He would never have said anything to anyone, let alone Carter. First Platoon will take care of this."

Captain Moore came down the trail. "OK. Battalion wants us to move further down this trail and see what we can find. We'll move in thirty." He gave McKenzie a wink and a big, knowing smile as he walked by.

The rest of the day was quiet except for discovery of a large, recently evacuated headquarters with ten reinforced bunkers dug deep into the hill. They were A frame living quarters, under ground, with smoke funnels, obviously intended to be long term and strong enough to withstand not only artillery but air strikes. It was impressive engineering. The larger bunkers measured thirty by fifteen feet. Around fourteen hundred hours, as they were clearing the last bunker, someone spotted movement up the hill. Quick pursuit by Kemper and two others produced nothing.

CHARLIE WILD ONE

Captain Moore decided the platoon would move a click to the West before setting up their night ambush. If the trail truly led into a narrow draw ahead, as the map showed, it would provide a perfect location where the draw ended. They were in position by dusk and listened as battalion artillery hit the NVA complex with bunker busters.

The platoon set up just off the trail where it came up out of the draw onto a side hill and split in two directions. One trail cut to their left front and straight back across the draw, going away from their position. The other went up and over a small hill to the right. There were only a few trees on top of the hill. The trail also split off and went back down into the draw the way they had come. It was thus possible for them to cover traffic moving in all three directions. This was a major intersection.

Claymores and trip flares were carefully set out. The men worked in a misty rain that had continued all day. Low clouds were now gathered into a heavy ceiling. Second Platoon called in and Captain Moore told them to sit tight until they could be picked up. There was a possibility they might be needed. At the moment, however, all birds were grounded. The monsoon season had begun.

McKenzie positioned his command group just behind an M-60 set up behind a log to cover the convergence of all three trails. Extreme fatigue was beginning to set in, a let down from the earlier adrenalin. Battalion had been euphoric about the possibility of more contact and Black Knight had called right after the morning ambush. He wanted the entire company back together for a major push but Captain Moore had asked where exactly was he supposed to push. There was another angry exchange over the radio.

"I'll be God damned if I'm going to march a whole company up and down these trails single file any more. We are tops in ambush kills the way we're operating now. Mr. Charles can't deal with us," he said as they moved along the trail, more to himself than to his RTO, who was now Navorski.

Losing Navorski was a huge blow but it would give McKenzie a unique connection to Six. Navorski promised to train his replacement. The man who would be the new One Six India would also share McKenzie's foxhole, his tent and his food. He had to have courage and calm under fire. He would have to learn how to call in artillery, air strikes or direct gun ships. In the end,

McKenzie selected a new man from San Diego who had immediately impressed him.

John Orson was a college graduate from San Francisco State, quick to learn things. He was interested in what was happening and why. He was big and strong, with broad shoulders at about one hundred and ninety pounds, standing around six feet. He had no trouble packing the extra weight of a PRC-25 radio. Although he didn't appear to be too gung ho about it, he understood the most important feature of an RTO was to be near and yet, stay out of the way. Navorski showed him how to calibrate and set frequencies.

McKenzie flops down next to Orson and digs into his pack for a can of peaches and a rubber poncho to ward off the rain, which is beginning to come down harder. He watches Orson complete a very, long yawn, arms outstretched and back arched. A bullet enters his open mouth and bursts out his left cheek, pushing blood and flesh through the air. It looks like a comic book shooting - red gore flying out and spreading like shotgun pellets.

McKenzie grabs Orson as he falls over, head first into his lap, knocks his helmet off and reaches inside his mouth to clear his airway of any bone, teeth or whatever else might prevent him from breathing. There's nothing. Miraculously, the bullet missed everything. Doc Watson crawls over and puts a patch on Orson's face to stop the bleeding.

"One lucky bastard," he shouts.

Around them, bullets are streaming down from the hill top and the platoon is returning fire. Green tracers hit the ground in front of McKenzie as his machine gunner puts red tracers back up the hill. He watches the color exchange, mesmerized and not moving. Mack, the machine gunner, jumps back and rolls over grabbing his right knee. More green tracers come from the right. McKenzie grabs the big gun and begins firing at tracers until the ammo belt runs out. Doc Watson lays on top of Mack trying to bandage his leg. Captain Moore appears from out of the dark.

"We got to get these men out of here, One Six. We can't stay here. They got us in a bad enfilade position. If they start coming down that hill, we're all in trouble."

McKenzie turns and yells at Casey. "Give me two men!" Then he yells at his captain, "I'll take the machine gun and the radio. We'll move up to that tree snag and see if we can hold em off. You move the platoon across the draw and set up a firing line, then we'll come across."

Six doesn't answer, he is already moving. He pulls Mack down the hill with him and disappears. McKenzie rolls over and pulls the radio onto his back, grabs the M-60, as much ammo as he can hold and crawls to the downed tree, pulling the gun behind him. Laying on his side, he opens the breach and slaps in a new belt of ammunition, swings the gun's front end over the tree trunk and starts firing.

Casey and Kemper appear beside him. Kemper has brought another can of M-60 belted ammunition. McKenzie sweeps the hillside from left to right as fast as he can, where ever he sees green tracers. The incoming is getting worse. Bullets thud into the tree trunk and whizz past his head. Casey pops magazines in and out of his M-16, firing on full automatic. He and Kemper have brought as many bandoliers full of loaded magazines as they could carry. Kemper is firing short bursts at muzzle flashes.

McKenzie screams at them to make their shots count but he knows there is no way to do that with what they are facing. They cannot see the enemy who appear to be moving down and across the hill. The fight ebbs and then renews itself. The NVA are trying to maneuver around to the right and cut them off from the rest. Kemper crawls off to the right, killing three coming up from the far end of the draw. Casey kills a sniper who has climbed into a tree on the ridge line and McKenzie sprays the upper trail at two new sets of green tracers.

The fire fight seems to go on and on and time gets suspended in the noise. McKenzie rolls onto his side, grabs a new belt and burns his hand on the barrel. Suddenly, a heavy volume of fire comes out of the upper tree line. It's moving in their direction and he suspects the NVA have decided to assault directly down the hill.

He rolls back to look and prays for a miracle. He fires short bursts back and forth as fast as he can but there are so many. The radio on his back begins to squawk. He reaches back and grabs the handset.

"Double Time, this is Charlie Wild One, inbound. Can I be of assistance?" It's a gun ship. McKenzie answers.

"This is Double Time One Six. We need help and you only got one shot. I'm going to throw a trip flare. There's beau coup bad guys on the hill to our front. I can hear you coming in from the West. Stay on course. They'll be east of this flare."

"Roger that, One Six. I see green tracers. Throw your flare. I'm rollin' hot."

Kemper takes the machine gun. McKenzie rolls onto his back. He had seen a trip flare laying carelessly on the ground earlier and put it on his belt. He pulls the pin, lobs it back over his head and rolls back to his stomach. What he sees takes the air out of him. It feels like an elephant standing on his chest, preventing him from breathing.

Caught for a moment in the flare's light are fifteen to twenty NVA soldiers coming down the hill with their weapons held waist high and firing. It is only for a moment because the hill side explodes as rockets and mini-gun bullets rain down upon the advancing enemy. A line of red comes from the helicopter's mini-guns, like a giant pissing blood. Even though his tracers are one in five, there seems to be no separation. Rockets explode across the hillside as the pilot swivels his tail to get a better angle, looking like a dragon fly in the rain.

McKenzie, Kemper and Casey slide backwards and drop over the edge of the draw. First Platoon opens up with everything they have. Kemper is in front leading them up the draw to the left and up the other side past the last man in the firing line where they fall down behind, breathing hard.

Charlie Wild One is screaming into his radio like an Indian warrior as he banks left over the tree line and comes back. Hovering just south of the hillside, he fires more rockets and mini-gun. There is no return fire but he keeps firing. Six yells cease fire.

They lay there watching the pilot expend every last bit of his ammunition on the hillside. Captain Moore thanks the pilot and moves the platoon back to a clearing for extraction of the wounded and for a better defensive position.

~~

THE ELEPHANT

They waited an hour for the Medivac until Captain Moore got mad and told battalion he didn't give a shit about the weather or the order to ground birds, he had two men that needed to be out of there and he wanted resupply of ammunition and water and he wanted it now. His vehemence paid off. Top not only got water and ammo onto a bird, but he was sending food and a much needed mail bag.

Captain Moore also asked Top to see if he could get the pilot's real name but when Top called back he said it was an unauthorized flight and battalion did not know who the pilot was. Charlie Wild One was not a call sign they knew. Six shouted at him, "Well, by God, you tell those fly boys I want that pilot's name." He came over to McKenzie.

"I will get that pilot's name if it's the last thing I do. You and I need to buy that guy more than a few drinks."

McKenzie sat under a poncho for a long time and shook. No one but the Captain came near him. He sat with his knees up, listening to the rain bouncing on the rubber poncho. It seemed like the only reliable thing in the world. The diverse staccato of drops was soothing. Even being wet was a message that he was alive. He had made it.

Kemper came over and gave him a Salem cigarette. The menthol reminded McKenzie of the air he'd breathed while camping in the Oregon Cascade Mountains with his Indian grandfather. It helped to calm him. He thought about the elephant that had stepped on him again. Fear and adrenalin combined to produce in him a sudden inability to breath, like an elephant was standing on his chest. Koop told him to sleep. They would cover his watch.

Somehow he got through the night. Black Knight called in the morning and said he wanted the platoon to cross back over the draw and do a damage assessment.

"Why the hell are we going back over there with one platoon? Charlie knows we're here. Why don't we just beat a brass drum when we go back over there and have a party?" He was raising his voice at his commanding officer, but McKenzie felt wrung out and didn't care.

"Because that's the orders, One Six. I may execute movement in my own way but I don't question orders. Now, let's pack up and get moving." Captain Moore said it calmly, not letting McKenzie rile him. He reached down and patted McKenzie on the head like you do to a young boy who needs assurance.

Both Kemper and Casey had come by earlier in the morning to revisit the night's events. They talked about it as soldiers do, wanting to know if the others remembered it the way they did, comparing actions and details as if to reorder their minds. The whole thing was remembered by McKenzie in slow motion, a phenomena he was still not used to. Why, he asked them, when a fire fight was so chaotic and out of control, did he remember it in slow motion? That's just the way it is, they told him. He saw them with new eyes. They were so old and so young at the same time. The ambush had bonded him to them in a new way.

WONDER BEACH

There was little evidence of how many dead or wounded the enemy had suffered. Blood trails were everywhere but they found only one damaged AK-47 and no bodies. Around thirteen hundred, battalion called. Delta Company was told to move one click to the East. They were going to be picked up and taken back to LZ Jane, then on to Wonder Beach, a make shift landing for cargo, operated by the See Bees. The old ones were giddy. They had been there before and described white sand, body surfing and something even more important. At Wonder Beach, they could parlay a ton of beer, get cleaned up and rest away from all they had been through since leaving Bien An.

McKenzie prayed for no more contact as they made their way to the pickup zone. He was the last man on the last chopper. He wanted his men out of there. He imagined Charlie watching from the trees as they flew away.

The enemy could return to moving troops and equipment without Delta to worry about. No one else was going into the area. We sure gave that up quickly, he grumbled to himself. Sitting on the edge of the chopper floor, he wasn't the new guy any more. He leaned out to let the cool air hit him directly in the face as he watched the ground race out from under him and wondered what was next.

CHAPTER FIVE - WONDER BEACH
(JULY 18, 1968 - 335 DAYS LEFT)

McKenzie's bird dropped down and landed outside LZ Jane. Delta's men were making their way from the grassy area, snaking through the concertina wire. Many seemed to be heading for certain bunkers as if automatically returning home. They were a rag tag group. Most needed new boots, pants, shirts, socks or all of the above. That would be difficult because there were superstitions to think about that prevented changing anything that had the feel of good luck about it.

He had an undershirt, the kind with no sleeves, just straps over the shoulder like his Grandpa used to wear. He had worn it every day and he was beginning to believe it had special powers, like eagle feathers. Dyed Army green, it was now well worn but he continued to wash it in his steel pot and wear it every day. He'd thought about how he could continue wearing it when it started to dissolve the way clothes did in the jungle. He would wear it over another full tee shirt. There was no way in hell he was going to get rid of the one shirt that had taken him through the last month and a half.

TOP'S WISDOM
He found Top standing outside the company tent with piles of new gear, ammunition, food and most importantly, beer.

McKenzie walked up, dropped his NVA pack and weapon next to the front entrance and walked in where he had spent those first two days so long ago. Top gave him a big grin and followed him in.

"Good to see you again, One Six. Sounds like you and my boys are getting along OK, huh?"

"They haven't fragged me yet, Top, if that's what you mean. I guess that's a good sign."

"I hear you got nothin to worry about, sir. Koop tells me you're gonna make it. You've been through a lot in a short time and you forget, I'm listening to that radio all the time. You just keep doin what you're doin. With One Five and those squad leaders, it's a good platoon. They went through some hard times waiting for you to come along and step up. They're not about to let anything happen to you."

Top walked over and put his left hand on McKenzie's shoulder. It felt like going home after a football game and hearing his Dad say he played a good game. Top was probably close to fifty years old with many young lieutenants under his belt.

"There's still a whole lot I don't know, Top. I'm losin' Kemper soon and Carter and sometimes, well, it gets to me out there."

Top grabbed McKenzie by the arm and pulled him out through the back tent flap . When they were far enough away, he stopped and stood quiet for a moment. Then he stepped closer, his face only inches away. He spoke in a low voice.

"You don't say that in front of anyone, sir. It gets to everyone out there but you can't show it or let them know it. I heard you had a hard time after that ambush and that's OK but, you got a long way to go and you better gather up. These kids are all scared. They just don't tell you about it. You're their leader. They're gonna talk among themselves or bitch or whatever. One thing I know is they're gonna do a whole lot better if they can believe in you.

Why do you think Six is such a hard charger? He's trying to set an example more than anything. That man's a saint. Believe it or not, he's a very sensitive person. Every time he loses someone, he hurts way down deep. He writes to every family personally. Not just for a KIA but for every WIA. I'll show you the letters he wrote for your two guys if you wanna see them.

And, by the way, he doesn't just leave his soldiers in the hospital by themselves. He makes sure they get what they need. In fact, sir, you're going down to Qui Nhon and Danang tomorrow to pay some of the troops in the hospitals."

"Where'd you hear that, Top?"

"Six just cut your orders. He hasn't had time to tell you yet, so I'm tellin' you. You better get cleaned up and resupplied today because when you come back, the company will already be at Wonder Beach."

"Top, I gotta find out who that pilot was that saved our butts out there. I owe that man a lot."

"Forget about it, sir. I already tried. That man took a helicopter on his own because he heard you were in trouble. They're not gonna give up his name. If they did, he'd lose his wings for disobeying orders on a no fly day." The pilot had not only risked his life for them but he'd also risked his career. McKenzie was speechless.

After Top shared a little more of his special wisdom, they stepped back into the tent. Koop was inside, having already shaved and bathed. His hair was wet and combed back in a pompadour and he was wearing glasses. He resembled a college professor as he studiously looked through a stack of new pants. When he saw the two of them, he stopped and came over to where they were standing.

RED LEG LIEUTENANT

"One Six. We got a problem. There's a first lieutenant who's been jumpin' the guys about how they look. The showers are backed up so its gonna take several hours before we can get everybody clean enough for the rear. He told Andrews from First Squad that his boots were a disgrace. No shit. I had to calm Sergeant Casey down to keep him from going after the guy."

"Who's this you're talkin' about, One Five?"

"I don't really know. He's some new officer who came in country while we were out. One of the artillery guys told me he's been like that since he got here. He's in charge of the 105s."

"You mean, he's a red leg and he's jumpin' my men who just came in from the boonies? Where's he at?" McKenzie said. He was feeling like he wanted to stomp somebody's ass. It might as well be a first lieutenant's.

"I just saw him up at the officer's mess by the TOC," Koop said. "I think he's eatin' lunch. But -- there's a whole bunch of senior officers up there. I'd wait if I were you."

McKenzie started for the door. "Just point him out to me, One Five. I'll take care of this."

Top said something about being careful as they went out of the tent. The mess table was up a slight incline past the other company tents, which were set in a row, Alpha through Delta. Each tent was a mixture of bleached canvas with ground in red clay covering the part that touched the ground. At the top of the incline, just past Alpha's tent, several long tables were lined up under a sun tarp where officers took their meals.

To the left, cooks had set up a serving line with several enlisted men dishing out food. Two majors, a lieutenant and one captain were already sitting at the tables. Four other senior officers were going through the line. McKenzie had not realized that so many staff officers would be around. He looked for Lieutenant Colonel Fishmuth but didn't see him. Koop pointed to the lieutenant, sitting on the end of the bench next to the S-3, Major Broughten. McKenzie walked up and tapped the lieutenant on the shoulder.

"Excuse me, sir. May I talk to you?" Without turning around, the officer said, "Whadaya want?" McKenzie took a step to the man's left where he could see the side of his face.

"What I need, sir, is for you to get off my troops. They just came in from the field. They're dirty, tired and frankly, not in a very good mood. From now on, if you have something to say to one of them, you come and say it to me or you and I will have a problem. Are we straight, sir?"

McKenzie put extra emphasis on the sir and waited for a reaction. As he said it all, he watched closely out of the corner of his eye to see if any of the other officers would react. He was not sure whether they would defend the guy or not. Not one of them

stopped eating or even looked up. There was a long silence or at
least, it seemed that way.

The First Lieutenant turned his head to the left where
McKenzie was standing, still dirty and unshaven like his men, then
he turned back and looked around the table. When he saw there
was no help there, he looked down at his plate full of meat and
noodles, swimming in a pool of runny gravy. He spoke in a low
but strong voice without looking up.

"I understand, Lieutenant. Thank you for speaking directly
to me about it. I'll certainly let you know if I have any other
problems."

"Thank you, sir. I'd appreciate that," McKenzie said.
When he turned around, Koop was still there. They walked back in
silence. After they had gathered up what equipment each of them
needed, Koop showed him the command bunker for First Platoon.
Unfortunately, the big eight inch gun emplacement was located
just behind. If called upon, it would be firing right over their heads.
Koop said he did not think it was fair to change now and put
someone else there. He, McKenzie and their RTOs would just have
to get by. So be it.

BEER TENT

"I suggest you might want to get cleaned up yourself, One
Six," Koop said. "The platoon has invited you down to the enlisted
men's beer tent for a cool one. They don't ask just every officer.
It's kind of an honor. You and me can meet later and get that Army
Commendation Medal written up for Hampton. It's that far tent
down the hill."

"Shit. I almost forgot about writing up Hampton, One Five. Thanks."

McKenzie felt bone weary walking to the officer's shower area and was thoroughly chagrined when he saw that while his men waited in long shower lines down below, the officer shower was empty. It was not the first time he had felt guilty about special privileges given to officers. Especially in the field, he thought everything should be equal. By God, he would go down and have a beer with his men.

After a long shower, he put on new clothes and walked down to the beer tent. It was already full of rowdy men from Delta. Some had yet to make it through the shower, filling the tent with their extreme fragrance. Calling it a beer tent was humorous. It was definitely not a bar. The men simply pooled whatever beer they could scrounge because the battalion sergeant major had decreed early on that all beer drinking would be confined to one place.

Sergeant Doll looked up. "Hey, One Six. Grab a seat. Can I buy you a beer?"

First Platoon had set up beer operations along the far wall with an ammo box full of melting ice, the beer wrapped in plastic. Empty cans of Black Label beer were scattered about on a green Army table.

"I thought Black Label wasn't made anymore?" McKenzie's question got a big laugh.

"One Six, the United States Army must have bought all the Black Label that was left cause that's all we've been drinking since I got here six months ago," said Private Malone, obviously several beers ahead. Over the next two hours, men from First Platoon came and went. When the beer ran short, one of the men went up to beg Top for more.

They told many stories during the afternoon. Word had already spread about McKenzie's trip to the officer's mess and his short speech to the rear echelon lieutenant who had been harassing them. He got a big "hoo rah" all around. Some talked about home and girlfriends, some did a little combat bragging and some just griped. He felt accepted.

When he told them he had volunteered early so he could come to the First Cav, the story got hoots and more "hoo rahs." They were proud of the Cav.

Sergeant Doll stood up. "I propose a toast to One Six for being stupid enough for not only wanting to come to Vietnam but for volunteering to come early. The men stood and gave another "hoo rah."

Then Doll said, "We're glad you did it, One Six. Just don't get yourself killed. We got you trained just how we want you."

That put a lump in McKenzie's throat, which he quickly hid with a big gulp of beer. He explained that he would be flying out the next day to pay troops and promised to get back as soon as possible. Then he left. He had to pee and the tent was unbearably hot, even with the end flaps open. There was no breeze coming through and between the cigarette smoke and rank sweat, it was suffocating in there. The men, however, carried on.

He would have to send Koop down shortly to make sure they got something to eat and sobered up enough to maintain perimeter security. After relieving himself at one of the piss tubes sunk in the ground, he headed back. Koop, as usual, was taking care of business. He was sitting outside their command bunker on a sand bag, writing on a yellow note pad. It was legal size, the kind an accountant would use. A bottle of Jack Daniel whiskey was stuck in between two sandbags in the shade.

"You toasted yet, One Six?" he said, looking up.

"No, One five. I'm OK. What are you up to?"

"Nothin much. Just giving you something to submit for Hampton's medal. Its tricky business. We got to beef it up so the medal police don't knock it down. We want Six to approve it, so we're gonna get it right the first time." He smiled, reached back, picked up the bottle of whiskey and handed it to McKenzie who took a taste.

"Oh, and One Six. Six was looking for you about an hour ago. He heard you were in the enlisted men's tent and he was not happy. He asked me to let you know he wanted to see you when you got back."

"What's his problem? I can go down and drink with my men if I want to."

"Well, now, that's debatable. Most of the officers come into camp and only associate with other officers. Its like their men got lice or something. You're never gonna see Two Six or Three Six in that beer tent."

"That's their problem. You said it was an honor to be invited and I agree. If I can live and die with these guys, share their food and sleep with one at my back for weeks at a time in the boonies, I sure as hell can go drink with them. Where did you say Six was?"

CARTER

"I don't know. I heard he's been up at the TOC having it out again with Black Knight. You might find him in the officer's beer tent or maybe up with Top. I got all the security assignments set out and Carter volunteered to go out on a surprise ambush tonight to see if he can catch a couple of Viet Cong they spotted a few nights ago scouting the perimeter. Top offered him a case of beer if he gets em."

McKenzie decided he better go find Carter first. He was intrigued by a man who would volunteer to go out alone and risk his life for a case of beer. After the ear business, Carter had steered clear but it was obvious to McKenzie, he was more than just a loose cannon.

Earlier in the year, Carter had briefly served as platoon leader before Koop showed up. He was awarded a Silver Star for action during the Tet Offensive in January. McKenzie found him sitting inside a bunker honing the blade on a K-bar knife, the kind usually carried by Marines. It looked like a bowie knife, with a serrated edge on top and a curving razor sharp blade attached to a knobbed handle wrapped in leather.

"Sergeant Carter, you busy?"

"Uh, no LT. Come on in. What can I do for you?" He said the words slow with more than his usual southern accent.

"I heard you volunteered to go outside the wire tonight and see if you can catch a couple guys who've been sneakin' around out there. That right?"

"Hell, LT. Top offered me a case of beer if I could get rid of those two guys and I thought, I ain't got nothin else goin on tonight. Funny thing is, I think he was just joking and I took him up on it. Sort of like them good ol' boys back in Tennessee who was always braggin' about having great cock roosters until I looked em in the eye and said, ya all come over yonder where mine are and we'll see who's teachin' who a lesson." Carter was freckle faced with red hair. He always had a big smile on his face. He finished the edge on his knife as he said it and slid the K-bar into its scabbard, which was wrapped in black tape.

"You taking anyone with you?" McKenzie asked, sitting down.

"No, LT. I work best alone when I'm sneakin' and peakin'. Don't worry none about it, I ain't aiming' to get myself killed tonight. Mr. Charles is the only one who's gonna be hurting'."

"Six know about this?" McKenzie said.

"I reckon. Top said it right in front of him and he never said a thing. I don't see what year gettin' all riled up about. I done this plenty a times before. I know what I'm doin."

"Well, you better be careful. I'm gonna put a quick reaction team together and if you get into any trouble, I want you to whistle and we'll come out to get you. Is that a deal?"

"Ok, but you ain't gonna hear no whistle. You jest keep those boys on the wire from shooting' me when I come back and we got us a deal."

ENIGMA

McKenzie located Captain Moore in the company tent going over the roster with Top. The CO was asking Top if there was any way they could get more men.

"You know, sir, no one's any better off than we are," Top said. "Its just the way it is. They can't process 'em fast enough to keep ahead of our losses. We got five men leaving country in two weeks and I gotta bring 'em in a week ahead of time so they can get cleaned up and get down to Cam Ranh Bay in time to get on that big Freedom Bird. I got Bailey and Shaw staying back now and not going over to Wonder Beach. Division says they can send seven new guys next week. That's the best they can do."

Top scratched his bald head and looked at the company roster on his big grease board. McKenzie thought it best not to interrupt and turned to leave but kicked a footlocker by the door.

"Hey, One Six. You looking for me?" Captain Moore said as he stood up and walked toward the door.

"Yes, sir. One Five told me you were lookin' for me earlier, something about being down at the enlisted men's beer tent?"

McKenzie tried not to sound defensive or like he was challenging his Captain but he had it in his mind not to apologize either.

"I heard you went up to the officer's mess earlier today and had a conversation with a certain first lieutenant about your platoon, One Six. Is that right?" Captain Moore looked serious when he said it. Then he smiled. "I got to give you credit, One Six. You sure as hell got a set of balls on you. Right in front of a bunch of majors and captains. Is that right?"

"Uh, yes, sir. That's my platoon and unless it's you or me, sir, I don't want anyone messin' with 'em. He's some LZ red leg who's ...."

Captain Moore interrupted him. "You don't have to explain anything to me, One Six. The way I heard it, you handled it just right. When I got up there for lunch, they were still laughing about it. That guy's been walking around here swelled up ever since he arrived and you were the first one to take him down. And, a second lieutenant at that. Ha, ha, ha," he laughed. "They all thought it was great. I would say you earned the right to go drink with your men whenever you want. Just don't make a big deal out of it. Black Knight doesn't like it."

"Sir? You know about Carter goin' out tonight?" McKenzie said.

"Yes, I do. You got a problem with that? He knows what he's doin'."

"No, I guess not. I'm gonna put a quick reaction force together and stand by in case he gets in trouble, if you don't mind."

"I wouldn't expect anything else from you, One Six. Stop worrying. Top's got a case of beer getting' cold already."

McKenzie looked over at Top, who conspicuously turned away as if he wasn't a part of the discussion. Damn! Now he was confused. Who was Captain Moore anyway? Was he a gung ho fighter and a strict disciplinarian or was he a cowboy willing to let Carter be a one man John Wayne on some yahoo escapade for a case of beer? The way Koop had put it, Captain Moore was mad as hell about McKenzie going to the enlisted men's beer tent but once he heard about the first lieutenant story, it was no problem. Was the captain strictly US government issue or was he not? McKenzie couldn't worry about it now, he had a quick reaction team to put together.

CARTER'S PATROL

Carter slipped out of the concertina wire one hour after dark, his face painted with camo stick, a camo bandana wrapped around his head and leg elastics to keep his pants tight at the knee and calf. Kemper and Doll had their best men there for quick reaction and Koop put the mortar crew on alert, although they would probably not be able to help Carter, who had no radio.

There were three exit and entrance openings in the wire and men were posted at all three. Carter had a hand flare he could send up, he could whistle or they could just react to gun fire. He was carrying only an Army 45 and his razor sharp K-bar.

The night moved very slow. McKenzie gave strict orders that no one was to fire at a target outside the wire unless fired upon and not before putting up an illumination flare for proper identification. Carter's password to reenter was "fruitful," a difficult word for Vietnamese to pronounce.

Around two in the morning, Carter came walking by McKenzie's bunker. He'd come in down by Second Platoon and Kemper was escorting him. McKenzie fell in behind. When they arrived at the company tent, Top and Six were up sitting by the radio.

"Hey, Top. How's about that beer?" Carter said, as if he'd just happened to pass by.

"Where's your bona fides, Carter?" was Top's calm answer.

"I pulled them guys up by the wire. Y'all kin pick em up in the morning if Charlie hasn't already got to em. They was setting up a forty-two mortar when I got there which I left behind with a little surprise for anyone moving it without first looking."

He looked around at McKenzie and said, "Oh, yea and these are both right ears." Carter pulled two bloody ears from his right pocket and held them up at eye level.

"Jesus Christ, Carter!" McKenzie said angrily as he stepped forward.

"Its OK, One Six," Captain Moore said raising the flat of his hand to stop him. "Good job, Sergeant. You earned the beer. Its on ice in that foot locker."

Kemper and Carter each grabbed one side and out the door they went. McKenzie was furious.

"Six, you know that I gave that man a direct order not to take any more ears."

"Well, I'm the CO in this company, One Six and I need a man who can go out on his own and kill Charlie like he did, with no noise. It scares the hell out of them to know we got men like that. When he does what he did tonight, he gets his ears. Capeesh?"

McKenzie whirled around and walked out of the tent without answering. He grabbed Koop and two members of First Squad and headed out the way Carter had come. There they were, two Viet Cong in black pajamas, one laying on top of the other just outside the wire. Carter had cut the throat of one and stabbed the other directly in the Adam's apple from the front, probably as he turned. McKenzie imagined how the movement of Carter's K-bar must have been lightning fast. It made him swallow hard. He stood there examining the evidence with his flashlight.

"One Six," Koop whispered. "Let's get em inside the wire so S-2 can have a look at em. You don't want to be standing out here with your flashlight on. Sir?"

"Don't call me sir," McKenzie said as he walked past Koop. The whole thing left him with bile in his throat. He had promised himself it was his job to be the last line of defense of civilization's ethics even if they were out there killing people. By God, that's the way it was going to be, CO or no CO.

GREATEST EVIL, HIGHEST GOOD

On the return trip, after paying troops in Danang and Qui Nhon, McKenzie traveled by truck to Cu Chi and caught a short hopper to An Khe where he hitched a direct flight on a resupply helicopter headed for Wonder Beach. He'd had four days to think about who he was and whether he felt strong enough for combat as the platoon leader of men who seemed at times to need him so much and at other times, able to live without him.

McKenzie's paternal family history was Quaker, traceable all the way back to England when George Fox was desperately trying to establish a church around the ideas of peace and love and a time when Quakers were the subject of persecution where ever they went. Although McKenzie was not raised to be a Quaker, his father was and he was a gentle soul. Enough had rubbed off on McKenzie that he had spent considerable time in college thinking about religious beliefs.

He'd read "The Seven Story Mountain" by Thomas Merton, a Trappist Monk, who had converted to Catholicism in his 20s and withdrew from the world to become a contemplative. One passage stayed with him. Merton wrote that the greatest evil is found where the highest good has been corrupted. McKenzie had also found truth in Emanuel Kant's categorical imperative. A man should be compelled to treat others as he would be treated. He knew that was not applicable in war. The idealism of a noble cause seemed absolutely contradicted by giving men permission to kill.

Was war the ultimate corruption of good or was it, as his Indian maternal Grandfather had explained, an honor to prove oneself in battle? That was the other part of him - the Indian part with a warrior legacy. If a country gives young men guns and all other forms of killing, brain washes them in basic training to do what they are told and teaches them to follow their government right or wrong, how are they supposed to know what is right? Add in resentment to the draft, a country that does not seem to appreciate the fact they are putting their lives on the line every day and the age old belief that if you do wrong to me or my buddies, you are my enemy and you end up with guys like Carter who are capable of doing things they would never do in civilian life.

It occurred to McKenzie that maybe what he was really worried about was what was going to happen to Carter when he went home or even, what was going to happen to him. Maybe that was the conundrum. Swirling around in all this philosophical mumbo jumbo was a developing hatred for Colonel Fishmuth that was festering in his gut.

As the chopper dropped toward Wonder Beach, he decided that his most important duty and maybe his only duty would be to bring as many of these young boys home as he could without letting them get completely ruined by the war - if that was possible.

REMFS

Delta Company had been at Wonder Beach for two days. McKenzie had been gone four. He knew First Platoon would be very curious to hear about Danang and Qui Nhon and he was eager to explain how different life was for REMFs (short for Rear Echelon Mother Fuckers) that he had seen in those two places. Their life was alien to combat soldiers. They were supposed to support the guys in the field but how many really knew anything about the constant dirt, the cold in the mountains, the heat on top of one hundred pound packs and the numbing fingers of fear that warped perception. McKenzie had been amazed at the various shops and the relaxed soldiers walking around in civilian clothes without weapons.

He landed at Wonder Beach around mid morning. A game of touch football was being played in the sand. The whole area had a relaxed feeling. Wonder Beach consisted of rolling sand dunes, which gradually diminished and tapered down to a beach with good incoming waves from the South China Sea. Two naked soldiers were body surfing while others sun bathed on the sand. To the South, a large cargo ship was being unloaded.

He found Koop going over security assignments and figuring resupply needs for their return to the boonies. Having procured a plastic lawn chair that folded back, One Five was stretched out looking very relaxed.

"Hey, One Six. Welcome back. How's life down south?" Koop said. McKenzie sat down on a sand bag and took a long, deep breath.

"It made me nervous as hell, One Five. There was no way to tell who was who. I had to fight off the MPs in Danang 'cause they wanted to take my weapon. When I asked them what they wanted me to do if Charlie started firing B-40 rockets and attacking the base, they looked at me like I was from Mars. I kept waiting for sappers to hit the place all night. All I could think of was how and when I could get the hell out of there."

"I'm not surprised, LT. Not the first time I've heard that. Out here it's simple. You see em, you shoot em. Down there, how the hell you know what's going on? So did you find Hampton? He's probably back in the world by now, right?"

"No. He hasn't left yet," McKenzie said. "He found me. He came charging into one of the wards after he heard I was there. He's got a great attitude but his elbow is real bad and he's going home for more surgery and rehab. We won't see him again."

"Well, shit. A million dollar wound," Koop said with a slight smile. "That lucky bastard. By the way, they approved his Army Commendation medal."

"Great. You obviously did a good job writing that up, One Five. So, what's new? You hear how long we're gonna be here?"

SOMETHING BREWING

"Six says five days total but I been hearing some scuttle butt about him and the old man. Something's brewing. Six has only been in the field four and a half months but Black Knight is so pissed off at him, we may lose him."

"Who told you that?"

"One of the staff sergeants in operations. There's gonna be a big push toward LZ Barbara. He heard the Colonel yelling that he wants all his company commanders on the same page. That means they gotta be willing to operate only in company strength, not with platoons split up."

"You talk to Navorski lately? He's gotta know something."

"I haven't been able to get him alone but I will. In the meantime, we found a couple of See Bees willing to exchange a case of steaks and a case of new poncho halves for an NVA belt buckle and a captured flag Third Platoon has been carrying around. I'm working' with Navorski on that. Doll came up with a whole lot of beer but I told him I didn't want to hear how he got it." Koop laughed a knowing laugh that made McKenzie think a midnight operation might have been in the works.

"Well, don't tell me either. I never heard that."

Koop winked at McKenzie. "We're gonna have a big blow out tonight. Six OK'd it and you're cut loose. Six hasn't called any meetings so I think we got a couple of days to ourselves. I'll take care of the perimeter assignments and I'm not including you or me. We're gonna sleep, sleep, sleep. Go find yourself a drink or something, LT. I hear there's an officer's tent somewhere. You might even decide to get drunk tonight."

"You never know, One Five. You never know."

McKenzie walked to the beach. Pallets of supplies were stacked up or being unloaded by various military personnel, both Army and Navy. Off to the left, two more naked soldiers walked into the surf where the sea began to break and attempted to body surf, laughing and swimming. He stood and watched them for a while before realizing he was hungry.

PETERSON

Wooden walkways ran between tents, probably for the monsoon season that was growing in strength. Bunkers were scattered here and there but their locations appeared to have neither rhyme, nor reason. McKenzie stepped up onto one of the walkways to look for a mess hall.

Up ahead he saw a soldier come out of what appeared to be a beer tent. He wasn't from Delta but his face was familiar. Where did he know this guy from? No way. It couldn't be Berry Pederson from home but it was. All the Pederson boys had bright, red hair, which made them hard to forget. He got in the soldier's path so that he had to stop and look up to see who was standing in front of him. They were six thousand miles from Oregon and it took a few minutes for recognition to register on Pederson's face.

"Holy shit! Kenneth McKenzie. Well, I'll be. You're the first person I've seen from home since I been in the Army. You a grunt?"

"Yep. Couldn't get out of it. What are you doing here?" McKenzie shook Pederson's hand.

"Supply, man. We get all this stuff and send it out to you grunts in the field or anywhere else it needs to go."

"Nice," McKenzie said. "You guys ever have to worry about Charlie here?"

Pederson smiled. "Nah. We had a couple try to sneak in last month but the guys on the line blew them away with a claymore. There wasn't much left. Hey! Can I buy you a beer?"

"Sure," McKenzie said. "I was lookin for a mess hall but that can wait." Pederson was already walking back down the board walk. He looked back. "You make PFC yet, Kenny?"

McKenzie had not worn any sign of rank since Koop had cut the bars off his shirt. He didn't answer Pederson's question. Inside the tent, he saw only enlisted men but what the hell. If he could dodge the question, maybe it wouldn't be an issue.

"You know anyone who wants to trade beer for a Chi Com grenade I liberated a couple of weeks ago?" McKenzie said.

"Are you kidding? Those things are too iffy. No one wants em. You been carrying that for two weeks? Wow. You got some kind of death wish, Kenny?"

"Not any worse than being out in the boonies with Charlie." McKenzie said. He took a long drink from the beer Pederson handed him. It wasn't Black Label. It was a cold bottle of San Miguel from the Philippines and it tasted fantastic.

"How the hell did you get this way up here?" he asked, holding the bottle up to examine it.

"There's this guy who makes runs down to the Philippine engineers and trades for it. Good, huh?"

"After Black Label, this is heaven," McKenzie said.

Pederson was full of complaints about the Army. He didn't like officers and he didn't like all the rules and regulations and he especially didn't like the sergeants who were constantly pushing him and his buddies around. He spent most of his time trying to figure ways to get out of work details. Just that morning, his supply sergeant had tried to send him over to the officer's mess because some big shots were coming in this afternoon and they wanted extra bodies to help clean up.

"So, do you know who's coming in this afternoon?" McKenzie said.

He had not heard anything about a visit from Koop. Maybe he should find some chow and get back to Delta.

"I don't know. They never said but it sounded big the way everyone was running around this morning. I did hear something about a general," Pederson said.

"You're kidding, right? I better get moving." McKenzie finished his beer and started toward the door. "Which way to the mess hall?"

"I'll go with you," Pederson said. "You don't want to walk into the officer's mess."

"Well, actually - I do. I'm a second lieutenant. I kind of skipped over PFC." McKenzie laughed when he said it and put his arm around Pederson, who had a look of complete shock on his face.

"What? You're a fucking officer and I been buying you beer in my enlisted man's tent?" Pederson looked like he was about to explode.

"It didn't make any difference a minute ago." McKenzie said, cutting him off. "We're just friends from back home, glad to see each other. Why don't you come over to our barbecue tonight? Delta Company, First of the Fifth, over on the North end of the perimeter. Ask for First Platoon."

"I'll be damned, an officer." Pederson was standing there shaking his head as McKenzie walked away. He looked back and waved at Pederson but got no response.

COMMAND VISIT

Half way back to the bunker area, McKenzie realized he was supposed to be looking for the officer's mess tent. He was really hungry but he would just have to scrounge up a LRRP meal or some Cs. He needed to find out who was coming in and if it was going to involve Delta Company. For some reason, he had a strong feeling it was.

Where the football game had been was vacant. Wind sprayed loose sand off the tops of surrounding dunes. Heat waves distorted the air ahead but he could see activity around the bunkers. Koop had gathered all three squad leaders.

"It sounds like Black Knight is coming in with one of the Assistant Division Commanders," he was telling them. " We don't know which one but he may want to come around, talk to the troops and see how they're doin. Hey, One Six, you heard?"

"Not before just now. No word from Navorski?"

"Yea, I talked to him," Koop said. "You and the other platoon leaders are supposed to report to Six around fourteen hundred. Black Knight is due in about an hour later. Navorski says it's got to do with the big push toward LZ Barbara."

McKenzie nodded his head and entered the bunker. He sat down on a cot inside the dark where it was cool and listened to One Five finish telling the squad leaders how he wanted things cleaned up. Coming out of the glaring sun, his eyes would not adjust. He reached into his rucksack and located a can by feel, then found his P-38 can opener in a side pocket. After two bites of cold ham and eggs, he threw the can in the corner and drank some warm water from his canteen. Was Black Knight after Six? He jumped up and headed for the company command bunker.

"Is Six around?", McKenzie said to Navorski as he walked up. Startled, Navorski almost fell off the box he was sitting on.

"Jesus, LT, you scared the shit out of me. No. He headed for the shower to clean up after the football game. How was your trip?"

"Not much fun except for seeing our guys. How long ago did he leave?'

"LT. He'll be back any minute. Sit down and take a load off."

The sun felt hotter. Navorski was sitting under a small door tarp attached to the bunker which he had pulled up and supported on the end with two metal poles. McKenzie grabbed a canvas stool from inside the bunker and sat down in the tarp's shade just as Captain Moore arrived with only a towel tied around his waist. He was the epitome of West Point - blond, good looking and confident with not an ounce of fat on him.

"I know why you're here, One Six," he said as he passed by and ducked into the bunker. "You wanna know why Black Knight is bringing in the ACG, right?"

"Yea. I want to know if this has anything to do with Delta or you."

"I can't say but I wouldn't doubt it. I had another heart warming conversation with Colonel Fishmuth last night on the radio. This push into the mountains is a big deal with him and he wants my assurance Delta will operate only in company size formation. I told him I wouldn't know until I saw the terrain, considered the intel and reviewed the operations order. He started screaming at me and said if I needed to understand his orders more clearly, he'd see to it."

"That's not why the ACG is flyin' in, is it?"

"I don't think Black Knight has that kind of pull. The Brigade Commander, Colonel Kinsey, is not one to put up with bullshit from his battalion commanders, so my guess is, its just coincidence."

"Is that Colonel Joseph Kinsey?"

"Yep. That's him. Why? You know him?"

"Six, he was my Brigade Commander at Fort Benning. I did a special job for him getting the brigade ready for a command inspection. Can I say hello to him sometime?"

"He's flying in to be here when the General shows up, so I guess you can. They want all officers and senior NCOs at the officer's mess when they arrive. Let One Five know. I want platoon sergeants and all squad leaders in attendance. We're the only Cav unit here, so we're gonna make a good showing."

GENERAL SHADWICK

McKenzie heard the choppers before he saw them. Two Huey Cobras circled above the two slicks which were dropping down for landing. Cobras always reminded him of circling sharks the way they were shaped and how they circled. Sleek, tapered at the nose and armed to the teeth with rockets and mini-guns, each had a pilot and copilot sitting on top, one behind the other under a glass canopy, the way jet pilots did.

One of the slicks had a star on a First Cav patch which was painted on the nose. Within minutes, both slicks were on the ground, rotor blades slowing and officers climbing out. The General climbed out of the pilot's seat, handed his flight helmet to a lieutenant and took a steel pot which he put under his arm.

McKenzie had been sent to the landing pad to guide him back to the officer's mess. He started walking toward the General who was being followed by Black Knight, two majors and a lieutenant. The General was impressive. Well over six feet tall, he had pepper gray hair, an easy smile, a straight nose and did not seem in a hurry. Around his waist was the General officer's distinctive black belt with a shiny round gold buckle, such as McKenzie had seen on other generals at Fort Benning. His fatigues were starched, creased and clean. His boots were spit shined. His name tag said Shadwick. When McKenzie stopped and saluted, General Shadwick returned the salute.

"Welcome to Wonder Beach, sir. I've been sent to direct you to the officer's tent," McKenzie said. A voice behind the general said, "General Shadwick, this is Delta Company's First Platoon leader." It was Colonel Fishmuth edging around to a place where he could be seen.

General Shadwick reached out and shook McKenzie's hand. "Do you have a name soldier?" he said, looking where a name tag should have been.

"Yes, sir. Back home I'm Lieutenant McKenzie. Out here, I'm just One Six."

"How long you been with Delta, Lieutenant McKenzie?" The General had begun to walk slowly toward the tent area and McKenzie walked to his left.

"Since June, sir."

"I hear good things about Delta. Your Six is Captain Moore, right?"

"Yes, sir. He's the best, sir. My troopers have confidence in him and the way he operates. So do I, sir."

Black Knight was giving McKenzie a look that could melt cold steel. He started to say something but the General interrupted. He stopped walking and turned toward McKenzie.

"According to the numbers, your company has more ambush kills than any other company in the division during the last two months. What's your secret?"

"Frankly, sir. We just out Charlie, Charlie. We work in small units and we pick our fights instead of waiting for Charlie to surprise us. Six is a master at setting ambush sights and the men are well trained."

"That's good work, Lieutenant. Now let's go have that briefing. "

DELTA'S ASSIGNMENT

Captain Moore called everyone to attention when they entered the officer's mess tent. Standing to his left was Colonel Kinsey. Two tables had been set up across one end of the tent with four chairs behind. The General's aide unrolled a large map and attached it to a piece of plywood with thumb tacks while the General said hello to Colonel Kinsey and Captain Moore. The General also shook hands with Two Six and Three Six before inviting everyone to have a seat. One of the majors stepped up to the map and began the briefing on what was planned for the area around LZ Barbara.

Reconnaissance reports indicated scattered base camps had been established in the area. Delta would be working close to the Laotian border in an attempt to catch smaller units before they could move out of the mountains. They had been selected for this critical operation because of Delta's recent success with ambushes. Intelligence gathering would be a major part of their mission.

At the conclusion of the briefing, General Shadwick walked around the tent and talked with each platoon leader, platoon sergeant and squad leader. McKenzie said hello to Colonel Kinsey who was delighted to see a familiar face. While they were reminiscing about Fort Benning, McKenzie noticed Colonel Fishmuth say something to Captain Moore. Neither of them looked happy. The briefing was over at seventeen hundred. It was time for barbecue and beer.

The party was loud and raucous. Pederson showed up with a case of LRRP meals and a bottle of Scotch and stayed to the bitter end. He forgave McKenzie for being an officer. He would be going home in four months and promised to tell everyone hello.

Several squad leaders performed an impromptu skit about all the stupid things new guys do and had everyone laughing so hard, beer came out of Doll's nose. McKenzie was thankful he had been spared from being the brunt of their jokes. Delta was going back to the boonies in three short days. Tonight, they were safe and too drunk to remember the fear.

DELTA'S SUCCESS

Over the next two days, Captain Moore told McKenzie what had happened. The G-3 (Division operations officer) told him that Black Knight had gone over Colonel Kinsey's head about Delta. He wanted Division to put out a general directive that all companies in I Corps were ordered to operate in company size only until informed otherwise. Of course, the major told Six that Division thought that was ludicrous. They would never think of issuing such a directive. Commanders on the ground have to adjust to the situation.

When the G-3 realized it was Delta Company that Black Knight was talking about, he remembered a report he'd seen on ambush success. He did not like the idea of Black Knight jumping over his own Brigade S-3, so he decided to have a little fun. He called Colonel Kinsey and requested permission to designate Delta for this special assignment and suggested a special briefing.

As it turned out, when he shared the ambush report with his boss, General Shadwick was so impressed that he decided to attend also. G-3 then called Colonel Kinsey again and invited him to come along. Kinsey indicated he had taken steps to ensure Black Knight would not be contacting Division operations directly in the future. Black Knight was furious and told Captain Moore quietly that he was not through with him and that if he did not do everything Black Knight told him to do during the upcoming operations, regardless of what anyone else said, he would get rid of him.

McKenzie wandered over to the company CP the last night to see if Captain Moore was awake. He was - studying maps and thinking about the new AO.

"So, what do you think, Six?"

Captain Moore looked up at McKenzie. "Like I been saying for the past two days, the terrain around LZ Barbara is extremely rough. If the Colonel thinks we can operate in this terrain looking for a large confrontation, he's got another think coming. You know I'm willing to follow orders I'm given but they gotta make sense, for Christ's sake. The draws down off the ridge lines around Barbara are very steep. If this map's accurate, trails are gonna snake in and around these hills, up and into side draws. It's a perfect area for bunkers to be buried along side the trail, around every corner. It gives me the chills just to look at it."

"So, how are we going to operate, Six?" McKenzie's mind raced as a little adrenaline leaked into his blood.

"G-3 wants us to interdict small groups filtering out of the mountains toward the low lands. That's what we're good at but

I'm concerned we're gonna find big bunker complexes in there where the NVA can keg up for rest and resupply. We know what those look like and they're usually well fortified. One mistake and Charlie will bring the hurt down on us. We're gonna have to be real cautious about when we work small and when we work big. Going either way at the wrong time could be disastrous."

BLACK KNIGHT

"What I want to know, Six, is why Black Knight keeps fighting you? You're the guy on the ground."

McKenzie had never probed this hard but he was hoping to understand the constant turmoil between Six and Black Knight.

"I'm gonna tell you a few things One Six but I don't want it repeated. Have I got your word?" Captain Moore said in a low but serious voice.

McKenzie nodded. Captain Moore laid the map onto the ground and leaned over with his elbows on his knees, head down. After a few seconds, he looked up as if he was searching for the right words. McKenzie sat down on a sand bag.

With a big sigh, Captain Moore said, "Black Knight's an ROTC officer who started out in signal corps. For whatever reason, he decided to switch over to the infantry, probably for his career. He managed to get into jump school first and after he got his wings, petitioned for transfer to the infantry. Like many battalion commanders right now, he was commissioned after Korea and has never led a platoon or a company into combat. It's just a freak of timing.

You know what the CIB means to a career infantry officer. Now he's got four line companies and a recon platoon and he thinks if he can just get a company from First of the Fifth into a big battle with a large enemy force that results in a high enemy body count, it will go a long way toward making his career.

He wasn't here when this battalion went through Tet, Khe Sanh, Hue, Dong Ha or the A Shau Valley in a six month period. Some companies lost enough men over six months to fill two companies. He probably thinks he got cheated. Its awfully easy giving orders over a radio when you're flying a thousand feet in the air above the shooting, traveling ninety knots over triple canopy jungle with a map on your lap.

I know that sounds disrespectful but I can't help it. I'm going to continue following the admonitions of the Vietnam Primer, written by Colonel Hackworth and S.L.A. Marshall, which they published in April, 1967. You ever read it? They learned early on that the most useful intelligence in this war is gathered after a unit is deployed. Exploitation of information supplied before deployment depends upon what the tactical unit learns and does." Captain Moore stopped talking and set his jaw tight, flexing his facial muscles.

"I have the Primer with me, Six. My company commander at Fort Benning gave it to me before I left."

"Doesn't surprise me, One Six. Any CO worth his salt should know the lessons learned in that publication by heart. There is always that delicate balance for the commander in the field. One that you might have to face someday. A good soldier honors and follows the chain of command and a good officer completes the mission. He also takes care of his men. Sometimes those two principles compete.

That's when the responsible officer on the ground goes back to the basics of duty, honor and loyalty. You find a way to be true to both principles if you can. Further more, a good senior officer will let his commander on the ground do that. Unfortunately, that's not what we've got here." It was obvious by the tone in his voice that Captain Moore was sad.

"You think Black Knight would really try to get rid of you when we have the best record going right now?" McKenzie said.

"I wouldn't be surprised at anything right now. A couple of weeks ago, I got a message I was being considered for a job in Saigon." Captain Moore sighed.

CHAPTER SIX - LZ BARBARA

(JULY 25, 1968 - 328 DAYS LEFT)

LZ BARBARA

Lift off to LZ Barbara was scheduled for ten hundred. Captain Moore indicated they would not be staying on Barbara but moving out after they picked up resupply. Brigade S-3 described a punch bowl valley off to the north of Barbara where scout helicopters had spotted a large bunker complex. One of the bunker openings looked big enough to drive a jeep into. That's where Delta was headed.

Flying into LZ Barbara felt to McKenzie like floating up out of a valley of despair toward mountains of the unknown. The helicopters rose through the morning fog hanging over the forest in a long line of whirling, popping blades and headed straight at the imposing mountains. Up, up, the helicopters climbed, as if there were castles to be assaulted or Himalayan monasteries to visit. McKenzie had not yet operated in forests this thick. He felt a foreboding. The monsoon season was gaining ground. Maybe the world down there would be like the rain forests he'd hiked through on the Olympic Peninsula in Washington State.

LZ Barbara was definitely perched on a fine mountain. Higher than any of the surrounding hills, there was only one access route along a thin ridge line to the East. All the rest of the perimeter looked down a steep hillside which no self respecting enemy would be fool enough to attack up. Barbara was so high, clouds floated below its line of defense. A new command bunker, three artillery pieces and several mortar pits occupied the denuded top. Bunkers were sand bagged and reinforced in every way imaginable. Alpha Company was already in place, having come in as early security and Echo Company, the battalion recon platoon, had been working off Barbara for two weeks.

While Koop directed his squad leaders over to a pile of resupply, McKenzie walked to the crest of the hill and watched a line of soldiers move along the ridge line, turn south and disappear down into the jungle canopy. Later that afternoon, when the patrol returned, he watched them walk through the perimeter wire, tired and wet. The trail was steep and bumpy from rain wash. The point man stepped out of the cloudy mist into the sunlight where the cool breeze, coming all the way from the coast, could be felt. Relief spread over each face as they walked by. All patrols used the same trail, going in and out like ants foraging for food and returning to the same anthill.

Around sixteen hundred, Delta received word they would not move until morning. McKenzie relaxed and began unpacking for the night. Koop yelled at him from the crest of the hill.

"Hey, One Six, you want to fire a 50 caliber machine gun they got set up in case the NVA decide to come up that ridge line? Six wants a little show and tell to make sure the troops refresh their memory on the fifty and then he's gonna demonstrate a flame thrower. He told me to ask if you want on the 50."

"Hell, yes," McKenzie said. "I haven't fired a 50 since OCS. Now?"

"Yep. He's waitin'."

The 50 caliber had been set on top of a bunker aimed so it could sweep the ridgeline. Sand bags stabilized its tripod legs. The platoon gathered around as McKenzie climbed the side of the bunker and stood behind the big gun. Unlike the M-60 machine gun, which had a pistol grip with a forefinger trigger, the 50 had a butterfly looking trigger in the back. McKenzie gripped the big metal handles on each side, placed his thumbs gently on the wings of the butterfly and pushed.

The gun was set flat so the bullets fired straight out with a noise that rattled his teeth. It was not fast like a 60, more of a heavy, ominous thumping at four to five hundred rounds per minute. The bullets were so big he could see them going out into the jungle and arching down. This was a gun that could destroy a truck engine block at three hundred meters.

He imagined pouring 50 caliber bullets down the hill into a charging enemy. It frightened him and yet gave him an exhilarating feeling of power. When he stopped, his ears were ringing and the platoon was yelling and hooting. They all gathered around closer as Koop went over loading, operation and cleaning requirements. Doll and Casey were then allowed to fire the big gun.

Captain Moore walked to the end of the hillcrest where it started to slope sharply down. He carried the flamethrower on his back with the nozzle end in his right hand. When he hit the trigger, it popped and a line of liquid fire shot out, dripping on everything in its wake. McKenzie could feel the heat. There was no doubt LZ Barbara, with only one route of access and steep sides around the perimeter, could be defended with these two awesome weapons.

Was Black Knight asking Mr. Charles to attack them? If there were that many NVA in the area, how the hell was the Cav going to continue walking off this hill and fight a pitched battle down at the bottom?

WALKING OFF BARBARA

The next morning, before leaving, Captain Moore walked with McKenzie and Koop half way down the ridgeline where he pointed to a hidden trail to the left.

"Are there other trails around here we can't see?" Koop said.

"I'm told there are One Five but this is the one we're taking," Captain Moore explained. "It drops down into the head of a draw that may be the start of a long canyon. It then circles around to the left and crosses a small creek on the other side before heading directly into a bunker complex - the one with the large cave like entrance. First Platoon's got the lead. Because I don't know what we're walking into, the whole company will move together this time."

McKenzie caught a sideways glance from Koop. So did the captain.

"There's a small knoll right after we hit the bottom. Second Platoon will circle around to the right and cross the creek at the same time as First. You'll see the knoll when we get down there. Third Platoon will follow as a quick reaction force," he said looking at Koop.

McKenzie walked over to look down the trail. "Looks kinda scary to me. Point man's gonna be all alone when he steps onto the floor below," he said.

"Yep. Just like every other patrol that heads down off this bad mother. You just gotta take it slow and easy. Make sure Kemper's got the point. Maybe he can smell 'em before we walk into them." The Captain grinned but didn't wait for a response. He turned and headed back through the perimeter.

McKenzie heard and then saw Black Knight's chopper. The helicopter created a dust storm on top, sending clean clothing, which had been washed and laid out on bunkers to dry, up into its rotor wash. Soldiers near the top had to duck down and cover their heads from the swirling dust.

Kemper was incredulous after McKenzie and Koop described the operation. "One Six, that sounds hairy and scary to me. What if Mr. Charles is waiting for us right at the bottom? We're not gonna have a chance."

"Mr. Charles knows we're here, Kemper. By now, he probably knows how many and all our middle names. If he's at all interested in a fight, he's gonna want more than a hippy with an earring and a few of his buddies. Your job, as always, is to smoke him out before we walk into the big one." McKenzie grinned.

Kemper did not. "You know this is another screw job from on top and we're the ones getting hosed."

"Six has put his trust in us to lead out and we're gonna see to it that doesn't happen, aren't we?" It was the kind of answer McKenzie would not have given when he was new but now, this was his platoon and he knew what they were capable of.

As it turned out, First Platoon was completely on the valley floor by eleven without any sign of Mr. Charles. Captain Moore had returned from meeting with Black Knight with orders to stay down off LZ Barbara until Delta made significant contact, an idea he dismissed with perfunctory disdain. McKenzie noted, however, that Six had marked three possible night positions and several potential landing zones on his map.

After First Platoon's last man touched down off the descending trail, McKenzie put them on one knee with flank security and sent for Kemper. The small knoll was only one hundred meters ahead. Second Platoon began to peel off to the right as Kemper came back.

"This is one, bad mother, One Six," he said. "You never been down in something like this. These are dark, thick jungles, like the A Shau. The trail up ahead, dips down into the creek, crosses over, and then turns a sharp left on the other side. We're gonna be absolutely blind the whole way."

RECON BY FIRE

"You want to recon by fire, don't you Kemper?" McKenzie said.

"That's what I'm thinkin'. Let's bring a 60 up and work over that other side. You said yourself, Mr. Charles already knows we're here anyway."

"OK. Let me clear it with Six." Five minutes later, Kemper was told to set up his 60 on a small rise to the right of the trail, before it dropped into the creek bed. McKenzie put a fire team on the down hill side, on line, in case something happened while Kemper was getting set up.

McKenzie signaled for his RTO to give the word to get down, then he nodded to Kemper. The jungle silence was ripped apart by long bursts of 7.62 mm rounds as flame shot from the air-cooled muzzle. Limbs on trees shattered, jungle plants exploded in shreds and dirt erupted into the air as if propelled from below by small explosions.

The gunner began in the middle of the trail and raked bullets back and forth. Empty cartridges flew up hot to the right. Bark jumped off the trees followed by splintered wood. Red tracers every five rounds helped McKenzie follow the path of firing. He yelled ceasefire to Kemper. There had been no return fire.

DEEPER FOREST

First Platoon got up and Kemper led them across the creek toward a deeper forest. This was the dark, back woods; the kind American children were raised on in nursery rhymes and in stories where trolls lived. It was where the big, bad wolf went after Goldilocks and where Hansel and Gretel were imprisoned by the nasty, old witch. It was where Davy Crockett fought the Mohicans and it was the dank, foreboding cavern from which sprang the headless horseman of Sleepy Hollow. Until Benjamin Franklin invented the light bulb, darkness was where evil dwelt in the American psyche.

Childhood fears, thought to be eliminated by adulthood, could revisit a man in such a stifling, pungent jungle. After all, this was an army of boys, trying to be men, drafted or recruited away from their adolescence, with no adult experience to weigh in against those fears.

First Platoon was a microcosm of the American army in Vietnam. It was being asked to seek out an enemy who had spent generations learning to live and fight in its own back woods - a tough Asian army that moved and lived comfortably in the darkness with none of those western fears. They had defeated the Chinese, the Japanese, the French and now, maybe the Americans.

Movement was very slow for the next two hours. Six ordered a short lunch break before Kemper moved out again. He spotted a bunker complex an hour later that did not appear to be occupied and sent word he could see a cave opening and it was huge. First Platoon moved in. The company spent another hour clearing bunkers and sending recon patrols in all directions. Captain Moore approached the large cave entrance just as McKenzie was getting ready to go in.

CAVE

"What the hell do you think you're doin'?" he said grabbing McKenzie by the arm.

"I think its my turn, Six. I don't think I should ask my guys to do what I'm not willing to do."

McKenzie had taken off his fatigue shirt and helmet. His green, faded tee shirt was full of holes but still viable. He double checked the square shaped 45 caliber pistol in his right hand to see that he had a round chambered and the magazine was full and then clicked the flashlight in his left hand on and off. Kemper had shown him how to hold it straight up since the light was at a right angle from the handle.

"I'm not real gung ho about this, One Six but it's your call," Captain Moore said.

"Good. Kemper and I have talked about it and he'll be my back up."

As he turns to go in, McKenzie feels a rock in his throat. His mouth is dry as alum. Flies buzz around his head from something dead lying next to the entrance. He walks up to the right side of the large opening and runs the flashlight beam up the side of the opposing wall and then down again. He pushes hard against his fear, trying to put it down into his gut where he can't see it. When he's explored the wall as far as he can see, he shines the light over the floor, which does not show evidence of recent occupation. He inches forward enough to look in and runs the light up the near side.

The tunnel has been dug into the hillside about twenty-five meters before it turns back to the left as if curving toward an exit. Fifteen meters inside is an opening on the right side. It's a room dug off the main tunnel. He approaches and cautiously looks inside. He scans the opposite wall up and down, then along the ground without exposing himself. He inches around and moves the light up and down. Further along the opposite wall he sees a back wall. There are old shovel marks in the dank, rich earth. He examines the back wall and determines no one is there. He is soaking wet in spite of the cool air, his tee shirt clings tightly as if it too is scared.

He looks back for Kemper who is not there. Soft, fluffy dirt covers the floor like a layer of fine but thick, talcum powder. The air grows mustier. McKenzie moves deeper into the tunnel. He comes to a second room.

Repeating the same method, he works the light beam down the left side of the room, along the bottom of the back wall, then clearing the floor and right wall. This is a larger room. He slips inside pressing his back against the dirt, hoping to find some indication of past use. He inches along the right wall - keeping his left hand with the flashlight upright and his right pointing the M-19 automatic Colt at the darkness.

He raises the light slowly to examine the upper ceiling. Something explodes in his face. He hears a noise before he feels anything. It is sudden. He has no time to react. Multiple, tiny, beating explosions drive him onto his back. He fires in the direction of the wall as he kicks his feet into the floor to move backwards. He keeps firing and kicking. Light suddenly blinds him.

McKenzie did not know how he got outside. He felt no pain but waited for it. As he lay in the dirt, on his back, his mind reran the movie of what had just happened. Bats! Hundreds of them had exploded off the back wall and flown into and around him in a move so instantaneous he had no time to discern what it was. He only saw it now as a flash back. Far off somewhere, he could hear laughing.

Someone said, "Did you see One Six come out of there on his back? He was flying."

McKenzie rolled over onto his left side and looked at Captain Moore, who had sat down. Koop came over and kneeled down on one knee.

"Breathe," he said. "Come on, One Six, breath." Koop wasn't laughing but he had a huge grin on his face. McKenzie rolled back and looked up at the sky, trying to get his heart to stop careening off the inside of his chest and trying to get a little air. Cirrus clouds floated, separated and disappeared into the steel blue atmosphere a million miles above him. He could see Kemper and Doll standing over him with others on the periphery. Koop looked up.

"Move back, you guys," he said angrily. He looked down, sympathetically. Then he reached down and pulled up on McKenzie's belt to help him breathe, like when a football player gets hit in the family jewels.

"Say something, One Six," Koop said in a low voice.

McKenzie was taking air in big gulps but he could not talk. He knew he should be dead. It was unfathomable to him how unprepared he was in that cave. Anyone there would have killed him easily. He was an idiot to go in there. Now he looked like an idiot to his men. This was nothing like the adrenaline rush of an ambush or a fire fight. This was raw, jagged fear and a sudden knowledge came with it. If he was going to make it out of the Nam

- just if - it was going to be dumb luck or the grace of God and nothing else.

His vulnerability had smacked his psyche hard and he had no words. His flimsy life was suspended in the war like a single strand of spider filament swinging in the midst of a hurricane. So fragile, so delicate, that single strand would only stay in place if providence wanted it to. How long, he asked himself. How long?

"Hey, One Six?" It was Kemper. "You came by me so fast, I thought you were on rollers. I thought there might be bats in that cave. I guess I should have warned you. I cleared the rest of it. The end comes out over there by those two trees. It's very well hidden. Doesn't look to me like any one's used it for quite a while. You want us to blow it?"

McKenzie stared up at him. "I don't know Sarge. Ask Six. My heart feels like it's going to explode. How the hell do you do that?"

"It don't mean nothin', One Six."

McKenzie rolled over onto his stomach and pushed up to his knees and elbows. Standing slowly, he found his way over to some shade and sat down. Across the way, several men checked out one of the bunkers which contained a freshly dug mortar cache. He poured water over his head and thought about men like Kemper. He'd always looked at them with respect but now he knew they were different, maybe in some unnatural way. They had been given quickness with total concentration and confidence. They either did not feel the fear in the same way when it crushed the breath out of a man or they were able to bury it for the moment and deal with it later. He thought he'd done that but it was evident, no amount of training or experience could create that. You either had it or you didn't. Why did he not have it?

The afternoon was spent digging up the buried mortars while Six argued with Black Knight whether to blow them with C-four plastic explosive or move them somewhere so they could be picked up and taken back to Division. Captain Moore wanted to blow them in place while Colonel Fishmuth wanted contact and did not want Delta to give their position away.

In the end, Captain Moore acquiesced and the company set up three large platoon size ambushes. The first two, designated A and B, were set about one hundred meters further up the trail where it split, with A to the left and B to the right. Ambush C was back behind the tunnel complex in the hope someone might try to come back for the mortars.

People left McKenzie alone. It was August, Seventh, a Wednesday. Athletes back home were thinking about how to get in shape for football. August weather along the Columbia River was dry and hot, pushed back and forth by a desultory wind. Seldom did it cool the air. His mind wanted to go back to the gorge, sitting on a rock with his high school girlfriend, talking about life. So long ago, it seemed like someone else.

SACRIFICE

McKenzie didn't see Kemper approach through the darkness until it was too late. He reached for his weapon. Kemper sat down next to him.

"Evening, LT. You feeling a little better?" he said.

"I guess. That wasn't your fault, Kemper. I should never have gone in there like that. What the hell would I have done if someone had been in there?"

"I don't think of it as my fault. Anyway, there wasn't much chance of anyone being in there. The area hadn't been used for a long time. People might pass through and dump supplies like those mortars but they aren't staying long. Just little things you begin to notice when you walk point. Bunkers here are in need of repair. No sign of recent camp fires and I couldn't smell 'em." He laughed as he said it.

"So is that why you let me go in there? You just wanted to see what would happen?"

"Hell, LT, you wanted to go in there. If it had been real bad, I wouldn't have let you. It's not your job but I figured you could learn something. Did you?"

"Now you're being patronizing, Sarge. Fuck you and the horse you rode in on."

Kemper looked at McKenzie for a long time without saying anything.

"No. I'm not patronizing you, One Six. I'm your sacrifice. Don't you know that? I'm the guy who's decided to be there first so the rest of these yokels can go home and make babies. I didn't want to be here in the Nam but you know, the draft had other ideas. I decided about half way through basic training that I was not the same as the rest of these guys and I was gonna stay different. They weren't gonna dumb me down, strip me of who I was and ship me off to this shit hole just to become a statistic.

This earring's not just my wanting to be a rebel. This red bandana's not just spitting in the Colonel's face. Its sayin' I'm different. I'm not Army green. I'm not standard issue. I'm me. Just like that holy tee shirt you keep wearing and those Indian beads you got around your neck. I got two months left, LT. Walking point and jumping into tunnels is my way of saying I'm different. I don't know what happens but when I'm doin' that - I'm more in tune with this place than at any other time.

You know how long we been waitin' for an LT who loves his men and who isn't an arrogant asshole? A long time. Since Lieutenant Gordan got it during Tet. That was February and here you come along in June. Between that time, we had two others. One got himself killed by playing hero during an ambush and well, you heard about the other. Now, we got One Five, Six and we got you. I just wanted you to appreciate what guys like us do."

"You thought I didn't?"

NIGHT ACTION

Kemper looked down at his bandana, which he had removed and was refolding just right. He never got the chance to answer. Off in the distance, toward ambush B, someone yelled, "Hey!" then a burst from an M-16 could be heard in the area of ambush A. Kemper looked at McKenzie. "Let's go get us some bad guys, LT." He left as sudden as he had come.

McKenzie moved over to Daley, his new RTO, who told him that a squad leader from Second Platoon reported they saw movement. One of his men yelled and four NVA ran toward A. They killed one but the others got away. When McKenzie found

Captain Moore, he was on his radio, asking the squad leader to come back and lead him to the bunkers.

Within minutes, they were all approaching the area. A full moon was up and showing through parted clouds providing just enough light to allow them to move without flashlights. Captain Moore pointed to a small bunker with logs securing the overhang and crawled up to the left side of it. McKenzie looked at Kemper who shrugged and motioned McKenzie to the other side before moving in behind the captain. Without warning, Six jumped in front and began firing on full automatic. There was no return fire.

Around one thirty, the sky turned black and heavy rain drops began to splat against the ground, quickly increasing to a thick down pour, soaking everyone. Huge rats came out of the bunkers and ran among the soldiers. Unable to sleep, McKenzie leaned up against a tree with his poncho pulled around him and his weapon between his legs. Some time around three he heard movement to his left. It sounded like a rustling of leaves. He turned to see a rat about six inches in body length chewing on his captured ammo pouch strap. He struck at him with the butt of his weapon and missed. "Shit! Can't even get a rat," he said out loud to himself.

Battalion S-3 called at first light. Charlie Company, First of the Fifth, was in trouble. They were in a deep ravine, cut off on both sides by a larger force and being harassed by snipers. Delta moved out of the area toward the pick up zone. Third Platoon set C-four around the ammo dump and timed it to blow after the company moved up the trail. The explosion rocked the ground.

McKenzie looked back at the smoke and dust rising up through the trees. So much for what Black Knight wanted.

First Platoon had the lead. They came out of the deep forest later that morning as the trail turned gravely and hard, evidence it was being heavily used. The sun was white hot and high, melting the clouds away and causing steam to come off the wet vegetation. They crossed a small stream running full from the night's rain. The point man spotted three NVA on the other side, at the crest of the hill. He fired on full automatic without success.

Koop came up. "You think this is a trap, One Five? Trying to suck us in?" McKenzie said.

"It don't look good to me, LT," he said. Kemper had a hold on his point man's collar as if he was afraid the soldier might go running up the hill. Koop waved his hand at everyone to get down.

"We got a Charlie, Charlie bird coming in, One Six. Let's let him go in and see what's on top of that hill. That's where our pickup area is, anyway." Before McKenzie could answer, Koop grabbed his radio handset and began talking to the inbound pilot.

"Roger that, Traveler One. We just spotted three, november victor alphas on the upper trail, in the area of our papa zulu. Can you have a look around? Thanks a lot, over and out."

SAY GOODBYE

They could hear the scout helicopter approach the hill but couldn't see him as he had come in from the other side. There was definitely someone up there. AK rounds snapped at the light helicopter, which returned fire with mini-guns. Behind McKenzie, someone shouted, "Get down. Get down!" He turned around to see who was yelling. Sergeant Doll pointed down toward a creek bed off to the East. Second Squad's machine gunner stood up and began firing from a standing position. M-79 rounds exploded and small arms peppered the area as others joined in. When there was no return fire, McKenzie yelled for a ceasefire.

The world became quiet except for his ringing ears. McKenzie's heart was pounding. He had no idea what the hell just happened and needed to take control. He turned back around. Sergeant Koop was on the ground. He saw but didn't believe it.

Doc Campbell was next to One Five, cutting off his pant leg. A bullet had hit his left shinbone and exploded out the back carrying skin and muscle, shredding it in all directions. Doc used the good part of Koop's pant leg to tie off the bleeding and gave him a shot of morphine. He sprinkled disinfectant powder on the wound and placed one field dressing on the front, two more on the backside where the leg looked like hamburger.

McKenzie stood watching. He heard Brady request Medivac. No! No! This wasn't happening. He dropped to both knees beside Koop and reached for his right hand.

"What the hell happened?" He was almost choking. Sergeant Koop, no longer his One Five, opened his eyes slowly, already feeling the effect of the morphine and smiled.

"Sniper, One Six. Guess I'll be seein' ya."

McKenzie looked at him through tear filled eyes. "Yea. Looks like that million dollar wound you're always talking about, Sarge. You're gonna be looking at some ugly nurse in no time and wishin' you were back out here with your boys. Shit. What am I gonna do without you?"

His throat was tight and tasted like metal. "Damn," he said as he gripped the hand tight and looked at this man who meant so much to him. Sergeant Koop's thin face looked as calm as ever, his head laying in the dirt, eyes closed and his unruly hair sticking out in all directions. How could this happen? Koop opened his eyes.

"You'll be all right. Doll is ready. So are you, One Six. You don't need me anymore. Its your time."

Third Platoon moved up to secure the pickup area. McKenzie stayed with Koop while Doll shouted commands off in the distance and led a team down to the creek bed in search of the sniper. A few shots were fired, then silence. The scout helicopter continued to work the area without any more return fire. Brady tapped McKenzie on the shoulder. "Medivac's in bound, One Six."

Kemper brought a poncho rolled out for a litter and slipped it under Koop. McKenzie, Kemper and two others each grabbed a corner and carried Koop up the hill where they laid him down. McKenzie got down on his knees and leaned over the top of his platoon sergeant to protect him from the dirt and rocks being thrown around by the helicopter's down wash. He put his cheek on Koop's chest and held him.

The Medivac crew jumped out with a litter stretched tight between wooden side poles and placed it next to Koop. They transferred him to the stretcher and lifted, placing him gently on the floor of the helicopter. Someone brought Koop's pack and weapon.

McKenzie walked backwards, away from the door. Sergeant Koop rose up on his left elbow to look at him as the pilot began to lift off. He raised a closed fist at McKenzie and smiled. The helicopter, with a big red cross on it, floated up over the trees, taking Koop away forever. First Platoon stood immobile until the sound of rotor blades faded into the shimmering sky.

"Sergeant Doll, you're the new One Five. Pick your replacement for Second Squad," McKenzie said. "Don't mean nothin'." He spent the next hour making sure Doll knew what resupply he and Koop had discussed that morning. Every time he brought up an issue, however, Doll was ahead of him. Koop had picked the right man to replace him. Doll still had five months in country and Kemper needed to stay where he was.

BUGGS

Lift helicopters arrived with water and resupply around fourteen hundred. Delta was picked up and dropped onto an old FOB above the valley where Charlie Company was. Captain Moore gave platoon sergeants time to break open cases of C-rations and pass around the resupply of ammo and claymores before moving out.

"I'm gonna have Second Platoon take over lead," he told McKenzie.

He started to say something else but was interrupted by the sound of AK fire down in the valley. A log bird had just flown over Charlie Company's position and taken fire. They watched as the bird swung around, climb to their level and turn toward them. It was apparent the pilot intended to land. Harvey from Third

Squad walked into the middle of the hill and raised his arms to guide the pilot.

"You expecting another log bird, Six?" McKenzie shouted.

"No! Get off the hill!" Captain Moore shouted back, waving his arms.

~~

The helicopter is coming in fast, not slowing down to feather its landing. At about one hundred fifty meters it begins to wobble, then dips sideways, then swings back and forth. McKenzie stands frozen for another second watching. Harvey continues to waive the pilot in, then ducks. McKenzie takes a step backwards toward the edge of the hill launching himself in a somersault as the main rotor blade on the tipped helicopter hits the ground and the tail rotor comes around looking like a saw blade in a lumber mill. The whole bird lurches upward, ass end in the air and rolls over spitting out both door gunners. The pilot and copilot are strapped in and left hanging upside down. Jet fuel begins to run down the fuselage creating a wide spill on the ground. Boxes of ammunition slide out and break apart.

Kemper and Private Juarez run to the cockpit and begin yanking on the upside door where the copilot is slumped over. Blood splatters dot the windshield between several bullet holes. Kemper steps in and pulls the copilot out, handing him to others who carry him off the hill. Juarez climbs in further, unbuckles the pilot and heaves him up to the copilot door. Kemper grabs an arm and half carries, half drags, the man away. The pilot's other arm is soaked in blood and hanging limp. McKenzie moves toward the tail looking for Harvey.

Juarez jumps free as something explodes inside and a belt of ammo begins to cook off. Bullets ricochet out. McKenzie retreats down the hill and makes his way along the under slope until he sees Doc Morris covering someone with a poncho. It isn't Harvey, its Buggs. Doc says the tail rotor completely severed Buggs' head as it swung off the side of the hill. Doc tries holding the head on Buggs' shoulders talking to himself. Harvey is there, lying on his back just above Buggs.

"You OK?" McKenzie says kneeling next to Harvey who looks up.

"I don't know how the hell it missed me, LT. I thought I was a dead man. I got lucky I guess." His face is ash colored. McKenzie turns back and tries to help Doc wrap Buggs into a rain poncho but his head won't stay put and Doc keeps doing it over and over, trying to get it right. Doll shows up and tells Doc to help others who are injured. He and McKenzie pull the heavy poncho down to a flat spot where they can manage it better.

Second Platoon has two men with broken bones. It's not until late in the afternoon when the two pilots and Delta's two soldiers are picked up by Medivac. The door gunners go out on a second lift along with Buggs. Night comes before anyone is ready but luckily, Charlie Company reports no more contact.

Days are beginning to run together for McKenzie. This day, however, would be a marker. His memories of some days were brown and cloudy as a dust storm while others, like today, were bright and jagged and painful. They stayed sharp in the front of his mind until he was able to force them away, promising himself to deal with them later. He saw others do it but the process always left him feeling opaque with eyes that did not blink.

After morning chow and limited clean up, Delta moved out toward Charlie Company amid a sudden rain shower. There were no KIAs, only two wounded. The area was dark and gloomy. Their position was surrounded by a plethora of tall trees rising off the banks of a sharp ravine, blocking out the sunlight. McKenzie was beginning to feel the anger. How many times did he have to see this before he puked?

Another Medivac. Charlie Company moved off to the South while Delta climbed back the way they had come to give security for a huge flying crane sent by Division to take the damaged and burned helicopter shell off the hill. Delta was slogging toward a far off ridgeline by afternoon in what had become a full-blown, torrential monsoon storm, the cold rain blowing sideways.

MOROSE

Captain Moore finally decided to stop for the evening. The freezing downpour had had its way with them. McKenzie dropped his pack onto the muddy ground and looked down at his hands, shriveled and wrinkled from the wet. They had walked through the grayness of low clouds, rain and no sunlight, unable to see. They had walked on as if there was no enemy and no danger.

The usual foxholes were dug and preparations made. Delta Company appeared to operate in an aimless dance of habit. McKenzie found it hard to pay attention. He went to see Sergeant Doll when the rain slacked off. His new One Five was resting comfortably under a lean to, water dripping off a roof of clear plastic into a small ditch he had dug around the base that directed the water down the hill. Rain had finally slowed to a drizzle but the air was mountain crisp and cold.

"What do you think, Sarge?" McKenzie said, sitting down under the lean to.

"Hell, I have no clue, One Six. This whole thing's been a cluster fuck since we left Barbara."

"You think Mr. Charles has got many people in here, Sarge? I mean, everything seems so on and off."

McKenzie had brought an empty cracker can, opened at the bottom on three sides for a stove. He placed a heat tab inside, lit it, opened a can of beef stew and sat it on the other can and then looked at his new One Five who was watching him without expression.

"I think we been lucky, LT. If we don't watch our ass, we're gonna get it wiped," Sergeant Doll said looking away.

"You think Koop's on his way to Japan yet?" McKenzie tried changing the subject.

"I talked to Top when you were up with Six earlier. They took Koop directly to Danang where he got some quick surgery to stop the bleeding but they're sending him on to Bien Hoa to see if they can repair the shinbone. Top didn't know anything more than that but he said Koop sent word, he's gonna write when he gets settled."

"You ever talk much with Koop, Sergeant Doll?"

"Yea, some. He was one to always keep to himself just because he didn't want to make friends. He had to run this platoon every time we had no platoon leader. That was before you got here. I think he just wanted to go home and get his degree in accounting.'

"You're shitting me. I knew it. Mr. Cool under fire wants to be a CPA. I always kinda thought he looked like one." They both laughed and reminisced about Sergeant Koop. McKenzie finished his beef stew and crawled out to throw the empty can into the nearest garbage hole. He was startled to see a small campfire blazing at the company CP. He almost ran over a couple of soldiers on his way over.

"Six? What the hell are you doing? Put that fire out. You want us to become a lighthouse for mortars? Six? Put that out."

TRANSFERS

Captain Moore was laying down on an air mattress with his back to the fire. He sat up and told Navorski to put it out. Smoke began to rise in a billowy plume as dirt was thrown on the flames. McKenzie kicked wet dirt onto the fire from where he stood. He was confused. Six was acting like he didn't care. He turned and walked away a few steps, stopped and turned around. Captain Moore had laid back down. He would have to wait and talk to him in the morning.

Navorski followed McKenzie back across. He told McKenzie Black Knight had made good on his threat. Captain Moore was being transferred to Saigon. Six had received the call earlier in the day. It explained the melancholy march all day. McKenzie had thought it was the loss of Buggs. Navorski said Six had pulled out a bottle of Scotch he'd been carrying as soon as they set up camp. He said he didn't give a shit any more.

"At first, Six was mad but then he just got sad because he knew Black Knight had done it and there was nothing he could do about it," Navorski said in a low voice.

That wasn't the only news. Navorski told McKenzie he was being transferred to Echo Company. Orders were cut. There was no discussion. McKenzie went back but Captain Moore said he didn't want to hear about it. Delta would be moving toward a pick up area in the morning. They were being sent in to LZ Jane for a stand down and the transfers. Bravo would come out on the pick up birds to replace them. That's all he could get out of his company commander.

What the hell was happening? Koop was gone, Six was leaving and McKenzie was being transferred away from his men? His world was coming apart. Everything they had built in the past two months was being shredded by an arbitrary war and a malevolent command. It left McKenzie feeling weak. He wanted to get mad but he had no energy for it. His lifeblood was being drained away and the ground he thought was finally feeling firm was rolling under his feet like the night of his first arch light.

KEMPER ON POINT

First platoon was back on point the next morning. Kemper's squad slowly worked their way back off the ridge where the terrain turned into rolling hills and then flattened out. Kemper stopped the march and came back.

"This is a perfect area for Bouncing Betties, LT. Its a form of mine set to pop into the air when you hit the trip wire. The blast can blow your balls off. '

"I saw them at An Khe when I came in country, Kemper, but we haven't seen any out here. Right?"

"Well, I'm taking point, LT. If they're here, I know how to spot em."

"OK, but you be careful, Sarge," McKenzie said.

Kemper had been glum all morning after he's heard McKenzie was leaving. They had talked it over and agreed to drink a few when they got back to Jane. Maybe this would take his mind off the future for a while. Movement slowed to a crawl as Kemper carefully examined the trail in front of him. Tall, thick cheat grass grew close to the trail. The rain had stopped but a moderate wind was blowing the grass back and forth making it difficult to see what was there. The air was humid after the rainstorm and they could feel a new weather system coming out of the mountains.

McKenzie moved to the middle of First Squad to watch Kemper work his magic. He would get down on all fours with his rifle beside him to look and look. Then he would slowly get up and move on.

McKenzie began to think about his transfer. What would his new platoon look like? It staggered him to think about it, especially when he felt his own move had something to do with the conflict between Captain Moore and Colonel Fishmuth.

He felt the explosion before he heard it. Hot air pushed him backwards before the sound filled his head. When he got to Kemper, he could see the back of his right pant leg, just above the knee, was thick with blood. Smoke floated in the air. Kemper who was down on his left side, had tears in his eyes but did not cry out.

~~

"Doc! Medic! Someone get Doc up here." McKenzie drops to his knees. Not again. He pulls a field dressing out, rips it open and holds it against the leg to stem the bleeding.

"Walker, get out in front and set up security," he says as he looks back for Doc. "Brady, get Medivac on the phone - now!"

Captain Moore and Doc Watson show up at the same time.

"Shit, shit, shit!", Six says. Doc sticks Kemper in the arm with morphine, then rolls him over flat onto his stomach and begins cutting his pant leg apart with a pair of surgical scissors. Black, jagged pieces of metal are buried in the muscle and sinew of his back thigh, which is torn apart. He pulls them out, one by one, with large tweezers.

"Damn, Kemper. You be goin' home or at least, out of the field," Doc says. "This is your third Purple Heart, man, and its gonna be a while 'for this gets healed up. But - you are definitely gonna live, my man."

Kemper crossed his arms in front and put his forehead on them. "Fuck you, Doc. You wanna trade places?" He turns his head slightly and looks up at McKenzie, who is still beside him. "LT, I'm sorry. I missed that one." The morphine makes him slur his words.

"Forget about it." McKenzie bends lower so he can talk quietly to Kemper. "I have learned so much from you, Sergeant Kemper. You have done far more than your share. You get the hell out of here and don't come back. Let me know where you are and maybe I can come down and see you. I won't forget you." He says it all before his throat tightens up. This time, he feels sure he might cry so he stays down next to Kemper with his arm over his shoulder until he can talk again.

"I'll write your parents when I get back to Jane and I'm damn sure gonna drink a few to you and the rest of your life. You take care of yourself."

Kemper did not look up any more. He just lay there while Doc put a compression bandage on. McKenzie looked up. All of First Squad had gathered around but there were no expressions on their faces. They just stood and looked. It was like that. Men were killed or wounded and taken away. New guys arrived and after a few weeks, became members of the team. How could he get through his tour when he always felt so bad? He saw how the others had learned to protect themselves with "it don't mean nothin'." He had tried to get there and even said the words from time to time but he was not there yet. By God, after Kemper, he would get there.

CARTER ON POINT

After the Medivac, McKenzie told Carter he was replacing Kemper whether he liked it or not. They were heading into a sparse mountain forest, more open than a rain forest. Carter started to move first as the point man. McKenzie hollered at him.

"What are you doing, Carter? I just lost one squad leader walking point."

"My choice, LT. I don't want any more of these Yankee suckers getting hit. We're goin' in for a stand down and I'm tired of watching guys leave on choppers. Y'all need to let me do it, LT. I need to do it." He stood with his weapon held out as if he was physically stopping McKenzie from advancing upon him.

"OK, Carter. I'm tired of losing guys too." McKenzie didn't have the strength to argue.

"No problem, LT."

There didn't seem to be any end to it.

Delta headed up the trail into deeper forest. It looked curiously familiar. The incline was gentle and the side hills sloping. McKenzie's mood was abject after losing Koop and Kemper and it was difficult for him to pull his thoughts out of the misery he had succumbed to. That little voice raged at him. What are you doing? Pay attention. This is just like the place you learned that lesson when Wright was killed.

A blast from Carter's weapon let him know the voice was correct. Carter continued to fire as he hit the ground. McKenzie rushed forward to where Carter and two others had made it off the trail behind a fallen tree.

~~

Enemy fire smears itself across the air, coming from a bunkered Chinese machine gun. AK fire is coming from both sides, digging at the tree bark and slamming into the earth around them.

Dammit, McKenzie cusses to himself. He radios Doll to move the other squads up and tells Brady to call for air support. When Doll tries to move to the other side of the trail, the AKs turn on him. McKenzie moves two machine guns up where they can get some fire on the AKs but the bunkered guy continues to fire short bursts at anything that moves. Six calls to say that gun ships are inbound and Black Knight is on station.

McKenzie rolls over and pulls the pin on a yellow smoke grenade, pops the handle and rolls it up the trail. Brady asks for identification of the color but gets no answer. They can hear a helicopter directly above them. There's an explosion to the right and two more up the trail. He looks to see if Carter is throwing grenades. He isn't. Another explosion occurs behind him. What the hell?

"Brady, get Black Knight on the horn," he says as he inches back to take the hand set. "Black Knight three, this is Double Time One Six India, my Six needs to talk to your Six. Here you go, One Six." Brady stretches the cord out so McKenzie can grab it.

"Black Knight Six, this is Double Time One Six. I got incoming but I don't hear a mortar. Can you spot the incoming for me? Over."

McKenzie waits but there is no answer. "Black Knight Six, this is Double Time One Six. Do you read me? I got incoming. Can you see where its coming from? Over."

A weak voice comes back. It's Black Knight. "Double Time One Six, that was us. We threw out a few grenades to assist you since no gun ships were on station yet. Over."

"Jesus Christ! Black Knight Six, you can't see us. You're throwing grenades on top of us. You throw another one and I'll personally turn my sixty on you. Over and Out. Damn!" McKenzie hits the dirt with his fist, putting his head down on the ground. "Damn, damn, damn!" He can hear the helicopter turn and fly off to the East. Finally, Black Knight answers, " This is Black Knight Six, Out."

~~

MALIGNANT ENMITY

McKenzie was crazy with anger. Luckily no one was hurt that he knew of. He wanted that Colonel there on the ground so he could sit on him and choke him. He pictured himself stomping into the command bunker and blowing the thin lipped idiot out of his chair, firing his weapon on full automatic. Brady tapped him on the back.

"LT, we got Patch One, a pink team on station." McKenzie rolled over and pulled another smoke grenade from his pack. This one was red. When the pilot identified the color, he directed him to the bunker and within seconds, rockets were flying down like a meteor shower. His blood was hot and he felt exhilarated with the full power of the Cav's arsenal being brought to bear. "Take that you sons a bitches!" he shouted. "This is for Koop and Kemper and Wright and Buggs and every other good man just trying to get home." He jumped up and began a loud Indian war hoop dance. Brady pulled on his pant leg until he kneeled back down.

He could feel himself starting to develop a sort of malignant enmity against these little bastards from the North. The small LOH helicopter hovered overhead firing his mini-guns at the crest of the hill while a Cobra sat off to the right, firing rockets across the hillside. He didn't care anymore what it felt like to be the enemy on the ground. They were the ones who kept killing and shooting his friends.

Carter pulled his wounded man to safety and carried him past McKenzie. "Thanks, LT. I thought we were up a crick," was all he said as he passed. McKenzie was dripping with sweat, ramped up and still furious when Captain Moore walked up.

"Brady, have those guys put everything they got on that hill before they leave," he said.

When the Pink team left, McKenzie got to his feet and moved the rest of First Squad up the hill to the right and onto the top, behind the bunker. Doll reported two dead NVA on an escape trial where the Cobra had caught them.

McKenzie had Smith, one of the new kids, lob two grenades into the bunker and then he jumped off the top to the ground and fired over the log berm, into the blackness. No one home. They found the Chinese machine gun, which had been damaged and left behind with about two hundred rounds of ammunition. McKenzie looked around frantically for something else or someone to shoot but there was nothing.

After Medivac, Delta moved away to the West until Captain Moore stopped the march. They would move to the pick up area in the morning. McKenzie ate a few crackers and peanut butter but he wasn't hungry. He wrote letters to the families of Koop, Kemper and Blandon, the kid wounded that afternoon.

SCOTCH AND CIGARS

A couple hours later, Captain Moore came over and sat down. He motioned the others away. He'd brought a lit cigar in one hand and a bottle of Scotch in the other. He poured at least two shots into McKenzie's canteen cup and took a long pull on the bottle.

"So what the hell do you think you were doing today threatening the old man, One Six?"

McKenzie did not answer.

"The problem is, One Six, I'm leaving and I'm not going to be around to protect these guys from that man like I been doin'. You're goin' over to Echo where he's really gonna have his way with you. You can't go around threatening the chain of command every time you don't like what they do."

"Shit, Six. That was the dumbest thing I've ever seen. If he would have killed one of my guys, what do you think Division would have thought about that?"

"Then that would have been up to Division, not you. I know its hard to keep the military rules straight when you're out humping the boonies but you're an officer. That's your job. You were not a good example for your men at that moment and you know it."

McKenzie looked his captain straight in the eyes. " Are you kiddin' me? They loved it. They saw me willing to do whatever I needed to do to take care of them. That's my relationship with them. That's our bond."

"Well, its wrong headed." Six said, pouring McKenzie another double shot. "I want you to have that bond with your men but you also represent military discipline and if you lose respect for the system and I'm talking about how its supposed to be, you will find yourself marooned with your men, plus, you will lose control. More than that, you won't be there for them if they court-martial your ass. I know what I'm talking about. I was in your boots back in '67'. It's hard but that's your job."

Captain Moore stayed talking for another hour. He was disillusioned but not with the military. It was hard for him to accept that he had been taken out of the field early. He was a soldier, however, and if that was the way it was, that was what he would do. He gave McKenzie a few tips about operating a recon platoon. He also said they would not be going directly to the pick up zone in the morning. Instead, they were going to check out a hillside that S-2 suspected contained a hidden arms cache. Unless they got into a fight, they would still be able to make the pick up.

MORE OF THE SAME

It was hard to swallow words like honor, obedience and military discipline when there didn't seem to be any in the chain of command above. Every time McKenzie tried to move his mind in that direction, it would snap back to thoughts of vengeance and retribution. He could see Black Knight's helicopter spiraling toward the ground, followed by black smoke. It was a plan he ultimately dismissed because he did not want to kill the other pilot or the door gunners but there had to be another way.

The next day was August, Sixteen, a Friday. There were only a few clouds, a break in the monsoon weather. McKenzie sat on his poncho liner eating C-ration ham and eggs, drinking coffee to drown the taste of the food and thinking about football daily doubles that would be starting back home. He would love to put on a full set of pads and hit someone.

The summer before his junior year, Coach Tucker told McKenzie he wanted him to switch from the backfield to the line but he would have to get stronger. He told McKenzie to do twenty-five push-ups the first day of June and add one every day until he got to one hundred. He also had McKenzie report to his house every Tuesday and Thursday for one on one blocking and tackling drills in the back yard. He told McKenzie that making the team was up to him. He wouldn't get the job unless he earned it.

Coach Tucker knocked McKenzie on his ass more than once during that summer. He loved it. McKenzie did those hundred push ups every morning and night until he graduated, and as a result, was a starter during the next two seasons. Coach Tucker had confidence in him and he had developed confidence in himself. As he ate his ham and eggs, McKenzie tried to apply the lessons of Coach Tucker to where he was.

The United States Army had given him their confidence when they commissioned him. They were relying upon him to lead men and uphold the principles of leadership. They had trained him and they had expectations. Yet, there was still an unanswered ethical dilemma. Was his first priority to his men or his mission? What if he could not serve both at the same time?

In the midst of his reverie, someone yelled, "inbound" and he looked up to see green smoke drifting across the hill and heard the first sounds of a helicopter blade popping. It was Black Knight. A runner informed McKenzie that Six wanted all platoon leaders up at the CP. He walked slowly toward the group, anticipating he might be the main topic but when he arrived, it was not so.

Colonel Fishmuth was standing in the middle of the other platoon leaders fitting a cigarette into what looked like a new silver holder. He let Two Six light it and then explained that he was bringing Alpha and Charlie companies in. Delta would move toward a small knoll about a click west where they would await further orders. Artillery batteries on both LZ Jane and Sharon were available to provide support if needed. The mission was to capture the ammunition cache without destroying it. In other words, he wanted an assault on the enemy without much prep. A more specific plan would be laid out once all three companies were on the ground.

"That's all, gentlemen. I want that cache in tact," he said pulling the butt end of the half smoked cigarette from his holder and field stripping it. "I am depending upon you men to make this mission the great military success for Fifth Battalion that it can be. I will be on the ground to help coordinate and lead the assault." Black Knight turned on his heals in a perfect about face and marched back to his helicopter.

SIX IS STILL IN CHARGE

Captain Moore watched the helicopter lift its ass end and drift into the morning sun, then he walked the officers off to one side, away from his own CP and spoke to them in a secretive voice. "This has the makings of a very dangerous operation. I want you all to stay on your toes once we get into position and hold fast until I have time to confer with the other company commanders. Don't scare your troops. We'll let them know more when the time comes."

It was an odd directive. McKenzie told Doll and his squad leaders they were headed for the pickup with a possible detour along the way. That was all.

"One Six, you ready for me to lance that boil?" Doc Watson said as McKenzie rooted around inside his poncho tent looking for the half eaten can of ham and eggs. He had been nursing a boil on his right forearm for a week but Doc refused to lance it until it was ready. " It looks real ripe now," he said looking close at it.

"Can I finish my meal first, at least? Jesus, how come you're so cut happy? You wouldn't do it two days ago." McKenzie said.

"Like I told you, LT, this way I can clean it out real good, pack it and let the sucker heal from the inside out. Almost no scar; I promise."

McKenzie was not only suffering from the boil but he had trench foot and a roaring case of crotch rot. He tried to dry out as much as he could at night but it had been raining off and on for weeks. Sometimes the smell of his own rotting flesh was almost overwhelming. It had a grayish, mottled look to it and it stunk.

Before he could finish his meal, Doc was back. Surgery was swift and without anesthetic. A long, yellow core came out of his arm as thick as heavy wool. The hole was huge. Doc stuffed it with string gauze and then covered it with a thick bandage and tape. The procedure was so simple and quick - McKenzie was amazed.

"Keep it covered and clean and I'll repack it every night. That way, when we're through, you won't hardly know where it was." Doc Watson laid his hand on McKenzie's shoulder.

"Thanks, Doc." McKenzie said. The arm had suddenly stopped aching. "You know I'm leaving, right?"

"Yes, I heard that. I'm gonna have to do a ton of counseling around here after you're gone, sir. It ain't right. I figure we lost glue when Koop and Kemper went out but you, that's just not right. I'll clean that hole as long as you're here, LT. Then it'll be up to you." Doc took a deep breath, the kind that comes from your guts.

Brady came over with his radio. "Listen to this, LT. I got us tuned in to the battalion frequency." He turned the speaker volume up a little.

"Black Knight Three, this is Black Knight Six, say again. I need to know why Alpha and Charlie Companies are not in the air. Over."

"This is Three. Yellow Horse has given lift priorities to Second of the Fifth and Second of the Eighth. Both have heavy enemy contact at this time. Over."

"Division is Yellow Horse, LT," said Brady. " I know," said McKenzie.

"This is Black Knight Six. When can I expect that to change? Over."

"Not today. Maybe tomorrow. Over."

"Roger that. Double Time, Six, this is Black Knight Six, what's your location? Over."

Captain Moore said they were about a click away and Black Knight instructed him to call when Delta was in position.

Sergeant Doll had walked up to hear part of the conversation. "What was that all about, One Six?"

"We're going in to look for a cache, Sarge. Right now, I don't know if that's a problem or not. Just hang fire and we'll see what develops."

"Something smells, LT. You gonna let me in on what's coming down or not?"

"All I know, One Five, is that Black Knight thinks there's a big cache of arms and its a big deal. It may be defended by a large enemy force or not. He wants us to go in and capture the cache without destroying it. That means, little or no prep and we're on our own."

"You have got to be shitting me! You want a mutiny on your hands, LT?"

"Hey! You know Six is not going to hang us out to dry. Let's see what develops. Now get everyone ready, we'll be moving out in about fifteen."

Sergeant Doll was a different One Five. Koop would have shrugged his shoulders and made it all seem like a walk in the park. Doll was calm under fire but edgy, chain smoking and furtive the rest of the time.

The rendezvous site was more like a small mound than a knoll. It sat in the middle of a green meadow, water fed from the mountain range to the West. About fifteen hundred meters in the direction of the mountains stood a much larger hillside covered in scrub brush and capped by trees. Captain Moore directed the company to spread out in a large circle around the knoll while he brought his platoon leaders and sergeants together.

"Black Knight is inbound. I don't know what he's got in mind but the cache is supposed to be over on that hill. Let me deal with him and try to keep your mouth's shut." He looked directly at McKenzie. "I'm not crossing that wide, open son-of-a-bitch without some kind of protection. I'm sure Charlie's watching us right now," he said.

UNWELCOME VISIT

When they could hear the helicopter coming from far away, everyone walked back to the north end and waited for the landing. The pilot slowed the rotors but did not shut down. Black Knight exited. McKenzie heard the distinctive bloop of a mortar round being fired from the far hill. Sound traveled faster than a mortar round but not much.

"Incoming!" more than one person yelled. McKenzie hit the ground and looked for his company commander. Colonel Fishmuth was bent over as if he didn't understand what was happening. Captain Moore pulled him to the ground by his belt just as a round hit to the West about one hundred meters away. There was no place to hide. Men scrambled around to the East side. Captain Moore was instantly on the horn giving LZ Sharon artillery coordinates. Another round hit closer. Adjustments were being made from the hillside.

Black Knight jumped up and ran toward his helicopter in a zigzag pattern as his pilot increased the rotor's RPMs. The bird lifted clumsily off the ground, wobbling, trying to get enough purchase on the humid air to fly. The tail swayed back and forth, then came up slightly higher than its nose, the skids still almost touching the ground. The company watched in disbelief as the helicopter started skimming the earth in a death defying effort to get away. Somehow, the pilot managed enough speed to gain lift.

Brady looked over at McKenzie. "That was a fine piece of open field running, don't you think? Looked just like Jim Brown."

"The man's a coward, Brady. I thought sure they were going to crash," McKenzie said without caring who heard.

Captain Moore placed a marking round near the hillside as another mortar round exploded closer. He yelled into the hand phone, "Adjust one hundred echo and fifty sierra. Fire for effect." Then he bent over and picked up Black Knight's flight helmet, which had been left at his feet. He held it in the air toward the departing aircraft. It would have to be returned. For the next twenty minutes, Six called in enough artillery to decimate the hillside. He didn't ask permission and he didn't appear worried about destroying any cache.

When it was over, Delta Company moved across the open space to inspect what might be left. They found two blown up rice bags and some foul smelling fish product. That was all. Third Platoon found the mortar tube and its two dead operators in a small foxhole in front of a tree. Three Six placed C-four inside the tube and blew it as the company walked away toward the pick up zone.

The next morning Captain Moore found McKenzie.

" Operations wants someone in Delta to write up Colonel Fishmuth for a Silver Star for bravery under fire."

McKenzie did not answer, he just looked at his company commander in disgust.

"That's what I thought," Captain Moore said with a laugh. They agreed that neither of them would write anything. McKenzie did take the time, however, to write up a few more medal recommendations for members of First Platoon.

CHAPTER 7 - ECHO COMPANY
(AUGUST 17, 1968 - 305 DAYS LEFT)

It was a group of somber men who waited for choppers to take them back to LZ Jane. Captain Moore and McKenzie were leaving. Koop and Kemper were gone and Carter was short. Three Six was getting out of the field and would be leaving after they returned to Jane. Second Platoon had three guys going home. One was their second squad leader. Both Navorski and the other company RTO were being given rear jobs. McKenzie looked around at the sour faces on soldiers sitting and standing. Carter shouted across the pick up zone at him, "Bravo Company inbound."

McKenzie had heard rumors about Bravo's company commander. Too much drinking and fraternization with his men. Although such talk was probably idle gossip, he found himself curious to see the man, who, as it turned out, was on the first helicopter. Black Gold Six was black, thin and about six foot two inches tall. He had an air of take charge but his handshake with Captain Moore was weak, the kind where someone grabs your fingers before you can get a good hand full. He walked over to a tree, put his helmet on the ground, rubbed his head and sat down on the helmet, looking at the ground.

His soldiers did not seem to be in any bigger hurry. Black Gold Six made no effort to replace Delta when Six pulled in his security,. McKenzie waited and climbed into the last bird. As the helicopter lifted off, he looked down at Bravo. The entire company was standing around the pick up zone. He felt grateful to have served under Captain Moore who was a true professional.

BLACK KNIGHT'S AGENDA

Navorski came over to McKenzie just before lift off and said Black Knight wanted to see him when he arrived. He also said things were changing at LZ Jane. Battalion headquarters was moving and splitting up. Intelligence or S-2 was moving to LZ Sharon along with supply, command and the company tents. Operations or S-3 had already moved to LZ Barbara.

McKenzie dropped his pack at the platoon bunker after he landed and promised Sergeant Doll he would be back to say goodbye. Captain Moore was no where to be seen. McKenzie headed for the old Battalion command bunker. He found Black Knight laying on a bunk over in a dark corner while several enlisted men worked the radios. McKenzie stood silently for a moment letting his eyes adjust.

"Sir, Lieutenant McKenzie reporting," he said, throwing up a halfhearted salute. Black Knight looked sideways at him and wrinkled his nose.

"Grab a stool and sit down, McKenzie."

McKenzie did as he was told and waited. After a few minutes, Colonel Fishmuth swung his legs sideways and sat up rubbing his eyes with the back of his hands like a small child does.

"I remember when you first walked in here and it shocked me that you were a Second Lieutenant. You gave me that bullshit about why you had refused any further training before arriving in

Vietnam and I was convinced you would be dead in thirty days. It seems, however, that you have adapted well. Are you aware that your platoon has the best record for number of enemy killed?"

When he finished the question, he got up and reached for a cigarette, placing it carefully into his silver holder. He bent over to retrieve a lighter off the foot locker next to his cot and lit it bent over, his back to McKenzie, who could have easily shot the man.

When Black Knight turned around and sat back on the cot, McKenzie said, "No sir. I did not know that although I knew Delta had the best record in the battalion but we have had our losses."

"I'm not talking about the company, Lieutenant. I'm talking about First Platoon. Oh, you have had some unfortunate losses like Sergeants Koop and Kemper but no one was killed in First Platoon."

He went on talking as if McKenzie had said nothing. It was just words. The real issue was Captain Moore's leaving and McKenzie's transfer to Echo and there was the matter of his threatening Black Knight for throwing grenades out of his helicopter. Maybe they would even talk about his refusing to write up Black Knight for a medal. McKenzie was certain this quiet talk was building toward something he would not like. The bunker smelled of mold and wet boots.

"I've tried to make this battalion the best fighting unit in the First Air Cavalry Division and from time to time, changes have to be made to achieve that kind of success." Colonel Fishmuth stood up, pulled his shoulders back and looked down at McKenzie who quickly stood up, almost bumping into the colonel, who was closer than he thought.

"I'm transferring you to Echo Company because you have presented me with a strange mix of leadership. It seems you are not afraid to fight but your association with Captain Moore has made it very important that I cannot leave you with Delta. They need a fresh start and Echo needs a new platoon leader. Their mission is long range recon and they work in smaller units, which, apparently you like. So, you're going over to Echo. We have a big push that will come in from the coast and drive straight toward LZ Barbara. Your platoon will act as a blocking force, ambushing and harassing the enemy as they are pushed back into the mountains."

McKenzie was seething. He gritted his teeth and looked at this officer who had done exactly what he and Captain Moore had suspected.

"Sir, I don't want to leave my platoon. I have an effective group of troopers who work well. Delta is not only losing its CO but one of the other platoon leaders is leaving country. If I go, that will mean a new company commander and two new platoon leaders. First Platoon is already adjusting to a new platoon sergeant and that's an awful lot to ask. I would like to stay and help them get through this transition."

"Lieutenant, it's not your decision. While I appreciate your warm feelings for your men, its my job to do what is best for this battalion and what I have done is just that. Don't you dare question or challenge me. You understand?" His voice was loud enough that one of the radio operators turned around to look.

"Is that it, sir?" McKenzie said loudly.

Colonel Fishmuth took a step closer. His eyes were puffy and his breath stale with cigarettes. He took the holder out of his mouth, now with a spent cigarette lodged inside, and started jabbing it toward McKenzie with his right hand.

"No, Lieutenant, that is not all. You are skating on thin ice with me. You make one mistake and I will have your ass. You understand?" Jab, jab went the cigarette holder. "I know you can do what I want you to do. You just have to get your head in the right place." Jab, jab. "I have requested a new company commander for Echo. He's a special forces veteran and he will be arriving in two weeks." Jab, jab. "In the mean time, you will have Sergeant Smythe, the recon platoon sergeant, who is also a Green Beret with three tours under his belt. They both will know how to implement my plan and you will do your job." One last jab. "Dismissed."

McKenzie spun around and stomped out into the bright sunshine, stopping just outside the door to let his eyes adjust. He wanted to go back and do something violent but he was not yet ready to confront authority that way. Koop and Captain Moore were gone. Kemper would not return and who knew how good the new company commander would be. His heart ached at the thought of leaving Doll and Casey. Black Knight knew nothing about those kind of feelings. He decided to go find Captain Moore.

"Captain Moore's gone," Top said. "The Colonel scheduled to have him picked up the minute he returned. He barely had time to gather his things. Any pending reports are to be submitted from Saigon. Captain Gandell is the new CO. No word who will replace you."

McKenzie sat down on a foot locker and put his head in his hands. He wanted to say goodbye to Captain Moore in person. Top handed him a forwarding address so he could write a letter. After sitting for a long time, he stood up and headed over to Echo Company's tent to check in.

FIRST SERGEANT FINSTER

First Sergeant Finster, who had one star on his CIB, was small and wiry, not quite the commanding presence of Top Kauthorn but it was obvious he knew what he was doing.

"Welcome to Echo Company, sir. I heard you like ambushes. You're gonna get your share of them with Echo."

"Thanks, Top. I don't know. I'm coming from a line platoon, so I figure I got a lot to learn." McKenzie looked around. There was no grease board with rosters or names crossed off.

"Well, that's OK, sir. We got a good crew out on LZ Barbara. Lieutenant Davis is short, so he'll be coming in tomorrow. I hear Delta's going to Barbara, so you might as well ride out with them. Unfortunately, you and Lieutenant Davis are gonna pass going and coming. I guess you'll just have to rely on Sergeant Smythe. He knows what he's doing. He's a former green beanie with two tours in Thailand and one in country. He's very experienced. You let me know if you need anything before you leave and I'll see if I can't get it for you. I already got your transfer orders."

"Oh, yea? Black Knight doesn't waste any time, does he?" McKenzie said. "Actually, I'm probably gonna spend the rest of the day and night with my old platoon at Delta. I got goodbyes to say. I could use a new pair of boots and socks if you got em. Ten and a half on the boots. I always carry an extra radio battery myself, so if I could get a fresh one, I would appreciate that."

"No problem, sir. I can tell you're not real happy about this transfer. Try not to bring my boys down, OK? They're a good bunch and you come with good recommendations, so they're looking forward to meeting you."

"Who's recommendations?"

"I talked with Top Kauthorn and Lieutenant Davis called your Six before he left. He's protective of the guys he's leavin' and wanted to make sure the platoon leader replacing him was not an idiot. Pardon the term, sir."

McKenzie turned and said over his shoulder, "No problem, Top. I'll see ya later."

GOODBYE TO CARTER

After a long shower and a trip to the medical tent to have his boil checked and repacked, McKenzie went back to Echo for a new set of fatigues. Getting the boil lanced had given him such relief. His arm had ached incredibly at night and it was often difficult to hold his rifle. His mind turned to Black Knight. There had to be a similar solution.

His life was in limbo - not with Delta and not yet with Echo. Of all the people he had to say goodbye to, Carter was gonna be the hardest. He was short and Top had decided to hold him back when the company returned to the boonies.

Carter had managed to worm his way into McKenzie's feelings. As a soldier, he had received two Bronze Stars for valor, a Silver Star and two People Hearts and yet, he was a country boy from Tennessee who liked to laugh, live life on the edge and would do anything for his fellow troopers. By some special magic, he appeared to be in total control of his fear.

The Silver Star was awarded for saving two wounded buddies in the City of Hue during Tet. Top had let McKenzie read a copy of the medal recommendation. The Cav had been working with Marines to clear neighborhood streets when First Platoon ran into a sizable enemy force holed up in a half demolished school. Two point men were hit as they entered the town square in front of the school. They were laying exposed between a brick well and the school.

Two Chinese machine guns fired at Carter when he ran into the square carrying LAWs (light antitank weapons) in his right hand and firing his M-16 with his left. He knocked out both machine guns with the LAWs, then ran out, grabbed one soldier and pulled him to safety. The NVA quickly reorganized and were coming out of the right side of the school when Carter returned. He killed the first two before grabbing the second soldier by the arm as bullets whizzed around him. A Marine sniper killed two more enemy coming out of the building. Kemper ran to the well with an M-60 and began hosing down the side door. His action attracted a counter attack from three sides but fortunately, a tank appeared and demolished the building. Both wounded soldiers survived. Kemper was given a Bronze Star with a V for valor.

It wasn't necessarily what Carter did. It was the speed at which he could size up a situation and react while others were taking cover or trying to get the elephant off their chest. He did not hesitate, ever. McKenzie found him packing. A case of beer sat nearby. Carter had already done some serious damage to it. He was sitting on the ground, crossed legged, with all his stuff laid out on a poncho, including a pile of black, dried up ears.

"So - Sergeant Carter - you're going home, I guess. Who's gonna do the suicide missions after you're gone?"

"Hey, LT. Grab a seat. Hell, I never did nothing but screw with Charlie's mind. Once you figure them little bastards out, it's not so hard. They act like they ain't scared but they are and its easy to get the jump on em. Sort of like roundin' up frogs in a swamp."

"If it was so easy, everybody would do it. You gonna drink all that beer by yourself or offer me one before we part and never see each other again?"

Carter reached over and underhanded a can of Black Label toward McKenzie who snagged it with one hand. "You never did like me, did you LT," he said as he went back to sorting.

"Just the opposite, Sergeant Carter. I have grown to both respect and like you. Did I agree with your ear collection? No. I didn't win that one, did I? Right now, I think this war stinks. I hope you go back to Tennessee and have a good life and maybe leave those ears behind."

"You know, LT. Them ol' boys back in Tennessee'd get a kick out of these here ears but I ain't takin' em. Don't worry none. When I finally step back on good ol' Tennessee dirt, I'm gonna forget I was ever here. This here country is in a sorry mess and the only people who are gonna figure it out is the people who live here. I done what Uncle Sam asked me to do and I survived. That's all that counts in my book. I just wish you was stayin' with Delta. They need you." When he said it, Carter did not look up.

McKenzie didn't know what to say. He sat there for a long time drinking the warm beer and watching Carter sort through his belongings, creating two stacks - one for going home and another for the burn barrel. He knew Carter would not forget the Nam or the guys he served with. He finally stood up to go. Carter got up and put his left hand on McKenzie's shoulder, looked him in the eye and wished him good luck.

After the awkward silence earlier when Carter had told McKenzie he wished he was staying with Delta, he'd shared what he knew about Echo. It was surprising how much he had gleaned from just listening. He said the previous platoon leader insisted on walking point every time the platoon went out.

"Not your job, LT. You let them kids walk point and watch what they're doing. They gonna be a lot better off if you do your job figurin' out how to out smart Mr. Charles and don't git your ass kilt walking point."

DOLL AND CASEY

After leaving Carter and making the rounds to say goodbye to his platoon, McKenzie found Doll and Casey at the command bunker. It was obvious Casey was down.

"The whole company's fallin' apart, One Six. These last two months, we had a unit that knew itself. Now there's only gonna be a few of us left. With Koop and Kemper and now you gone and a new CO coming in, what the hell do we tell the guys?"

Sergeant Doll spoke up before McKenzie could answer. "Don't you be fallin' apart on me, Casey. I told you, it don't mean nothin'. All you gotta do is take care of yourself and your men and I'll do the rest."

Doll was a big man who had a habit of sticking out his chin when he was serious. A sparse mustache revealed his young age but he also had tired eyes. The kind of combat weariness that saps the soul no matter how strong a leader tries to be. McKenzie had begun to feel the same weariness.

In the beginning, he could remember every minute of every hour, day after day. He was able to keep vivid memories of what happened and replay them with total recall. Lately, his memory was slipping. There were holes. It had become easier to focus only on the present. Just get through the day and tomorrow will take care of itself.

"Look, Casey. I only got to spend two months with First Platoon and Captain Moore. You guys had more. I gotta say, I learned so much from all of you. The strength of this company and First Platoon is the standard set by the good ones, like Koop and Kemper and Six and all those that were here before them. Its a good feeling and its in you. Just keep up that feeling and every soldier who comes in will automatically know what's expected. If you find yourself gettin' down or lost, just ask yourself what Koop or Kemper would do?"

"Well, you keep your head down too, LT. We're not gonna be there to cover your ass any more," Casey said.

"You know, Sergeant Casey. You and me got a history together - all the way back to Fort Benning. I don't intend to let the bastards get me now and I expect to hear you made it out of here. Otherwise, I'll feel like my training in boot camp was a failure."

Casey looked up. "So, I guess we're even cause we trained you here," he said, still looking sad.

TOP'S BEER

"I guess we are. You guys gonna buy me a beer or do I have to go down to the enlisted men's beer tent one more time just to see who I can piss off at battalion?"

"We haven't got any beer One Six but we know where you can buy us some. Top's got a whole bunch stashed behind his tent which, right now, he's not willing to cough up. I think that's the least you could do for us and all our training." Casey's mood began to improve. By the time they hit the company tent, he was walking with his usual bounce. Top was on the radio trying to find out when the new CO and platoon leaders were coming in.

"That's horse shit, Kelly. You guys down at G-1 (personnel) need to get your shit together. I got a company headed back out tomorrow with no CO, only one platoon leader and shy about ten men and you can't give me any idea when to expect replacements? Fine. I'll contact the personnel depot in Cam Rahn Bay myself." He slammed down the radio hand set into its carriage, turned around and found three soldiers standing in his entrance.

"We're going out tomorrow? Already, Top? We just got here." Doll sounded very tired. "That's the first I heard of that."

Top Kauthorn snorted and sat down. "So, when are ya gonna stop being surprised by the Army, Sergeant Doll? Word came down earlier that you guys are going back out to LZ Barbara. That's why I'm trying to find replacements. You better have your squad leaders check their ammo and chow. So what can I do for you guys? Sir, aren't you supposed to be hangin' around Echo Company by now?"

"Wait a minute," Casey interrupted. "Who's gonna be the acting CO? We don't have a Six, we don't have an XO and we only got one platoon leader."

"Two six will have to be the CO for now. You, Sergeant Doll, are now the acting platoon leader for First. You all been through the drill. Deal with it. Just run you platoon and your squads like you always have. The rest will take care of itself. I'm sure as hell not goin out to run the company." Top spoke with the voice of authority and many years. He made it sound like it was just stuff that should be understood.

"Wait a minute, Top. I think that would be a great idea. You got more experience than anybody in the company. You got two stars on that CIB. Who better to lead Delta?" McKenzie tried to look very serious as he said it. He walked over to a foot locker and sat down across from Top, putting his right elbow on his knee and his chin in his hand like he was thinking.

Top stood up, took two steps backward and picked up some papers as if he had work to do. "Now, sir. Don't you be giving anyone stupid ideas. I humped my share of hills and anyway, I can't leave these lame brains I got working for me alone. They would be drunk inside of an hour and never get the resupply out."

"Top, that's not fair," protested Sergeant Bush. "I could run this place in my sleep."

"You probably would. Now listen up, all of you. I ain't goin nowhere but here. Sir? How come you're stirrin' up my men anyway?"

"I'll tell you what, Top. I'll refrain from marching over to the Battalion Sergeant Major and puttin' in a special request for you to go out to the field until the new Six arrives if you'll divest yourself of some of that beer you got stashed in the back."

"Well, I'll be go to hell. I'm being bribed by a Second Lieutenant and one that's not even in my company any more. I thought you had ethics, sir."

"I'll tell you what, Top. I'll pay you for it even though I know you paid for it out of the company's slush fund. How much you want for a case?" McKenzie pulled a roll of military script out of his pocket.

"I don't want any of your officer money! Just take a case and get the hell out of my hair. I got work to do and you two," he said pointing at Doll and Casey, "get your shit together. If you need something for yourself or your men, you better let me know now. I probably won't have everything you need but I can get it on a bird by tomorrow or the next day. Sergeant Doll, your mailbag is sittin' over there by the desk. Now all of you, get the hell out of my area." By this time, Top was standing with hands on his hips.

McKenzie walked up to him and stuck out his hand. "It's been a pleasure knowing you, Top. If I can, I'll drop by when Echo comes through."

Sergeant Kauthorn relaxed and grabbed McKenzie's hand. "Sir, you know where to find me. You be smart out there. Don't be no hero. I don't want to read your name on some casualty list."

On his way out the back, McKenzie stopped and erased his name off the board, then he rounded up a block of ice and a large plastic bag from the mess sergeant. By the time he got the ice broken up with an entrenching tool and the beer laid in, Doll and Casey returned after taking an inventory for the field. An hour later, they were well on their way to getting seriously drunk. Carter and a few others showed up and quickly organized a recon to liberate another two cases from behind Delta's company tent. Top spotted them and just shrugged. Carter contributed a bottle of one hundred percent Tennessee home brew which tasted very similar to Georgia white lightning. The mixture of beer and home brew was enough to tank everyone. They finished up around midnight and it was a slow bunch of soldiers who boarded the helicopters headed for Barbara the next morning.

SERGEANT SMYTHE

It was obvious as they were flying in that Barbara had changed. Engineers had constructed a large battalion operations bunker for the S-3. Two large antennas were added to the skyline. Perimeter bunkers were rebuilt and pushed out. There appeared to be an ongoing attempt to reinforce each with timbers and sandbags. McKenzie grabbed his pack and rifle, exited the helicopter and walked over to Echo's area where he found a soldier sitting on top of a sentry like bunker next to the perimeter entrance.

"Good morning, Private. I'm Lieutenant McKenzie, Echo's new platoon leader. Can you tell me where I can find Sergeant Smythe?"

"Yes, sir. You the new One Six? We been waiting for you, sir. I'm Wallace. Sergeant Smythe is over there checking out bunkers. You want me to get him?"

"Nope. That's OK. I'll wander over there in a few minutes. How long you been with Echo, Wallace?"

"About a month, sir. Good outfit. I came over from Alpha. They come through askin' if anyone wanted to go to recon and I jumped at it. Lot better'n wandering around in the jungle with a whole company waitin for the NVA to ambush us. I always figured we might as well be doing the ambushin'. Did you volunteer for recon, sir?"

There it was, McKenzie thought. One of those questions he hadn't thought about.

"Not really. I was transferred from Delta to replace Lieutenant Davis. My company commander believed in working with smaller units and I guess the battalion commander thought that recommended me. Mind if I ask you something between you and me?"

"Sure, LT. I got no secrets." Wallace was refreshing. He was clean, energetic and easy to talk to. He had a baby face with no facial hair and auburn hair which sat in curls as if he'd just had a perm.

"I heard your previous One Six always walked point. Is that true?"

"That's affirmative, sir but the guys weren't too gung ho on it, to tell you the truth. Sometimes he moved too fast and it didn't give the rest of us much of a chance to learn how to sneak and peak."

"What do you think the guys would say if I decided not to walk point?"

"Hey, LT. That'd be cool. It's your show. Everybody does things different. As long as we're being honest, your biggest problem is gonna be Sergeant Smythe. He's a lifer, man. He talks more about killing gooks than anybody over here. He's already done three tours with the Green Berets and he's trying to win the war all by himself."

"Whadaya mean?"

"He was always right up there with One Six because he was afraid of missing something. We just knew that someday we'd get hit and they'd both be gone in the first ten seconds."

"I see. OK. Thanks. I would appreciate it if you kept our conversation between us. I don't want anyone to think I'm critical of either Lieutenant Davis or Sergeant Smythe. I'm just trying to get the lay of the land."

"Yea. We're cool, LT. I don't want no trouble. Lieutenant Davis told us he thought you would be good from what he heard, so we told him we'd take care of you as long as you take care of us."

"Like you say, Wallace, that's cool. I'll see you later."

McKenzie located his new Sergeant Smythe down in a freshly dug bunker helping to place a log on the front downhill side. It was easy to see why. He was over six feet tall and had to be close to three hundred pounds. He was heavy but most of it was muscle. Two soldiers were on one end of the log while the big sergeant handled the other end. Several others were standing around. He was bellowing at the two soldiers who were struggling to keep up.

"Lift! Come on girls, move!"

A thick layer of mud had rendered the ground difficult to stand on and when they tried to throw the log up on the berm, one soldier slipped causing that end to dip lower than the edge. Smythe threw his end onto the berm and quickly moved to the middle of the log, reached under it with both arms and carried it into place. He turned and looked at the soldier who was down on both knees and growled at him. There were two other logs precut and laying to the side. He turned to grab one and saw McKenzie standing on the up hill side.

"Welcome, sir. Didn't see ya standing there. If you wanna come down and join us, I could use a little help." Smythe waved McKenzie toward the hole.

"No thanks, Sarge. You look like you don't need any more help than you got.
When you finish up, I'm gonna be at the TOC trying to learn what's going on in the AO. I'd like you to come up and brief me."

"I can do that, sir. Mind if I bring along my squad leaders?"

"The more the merrier. I'll see you later."

McKenzie was almost to the next bunker when he heard Smythe exclaim to those around him, "Well I guess that's him. They didn't waste any time did they?" There was no response from the others. McKenzie was being challenged, even though it was subtle. Smythe did not show up at the command bunker. McKenzie returned and found him still working on bunkers around seventeen hundred.

"Missed you up at the TOC, Sergeant Smythe. Think you might be able to spare me some time this evening?" McKenzie did not want to chastise his new platoon sergeant in front of the other soldiers. Smythe was digging with a long handled shovel. He stuck it into the mud and leaned on it.

"I believe you said when I finish up. You can see I haven't finished what I was doing. I should be done in about a half hour and then you and me can have a nice visit." His voice sounded a little too syrupy.

"Sergeant Smythe, I'll expect you to show up at nineteen hundred sharp at my bunker. Are we clear?" McKenzie said. He turned and left. Again, he heard a comment as he walked away.

"I guess I better finish up here in a hurry cause I just got a direct order," Smythe announced to his audience. He let out a big belly laugh but no one else joined in.

"I hope he's as tough out in the field as he acts when he's on the LZ," McKenzie said to himself.

Sergeant Smythe showed, exactly on time, dressed in a clean Tiger striped camouflage fatigue jacket, although his pants were dirty and faded. He wore a wide, black belt with a Bowie knife in a hand made scabbard on the left and a captured Chinese pistol in a black holster on the right. On his right shoulder was the insignia of the Fifth Special Forces and on his head, the traditional green beret, cocked over his right eye. He had washed up and brought a plastic bag containing maps and a tablet.

Smiling as if he hadn't a care in the world, he said, "Good evening, LT. You getting moved in and settled? If you need this bunker fixed up, me and the boys can do that for ya."

Evans, his new RTO, had filled McKenzie in on the former Special Forces advisor earlier. He said Smythe was a very knowledgeable soldier, unafraid but that he bragged about his exploits in the Central Highlands way too much. Sometimes his descriptions of killings were extreme but so far, the platoon had not witnessed any of it. He'd been with Echo only a couple of months and, on more than one occasion, had clashed with Lieutenant Davis over tactics. Usually, it involved Smythe doing something that had not been discussed or agreed upon.

McKenzie looked up at the big man standing above him. "I think I have everything under control, Sergeant - except you. Are we going to have trouble knowing who's in charge here?"

"No, sir. I'm not sure what you mean, sir." Smythe jumped down into the front of the bunker which, like all the others, was perched on the side of the hill. He had a way of taking up space and it felt to McKenzie as if he was being physically threatened. He got up from the cot he was sitting on and walked past the sergeant out of the bunker.

"Let's you and me go over to the command bunker where I asked you to go in the first place," he said over his shoulder.

MAJOR BROUGHTON

McKenzie did not look back to see if Smythe was following but there would be hell to pay if he was not behind him when he got to the TOC. He was, however, and the conversation was polite but tense. After about ten minutes, the S-3, Major Broughton, who was monitoring movement of Alpha Company over the radio, stepped over and interrupted.

"Sergeant Smythe, are you getting a clear picture of this operation? I had an opportunity to explain it fully to Lieutenant McKenzie this afternoon. It was a shame you were not here. Do you have any questions of me about what you've learned so far?"

Major Broughton was not a huge man but he was stocky in a way that indicated big, solid bones as if he might have wrestled in college. His forearms and hands were massive. He had a ruddy complexion and tended to squint when making a point. It was generally known he was very bright and ran the battalion for Black Knight. He was standing within an arm's length of Smythe.

"Not at this time, sir. I think I get the drift." Smythe's posture got a little straighter just before he answered.

"Well, Lieutenant," Major Broughton said without looking away from Smythe, "if you need me to clarify anything, you just let me know."

"Thank you, sir. I will," McKenzie said.

The rest of the conversation inside the bunker went without incident. McKenzie requested that Smythe prepare a status report of the platoon including who would be going outside the perimeter that night for ambush patrol. There had been a few close encounters with no real contact, however, Major Broughton had the impression the NVA were increasing their efforts in the past couple of weeks.

McKenzie returned to his bunker and resumed his position on the cot inside. He finished writing a short note to Koop, who was being sent to Japan. Next, he began a thank you letter to Captain Moore. He also needed to write a couple of letters home. Why not wrap up all the emotional stuff in one session? If he did that, he could bury it and ignore it for a while. It would be like picking a scab off a painful, deep cut but he needed to get it all done.

LOST PATROL

He was surprised to see the ambush patrol exiting through the concertina. He had lost track of time and it was dusk. Smythe had not returned with his status report. "Evans, go tell One Five I want to see him." When Evans returned, he said Smythe was on a scrounging mission somewhere on the LZ and he wasn't able to locate him. McKenzie took out his notebook and wrote below the date, "This shit is going to stop."

The night moved slowly. McKenzie decided to go for a walk to see how Delta was doing. He could not sleep. It felt eerie sitting on a knob so far above the jungle. Mist had formed into dark clouds that floated below the perimeter. Barbara looked to him as if it had been placed on the high point of an island surrounded by a blue green ocean hiding dangerous things below the surface.

Australian civilians during World War II worked with natives to set up radio locations on the tops of island peaks in the

Pacific. Their job was to monitor the coming and going of Japanese war planes and send reports to Allied forces without getting caught. McKenzie felt a kinship with those brave men.

He found Doll going over orders for the following day. Black Knight was sending Delta off the South side of Barbara, down where a trail system was in constant use by the NVA. Alpha Company described the southern trail as dark, scary and very busy.

Lieutenant Janikouski wanted to work in company size in complete capitulation to Black Knight's wishes. First Platoon would be on point. McKenzie and Doll discussed order of movement, security measures and small unit tactics until Evans showed up around two in the morning.

"I lost radio contact with the ambush squad, LT. I can't even get a radio squelch," he said breathlessly.

"How long has it been?" McKenzie said as they hurried back to the bunker.

"Its been almost two hours. Our protocol is a squelch report every hour which was forty-five minutes ago. Since then, I have been trying but I can't raise em. Nothing. One Five wants to send a contact patrol out. I think he's putting one together now."

McKenzie stopped and looked at Evans. He sent his RTO back to the radio and went to find Smythe. He found his new platoon sergeant all geared up with camouflage face paint, wearing a tee shirt with ammo bandoliers strapped from each shoulder and his pants tied above the knees and just above his boots with leather string. He was carrying a Colt Commando, a shorter version of the M-16, designed for close quarter fighting and wearing his Bowie knife, Chinese Pistol and several grenades. He had recruited two others who were also getting prepared.

"Where do you think you're going, Sergeant?"

"Evening One Six. Me and the boys thought we'd take a walk and see if the gooks got our boys or if they was just sleepin'. Want to come along?" Smythe shot his biggest full toothed smile at McKenzie and looked around at those behind him.

"Sergeant? You think you might have discussed this with me before you got all charged up?"

"No, sir. I did not." Smythe reached down, picked up another grenade and attached it to his belt. When he looked back at McKenzie, his eye's flashed anger and his mouth flattened out. Then his lips parted as he bared his teeth in a mock grin. Stretching his neck without moving his body, he leaned his head toward McKenzie.

"Them boys out there is my responsibility and I'm going out that wire to see what's going on."

"I'm giving you a direct order, Sergeant. You will not move outside that concertina wire tonight unless I tell you to and if you do, I will bring charges. Is that clear?"

Smythe stood for a long interlude before answering through clenched teeth. "Yes, sir, I got that. Now, maybe you will tell us what you plan to do about an ambush that hasn't responded to radio contact in almost two hours?" His emphasis on the word you, was another direct challenge to McKenzie.

"I'm going over to the mortar platoon and ask them to put a couple of flares up in that direction. If they're dead you could be walking into a trap and in spite of your vast experience, I don't want to have to write letters home to grieving mothers because we made a mistake."

By three, McKenzie was feeling desperate. Two flares had not caused any response. Smythe was hovering around with his quick reaction team and had asked several times for permission to go see what the problem was.

"Sergeant, do you have an accurate location for the patrol? I mean, did you discuss exactly where they were going to set up tonight?" McKenzie asked.

"Of course I did, sir. That's why I know I can get to em without gettin' blown away."

"OK. I want your best M-79 man up here. I want him to put a round about fifty meters in front of that patrol. We'll see if that wakes em up. If that's not successful, you can go out. Agreed?"

"You testing me, sir? You don't think I know where they are, do you?"

"I guess we'll see."

Several minutes later, Smythe had a sleepy, half groggy soldier up by the concertina wire. Specialist Lemon questioned the assignment but was quickly rebuffed by Smythe. He carefully and slowly loaded a grenade round into the barrel of his shotgun looking weapon, snapped it shut and adjusted the sight. He aimed it almost straight up into the air for a high trajectory. The round landed with a deep, explosive thud. They waited. Nothing. After a few minutes, McKenzie ordered a second round in the same area. No sooner had it exploded than the radio came alive.

"Echo One Six, this is Echo three, we're taking incoming. Who's shooting at us? It sounds like mike seventy-nine rounds. Over," a voice whispered loudly.

McKenzie reached for the radio handset offered by Evans. "Echo three, this is One Six, give me your sit rep. Over."

The voice was shaky. "Echo One Six, this is Echo three. We've had negative movement in our area. But, but - we've had trouble with our commo. Over."

"Roger that, Echo three. Move back inside the perimeter immediately. One Five will contact you just outside the wire. You report to me when you get in. Over."

Smythe was already moving. When the squad leader showed up, McKenzie walked him over to the side, away from Smythe and the others.

"So, Sergeant Palowski, you want to tell me what was going on out there? I don't buy that commo crap since you were able to call immediately after you took a second round. You have a man go to sleep on you out there? Before you answer, I don't want to know who it was. I just want to know you're gonna take care of it."

"Yes, sir. We were having trouble earlier with the radio but I understand. I will make sure this doesn't happen again."

"Fine, Sergeant. I'm your new One Six. When we go out on patrol, I will expect you to have your squad ready and if you have any problems you need help with, you let me know."

DIRECT CONTROL

It was unusual for a platoon leader to make that kind of statement. It was the platoon sergeant's duty to run the platoon, to see that its organization and its men, were trained and ready to go. He could bring a serious issue to his platoon leader and they would agree on the best approach. Because of Smythe's defiance, however, McKenzie had decided to exert a little more direct control.

It only took a week for him to firmly establish command of the platoon. Enemy activity was increasing in the area and a recent sapper attack on LZ Sharon changed things. Battalion decided Echo would stay put and not venture out too far. Their mission was changed from long range recon to day patrols and helping secure the perimeter. Ambushes along the ridge line had been suspended even though the LZ was occasionally harassed by mortars, rockets and small arms fire at night.

One of Echo's day patrols wounded a courier and captured a satchel of important papers. Black Knight was euphoric and went to great length to complement McKenzie. Favor from Black Knight was anathema to him. It could only produce negative results.

The monsoon season expressed itself fully in heavy rains interspersed with winds and constant drizzle. Two of Smythe's reinforced bunkers washed down the hill after collapsing upon their inhabitants. Only a Herculean effort saved the situation. They met every evening. When Smythe tried to tell of his heroic past, McKenzie would interrupt and change the subject.

242

OUR OWN HELICOPTER

On September, Second, McKenzie walked out through the wire with a patrol of ten men. It was an unusually clear day. The gray skies and constant rain had temporarily abated. Warm rays of sunlight streaked through the trees like subtle spotlights in a theatre as the patrol made their way along the ridge line running away from Barbara. The trail had become wide and well worn, vegetation cut back for visibility.

McKenzie woke up that morning feeling so good he decided to personally lead a reinforced squad down into one of the gullies off to the Southwest where Delta had discovered signs in Vietnamese giving directions that had been carefully placed on trees at eye level. NVA soldiers would often place a forked tree branch to help others find their way. They'd also found an ominous sign in English warning American soldiers not to come into the area or they would die.

Operations had called for an artillery mission to walk through the area first. Echo would then go down to see if they had gotten lucky. McKenzie was buoyed by the idea of catching Mr. Charles with a surprise artillery round or two. The remaining men of Echo perched on top of their bunkers to watch the show. They reminded McKenzie of Ospreys perched on poles along the Columbia River.

The patrol stopped where McKenzie could look down into the forest and adjust the artillery. Evans called for the fire mission and McKenzie made two adjustments, working the artillery up and down where he knew the trail to run. The patrol was spread out to watch and relax.

He motioned the point man to move out when the barrage was complete, stood up, pulled an ammo bandolier over his right shoulder and looked up at the sound of a Huey gunship flying in from the Northwest. He reached down, lifted a claymore bag he'd converted to carry a larger load of fully loaded magazines, swung the strap over his head and bent over to pick up his weapon. Maybe the S-3 had called for the helicopter to follow up on the red leg.

~~

He hears the zing and ping of an AK-47 on full automatic firing at the helicopter. It's that high pitched AK sound that now sends chills up and down his spine. He hears it before he recognizes it but his automatic brain identifies the sound. McKenzie drops to the ground and rolls to his left. He estimates the shooter is just off the edge of the ridge at about seventy-five meters. The firing stops.

He hears the helicopter turn back. McKenzie looks up to see if it has been hit. The pilot banks and launches two rockets in the patrol's direction. What an idiot! He's trying to kill the NVA this close? Doesn't he see us? Both rockets explode on the opposite side of the trail as the helicopter swings over them from left to right. Dirt, rocks and shrapnel fly out of the impacts peppering helmets and bodies.

McKenzie grabs Evans by the arm and pulls him toward a large banyan like tree with flare roots large enough to get behind. He sucks hard to get air back into his lungs. The elephant has arrived. The chopper circles back and begins to spray the ground with his mini-gun and releases two more rockets into the midst of scrambling soldiers. Shrapnel smacks the tree root in front of McKenzie's face. He yells into his radio hand set.

"Black Knight Three, this is Echo One Six. We're taking fire from one of our own helicopters. Over."

"Echo One Six, we see it. We're attempting to make contact at this time. Over."

The pilot banks for a third run and releases two more rockets which look like torpedoes sliding toward them. They land on the trail as more bullets hit the trees propelling wood splinters in all directions. The explosions send shrapnel spinning and whistling at the patrol. Most of the men manage to get off the trail and behind trees except Private Mandell, who has been hit in the legs. He is lying just off the trail in an exposed position but is not hit again.

McKenzie screams into the radio, "You get that idiot off me or I'm turning my M-60 on him."

"Echo One Six, we got him called off. Maintain proper radio procedure. Over." McKenzie watches the helicopter disappear into the atmosphere.

Oh, yea. McKenzie was worried about proper radio protocol when he had one of his own choppers bringing the world down on him. He was scared and furious. He moved from the tree and sprinted out toward Mandell. Doc reported six wounded but no one killed as he was applying pressure to Mandell's right thigh.

He pointed to his own nose with his free hand and then at McKenzie. Evans appeared with an open gauze bandage. Only then did McKenzie realize he was bleeding profusely from the bridge of his nose. He held the bandage from Evans tight against the cut and looked around. Soldiers were yelling or swearing at the pilot in the helicopter which had drifted away into the blurry sky. The cacophony of complaints and cussing seemed distant to McKenzie, whose ears were ringing as usual. The only ones not swearing at the pilot were those in too much pain.

"What the hell was that, LT?" Anderson shouted at him. "I'm not doing this shit any more if our own guys are gonna take us out." He held his right arm up so his squad leader could wrap a field dressing around it. Tree splinters had sliced his forearm in several places.

Evans called for Medivac. Besides Anderson, two men had shrapnel wounds in the back and another had been shot in the leg. Both of Mandell's legs were ripped with shrapnel. Evans cut off Mandell's pant legs and helped Doc wrap strips for tourniquets. The first aid pack McKenzie held to his nose quickly filled with blood which was now dripping down his arm. He heard, then saw Smythe coming down the trail with the rest of the platoon.

"You OK, One Six? You got bad guys in the area?" he said, sounding ready to start a world war.

"Yea, I got bad guys. My own bad guys in the air. You see that shit from where you were? Somebody fired an AK at the chopper from over there and he thought it was us."

"Yea, LT. I was sittin' on a bunker watching you direct the red leg and ran up to the TOC when I saw the pilot make his first run. They had no info on him and he broke all the rules. He never asked for friendly locations or for permission to engage. Sit down over there and let me take care of this."

McKenzie walked over and sat down against the tree that had protected him and Evans. Smythe led a squad over the side to see if they could find the guy who started the whole mess. Mandell and another man with a leg wound were loaded onto litters brought by Smythe. The rest were walking wounded.

McKenzie had started to shake badly. Doc gave him a fresh bandage and Evans gave him a cigarette but when he tried to light it, his own hands were shaking. The other two soldiers who were not wounded came over and sat down as if to share their own fear. They were also shaking and trying to relax with smokes. McKenzie fumbled with his canteen, finally getting some water into a very dry mouth. No one spoke. They just sat and watched the others.

They were all back inside the wire twenty minutes later. Medivac came and left. Doc came over and put a butterfly bandage across McKenzie's nose. When he finally calmed down, he walked up to battalion operations where he found Major Broughton sitting on a stool watching the activity from just inside the door. McKenzie stepped onto the first ammo crate step built into the dirt and leaned against the frame of the door.

"Excuse me, sir but maybe you could tell me what the hell went on out there. I got six guys WIA by one of our own helicopters."

Major Broughton looked at the ground. "I don't know, Lieutenant. I just don't know. That guy was supposed to be flying back to base from a mission with Alpha Company. He was off our frequency and did not check in for a fly over. Rules of engagement are strict. When a pilot is fired upon, he needs to identify friendlies in the area and contact command before returning fire. I reported the incident to Division. They said the Assistant Division Commander will address the situation."

"Address the situation? Is that what you said? We could have been killed by that idiot." McKenzie was raising his voice but he didn't care.

"Lieutenant," Broughton said a little louder. "General Shadwick is the operations ACG and G-3 told me he is furious. He's promised to take care of this personally. I don't know what that means but my guess is it won't be pretty. That pilot will probably be grounded, maybe permanently lose his wings. I know that's not much of a consolation but that's all I got. I'm sorry. I know that was scary. Your new Six, Captain Macavoy, is coming in day after tomorrow. Until then, you guys stand down."

The Major did not wait for a response. He got up from the stool, picked it up with one of his big hands and walked back into the dimly lit TOC. McKenzie pushed off the door frame with his left hand but then stood there with his head down trying to think. The world was quiet now. His ears were still ringing but there were no helicopters and no artillery, only the constant buzzing of flies and people moving behind him.

He recalled General Shadwick from Wonder Beach and wondered if the General would remember him. He had to think about dealing with a new CO but the events of the day had shaken him. He did not want to be in recon any more. Had he lost his nerves? Until that day, even considering all the times the elephant had stepped on his chest and stomped the air out of him, he'd not felt the kind of panic he felt that morning. They had been helpless. Sort of like a bug under a soldier's boot.

It was nothing like a firefight where he could move and react and attempt to gain or regain fire superiority. More importantly, it wasn't the enemy. It was their own damned helicopter firing at them. Helicopters were the very symbol of the Cav. They were freedom birds to take you away. They were resupply and Medivac and mail and awesome fire power when the troops needed it most. The wop wop sound of the blades had always meant support and strength and reassurance.

There had been times when McKenzie would long to hear the air popping around the main overhead rotor blade or to be up in the air, next to an open door, looking down as the ground went by in a blur. When he was most afraid in the early days he often wished for a big hand to reach out of the sky, pick him up and put him in a helicopter that would fly him away. Now he was beginning to feel different.

He'd had one helicopter crash on his head and decapitate Buggs. Today, he'd been fired upon by a gun ship that became ominous and dangerous and no longer his friend. His mind was racing.

"You all right, Lieutenant?" Major Broughton had returned to the doorway.

McKenzie looked up. "I don't know, sir. I just don't know."

The next evening, both men who were not wounded came by to see him. They were also shaken. McKenzie encouraged them to talk their way through it. They also felt the helplessness. One said it was like getting invited to a turkey shoot without being told they were the turkeys. It didn't fit into the rules they had learned. They agreed on one thing - if that was a small sample of what Mr. Charles went through, they had a lot more respect for him than before. How the hell he endured that kind of terror and came back shooting was beyond them.

CAPTAIN MACAVOY

Morning arrived and so did Captain Macavoy. He landed around ten and finally wandered down from battalion to the platoon area for a quick visit. He was short and round, with a pleasant face, although his skin was tight like stuffed sausage. He told the assembled group he had ordered tiger camouflage fatigues for everyone.

"I intend to teach you the more advanced methods of long range tactics, using small groups of three to five men. Battalion wants a special ambush tonight and I want One Six to lead it. We need to do something aggressive to prevent enemy from harassing this LZ. If they are allowed the opportunity to get closer, shoot at our helicopters and maybe diagram the position of our mortars and artillery, as well as the layout of our defensive positions, it will lead to an all out attack much like sappers did at LZ Sharon. I'm asking for volunteers to go out."

Private Miller: "Private Miller, sir. There's nobody here that's not willing to volunteer, sir, but we don't know what you've got in mind."

Captain Macavoy: "Good question, Miller. When I was an advisor in the Central Highlands in 1965, the NVA did not want us establishing Special Forces camps near the Cambodian border. Once it became apparent we were being watched or that a build up was occurring in our area, we would send out night patrols who would double back and wait for the NVA to show up. As long as we didn't over do it, this method was effective. I would like to see if we can catch who ever is scouting us here. Do I have any volunteers?"

Smythe: "You can count me in, sir."

Macavoy: "Sergeant Smythe, you will be ready with a quick reaction force from inside the perimeter. I don't want both my platoon leader and sergeant on this one."

Smythe: "Sir, I am very familiar with this tactic and feel that I should have the opportunity to lead that patrol tonight."

Macavoy: "Well, I don't Sergeant. We need three men besides One Six. You men let him know who's willing to go and he'll decide. The ambush will move out thirty minutes before dark. If Charlie's watching, he'll see you go. You will move out along the finger, half way down the trail on the South side. You will then move off the trail far enough to catch anyone coming up the trail and sit there until twenty-three hundred. That's the time I understand the enemy has been moving into position. If no one comes up the South side, they will have come up from the North.

In that case, you will be able to move in behind them and get your kills. Questions?"

McKenzie: "Sir, I'm not so sure I like moving in the dark like that. Its a waning moon and if the cloud cover stays like we have today, its going to be very dark. Why don't we just move out to the end of the ridge line, set up off the trail and wait? If we get movement, we'll know it."

Macavoy: "If Charlie can move at night, so can we but OK. If that's what you want, I have no problem with it. Work with the mortar crew and preset your fire coordinates. If you get bad guys in your area, I want bodies."

Private Wallace, the first man McKenzie met when he arrived, quickly volunteered. He brought his two buddies, PFC Jenkins and Specialist Goytowski. All three were from Third Squad. They said they worked well together and were eager to get some payback for two soldiers wounded by incoming. No one else showed up. Wallace explained that he had laid claim to the patrol and no one challenged him. There was also a bounty for kills in the platoon.

"I got beers on this one, LT. The more we bag, the more beer those guys will have to pony up."

Wallace and the others were excited. None of them had been on the ill fated patrol two days before. Their enthusiasm gave McKenzie a boost. It made him feel positive again. They discussed weapons and gear. He told them to wear either a soft hat or Army green bandanna and camouflage paint on their faces. .

The cloud cover lifted by mid afternoon and the setting sun turned bright orange as if unwilling to let the night come.

McKenzie sat down against the back side of his bunker and leaned against sandbags looking at the mountain range silhouetted by the orange glow. Activity on the LZ was a calm preparation for evening.

Everything in Vietnam was an omen. The war was not just soldiers and weapons but the world in all its entirety. Everything had meaning. He looked for signs of discord or imbalance. Somewhere down in the jungle NVA soldiers might be making preparations to approach the LZ. How could he know? Were there more birds in the air? Less? Was it quieter than usual? Would the geckos talk to him tonight or would they scurry out of the way? He had no idea how dangerous this patrol would be.

CATCHING CHARLIE

Even after the orange sun dropped its blazing light reluctantly behind the mountains, night seemed unusually delayed. The small patrol waited, unwilling to move out thirty minutes before the expected darkness. McKenzie finally moved them out when he felt safe to do so. Several small ups and downs in the trail meant they would be blind as they topped each crest. It was important to be in place before full darkness.

Night dropped upon them like a theatre curtain, sudden and complete. There was no transition and no moon yet. The patrol bent tight to their weapons, crested the second rise and stepped slowly toward the end of the ridge. They were moving in a world of suffused carbon. Wallace, who was walking point, went down to one knee. McKenzie was behind him and unable to stop, ran into him, his weapon hitting Wallace in the head with a soft thud. He backed up and turned toward the others, "Psst - hold up." They were in a world of blind opacity. McKenzie waited. His eyes seemed unwilling to adjust, his pupils slowly dilating to maximum. When he was able to see the trees, some appeared slightly darker than others, every other one looking like a sentry holding his post.

"Can you see the trail?" he said to Wallace quietly.

"I know that it goes straight for another fifty meters or so," Wallace said in a breathy whisper.

"Let's do it then. Move off to the left at fifty. If you have to feel your way, I guess that's what you'll have to do." McKenzie was not sure what to do but they had to move.

Wallace did not answer. He began to move. McKenzie reached back and tapped Jenkins. "Follow me." Damn, he thought. He'd just used the OCS motto. Adrenaline had made him giddy. The blackness was so enveloping he felt off balance but he knew it was nerves. Slowly the four of them stepped softly through the obscurity until Wallace turned them and they reached a point inside the trees about fifteen meters off the trail.

Fire from the errant helicopter attack had eliminated most of the ground cover. They were exposed, protected only by a dark night. McKenzie looked at his luminous Army watch dial. They would move up the trail in seventy-five minutes if nothing transpired. The patrol tried to get comfortable with weapons ready.

When the time came to move, tension was extreme. They had heard noises over the first rise back toward Barbara. Unless it was a large animal, there were probably enemy soldiers between them and the wire. They moved back onto the trail. The quarter moon had come up and a diffuse light poked through porous clouds, making the patrol more visible than they wanted.

~~

McKenzie can see Wallace clearly now and Jenkins is visible fifteen meters behind. Dark trees stand watchful on each side as they move toward the rise. Will Wallace be able to distinguish an enemy soldier standing among the trees? They approach the crest. There is a quick flicker of movement to the right. Everyone freezes.

Wallace floats off the trail in that direction with his weapon brought up to his shoulder. McKenzie's heart flips over in his chest. He bites down on his lip and looks hard into the darkness. A faceless figure springs up and Wallace fires. The man is only four feet away and the force of bullets throws him backwards. AKs begin firing from the base of the next rise. There are five Chinese weapons firing at the patrol and five soldiers maneuvering toward them. Wallace hits the ground and returns a heavy volume of suppressing fire. The patrol spreads apart and joins Wallace on the ground, firing at the incoming.

Jenkins calls on the radio for the quick reaction force and mortars. McKenzie rolls over and waves at Jenkins who does not see him. Bullets hit the tree above them. He crawls over to Jenkins and hits him on the back.

"No! Jenkins! We're too close. Call off the mortars." McKenzie hears a mortar bloop. A round rises to the top of its arch and descends toward them. "Cease fire! Cease Fire!", Jenkins screams into his handset. The mortar round whistles as it travels and lands ten meters in front of Wallace without exploding. The enemy fire increases. Wallace and Goytowski spray bullets back and forth. McKenzie and Jenkins rejoin the fire fight, emptying full magazines with tracers, ejecting them and reloading.

Smythe and the quick reaction force arrive on the rise and begin firing down the slope and throwing grenades. Smythe is hollering like a Viking in battle. Return fire stops. McKenzie yells cease fire. The night is quiet except for the sound of Wallace and others gulping air. McKenzie rolls onto his back and lays there, eyes closed, mouth open.

"Holy shit, LT. That mortar would have killed me if it hadn't been a dud. I don't believe it. What the hell happened?" Wallace was jacked up and on his knees.

"Get down, Wallace. Jenkins, call One Five and tell him we'll move in their direction when he gives the OK. Police up your magazines and let's get the hell out of here. Tell One Five where the step on is. We're through for tonight," McKenzie says.

That was too damn close. The thought repeated itself over and over as McKenzie walked back through the perimeter wire and headed for his bunker. When Evens started to say something he said, "Don't talk to me." Don't never take a chance you don't have to. Wasn't that what he had promised himself in the beginning? This was the second time in three days he'd found himself in a bullshit situation he could not control and each time his life was put at extreme risk. They could be wrapping him in a poncho to load onto a helicopter right now, headed for graves registration and back to Oregon where his family would receive him in disbelief and horror. His Wy-Am grandfather and mother would dance, shake the rattle and sing to Coyote. His Quaker father would sit in silence and abject sorrow.

He was dizzy from the amount of adrenaline in his blood. He felt light headed, almost out of body. Walking around in the dark was stupid. How in the hell did he let Macavoy talk him into such a stupid thing? "Well, it was an order, wasn't it?" he said out loud to himself. Evens looked at him but said nothing. Maybe the idea of doubling back was OK but they almost walked right into their own death scene. On the other hand, they were able to jump Charlie and get one kill. It was just, well shit! This is where Black Knight had put him and he didn't like it.

Captain Macavoy came down the hill jumping up and down like a school boy.

"Excellent, One Six. Black Knight is coming in tomorrow. He wants to get a direct report. That was a damn fine job. You and your patrol preformed just like we planned it. A huge feather in Echo's cap." He slapped McKenzie on the shoulder.

"I don't know about that, Six. We almost got blown away by our own mortar. Are you aware of that?" McKenzie had sat down on the log berm. He pulled his ammo pouch over his head and threw it on the ground, picked up his canteen and drank the warm water, long and hard. He pulled the canteen away from his mouth and looked up at his new commander who was standing above him.

"It was as dark as black ink out there. We never saw that first guy until he jumped up right in front of Wallace. I think he was a sentry or maybe even a guide for more coming out of that draw to the North."

"Listen. You guys did a great job out there," Macavoy said. "Maybe you ought to write Wallace up?"

"Maybe I should. You know, I'm not sure I'm cut out for this sneakin' around at night. I liked it better when I was in a line platoon and we had more control," McKenzie said, looking down at the ground. The night air was fetid, no longer just humid. He pulled off his wet shirt and realized the smell was his own acrid sweat.

"Are you kidding? You guys were totally under control. You've just got the after action jitters. That's normal. I monitored the whole thing. Here comes One Five. Let's get a report on that kill," Macavoy said.

Smythe came walking toward them with an expansive grin, an Ak in one hand and an NVA pack thrown over his shoulder.

"You got more than one, LT. We found blood trails in two locations. They drug their buddies down over the hill. There's a trail that snakes down off that ridge on the North side," Smythe said with enthusiasm.

"I know, Sarge." McKenzie took a deep breath. "I was down there with Delta about a month ago. There's a big bunker complex down there."

Wallace, Jenkins and Goytowski were greeted like returning Trojan warriors. After a couple of beers, Wallace was regaling the others with his lightning fast elimination of the enemy. They were each given three beers based on three kills and Six indicated that would be his report to Black Knight. McKenzie protested that they only had one "step on" but that was quickly rebuffed by Macavoy who said that Smythe had confirmed the amount of blood on the ground indicated two additional kills. The discussion ended with McKenzie stating he would not put his name on such a report and Six exclaiming he would.

TELLING THE TALE

The next morning was disorienting to McKenzie. Black Knight landed around eleven. He was summoned to the TOC where he found Captain Macavoy and Sergeant Smythe already in attendance. Captain Macavoy went over the entire operation from beginning to end - the planning, the execution and the after action investigation. McKenzie said nothing.

That was supplemented by Smythe describing in detail how he had taken a flashlight and carefully examined the entire area. It was a wonder Smythe wasn't surprised by Charlie coming back to retaliate as he wandered around in the dark flashing a light, McKenzie mused to himself. Examining the body and returning the next day would have been wiser. At the end, Colonel Fishmuth turned and looked at McKenzie, who sat silent, not wanting to talk.

"Fine job, Lieutenant. I made the right decision sending you to Echo Company. Keep up the good work."

Afraid that Black Knight might come over and try to shake his hand or ask him to tell a story, McKenzie thanked him, saluted and asked to be excused. It was a quick exit which appeared to catch everyone off guard.

He stopped at the bottom of the steps to accept the sun's warmth. He did not like it inside the TOC. It was where myths were perpetuated and reality expanded upon. He kept to himself the rest of the day until a log bird arrived. There was no mail for him but Evans gave him a copy of the latest Army Times. He thumbed through it hoping for something that would take his mind off where he was and what he was doing.

INCOMING

Page three held a huge surprise. Twenty-nine OCS graduates from his class were listed in alphabetical order, soon to be arriving in country. Not one was coming to the Cav. The date of publication was August, Twenty-first. That meant they were probably already in country. Today was September, Fifth.

They would be arriving as Second Lieutenants, like him, at least until November, Twenty-second, when they would all be promoted to First Lieutenant. The Army must be moving assignments up due to the heavy loss of platoon leaders in the field. In the past, unless an OCS officer volunteered to come early, like McKenzie had, most landed in Vietnam one year after graduation, just as they were promoted to First Lieutenant.

He read through the names and visualized each face. Six months together in the crucible of OCS had left him with a clear picture of each. He was worried about some, especially the ones who did not seem physically strong enough or whose nature appeared too gentle of spirit. The orders did not state specific assignments, only units, so hopefully there was some natural order of selection that would place those on his worry list in jobs more suited to who they were. Rose, for example, was one of the gentlest men he had ever met.

"What a bunch of crap," he said out loud. Evans looked at him with a questioning face. "Nothing," McKenzie said as he folded the paper for safe keeping. There was a bigger problem. From now on, he knew he would be searching the lists of KIAs printed in the Army Times. "Shit!" He got up to walk the perimeter.

He had tried hard not to feel personal about the war. He'd already let the men of Delta get too close and he could feel it happening with Echo. Now he had really good friends, pre-Vietnam friends, who were going to be there in the maelstrom of killing and it made him sick to his stomach.

Monsoon rains returned with a vengeance. Nights became more difficult and walking the perimeter extremely perilous. Bunkers failed from the constant deluge and threatened to slide down the hill. On September, Twelfth, the battalion was informed the long planned but much delayed sweep would begin on September, Fifteenth. There would be a push in from the low land toward the mountains and Echo was still going to be used as a blocking force.

Macavoy said their first patrol in support of the push would be off to the North, back into the area McKenzie knew all too well. Macavoy would stay on top. McKenzie would be walking down with a full recon platoon. So much for learning to operate in groups of three or four. He tried to explain what he had seen with

Delta but neither Macavoy nor Black Knight were dissuaded. As far as they were concerned, Echo was a deadly weapon, capable of taking on the enemy, regardless of the circumstance. McKenzie's admonitions that the area was big enough to contain a large enemy force fell on deaf ears.

BLOCKING FORCE

At nine hundred hours, on the morning of September, Fifteen, McKenzie gave the order to saddle up. Sergeant Smythe showed up wearing his beret.

"Where's your helmet, One Five?" McKenzie said without looking at him.

"I don't wear one. All I need is my beret, One Six."

"Do you have a helmet or not?", McKenzie said turning and looking at Smythe directly.

"Yes, I do. Its in my hooch."

"Sergeant Smythe, go retrieve your helmet or stay behind."

Smythe gave one of his long looks and then turned. "Oh, for Christ's sake. OK, go ahead and move out. I'll pick up Third Squad as they leave the perimeter," he said.

McKenzie had seen more than one soldier saved from direct hits by the physics of a steel pot. A bullet would penetrate the pot but then be deflected around the plastic helmet liner inside, leaving the soldier only slightly wounded or better, totally unscathed. It was a miracle of physics hard to understand but appreciated by soldiers who had seen it.

The trail snaked back and forth at a steep angle. Once the platoon reached the bottom, McKenzie could see the lower trail was much more traveled than before. He moved quickly past the front soldiers until he reached Walsh who was walking point.

"We'll recon the sides before we move down the trail. Evans - you call One Five and tell him to move Third Squad off to the right about one hundred meters."

With Walsh and two others, McKenzie moved off the trail to the left. They immediately heard movement and saw approximately six NVA scoot down the trail away from them.

"Evans, call One Five and tell him to move back and keep an eye on our rear." Then he turned back to Walsh. "This trail circles the knoll coming back to the right. I've been down here before. It drops into a creek and up the other side to a bunker complex. See if we can move further off the trail to the left, down that short incline and up the other side. We might just catch someone coming around."

Movement through the wet underbrush was easy. No dry leaves to rustle. Walsh stepped cautiously toward a fallen log. Mist hung in the trees, lit here and there by slivers of light. Otherwise, the triple canopy of interlocking foliage kept the area dark and ominous. Evans pulled his antenna over into a loop. Walsh placed his butt on the log and swung his left leg over to a sitting position. Before he could move his right leg, a sniper fired hitting the log in front of him causing Walsh to snap his head back, hitting it on the log. He rolled off to the other side. Two men moved to the log. They waited but there were no more shots. McKenzie did not want to engage the sniper if they didn't need to. He sent Second Squad for a look. They were back in fifteen minutes. The sniper was gone.

Smythe showed up with his steel pot strapped to his back pack, still wearing his beret. After another angry exchange, McKenzie decided not to hassle the issue now that they were in the boonies for the reason he needed to work with this seasoned veteran and learn what he could.

He wanted to locate a good overnight position early where they could spread out and be protected from attack in any direction. It was obvious the area was full of enemy and they needed time to place claymores, trip flares, to establish good fighting positions and plan a route of escape if needed. Blocking force, hell.

The original plan he'd been given was that Charlie Company would escort them down through the area. Echo was then to have broken off into smaller units and set up effective ambushes while Charlie Company continued off to the North. That had been changed at the last minute.

His decision to stop early was met with opposition from Division. Yellow Horse Three, who was running the entire push, ordered Echo to move another two hundred meters east, which meant going on around the knoll, along the trail and closer to the creek bed. It seemed obvious that Mr. Charles knew where they were unless the sniper was only part of a small group moving through the area. McKenzie doubted that and said so. The order stood.

Walsh led out. It was a huge gamble to move another two hundred meters and set up later in the afternoon, however,

264

McKenzie understood that moving their location may have been important for a number of reasons. There could be conflicting locations of other units, placement of night artillery missions or ARC light already planned. There was no way of knowing.

Walsh cautiously approached the creek bed and dropped to one knee at the corner. He sent word back that he could hear voices off to the right, down in the draw. He also reported hearing clanking of metal, possibly mess kits or cooking utensils. McKenzie hand signaled the lead squad to spread out on both sides of the trail as security, so he could bring up the others for a hasty ambush.

"Once we're in position, you will move back behind us and we'll see what we get," he said to the squad leader.

It's difficult to move that many men without making noise. The enemy is only a hundred meters away, just beyond where McKenzie knows the trail drops into the creek. Smythe shows up. He takes charge pointing out locations for machine guns and firing positions with hand signals. He is efficient and very good at indicating what he wants. Once he has everyone in position, Smythe moves up to the corner toward First Squad.

From the other side, an AK opens up on full automatic and several lead soldiers return fire. It's over in seconds. McKenzie scrambles past Smythe to the corner. Walsh looks back and indicates with his right hand that four came up the trail and two are down. One is about fifteen meters from Walsh, right at the crest of the trail.

"I'll go see what we've got, LT," Smythe says.

McKenzie turns to say no but the big man moves away. Two others follow and several men from First Squad rise to one knee in firing positions. Smythe walks bent over holding his Colt Commando in his right hand and motioning First Squad to stay down.

When he reaches the dead NVA, Smythe looks down the trail, back and forth on both sides, then kneels down. He rolls the man over with his left hand and begins to pull off his pack when a Chinese machine gun fires three short bursts. Two Chinese rockets scream over First Squad, exploding in the brush behind. Walsh and the others are up running around Smythe, firing their weapons as they move. There is a short exchange and then it stops, just like it always stops. McKenzie moves closer. Two men are down - Smythe and Wilson.

Evans calls Cavalier, who is close by. McKenzie kneels down. He hears Evans place rocket fire on the hillside and then into the creek. He looks closer at Smythe as Doc Brown reaches for the big sergeant who is laying on his front with no visible sign of a wound. Wilson is shot badly above the elbow and in agony. Doc pulls off Smythe's beret which is beginning to show blood and turns the big man's head to the side. Smythe has a hole in the temple just above the right ear. He is dead. A steel pot might have saved him. McKenzie stands up and walks away.

"Shit, shit, shit," he says. "Damn it." He looks at his watch which reads seventeen fifty. They need a Medivac but there is no place for a helicopter to land. He has one wounded and a three hundred pound dead platoon sergeant. Wilson can go out on an extraction penetrator seat but Smythe will require a cable and litter basket. It's going to be dark soon and the whole place is crawling with NVA. He needs to stay calm.

Moving Smythe is very difficult even with three men on each side. They are barely able to move him back up the trail to an area of sparse trees with a clear path overhead. Doc puts a bandage on Wilson and shoots him full of morphine. Walsh maintains a security ambush back down the trail and Third Squad secures the other direction. Cavalier continues to work the ambush area and beyond with rockets and mini-guns. Evans calls for additional air security to protect the Medivac.

It took thirty minutes for Medivac to arrive. Walsh was extracted without difficulty but Smythe was a bigger problem. Six men struggled to move him onto the litter basket and strap him down as the triple canopy jungle began to darken. Forester, from Second Squad, hooked the cable to one end and signaled to the door gunner. Without warning, the pilot turned his spotlight on, shining it down on the men and Smythe. McKenzie raced over to Evans and grabbed the handset.

"Dust off, this is Echo One Six, can you operate without the spotlight? I got bad guys down here and they don't need any more invitation to my location? Over."

"Echo One Six, this is Dust Off, that's a negative. I've got to see those trees so I can pull your guy out. Otherwise, he's gonna get tangled up and we're all gonna be in trouble. You hang on down there. We'll be out of here in a few. Over."

"Roger that, Dust Off and thanks for your help. Out."

The men that had helped load Smythe looked up at the litter turning slowly in the spotlight, pulled up by a winch. The door gunner had grabbed the cable trying to control the swinging but once the basket started moving, it seemed to gain momentum. When the litter cleared the tree tops, the crew made no effort to load Smythe inside. The spotlight blinked off as they flew away, dangling the big sergeant below in the spinning, litter basket. McKenzie turned back to those who were still alive.

He had no other choice. He had to move the platoon back to the original overnight position and after some discussion, got Division's consent. They need high ground, which can be defended. Putting out trip flares and claymores was difficult in the dark. There was no time for digging good fox holes, so he ordered fighting depressions with an all night alert. Soldiers scooped away the earth with steel pots.

It was midnight before McKenzie finally sat down to eat something underneath his poncho, with a flashlight between his knees, pointed toward the ground. He was certain they would be probed and probably attacked at first light. He sat in his poncho cocoon and thought about Steinbeck's hour of the pearl which would surely come creeping through the night and present itself. He switched off the flashlight and raised the front of his poncho.

He could not see but could sense Evans next to him. "Call Cavalier and request they come on station right at first light," he said.

~~

Dawn's first light seeps in, stealthily and under cover of a wet fog. Although the light rain has stopped, water soaked trees drip a staccato drum beat on ponchos and helmets. The men strain to hear movement above the cacophony of drips. It's hard work and it stretches the nerves tight as piano wire.

A warning can with rocks inside rattles and someone blows a claymore which sets off a trip flare. Three NVA in pith helmets are crawling toward the West side of the platoon perimeter. AK fire comes into Echo's perimeter from several directions and the platoon answers. Both machine guns converge on the incoming until it stops.

They are sitting on a cement island on Forty Second Street in New York City, early in the morning. They have to move. Traffic is coming. Zakorias, a Greek soldier from Baltimore, volunteers to lead them out of there. He has proven himself to be incredibly reliable and careful. He seems at home in the jungle. McKenzie looks at him and imagines him walking the hills of Greece in a native costume looking for Germans during World War Two. They talked one night on Barbara about sitting down to a large Greek meal and drinking a ton of ouzo, an anise flavored liqueur consumed throughout Greece. The platoon leaves the hill, following Zakorias.

After fifty meters of movement, Zakorias spots a lone enemy off in the distance. Cavalier is on station and recons by fire with no result. McKenzie asks the pilot to stay as Zakorias leads them further down the trail, back toward the point where Smythe was killed. Everyone's nerves are balanced on a razor's edge. Zakorias' orders are to stop when he can see the creek. The platoon splits in two directions, coming at the depression from high ground on both sides.

Zakorias steps cat like around the bend in the trail, whirls to his right and fires on full automatic. Collins, who is behind him, drops to one knee and fires a full magazine. Zakorias scrambles to the hill side for cover and fires a second magazine. Return fire from AKs come across the creek as McKenzie runs forward. Collins jumps and makes a sound like he's been punched in the solar plexus and goes down. He reaches for his right foot, then rolls to his back and pushes himself back up the trail with his good, left leg.

Two more members of First Squad move forward with McKenzie, firing furiously toward the other side of the creek. One of the platoon's M-79 men begins to lob grenade rounds across the creek right into the enemy's lap as fast as he can load. Evans directs Cavalier toward the hillside.

∼∼

Two dead NVA lay on the side of the hill where they had been caught moving into ambush position. They would have fired on the lead element and then moved off down the trail, exactly what McKenzie and Captain Moore had discussed so many times. If the platoon had pursued, they would have walked into a lateral, enfilade ambush with nowhere to go.

WRONG PLACE

Cavalier reported as many as ten enemy soldiers in full combat gear moving away from the hillside. He killed one coming out of a spider hole but could not confirm any other kills. Echo was in the wrong place at the wrong time. They were stuck at the head of that valley, no place for a small recon platoon, especially one that had been in contact since arriving. Any element of surprise was gone. To stay would subject the platoon to nothing more than a running battle and further losses. Their mission to act as a blocking force through hit and run ambushes was totally compromised. McKenzie decided to act on his own.

He moved the platoon north to Medivac Collins. Once this was done, he moved the platoon back southwest and up the hill the way they had come, back to LZ Barbara without requesting permission or informing command. McKenzie was angry as hell about being stuffed down into that valley without support. He had tried to tell them what was down there. He knew he would be in trouble for walking out without permission but he had men to think about and the mission had been a disaster. He had a proposition.

Echo would go back down into that valley but only after Charlie Company went down to clear the area. The two units would then operate together as a team, becoming a reinforced blocking force for whatever was there. It was straight forward and he had hopes of convincing command until he walked back into the LZ. Captain Macavoy was livid, Major Broughton was speechless and Black Knight ranted and screamed over the radio. McKenzie held his ground.

Black Knight flew to Barbara in the late afternoon. He invited McKenzie to sit down with him in the corner of the TOC for a private discussion about what went on down in the valley.

"Lieutenant, do you want to be in my battalion or don't you?" Colonel Fishmuth pressed.

"Sir, I never wanted to be in recon but that's where you put me and now I'm here. They sent us down there to work as a full platoon. That's not how this unit has worked in the past. By definition, most recon patrols are small and operate through stealth and camouflage. A full platoon cannot do that. To further the problem, this platoon ended up trying to operate as a company blocking force. With all due respect, sir - that's ludicrous.

I informed everyone what was down in that valley before we went. I was down there a month and a half ago with Delta and there are NVA everywhere. We were promised Charlie Company would escort us down into the valley. Instead, they sat here on the LZ for two days while we got our ass shot up, lost three men, including my platoon sergeant killed. What with the helicopter fiasco and now this, I am down to twenty men. How would you feel sir?" McKenzie had rambled and Black Knight had let him. When he was through, the Colonel, who had been looking at the ground, looked up and took a deep breath.

"I only require one thing, Lieutenant. You follow my orders and if you are not able to do that, then we will have to figure something else out."

Colonel Fishmuth stood up as if the conversation was over. McKenzie stood up in a way that did not allow Black Knight to walk around him.

"Sir. I am willing to follow orders but I also have a duty to my men. That mission was ill conceived and I had to abort it. I suggest you send down a larger unit to clear the area. If that is possible, then we will go back down and set up blocking ambushes, in small units and do what you want. Although, at this point, I don't know. That little valley is crawling with NVA and they knew where we were from the moment we got down there."

The Colonel pushed by McKenzie and began pacing back and forth with his arms clasped behind his back as if he was pondering D Day. He stopped and stepped back close to McKenzie, his nose twitching.

"If you are not going to follow my orders, then I don't want you here. I have arranged for you to trade with a platoon leader from Bravo Company. He will be here in a couple of days. Until then, I will be sending Charlie Company down to see what's going on down there. Echo will stay behind and provide security."

"Sir, if its at all possible, I would like to go back to Delta."

"Its not and you will do exactly what I tell you to do, without comment. You are walking a very, fine line with me. Dismissed, Lieutenant."

McKenzie quickly exited the bunker. He was on a roller coaster. Taken away from Delta, he had begun to build a relationship with the kid soldiers of Echo. Who was going to protect them from Black Knight? Of all things, he was being sent to Bravo Company. He recalled his only observation of Captain Baskins and the word sloppy came to mind.

What was he doing out in the field? McKenzie had originally enlisted for four years with the Army's guarantee he would learn a language and be assigned to the Army Security Agency. After a series of broken promises, he'd ended up in the infantry, then OCS and now he was a platoon leader. He had tried to talk himself into believing he could be a fighter in the war but the real issue, once he was in Vietnam, was not the war. It was how to stay alive, do a job he never wanted to do and take care of his men. There was one more thing. A virulent, malevolent force was manifesting itself above him. Black Knight had put his thumb on McKenzie's neck and was pushing down.

CHAPTER EIGHT - CAPTAIN BASKINS
(SEPTEMBER 20,1968 - 271 DAYS LEFT)

Morning arrived as so many others had. McKenzie was up early waiting and watching for the sun to give light to the eastern sky. He stared where he knew the sun was hiding. He watched as the familiar faint hint that darkness would be going away appeared, then as he concentrated and wondered about it, a filament thin light appeared on the lip of the horizon as if a celestial painter was drawing with a college highlighter. It was always mesmerizing.

He watched and waited, and waited and watched, aware that time appeared not to move and yet move. This was the time he was supposed to be the most vigilant, watching the surrounding trees for enemy. Yet, when he could see the horizon clearly, as he could then, he was always distracted by it. It was one of those dangerous attractions people give in to when they know they shouldn't and yet do because there is a small thrill in taking the risk.

KNOW THE ENEMY

Did he know who the real enemy was? Was he being sent to Bravo as a punishment? Was there some relationship between Bravo's Six and Black Knight that would impose more misery by heaping unknown risks on him? He would need to be even more vigilant and wary. Where was the real danger coming from?

An orange-ish glow appeared where the sun was about to come up. It grew without seeming to grow. McKenzie looked away and then back. The orb was not there yet, so he fixed his gaze at the place until the glow puffed up and heaved at the night trying to push it away. Just when he began to wonder how long it would take, the sun broke through, like a new born chick pushing at its shell and came up fast, changing night into day. The sun had liberated itself from the dark side and so would he.

The mountains had become cold at night. Daybreak meant the return of warmth even though it would soon be hot under the Vietnam sun. McKenzie pulled off the blue sweatshirt his wife had sent from home.

He was set to fly out of LZ Barbara around noon. He said goodbye to Evans and waited up on top of the LZ. Lieutenant Parkinson from Bravo was evidently a willing partner to the trade and en route, having been picked up from Jane. McKenzie was curious why he was so agreeable. He had no opportunity to discuss it, however. When Parkinson got off the helicopter, he got on. They eyed each other and shook hands in passing. Parkinson was about five feet eight inches tall with loose blond hair and a beginning mustache. McKenzie would be taking over another First Platoon. He was still One Six and it was becoming a matter of superstition.

When he landed at Jane, he could see that dismantling had changed the LZ drastically. Only one company tent and one small battery of artillery remained. Bunkers were in obvious need of repair. Bravo occupied the entire perimeter.

SERGEANT FORDHAM

After checking in with Bravo Company's First Sergeant, McKenzie found Staff Sergeant Fordham, his new platoon sergeant, sitting shirtless on a raggedy lounge chair. He'd been told that Fordham had been promoted in the field, coming up from PFC, then E-3, to Staff Sergeant in just 10 months. At twenty-five, he was only two years older than McKenzie but he looked aged beyond his years. He also looked like he'd consumed a little too much beer over the years as the man supported a round, taut belly.

He was easy to talk to, born and raised in Michigan which explained his otherwise strong physique, reddish brown hair and ruddy cheeks. His eyes were sad looking, his beard grew fluffy upon his red cheeks, sort of like down on a baby chick. After he introduced the RTOs, both college graduates, and the medic to McKenzie, Fordham explained that he was not upset to see Lieutenant Parkinson leave.

"Let's put it this way, Parkinson was a cocky, give-a-shit drunk. He didn't have the balls to stand up to Six and he wouldn't listen to what I had to say. I spent most of my time just letting him step on his dick and trying to get out of his way. My question to you, sir, is why would you want to trade and come to Bravo?"

"Why do you say that, Sarge?" McKenzie was surprised at the question.

"Because. Our Six, Captain Baskins, is a kiss ass to Black Knight and a loose cannon in the field. He showed up in June and we haven't been safe since. Haven't you heard about Bravo? As far as I'm concerned, we just stumble around waiting to get our ass kicked. I got two months to go and I just hope I make it. Right now, I don't fight him. I just try to take care of my men. We've had good leaders. We know what they look like. He's not one of them. Question is, are you?"

McKenzie was silent for a moment. He took a deep breath and folded his arms across his chest looking at Fordham. It was clear to him the others were also giving him the once over and waiting to see what he said.

"Sarge, I'm going to answer that but I hope the rest of you can keep this to yourselves. I didn't pick Bravo. I just got kicked the hell out of Echo. If what you say is true, Parkinson's gonna have to get his stuff together and be willing to do whatever he is told because that's the way Black Knight is.

I've had a personal running battle with Colonel Fishmuth since I got here. I also came in country in June. Delta had the best record in the battalion but Black Knight wanted my Six to run only full company operations and Captain Moore, who was a damn fine officer, wanted to work platoon size or smaller. The Colonel eventually managed to get him transferred to Saigon to a teaching job and sent me to Echo. It didn't take long for us to start butting heads. That's all there is to it. He's the one who sent me here."

"So what was wrong with how they ran recon?" Fordham asked, lighting a cigarette in a way that told McKenzie he was being vetted.

"The first thing was, they wanted us to be a blocking force to the big push coming in from the coast. The second thing is they wouldn't listen when I told them I was familiar with a particular area and that there were beau coup NVA down off LZ Barbara to the North. We got hit three times in a day and a half and I walked recon back into Barbara and basically - told them to shove it. They had promised to send Charlie Company along until we could keg up and they didn't."

"So you haven't heard." Fordham said as he sat up in his lounge chair.

"Heard what?"

"Charlie Company got hit this morning - lots of casualties. Alpha Company is being air lifted in and we're on stand by."

"You're kidding me, right? Where did you hear that?" McKenzie was dumb struck.

"Sitting up at the company tent this morning. Top was monitoring battalion and we heard the whole thing. They figure Charlie Company tied into at least two companies, maybe more. Sounds like it happened just after you left."

"That's probably right, Sarge. They walked out of Barbara about an hour before I jumped on a resupply bird coming back to Jane. Jesus. Even though I was right, I hate to hear that. Well, I guess I need to ask you something. Are you combat ready?"

Sergeant Fordham scratched his belly, leaving red streaks from his finger nails.

"If you're lookin' to work in small sized units, you ain't gonna find it here unless you can somehow talk our Six into it but I doubt that. He does whatever Black Knight tells him to do."

He looked at McKenzie with sad eyes and shook his head. For the next hour, Fordham, the two RTOs, Lawrence and Harmon and the medic, Doc Thompson, filled McKenzie in on the status of First Platoon and Bravo Company. It was not good. Discipline was weak. There were a number of good soldiers but there were also a few cowboys who liked to talk tough yet had not really been tested. There were a few old ones and McKenzie made sure he found out who they were.

There was another problem. The rumors McKenzie had heard were true. Black soldiers in the company tended to congregate around Baskins at night and it was difficult to build platoon unity. Fordham stated emphatically, however, he thought they were all good men. They just needed a leader. The others agreed, including Doc Thompson, who was black. He offered some advice.

"If I was you, LT. I'd be for bustin' up the squads in this here platoon. For some reason, Third Squad is all bloods and they be hanging out together all the time doin their thing, like giving each other the dap and ditty boppin' to the tunes. I think its gettin' out of hand. That is, if you want my opinion."

"Thanks. I do, Doc. I really don't care so much about the dap or the music. I see all the soldiers getting into that now. Let me think about it. Where can I find the CO?"

BLACK GOLD

Specialist Lawrence, McKenzie's new RTO, offered to help him find Black Gold Six. He reemphasized on the way over how much Captain Baskins acted like he and Black Knight were buddies. It wasn't that the Captain was eager to fight. He wasn't. He just didn't discriminate between what Black Knight wanted and his own judgment. Ever.

"Fact is, LT, I don't think Six uses any of his own judgment," he said. "It's always the platoon leaders who do the fighting anyway. I never seen him even get close. He follows way behind. The Captain wants kills for his good buddy Black Knight but he isn't into exposing himself too much. You know what I mean?"

They found Captain Baskins sitting on a cot, which had been hauled outside one of the bunkers. A group of black soldiers were gathered around a battery operated tape deck turned up loud and playing James Brown. They were laughing and dancing. The captain's jungle fatigue shirt was completely unbuttoned and he had just put a can of beer to his lips. Without lowering the beer, he looked over at the approaching two soldiers.

"Lieutenant McKenzie reporting in, sir. I'm your new One Six."

Captain Baskins slowly sat up, bent over and placed the can on the ground. Still looking down, he rubbed his rather small, semi-bald head the way McKenzie had seen him do in the field. He looked to be around thirty years old.

Fordham had told McKenzie that Captain Baskins was an OCS career officer looking for promotion to major which he felt his association with Black Knight would get him. He had not been bashful in talking openly about his aspirations. He had a long face that appeared even longer when he looked up.

"Welcome, Lieutenant. I'll meet with you later. We're on - uh - standby to fly - uh - into LZ Barbara - if needed - uh - so I want you - uh - to get your platoon -uh - ready to move."

It was a slow, clipped way of talking; two or three words, then a pause, with just a hint of southern accent.

"Yes, sir. I already talked to Staff Sergeant Fordham and he feels ready to go."

Captain Baskins frowned. "Lieutenant, I didn't - uh - ask you what Sergeant Fordham - uh - feels. Now, you go back and - uh - see for yourself - uh - that they're ready to go - uh - and you report back - uh - to me at nineteen hundred."

McKenzie said, "Yes, sir," turned and walked back with Lawrence in numbed silence. He'd anticipated a private conversation where he would be told to watch his step or something similar, emanating from the antipathy between himself and Black Knight, but he hadn't expected to be treated in such a dismissive way. Clearly, he'd been dumped on Bravo Company, which so far wasn't very impressive

He spent the next hour meeting his squad leaders. Sergeant Gibney was a big, burly kid from Kansas who ran First Squad. He had thick, black hair, heavy eyebrows, a bushy mustache, a three day old beard and he appeared to be the type who led by quiet example rather than word. Sergeant Mack, from Gonzolas, Texas, was in charge of Second Squad and Sergeant Campbell, a black soldier from Detroit, who didn't seem to like Mack and made no bones about it, ran Third Squad, which, at the moment, was entirely made up of black soldiers. McKenzie and Fordham spent the rest of the afternoon rearranging squads and producing new hand written rosters for each squad leader.

Lawrence returned from talking to Top Balcom at the company tent and reported that Alpha Company had successfully extricated Charlie Company but not before suffering significant casualties itself. Bravo was taken off standby and told they would be at Jane for another five days.

During the afternoon, McKenzie learned a lot more about his new platoon sergeant. Fordham was an avid hunter. He loved the outdoors and appeared to have good instincts about terrain and movement which was evident when he related stories about Bravo. Several soldiers came to him with problems and McKenzie was impressed with his fatherly way of handling each issue even though he was clearly only a few years older.

"Let me ask you something, Sarge. If you had a chance to run your own show, how would you fight Mr. Charles, as my guys in Delta liked to call the NVA?"

Sergeant Fordham scratched his belly again, leaving long fingernail marks. His girth looked remarkably like a pregnant woman at around six months. He had a habit of looking to the side when he was thinking. He reminded McKenzie of an old hunter in Oregon who would look into his memory that way. Fordham also had a habit of clearing his throat with a deep reverberation. He reached up and picked something out of his reddish, brown hair.

"I'll tell you what, sir. You got to hunt Mr. Charles the same way you hunt game - patiently. Everything over here is in a big hurry. It's the Rube Goldberg war we got going over here. That's what my Daddy used to call anything that was made more complicated than it was supposed to be. We got so much fire power and we're so damned excited to use it, we spend all our time just trying to bait the NVA into a fire fight so we can blow him away with all our shit.

Well, you know what? He ain't goin away. We been blastin' away at him now for the last three years and he just keeps coming. As far as I'm concerned, I don't give a hoot about winning this war. I just want to get out a here alive. I would love to have someone let me fight on my terms for once."

He picked up a piece of wood he had been whittling on, grabbed the pocket knife he'd left stuck in the ground next to it and began using the knife for a pointer. He waved it a little and said, "You let me fight Charlie on my terms and you'll be my hero. But - that I gotta see."

NIGHT TRIP

The next two days were inconsequential. Squads were rearranged and integrated with some complaining but without mutiny. The meeting with Captain Baskins was benign and life slowed to a crawl as heavy monsoon rains returned to oppress the soldiers at LZ Jane. On the third evening, McKenzie was shocked to learn that Baskins had taken the only jeep on the LZ and headed for a place called Hai Lang, the District headquarters for Quang Tri Province, with one of the other platoon leaders and a platoon sergeant.

They were on a mission to pick up whiskey and would be traveling on roads gooey with deep mud complemented by ravines from heavy use. They left around seventeen hundred and were scheduled to return after dark. Bravo's supply clerk did say they had taken a radio in case of trouble. Sergeant Fordham laughed when McKenzie returned and told him about the expedition.

"Hell. That's not the first time Six has gone off on some escapade," he said.

"So, what happens if they run into trouble?" McKenzie said.

"I really don't give a damn, LT. If they get into trouble, they're on their own. That's Indian country out there and they're just askin' to get killed. If they get stuck, they can find their own way home. I'm not sending any of my boys out there to get ambushed." Fordham's face got redder when he was angry.

"They're probably after more than whiskey anyway, One Six. Boom, boom," he said.

"You mean their looking for whores?" McKenzie was incredulous.

"I mean they done it before and probably will again. You got a lot to learn about Six. Sometimes he acts like he's back in the hood."

"I thought he was a career officer? What about Black Knight? He ever get wind of this?"

"I don't know," Fordham said slowly, not as angry as before. "There have been a couple of close calls but I don't think Six has ever been caught."

McKenzie was flabbergasted. Throughout the rest of the evening, he thought long and hard about what he would do if called to go out and rescue them. He finally decided that if it was an enemy situation, he would go. If it was just three drunks stuck in the mud, however, they would have to fend for themselves.

He had been taught over and over in OCS about the high standards of the officer corps. One part of the OCS prayer had stuck with him. "We pray for humility, O Lord, that any existing selfishness, arrogance and vanity be removed from our lives." There were good officers in Vietnam. He knew that.

OREGON

Light from a full moon broke through the clouds and brought with it memories from home. Nothing in the Vietnam night, which had become more dangerous lately, should have brought an image of home to McKenzie as he sat staring into the night but it did. The moon seemed to blow the heavy clouds away as it rose higher into the sky leaving wispy clouds to skim across a blue night. It became bright and orange as a harvest moon in Oregon filling the sky and looking so familiar, like the ones he remembered in his youth and yet, there was no honesty in it.

Between that bright, full man-in-the-moon face, clearly visible on a night like this and where he sat, was one hell of a darkness. How could that face ever imagine the danger these dark nights held? Yet - it was the same moon that had looked down on the earth and all its foibles for thousands of years. Maybe it did.

He looked hard at long shadows cast toward him from a tree line across a narrow clearing in front of the perimeter wire. He squinted and thought he saw something move. Elephant grass resembled thin fingers where ever moonlight did not hit the ground. Where it did, the ground was buttercup yellow. Tents within the compound forecast strange shapes. Soldiers resting outside foxholes and fighting positions were lit up and visible. Sentries popped up here and there, like prairie dogs, to look into the night.

McKenzie thought about his first summer camp at the base of Mount Hood. He was eight years old. A full moon had provided enough light for older boys to crawl between tents and pull practical jokes on the counselor or scare the hell out of he and the other first year kids. They had stayed up scared and excited until four in the morning when the moon finally settled down behind pine trees west of the lake.

He remembered his high school graduation night, lying on a sandy beach next to the Columbia River, this very same moon reflecting off the river in a checkered pattern, scored by the waves and wind. Shale cliffs protected he and his high school sweetheart as they sat on a blanket dreaming of all the tomorrows. Her blue eyes had seemed translucent in the moonlight.

SIX ON THE HORN

"Hey, One Six, Six is on the horn and says his jeep is stuck in the mud. Sounds like he's drunk," Lawrence said with a grin. McKenzie took the handset to his ear and heard," Black Gold One Shix, this is Black Gold Shix, do you read me? Over."

"Black Gold Six, this is One Six. Over."

"Uh - Black Gold One Shix, this is your Shix. We - uh - need an escort. Over."

McKenzie picked up the radio by its straps and stepped outside the bunker. A warm breeze coming in from the coast blew the humidity against his face. He looked back at the others sitting inside. They looked back with unblinking eyes.

"Six, what's your location? Over," McKenzie said quietly into the mouth piece.

"How the hell do - uh - I know? We're on the road -uh - about a click away. The zjeeeps shtuck. You get a shquad out here, now. Over."

"Black Gold Six. This is Black Gold One Six. Do you have enemy contact? Over."

"What? No, we haven't got any God damned enemy contact but I need some shecurity. Now, that's an order."

"Six, that's a negative. Just follow the road and we'll keep an eye out for you. Over."

"What? What the hell you talking about?" Captain Baskins was talking too loud for being out in the middle of the night. Two Six broke in on the radio.

"Six, this is Two Six. We'll be there but its gonna take us a little time. Over."

"Roger that, Two shix. We're gonna shtay put so you don't light us up and I'm gonna take care of One Shix when I get back. You hear that, One Shix?"

McKenzie handed the radio back to Lawrence. "Better gear up boys. Six will be paying me a visit if he makes it."

It was foolish for Two Six to walk around on the road at night with the moon out. He was taking one hell of a gamble with his men to go out on a rescue mission for three drunk soldiers who were off limits. Although McKenzie felt he was only protecting his own men, when he heard Two Six volunteer so quickly, he felt a pit form in his stomach. Was he being disloyal or was he truly making the right decision?

BLACK GOLD'S VISIT

McKenzie put together a quick reaction force in case Two Six got into trouble. He also notified the artillery sergeant of the approximate coordinates and requested they stand by with night flares. For several hours, he sat waiting. Around four in the morning, he heard shouting from the northeast entrance of the perimeter. It was Black Gold and the shouting grew louder as he came stomping across the LZ.

"You snot nosed Second Lieutenant, where the hell are you?" he yelled as he came over a small rise in front of the bunker. He definitely talked faster when he was drunk.

One Five was awake as were the two RTOs and Doc Thompson. Captain Baskins charged into the bunker with a pistol in his right hand. Fordham slap grabbed his weapon and clicked off the safety as he raised it toward Captain Haskins who was pointing his pistol at McKenzie.

"Who the hell do you think you are, you shun of a bitch!" he screamed. "I ought to court martial your ass but that would be too good for you. I ought to shoot you right here. When I give you an order, you had better obey it or else." He moved closer, putting the pistol about a foot in front of McKenzie's face.

"I wouldn't do that, sir," Sergeant Fordham said in a loud and menacing voice.

Captain Baskins stepped back and looked over at the sergeant. "What? I got NCOs against me too?"

"Sir, I made that decision because you were off limits at night and I was not about to risk the lives of my men to come and get you." McKenzie was scared but tried not to sound like it.

"You lishen to me. Two Shix came out to get ush and nothing happened. Heez got balls and he knows how to obey an order. Thish iz not over. You and me are gonna come to an undershtanding and quick. I'll shee your ass in the morning." He turned and stumbled out of the bunker. McKenzie let out the air he was holding in.

"Well, that was a great start. I'm gonna go see if I can find out from Two Six what happened," he said.

Just outside his bunker, McKenzie saw the platoon sergeant from Second Platoon laying face down on the ground, passed out. When he found Two Six, he learned the passed out sergeant had continued to consume whiskey on the way back and it had been difficult to keep him quiet. Six finally told him to shut up. None of the rescuers had any sympathy for him, so they just left him where he fell.

Lieutenant Fromer, Two Six, had been with Bravo almost five months and was due to get a rear job in another month. He was overweight with a Yogi Bear face and an attitude that seemed to indicate he didn't care one way or another about anything.

"Why would you risk your men's lives to go out and rescue a bunch of drunks, company commander or not?" McKenzie said before leaving.

"Why not? If you got drunk and needed help, wouldn't you want your buddies to come and get you? Besides, one of those guys was my platoon sergeant," Fromer said.

"I wouldn't be wandering around in the dark out where Charlie owns the night and I wouldn't be running into town for whiskey or whatever else just because I felt like it." McKenzie said, surprised at the man's attitude.

"Don't be too sure, young lieutenant. You just ain't been in the field long enough."

"Like hell I haven't," McKenzie said angrily. On the way back, he observed two soldiers helping the drunk sergeant off the ground.

Morning did not bring a confrontation. McKenzie spent the morning with his squad leaders, trying to get to know them better and waiting for a meeting with Captain Baskins which never took place. Mack was beginning to remind him of Carter. Campbell was definitely not invested in sucking up to Six like some of the other soldiers. Just before noon, Fordham returned from a trip to the company tent. He had a wry smile on his face.

"So, what are you grinning about now, Sergeant?" McKenzie said. It was the kind of grin a person gets when he has a story that wants to be told.

"I'm not sure I really know where to begin, One Six." Fordham gave out a short, deep throated laugh and sat down on his lounge chair. Six had decided to have a party and not just any party. He had decided to have a barbecue to promote company unity and incredibly, had ordered his buddy, Two Six, to take a squad out into the rice patty east of the LZ and kill a water buffalo.

McKenzie looked at Fordham, not knowing if this was the truth or whether he was pulling their legs.

"Close your mouth, One Six, before you end up with a stomach full of flies." Sergeant Fordham lay back on his lounge chair and started to laugh, which made his belly shake and soon, tears were rolling down his ruddy cheeks. It was the kind of laugh that made the others laugh.

The laughing was interrupted by someone firing a machine gun outside the wire. Fordham sat up. McKenzie walked up the incline to the crest of the LZ and over to the eastern side where he could see what was happening.

He could see a dead water buffalo laying not more than one hundred meters outside the perimeter wire, stitched on the side with bullet holes, each leaking streams of red blood running down the animal's black hide. The assassination squad stood around talking and examining the product of their work.

McKenzie did not hear the unmistakable sound of a descending helicopter pulling pitch to land. When he did and turned around, Black Knight was already exiting the pilot's door and Captain Baskins was walking briskly over to meet him. McKenzie moved closer to see if he could hear what was said.

The gist of the meeting had to do with repair of bunkers. LZ Jane was in transition and Colonel Fishmuth wanted to tighten security. He wanted Bravo Company to repair all bunkers before they returned to the field. The two officers set out to walk the perimeter with Black Knight giving specific instructions on needed repairs.

This was going to be interesting. When they reached the eastern side where the water buffalo was clearly visible, all hell would break loose. The Colonel had come in from the West and apparently not seen the squad or their trophy. McKenzie followed at a distance with a sense of giddy glee. Captain Baskins was practically genuflecting as the two made their rounds.

When they reached the eastern side Captain Baskins explained the soldiers were out policing up the area. The squad had managed to pull cardboard from C-ration boxes away from a nearby dump and pile them around the huge buffalo. It looked like they were going to have a bonfire. McKenzie stopped in amazement. The two officers, the emperor and the sycophant, moved on, the emperor apparently not curious why cardboard was stacked in the middle of a rice patty.

McKenzie was incredulous. There was no frickin' way First Platoon was going to participate in any barbecue. He walked back and gave Sergeant Fordham his order. "Every man in First Platoon will, by God, stay at his bunker and any man who ventures near that barbecue will get an Article 15. This is not going to involve us."

Black Knight finally left. Captain Baskins ordered the Cave Killers who were still on LZ Jane to link up with each platoon. He wanted three bunkers repaired or rebuilt by each platoon and he wanted the engineers to see to it. Lieutenant Shmedley was in charge of the engineers. When he came by later he was pissed. He was aware of the drunken excursion into town because he had to go retrieve the stuck jeep. He was also sickened by the water buffalo killing and vowed to let Division know what was going on.

By late afternoon the buffalo carcass had been drug inside the perimeter by jeep, cut up and what was left, drug back outside the wire and buried. The entire butchering procedure was grisly. Flies swarmed around the dead animal and congealed blood lay in thick pools. Meat was cut off and wrapped into ponchos to keep flies from laying eggs into it. Chances are, some of it was hit anyway.

McKenzie stood vigil, mentally documenting the entire sordid ordeal. Baskins noticed his observation and approached. He inquired politely if McKenzie was looking forward to the festivities.

"No sir. Neither I nor any of my men are going to participate in this illegal killing," McKenzie said through a tight jaw. "If you'll excuse me, sir. I have things to do."

"You better watch your step, buddy boy. You don't know who you're messing with," Captain Baskins said in a half shout as McKenzie walked away.

"Asshole!" McKenzie muttered to himself.

Baskins words came out angrily but McKenzie thought he heard a hint of concern. A chasm had developed between the two men and he wondered what was going to transpire in the field. He also suspected that Black Knight had put him there knowing this would happen.

Bravo company walked out of LZ Jane on the fifth day. They were being replaced by Charlie Company, which was still trying to recover from the ambush off LZ Barbara. It was September, Twenty Sixth. Dark, threatening monsoon clouds had returned and hung overhead as the men navigated their way through the concertina wire toward a wet trail made of slick, red clay, resembling a wet summer baseball infield long ago played out by school children. McKenzie stood near the exit counting his platoon through the wire.

Next to him was Sergeant Fordham, who turned and looked over McKenzie's shoulder, behind him and said, "Oh, Oh, we got company." Advancing at a near run was Black Gold Six. McKenzie braced himself.

"One Six, get your damned men through that wire and quit screwing around. They don't need to be staggered so far apart until we get out on the flat."

He bumped McKenzie with his chest and then shoved him toward the opening with his left hand.

"I'm counting my men through the wire, Six. You need to let me do my job and go find your command group." McKenzie's voice was low and hard. It was disrespectful but that breech had already occurred. Baskins stepped closer in a way that threatened to turn into something more physical. Before he could say anything more, the company RTO hollered that Battalion was on the horn. Baskins left as fast as he had come.

IN THE FIELD WITH BLACK GOLD

The first week passed with no enemy contact. The company seemed to wander in circles with no apparent mission until it was picked up and inserted north of LZ Barbara to look for a heavy weapons company.

First Platoon took the lead on day eight. Sergeant Campbell selected Private Randall to walk point. Randall was a huge fan of the nightly gatherings around Captain Baskins. McKenzie moved up to watch him. He had a swinging walk and a cocky attitude. He wore green ties with loose ends on his arms and several silver necklaces which Fordham had ordered him that morning to tape together. He had a cat like way of moving, wary, never approaching a turn from the near side but always crossing over to open up his line of sight.

Forest birds were talking loudly to each other. That was a good sign. Monsoon's grip had loosened briefly allowing the sun to influence the day. It was a warm jungle, swollen full of fragrances and dank, decaying vegetation. The air buzzed loudly with a mixture of bugs and flies as the column of soldiers stole silently along. Thin water falls of sunlight filtered through the jungle canopy producing delicate curtain like shadows. Seductive memories of warm spring days back home crept into McKenzie's mind as he watched Randall approach a corner in the trail.

His movement was so quick, McKenzie almost missed it. Randall had deftly moved the barrel of his weapon to the right and fired a short burst on full automatic. That was it. Just one short burst.

"This guy was walking along like there was no one else around. He never saw me," Randall said calmly when McKenzie got to him. A dead NVA soldier lay in the middle of the trail.

After searching for papers, the column moved on until, an hour later, they discovered several large structures resembling American Indian smoke lodges. Inside the first was an SKS rifle, an old M-1 and a B-40 rocket. Second Platoon uncovered two booby traps on the uphill side. One was made from an M-60 mortar and the other lay at the bottom of a pit full of punji stakes, the points covered with human waste. Cave killers were flown in and worked through the afternoon blowing hooches and booby traps.

Bravo continued to work in and around the bunker complex for several days. On the morning of October, Tenth, they were picked up and dropped onto an old LZ. Their orders were to look for a radio station but Division did not have precise coordinates.

HUNG OUT

"Great," McKenzie said to Fordham. "Other than the fact such a mission would be more appropriate for a long range recon patrol, I can't help but wonder if this is just another lark assignment for Black Gold. Since leaving Jane, there hasn't been much purpose to our movements." Fordham gave him that sideways look.

The company spread out over the old LZ, soldiers discarding their packs and settling in while Black Gold Six waited for coordinates. Around eighteen hundred, the call came in to move fifteen hundred meters south before dark. Such a late move was perilous at best. McKenzie quickly gathered his squad leaders. He drew a map of the route and terrain in the dirt.

"This trail appears to move down into a steep draw. The lower we go, the darker it will get, meaning we're gonna lose light faster than if we were still on top. We'll be moving out last today. I want our point to give good separation from Third Platoon. If Second gets hit there's a good chance Third will get caught up. If we're asked to move we'll do it by squads.

Since Third Squad's our lead, I'll go with them and we'll move up on the left. One Five will stay with First and Second squads and move to the right. This may vary depending on the terrain but we're not gonna get sucked into a second ambush waiting to catch us moving up. If its too dark we may just keg up off the trail on both sides and defend our position until first light. I haven't got a clue about enemy activity in this area but frankly, S-2 doesn't either."

"What if Six orders us to move up on the trail?" Campbell said.

McKenzie grabbed him by the shirt. "You got a loyalty problem, Campbell? If you want to stay alive and go home to your Mamma, you will do as I say. Let me deal with the tactics. Are we clear?" He pushed Campbell away.

"You don't have to grab me like that LT. I'm not one of Six's lap dogs. I was just askin'. You wanna take Six on? That's fine with me. All you gotta do is tell me what you want and I'll do it. Are we clear?"

McKenzie smiled. "OK, OK. You made your point."

"All right, lets get moving," Fordham said stepping between McKenzie and Campbell as if he was unaware they were talking.

It was the first time in his tour that McKenzie had been that tough on a squad leader but he was genuinely concerned about the leadership in Bravo. In the last four months, he had never felt this out of control. The mission was unclear, the terrain was ominous and the order to move out at this late hour to an uncertain location was confusing. Thank God he'd just been reassured by his men that they were ready to stand by him. He sucked in a deep breath as he shouldered his own pack and looked around for his radio man.

Movement slowed to a crawl as the column of heavily laden men descended into the draw which looked more like a steep sided ravine. Third Platoon reported the trail ran directly through the bottom then up a long incline toward the top. While it would be difficult to attack the company laterally, an enemy pushing in from either end, or worse, from both ends, could box them in. The only escape would be a counter attack directly at one or both ends.

The trail in the bottom was wet and soggy from a small, run off creek. By the time Bravo reached midpoint they were in very dark surroundings. Baskins decided to stop where he was for the night. McKenzie grabbed the radio.

"Black Gold Six, this is One Six. I think we should continue out of this ravine. We're badly contained on both ends. Over."

"One Six, this is Six, if you don't like it down here, you can lead out. Over."

"Roger that. Out." McKenzie quickly moved First Platoon past Third and Second Platoons. He put Gibney's squad in front with instructions to take it slow, especially coming out at the top. Rain rivulets had created deep cuts in the trail, making ascent difficult. Gibney's point man slipped to his knees several times trying to negotiate the difficult trail in semi darkness while keeping an eye to his front.

McKenzie could see the sky getting lighter as they neared the other side. Within a half hour they were out. The setting sun loomed on the horizon in front of them, like an orange flare keeping the night away. Only a few hundred meters beyond was a perfect hill for night set up. McKenzie waited on top as the last member of First Platoon came out. No one was following.

"Black Gold Six, this is One Six. Over."

"One Six, this is Black Gold Six India, over." It was Black Gold's RTO.

"Six India, tell Six we spotted a perfect over night to our east about two hundred mikes. We'll move ahead and secure it. Two Six and Three Six can move in our direction. Over."

"That's a negative, One Six. Six says its too dark for us to move. You secure your location and we'll rendezvous in the morning. Out."

"What the hell?" someone said behind McKenzie. He turned to see Sergeant Fordham standing next to him.

"I think we just got suckered, LT. Can you believe that? Six had no intention of coming out after us," he said.

"Well, I'm thinkin' we set up on that knoll anyway, Sarge, with OPs all around on four corners and send out three man ambushes in each direction. A pinwheel ambush directly on the trail might work but that could leave us exposed from the knoll."

"I don't like it, LT."

"OK, how about this? Let's not put an ambush in Six's direction but set up a full squad ambush down the other way. You and me and the rest will reconnoiter on the knoll and angle the perimeter back the way we came. That way if anything happens, we can either pull the ambush in or react. I'll leave you to do your magic on the knoll."

"Sounds like a plan, LT," Fordham grinned as if he'd just won an argument.

"What? One Five? You like that or don't you?"

Sergeant Fordham kept on grinning while he scratched his belly and looked at the ground. Sergeant Gibney joined them. "He's got us up here on the flat, LT and he's down there with two platoons in the bottom of that ravine. Does that make any sense to you?" Fordham said, still looking at the ground.

"Listen, Sarge. You guys told me how it was in the field. Frankly, I like our position a hell of a lot better than his."

McKenzie turned and walked to the knoll. There were signs someone had been up there once but not recently. Old foxholes were scattered about. Maybe this was an overnight for French troops or even, Japanese soldiers during World War Two. He reminded everyone to be aware of possible booby traps.

Captain Baskins had given him a clear message. If McKenzie was going to challenge him he was willing to hang his platoon leader and First Platoon out on their own. He wondered what Coach Tucker would tell him to do?

Morning arrived pleasant and uneventful. Fordham approached carrying his canteen cup, as the sun began to heat the night's coolness to a comfortable level. McKenzie sat with his back to the rising sun, letting the warmth soak into his shoulders and stirring the hot water he had just poured into a LRRP meal of chicken and rice. Lawrence was brewing the ubiquitous coffee and hot chocolate that appeared where ever McKenzie went.

"Morning, One Six. I told the guys to take it easy. Clean up, write some letters, etc."

"Morning, One Five. You lookin' for some of Lawrence's Mo-Jo?"

"Yep. You know, LT, we're gonna have to wait here for a while. Old Sol's not gonna shine down into that deep ravine for a couple of hours. I figure Six and the rest won't be up on top before eleven hundred. Funny how things work out, ain't it?" He laughed and cleared his throat before taking a sip of steaming coffee. "Damn, that's good. You hear we got a log bird comin' in this afternoon?"

"Yeah. You give Top our list?"

"Of course. Are you aware our old forward observer is coming out on that bird to say goodbye before he goes back to the world?"

"No. I wasn't. Why?" McKenzie could hear concern in One Five's voice.

"Oh, I don't know. It's just another one of those deals. Aren't we supposed to be lookin' for a radio location or something important like that? Instead, this feels like a fiasco that always seems to turn into a loud party out here."

"I appreciate your concern Sarge but we're just gonna keep on keeping on. We're gonna mind our own business, make sure our security stays good and alert and if Six gets too loud, I'll just have to say something. I'm already on his shit list." McKenzie was learning that when Fordham used the word "deal," he was trying not to say what he really thought. His new platoon sergeant had a sixth sense and McKenzie tried to pay attention whenever he could see it was working.

The rest of the company did not arrive until late morning, as predicted. Captain Baskins went to the far side of the knoll, sat down on his helmet and rubbed his head. "Tell Two Six and Three Six to spread out. We'll be here for a while," he told his RTO.

Radio traffic for the next two hours was more about what was coming out on the supply bird, including the guest, than anything tactical. Orders came down to move toward a ridge line, establish an early FOB and wait for the log bird. Captain Baskins did not speak to or acknowledge McKenzie's existence except to send word that First Platoon was on point.

They spotted the log sight an hour later up on a far away ridge. The trail had become wider and showed recent signs of use. Point was all alone when he approached the near end of the ridge which flattened out on top. McKenzie was considering moving a squad up to secure when Gibney's point man opened up. Two NVA ran across the top and down the far side. First Squad moved up and reported finding another trail which crossed over and then dropped into cover on both sides.

Top called and said his log bird would be inbound around seventeen hundred. The landing area was close to a tree line on the North side with a steep drop off to the South, meaning the pilot's approach would have to be from either the East or West. There were trees too big to cut down so Fordham placed foxholes and night positions down on the hillside, among the trees. Third Platoon located east of the ridge line, Second Platoon went to the steep side and Baskins set up at the West end, leaving the top bare.

"One Five, move around the perimeter and coordinate with the other fives to lock in fields of fire and discuss responsibilities since this is gonna be a fairly loose perimeter. Make sure the trail entrances on all four sides are covered with night ambushes."

McKenzie said, not willing to wait and see what Six would do any more.

It was a dry afternoon and McKenzie felt relaxed. He sat down to make a few entries into his journal. Maybe writing down the sequence of events since leaving Jane would help sort out his disparate thoughts. As usual, there was too much noise but he tried to ignore it.

Mack returned after making a three hundred and sixty degree tour around the lower edge of the ridge. "Hey, One Six. That was good duty. This trail looks like a travel route. Its had some use but only a few at a time and we can take care of that with night ambushes. There's no other trails coming in from any direction except the one we came in on. We saw no bunkers or anything."

"Thanks, Mac. You put a night ambush out to the North and we'll get Second Platoon to cover the South. Let the ambush take One Five's radio. Our log is due any minute. We've got ammo and supplies coming in, so have a couple of your guys grab our stuff off the bird quickly and make sure I get my extra battery for the radio."

"No problem, LT. I hear Lieutenant Wasserman, our old forward observer, is coming out to say goodbye."

"Yea, that's what I hear and Bevans is coming back from R&R. Did you know Wasserman?"

"Yea. He's a great guy. He liked to party and didn't have his nose in the air when it came to the guys. Everybody liked him."

~~

The faint but familiar sound of a helicopter blade chopping through the air is heard. Movement around the perimeter stops. Like all CAV soldiers, they welcome the sound of an approaching helicopter, especially when it's time for resupply and mail from home. McKenzie is still gun shy after having one of his own helicopters shoot at him and another one almost crash on his head. He moves slightly closer to the edge of the hill.

He looks up to watch the aircraft growing larger. Above the dark fuselage, where the First Cav patch is painted on the nose, whirling blades blur as the pilot changes pitch causing the popping sound of the blades to grow louder. He drops the tail, exposing the under belly of the craft as he feathers in toward the hill.

Second Platoon has a man standing on top with both arms in the air directing the approach. Green smoke spirals up. The helicopter hangs suspended at the beginning of the ridge and then slowly drifts forward. This is always the time McKenzie worries about snipers and so, he listens. Inside, two soldiers sit on the drop down seat. One is waving as if he knows everyone on the ground personally. Door gunners on both sides scan the surrounding area as the pilot looks for his landing.

Hot adrenalin explodes inside McKenzie's circulatory system as he watches the pilot appear to lose control and drift left in slow motion until his top rotor blade hits a large tree, spinning the helicopter tail around to the left. Somehow it misses McKenzie, who launches backwards without regard to where he will land. Wood splinters strike his back as he hits upside down on his right shoulder, feet over his head somersaulting backwards down the slope until he's stopped by a soldier standing next to a foxhole.

Scrambling back up the hill on all fours, he sees fire coming from underneath the helicopter which is over on its side. Both door gunners have jumped free and the pilots are crawling out of the up side window. Pinned under the fuselage are Lieutenant Wasserman, who is not moving and Bevans, eyes open and conscious.

Ammunition begins to cook off and explode. Several soldiers run toward the trapped men. They grab underneath the door opening. They pull and try to lift up but cannot. McKenzie rises to his knees and starts to stand. Belts of machine gun rounds explode in staccato rhythm, sending bullets in all directions. A grenade cooks off and the two men trying to lift the helicopter run away.

McKenzie looks around for Captain Baskins. The number and frequency of explosions increase. A claymore, sitting on the passenger deck, explodes, ripping a hole above the two trapped men.

"Help me. Oh, God. Somebody help me!" Bevans screams.

He starts to cry and tries to twist around looking to see if anyone is coming. His legs and hips are pinned by the body of the helicopter but his arms and shoulders are free. He pushes them into the ground trying to lever his torso to the right. Soldiers yell at each other and jump up. Explosions send them back over the ridge line. Exploding bullets fire off and grenades detonate every five to ten seconds.

McKenzie makes his way over to Captain Baskins. "I don't think I can watch this, Six. We have to do something," he says and grabs Six by the shoulder, pulling him around so he can look directly into his eyes. Baskins has a glazed, frozen look.

"One Six, let me shoot him," Fordham says, from behind McKenzie.

Bevans is now screaming louder but his voice is difficult to hear amid the explosions of bullets and shrapnel flying out of the passenger area.

"I mean it, One Six. I'd want someone to do that for me," Fordham says. "He's not gettin' out of there and we can't just stay here and watch him burn to death." McKenzie looks around at Fordham who starts to raise his weapon toward the helicopter. He looks back at Baskins, who's eyes flash. Baskins pulls his pistol from the shoulder holster and points it at Fordham. McKenzie grabs the top of the barrel and pulls down on it. The two men glare at each other as if there is no other world around them.

"No one is shooting that man. If you do, I will court martial your ass for murder, do you hear me?" Baskins says to Fordham through clenched teeth.

"Six!" McKenzie yells into his face. "Are you willing to just stand here and watch that man suffer and scream until he burns to death? Are you willing to do that?"

"War is hell, One Six. I don't like it either but no one is shooting that man. Its my decision. Now, let go of my gun."

The danger of jet fuel exploding increases as the fire grows. A pungent, oily smell burns the eyes and noses of soldiers who have moved down the hill away but not so far they cannot hear Bevans' cries growing fainter and less often. It's hard to keep from crying and several cannot. Bevans was a popular member of Second Platoon, a good point man and someone who could always cheer up the men when things were bad.

By nineteen hundred, the fire has burnt itself out. No explosions have occurred since the first hour but the company waits another hour before approaching the damaged bird. Men lie on the side of the hill in silence and melancholy, some with their faces buried in folded arms, smelling now what they know is burnt flesh and listening to the popping and sizzling.

Medivac is called for the pilots and crew, all who suffered injuries in the crash. One pilot has a broken arm and the other a severe head laceration. One of the door gunners sprained his ankle but the other only suffered bruises and minor cuts. Extraction will have to be by penetrator seat or litter basket as the downed helicopter occupies the entire landing area.

Captain Baskins has Third Platoon pop smoke and tells his RTO to direct the pilot in from the opposite direction. A gun ship follows. As the Medivac swings around from south to a north west direction, an AK fires from the draw further off to the West, coming from an area reported to contain no trails. Within seconds, the Cobra swoops down from its perch, firing rockets directly into the draw.

~~

Extraction was complete by the time darkness set in. Bravo Company spent the next two days securing the area to allow Division time to send in a crane to retrieve the burned helicopter and graves registration to complete the grisly task of identifying and removing the burned remains of Bevans and Wasserman.

The men of Bravo found themselves morally and psychologically in trouble. More than one hushed and smoldering conversation occurred about the death of Bevans and Wasserman and what each man would want done if they were in the same predicament.

CHAPTER NINE - WHAT WOULD TUCKER DO?
(OCTOBER 24, 1968 - 237 DAYS LEFT)

McKenzie flew away from Bravo Company the evening of October, twenty-four, headed for LZ Sharon on orders from the company medic to get treatment for a kidney infection. After seeing the doctor, he headed for Delta's tent to see Top Kauthorn and found him inside looking over a new roster.

KAUTHORN'S WISDOM

"Hey, Top. Guess who?"

Kauthorn turned to look. "Well, I'll be damned. A face out of the past and still in one piece. How are you doing, Lieutenant? I hear you been bouncing around a bit since you left my protection." He stood up and shook McKenzie's offered hand. "Have a seat and spill your guts, I want to hear what the hell's been going on with you. Can I buy you a beer?"

"Sure, Top. Maybe I should ask what you've heard?"

"I heard you did well with Echo but you pulled out of a mission and asked to be transferred. Now you're with Bravo. How are you getting along with Captain Baskins?"

"You're right up to speed. You know I didn't ever want to go to Echo. I belong in a line platoon. I'm not long range material. I would have given anything to come back to Delta."

"Yes, sir. You would like the new CO, Captain Gandall. He's a lot like Captain Moore, except he manages not to get under the Colonel's skin as much. So, what about Captain Baskins? You getting along with him or not?"

McKenzie shook his head, sat down on a foot locker and took a long drink of the beer Top had just handed him. He'd been told not to drink while taking antibiotics but Top didn't know that. The First Sergeant stood up and retrieved two more. McKenzie also took an offered cigarette. He had started smoking again but couldn't remember when.

"Did you know he had a water buffalo shot at LZ Jane because he wanted to barbecue it and that he has a habit of going into town for whiskey and prostitutes whenever he's back for a stand down?" McKenzie said, trying not to sound angry.

"Let me tell you something about this man's Army, Lieutenant. There ain't nothin a senior NCO doesn't know. Our communication network is the best there is and I know all about Black Gold and the people who hang around him. I also know he's got his nose shoved half way up the Colonel's ass. If you want a pile of trouble, you're in the right place."

"You know, Top. I just want to take care of my guys and get through my tour alive. I don't want to be part of some other guy's shenanigans. He's a loose cannon out in the field and I'm just trying to stay out of his way which he makes damn hard."

"So, what are you going to do out there, young Lieutenant? I'm sittin' here lookin' at you and you still a second lieutenant. What makes you think you know everything? You're the lowest carving on the totem pole. Does that tell you anything?

Maybe Captain Baskins, who, by the way, already did one tour as an infantry platoon leader, is just plain tired. I don't really know what motivates him and I don't care. It's up to his commanding officer to evaluate his performance, not me and not you. Maybe you should figure out how to get the job done and quit trying to prove you know better'n everybody else."

"That's a little harsh isn't it, Top?"

"No, it isn't. You came wanderin' in here cause you wanted to hear what I had to say, didn't you? Well, that's what I think. You got the makings of a good officer but the Army's not much different than life. There's all kinds and you got to learn to deal with it. He's an infantry company commander and he deserves that much respect. My advice is, stop trying to take him on. Learn to work around him. How the hell do you think I got where I am?"

There were no helicopters leaving for the field until the end of the day, so McKenzie sat and talked and listened until it was lunch. Top had his clerk go to the mess hall and bring back two trays. McKenzie didn't want to socialize with any other officers. He needed as much wisdom from this old soldier with the gray military crew cut as he could get and they both seemed to sense it.

BRAHMAN

Mid-afternoon, Delta ran into an ambush and McKenzie stayed to listen to the radio as Delta's new Six calmly controlled the company. They maneuvered, broke the ambush and counter attacked. An electric bolt hit him when he heard Sergeant Doll's voice. Two enemy were killed. First Platoon suffered one KIA and one WIA. The wounded man was Brahman, the kid he'd caught sleeping at Bien An. Brahman was inbound on Medivac and McKenzie decided to go down to meet it.

Listening to the radio in Delta's tent, after months in the field, the war seemed unreal. When McKenzie had first arrived, back in June, combat was ominous, unknown and dangerous. Now, after seeing the war in its most frenetic, chaotic setting, this felt so sanitized. Just words and sounds over the radio. No wonder some senior officers could view the war on a map and think only of tactics. He knew there had to be good officers who suffered over their decisions but he could recognize truth when he saw it. This was exactly how Black Knight did it. He was out of harm's way and had no concept of what it was like on the ground. McKenzie exited into the glaring sun looking for the helipad and seething.

Medical personnel were already waiting. As the pilot carefully settled his aircraft, blood ran across the flat, corrugated surface of the deck and spilled over the edge in thin, red water falls. Two dead soldiers lay wrapped in ponchos. The medics were loading Brahmin onto a litter when McKenzie stepped along side.

"Hey, LT. What the hell you doin here?" Brahmin said, raising up onto an elbow, not showing any pain.

"I came over to see how you're doin. How bad is it?"

"Oh, it's not too bad but its my third and I only got thirty days to go, so hopefully, I'm out of the field."

"Well, I'm happy for you. How is it out there? You know, I worry about you guys since you broke my cherry."

"It don't mean nothin, LT. One Five's got us working good. We been through two LTs since you left. How you been?"

"I got moved over to Bravo but I'm still One Six. Listen. If I don't see you again, you have a good life, OK?"

"Hey, LT. I never did thank you for shakin' up my shit when you first came in. After that I decided to be a better soldier and I did. It was 'cause a you," Brahmin said.

"Like you say, Brahmin, it don't mean nothin. What ever you did, you did yourself. Take care."

Brahman lay back. His face had started to show the hurt. He didn't look back but he raised his right hand to say goodbye as the medics carried him up the hill.

WASHING UP

When McKenzie finally got out the next day, he found Bravo set up on the worst forward operating base yet. Everything seemed out of whack. He could hear laughing and shouting around the perimeter as the helicopter noise faded. It looked like one of the boy scout overnight camp outs on Mt. Hood. Smoke rose from a central fire pit and no one seemed to be on alert.

Captain Baskins was lying on his back, eyes closed, his head under the shade of a poncho half held up by stakes. McKenzie walked over to the forward observer, First Lieutenant Closter, to ask what the hell was going on. Someone in Third Platoon started laughing loud.

"Shut up!", McKenzie said. "All of you. What the hell do you think you're doin? Maybe we should invite Charlie into camp?"

"Cool it, One Six," he heard Baskins say in a low, deep voice. When he turned to look, Black Gold Six had not moved, his eyes still closed. "Did you get - uh - yourself fixed up or not?"

"Yes, I did," McKenzie said. He turned and walked away.

He found Sergeant Fordham going through new supplies.

"What the hell's been going on out here?"

"Same 'ol, same 'ol, LT. This is how it runs. We set up on bad FOBs, we wander around not sure what to do and hoping we don't find it or it don't find us. I got you a new, extra radio battery to carry," Sergeant Fordham said.

Top Kauthorn was right. Better for McKenzie to work on his squad leaders than to fight Black Gold Six. If the company was going to walk in circles, it was his job to see that they do so safely, even if they were trailing around the jungle under failed leadership. Fordham told him there was no urgent mission on the horizon. Second Platoon had discovered a large mountain stream and Six had decided they would stay put so each platoon could have baths.

"Meaning?" McKenzie said.

"Its my understanding, Second and Third Platoons are going over to wash up tomorrow and we're supposed to stay here," Fordham said.

"Let them do their thing, One Five. I'd just as soon stay away from whatever they're up to anyway. Have the squad leaders check weapons and ammunition and I'll do a weapons inspection while we got time," McKenzie said, looking around to see how the perimeter was laid out.

After he completed the weapons inspection, McKenzie lay down. His back was hurting from the fall he took after launching himself backwards to avoid the helicopter that killed Wasserman and Bevans. At first, he thought the pain was part of his kidney infection but now it was obvious this was different.

Morning brought a realization his back had not endured the ground well. No matter which way he moved, it would seize up. He watched Second and Third Platoons move out with Six in tow. Fordham shifted men to fill in around the perimeter.

"Hey, One Six. You should have seen that. You would have thought they were going to the beach at Vung Tau. They had their towels and soap out before they left. I hope they have sense enough to set out good security before they get all naked and stupid in this deal," Fordham said when he returned.

"I saw it, One Five but I bet Six isn't any more interested in getting his butt shot off than we are. They'll be OK. I guess, if the shit hits the fan, we'll just have to go riding in on our white horses and save their asses." McKenzie said, trying to sit up but only getting as far as his elbow. "Shit, my back hurts. I thought it was the kidney infection but I think I hurt it when I dove off that hill to get away from that damned, crazy helicopter," he said.

"You gonna have to go back in?" Fordham said.

"No! I just got back. I'll ask Doc to request some pain pills or muscle relaxers or something. If that comes out, I should be OK."

McKenzie lay back and closed his eyes. He thought about getting some breakfast but the next thing he knew, he was awakened by Second Platoon returning. They could be heard long before they arrived, talking among themselves and laughing. Their point man had his weapon held by the end of the barrel, resting on his shoulder. Most were in tee shirts or shirtless. Two Six came over and looked down at McKenzie.

"Your turn, buddy boy. Its a beautiful stream. By the time you arrive, it should be all cleared up. You're gonna love it," he said.

McKenzie rolled over, put both hands on the ground and got to his feet, then squatted down to stretch his lower back. One Five walked over and picked up his pack for him. What they saw when they arrived at the stream was unbelievable. Clothes were hung on trees and members of Third Platoon were still in the stream, bathing and splashing each other. Fordham moved quickly to check the perimeter and set out security posts.

Captain Baskins was sitting on the bank, in the one area where filmy sunlight had sneaked through the over hanging trees. He was smoking a cigar and leaning back against his pack watching the melee in the water. It was a good sized stream with a large pool created by a wall of rocks piled across to create a dam - probably a favorite location for traveling NVA.

Fordham came back. "Guess what, LT, no security on the incoming trail so I took care of that. I say we wash up quick and get the hell out of here."

"I don't like the whole thing but these guys are sure having a good time and maybe Six is right. Intel says there's no one in the area and the company's been through a lot losing Bevans and Wasserman. Get the men organized so they can bathe in shifts and then you and me are gonna walk the perimeter again," McKenzie said.

"You got it, LT. I'll get everyone lined up and then you and me can wait for the water to clear and enjoy the water by ourselves, alone."

"I like the way you think, One Five."

After walking the perimeter, they both sat down to watch the commotion. It was just as he had imagined flying in to An Khe months earlier. Only this wasn't a bomb crater. It was a stream in the Annamite Mountains, where naked soldiers from all over the United States, from every background, ethnic persuasion and experience, bathed together, stripped out of their military identity, tan torsos and untanned bottoms, cleaning up and enjoying the moment. There were no squads, no privates, no sergeants and no officers. These were only American boys, like they were before being sent to Vietnam.

Rank has its privilege they say. After the others were out and the water had cleared, he and Fordham walked into the pool with their bars of soap, towels hung on a nearby tree and enjoyed themselves. They got a few cat calls but they turned a deaf ear. McKenzie soaped up from head to toe and then slowly squatted down to rinse in the cool water and soak his back. Fordham had his eyes closed as he scrubbed his head, stopping to dig at his scalp. He was humming and scrubbing.

Men in the military are used to communal showers but this nakedness was something else. It was what they were reduced to if they wanted to bathe in the jungle. They had to take off their uniforms, lay down their weapons and rely on others to protect them. McKenzie allowed himself to succumb to the strength in that.

BUNKER COMPLEX

Bravo company wandered around for a few more days. On October, Twenty First, they made a combat assault into an area where Echo reported seeing seventeen NVA and hearing bunker construction. Both Bravo and Alpha Companies came into the same LZ. Each company was assigned an Echo soldier as scout. By mid-afternoon, Alpha Company, call sign "Foggy Day," was lost and Black Knight was growing impatient.

He called in naval gunfire on the complex. Both companies were told they would be going in for a damage assessment when the bombardment was over. Bravo sat and listened to the heavy, sixteen inch rounds arrive from the ship off shore and lumber overhead. They sounded like freight trains in the air and the explosions were huge. McKenzie looked at the area where smoke began to rise and reached for his binoculars.

"That's not where we were headed, is it?" he said to Fordham, who had come up the trail. "Check with Six and see where he's puttin' that stuff. That looks to be about a half click too far to the North."

After a short conversation with Black Gold Six India, Fordham reported, "That's right where he says the old man wants them."

"Great. Well, its a good thing Foggy Day is way to the South, out of harm's way. Its going to be an interesting day, One Five."

Bravo was then ordered to stay put while Alpha went in for the BDA alone. When they arrived late in the afternoon, Echo's guide immediately declared the area was not right, plus there were no bunkers there. Cavalier had come on station and reported taking fire from an area approximately five hundred meters away. When Black Gold Six demanded clarification, the pilot responded angrily that he knew AK bullets when he saw them and he could see partially built bunkers through the canopy.

The radio came alive. Black Knight instructed Bravo to move within five hundred meters of the correct sight, spend the night and prepare to move into the complex in the morning. Alpha was told to move and set up a blocking force. Bravo would then push through, hopefully driving the enemy toward Foggy Day. It was a plan that made McKenzie nervous. Bravo's Echo guide was Wallace. They needed to talk.

During the evening, Wallace described as much of the terrain as he could remember. It was a typical hillside camp with room for a full company or larger. He speculated there would be spider holes and slit fighting bunkers. McKenzie decided that Mack's squad would take point. He would move up and walk as their sixth man. He told Lawrence to tape down his antenna and walk two men back.

They moved out at eight sharp. Point quickly found an intersection of trails showing heavy traffic. They were still three hundred meters from the objective. Point man took a knee. McKenzie moved up. He heard an AK open up in the direction of Foggy Day. Then a Chinese machine gun began to chatter off in the distance and an M-60 answered. The fire fight grew. It sounded as if everyone was firing at once. Grenade launcher rounds mixed with B-40 rockets. McKenzie could hear men shouting in the background of radio transmissions as they always do.

Foggy Day reported they had three KIA and its First Platoon was pinned down. The bunker complex was larger than anticipated and Foggy Day asked Black Gold to move up. Captain Baskins instructed McKenzie to pop smoke when they reached the complex to avoid cross fire. McKenzie turned to Mack.

"This has got the makings of becoming a real cluster. We're not going to walk in on this trail. You take Second Squad up to the left. I'll move with Third to the right. If we make contact, do not try to move forward. Just deal with the contact first and we'll pop smoke. Go."

Black Gold Six suddenly moved Second and Third Platoons off to the left which put them in between First Platoon and Alpha Company. Gun fire slowed to sporadic. McKenzie stopped First Platoon. This was not developing well. ARA came in and put rockets directly onto the complex which allowed Alpha to pull out their KIAs but they paid a heavy price. Now they had five WIAs.

Black Gold Six orders Second Platoon to move directly into the complex with a frontal assault while swinging Third Platoon around to push in across the area where Alpha had been. He tells First Platoon to hold but McKenzie keeps moving closer. First Platoon stops on a small rise above the complex where they can see what's happening. They watch in disbelief as Second Platoon begins to move from their left across the trail and up the other side.

"Jesus! What are they doing?", McKenzie says out loud.

Three men walk across first. The lead soldier approaches an obvious bunker and stops. An NVA soldier raises up and shoots him in the chest. He falls backwards. Someone behind him kills the NVA. Cranahan, the Second Platoon medic, runs across the trail and up the hill. Another NVA soldier fires from the same bunker killing him. Second Platoon is now on the ground with two dead and three others looking for cover.

McKenzie motions Third Squad up as another fire team from Second tries to cross the trail and is hit by intense fire from further up the hill. Mack and two others run from the right toward the top bunker, firing directly into the opening. Watson pulls pins on two grenades, lets the handles spring free and rolls them in. The top of the bunker collapses. Gibney rises up and fires a LAW directly into the lower bunker which blows the roof straight up in the air. Three NVA exit a third bunker and run over the top of the hill. Cavalier spots them and follows with mini-guns blazing. It's over. The rest of the afternoon is spent clearing four other bunkers and medivac'ing Second Platoon's two KIAs and five WIAs. For what they accomplished and the men they lost, this operation is a bust. McKenzie cusses Black Knight in his head.

~~

WHAT WOULD TUCKER DO?

McKenzie's back had become worse. He informed Captain Baskins of the problem. All he got was a grunt. Matters between them were coming to a head. He thought about Tucker, his high school coach and wondered what he would do in this situation. He was a big man with an easy, infectious laugh. Tucker always knew who he was and what he expected of others. His discipline was swift but fair and his encouragements large.

McKenzie was smaller than most kids. All he did during his sophomore year in football was collect slivers riding the bench. The first time he met Tucker was his first day of PE. Another student threw a baseball glove hitting McKenzie in the balls and he had chased the kid down. Coach Tucker called him over to where the glove lay on the ground.

"Pick up the glove," he said.

"It's not my glove and I didn't throw it," McKenzie growled.

Tucker grabbed him by the back of the neck with a big hand and shoved his face into the dirt next to the glove. "Pick it up," he said. It took twenty minutes in that position before McKenzie's stubbornness was defeated by Coach Tucker's desire to make a point. He told his Dad about the incident that night. His Dad's only question was why hadn't he picked up the glove when he was told to. He'd said it without looking up from his plate of food.

Coach Tucker called McKenzie off the bench half way through the fourth quarter of the last junior varsity game. "Go in as a defensive guard," he said. McKenzie weighed only one hundred and fifty pounds, was slow and had wanted to be a fullback, not a line man. He was mystified by this opportunity to get beat up by bigger boys.

He was surprised to find he had a knack of getting around the opposing players and sacked the quarterback twice before the game ended. He'd even managed to get in on three tackles. He'd been shoved around good and had his face buried in the mud more than once but that wasn't important.

The faith Coach Tucker had placed in McKenzie that day changed his life. Most of the confidence he had, his ethics and how he defined himself as a person, were given to him by Coach Tucker. It was not an exaggeration to say that he felt he needed to live up to those expectations in Vietnam. When he considered his predicament with Captain Baskins and wondered what Tucker would do, the answer was easy. He would not have compromised his principles. McKenzie would follow orders unless his men were placed in unreasonable jeopardy, then he would find the right thing to do, even at risk to himself.

FAMILIAR TERRITORY

The company was in a stupor. They had no mission and soldiers were trying to put feelings of loss behind them with casualties piling up. The next day was October, Twenty Seven and again, there did not seem to be any real target or mission. The company moved east toward an area between LZ Jane and the mountains. First Platoon was last in line. Scrub brush covered sandy ground with clumps of grass here and there. The air hung heavy around them as the sun heated up the previous night's rain fall. Heat waves appeared even closer than normal.

"Its amazing how Six always makes the mission sound as if we're going to assault Mount Suribachi on Iwo Jima, especially when there's no real target," McKenzie said to Lawrence as they moved along.

Second Platoon reported a wide trail heading into an area of cultivated fields with no inhabitants. Farmers usually commuted from their village to the field early in the morning. There were none to be seen.

"This feels like we're sitting ducks, One Six," Lawrence said.

The column continued to move until they turned back west and McKenzie realized they were now headed straight toward the first area he had been in with Delta. When he called Black Gold Six and told him he was familiar with the valley up ahead and stressed the dangerousness of walking into the bottom, he got cut off.

A half hour later, walking through taller grass toward thicker trees, McKenzie knew they were heading into the same long valley where White was killed.

"This is idiotic." McKenzie said. "Lawrence, call Six again."

"Black Gold Six, this is One Six, India. My Six is sure of our location. Bravo needs to change direction of movement. Over."

"One Six India, that's a negative. I'm gonna call a marking round so you can get reoriented, Over." Captain Baskins sounded agitated.

"Roger that. Out."

McKenzie waved the platoon down to one knee. Within a few minutes they heard a marking round in the air but could not see it.

"Call Six India and give him the right coordinates, Lawrence." He pointed to the map. Soon another round came in from LZ Jane and flew directly overhead.

Sergeant Fordham, who had come up and was kneeling next to McKenzie, said, "Well, I guess that answers that shit." He chuckled the belly laugh McKenzie was starting to grow fond of. "There will be hell to pay for being right, LT," he said in a low voice.

RADIOS AND BATTERIES

Second Platoon secured an overnight position away from the valley approach. It was sixteen hundred hours before First Platoon reached the perimeter. Two Six had located near a small stream next to a trail which ran through a swale. Another example of Baskin's uncanny knack for picking one of the worst places on the map.

He needed a private conversation with his company commander and asked if they could move away from the others. They walked over to an area of the perimeter between positions. Baskins turned and said in a laconic voice, "Go ahead."

"I want an apology, Six," McKenzie said. "Every time I offer something you practically call me a liar. I know we started off wrong but I'm trying my best here and I cannot be an effective leader if you keep putting me down in front of my men. I knew where we were and instead of listening to me, you assumed I was wrong." McKenzie said it all as earnestly as he could. Baskins rubbed his head.

"OK. I'm sorry. Is that what you want? Let's see what happens with you from now on. I want you on my team and nobody else's. You're still on my shit list, so this changes nothing. If you defy me, you are gone. Are we clear?"

"Yes, sir. We are clear."

When McKenzie returned to his CP, Fordham was more animated than usual.

"LT, this is crap. We're right up against this tree line. Everyone else is out a hundred miles from here. I've walked out front and there are a couple of old trails coming right at us. They don't look like they've seen recent use but you never know. Second platoon is on the other side of that rock pile and Third is down the other side of that hill. If we get hit from any direction, Charlie will be inside this perimeter before we know it and we won't know who is who. I can't believe this." Sergeant Fordham was obviously worked up.

"Calm down, One Five. Second and Third have good NCOs and they'll do the best they can. Set up rallying points with those other platoons and agree on a signal to rally. That way, we'll have a better chance of defending if we get hit. Then, establish a second line of defense inside the perimeter. Load up on trip flares and claymores and make sure your fields of fire intersect deeper than usual with Second and Third and don't make a big deal out of it. I don't want another fight with Six. Just do it among the platoon sergeants," McKenzie said.

When Fordham returned, McKenzie was bent over a helmet full of heated water trying to shave with a Red Cross mirror and the available light. He was having trouble because of his back. He straightened up slowly and looked at Fordham who was grinning.

"They all agreed, LT. Since Six is sitting right in the middle of this mother, he won't have to move if we get hit. Three Six was there and so I let him in on it. I think he's tired of Six also. He called him Weird Harold. The rallying signal is a hand flair in the air."

"Good job, One Five." McKenzie said before slowly bending over to finish his shave.

"By the way," Fordham said in a manner that made McKenzie look up. "On my way back here, Six India stopped me and wants to know if you have that extra battery you always carry. Six also wants your radio."

"What?" McKenzie straightened back up.

"Both of Six's radios are dead. You believe that, LT?"

"He wants my radio and my extra battery? How does he know I carry one?", said McKenzie.

"Everybody knows that, LT."

"Well, there's a very good reason why. Anything can interfere with resupply and that radio is the only means we have of requesting a fire mission or ARA or Medivac or whatever. This company was resupplied yesterday and the company commander of an infantry company in Vietnam has two dead radios and no back up batteries? You gotta be shittin' me! Does either of our RTOs have an extra battery?" McKenzie said.

Fordham shook his head. "No, I already checked."

"Can we get resupply first thing in the morning? Top's sending a chopper out so I can go in and have someone look at this back. I'm not going anywhere if we don't get new batteries."

"Yea, I already called Top, LT. He's puttin' another resupply together as we speak. I also asked him for two extra batteries. I'm gonna start carrying one too."

"OK. Give Six my extra battery and take my radio. We still got your radio but no one goes out on ambush tonight without a good radio."

McKenzie pulled the battery out of his backpack, took it out of the plastic bag, handed it to Fordham and went back to his shaving. He was so angry, he cut himself twice. After rinsing his face, he threw the water on the ground, rinsed out his steel pot, replaced the helmet liner and sat down to look at his terrain map. There was no way he was going to send anyone out into the jungle at night without a radio and he wanted new batteries before they moved out the next day.

SECURITY AMBUSH

A half hour before dusk, Fordham came walking from the direction of the company CP. "I got more bad news, LT," he said. "Six wants us to send out a security ambush on this side and the battery on my radio is getting weak. I just checked it."

"Well, that's not going to work." McKenzie said. He stood slowly and went looking for Captain Baskins who was busy heating a can of ham and lima beans over an empty cracker tin filled with C-4 instead of a heat tab. It was a practice McKenzie was trying to break his own men of. Unless the company carried extra C-4, soldiers would rob the explosive from the back of a claymore mine by unscrewing the back plate. It burned hotter and faster than a heat tab but the practice rendered the mine useless.

McKenzie stood out of the light for several minutes watching the captain. He was squatted down on his haunches like a captured VC. McKenzie simply had no respect for the man. He stepped into the light. Baskins stood up quickly when he saw McKenzie approach.

"If I'm sending out a security ambush tonight, Six, I need a good radio. The one I have left is getting weak. I would like my radio back for the patrol. You will still have one with my fresh battery in it. Is that OK?"

"No. That's not OK, One Six." Baskins stood there with the plastic fork held gingerly between his right forefinger and thumb.

"Then, have Two Six or Three Six send out the ambush," McKenzie said, feeling the anger rise inside him.

"Not their turn," Baskins said dismissively.

The two of them were standing in the middle of the FOB. It had been raining for the past hour and palm shaped leaves were producing waterfalls, filling the air with dripping sounds. Others at the company CP stopped what they were doing and watched the two men. McKenzie hesitated for a moment, then reached for his radio. Baskins picked it up quickly and hugged it with both arms like a personal teddy bear about to be taken away from a small boy.

"Lieutenant, I'm giving you a direct order. Your platoon has perimeter ambush tonight and you get your men gathered up right now and get their asses out there. You understand? Don't tell me about no radio. The NVA and VC do it all the time," Baskins said.

McKenzie was furious. "Six! If they hit the shit, we will have no way of knowing what's happening. I will have no way of knowing if they're coming back inside the perimeter and someone might get shot. You failed to properly resupply, not me. Now give me my damn radio or my good battery and I will be happy to send them out on ambush." McKenzie reached out and grabbed the radio strap on the side.

"Lieutenant! Either you do what I say or you are relieved."

McKenzie let go, turned around and walked back to the area of First Platoon. He sat down with his back against a large, gray boulder. He wasn't sure this was the right issue to have a show down over but he was mad as hell. He unsnapped the buck knife he carried on his belt and removed the blade from its scabbard. It was one of those items he thought he needed when he went to the PX at Fort Benning. He had the sergeant behind the counter put a razor sharp edge on it. The blade was made of hard carbon steel that would not dull easily. He ran his thumb over the edge carefully and considering his predicament, then called his leaders together.

Most soldiers were finishing their sleeping areas, eating, cleaning weapons or writing home. Sergeant Mack showed up in a tee shirt and a green head band. Sergeant Gibney had been working and reported that the perimeter trip flares and claymores were all in. He was sweating hard. Sergeant Campbell came without a shirt, his wash time having been interrupted. A green towel was draped over his right shoulder.

McKenzie looked up at them, studying each in turn, taking their measure. Not one was a slacker. They were leaders in different ways.

"Here's the deal, men. Six wants an ambush out tonight and we have no radio."

"So. What's he want us to do about it, LT? said Mack. "You get us a radio and we'll be there but no radio and you can tell the old man to do it himself."

"He gave me a direct order, Sergeant Mack."

"Then I think there's more than one guy in my squad that won't go," Mack said. "I agree," said Gibney.

"Here's what I want," McKenzie said, pausing to look at each of them. "First Squad will put out an ambush but only about thirty meters, within sight of the perimeter. They will take a flashlight and if they need to come into the perimeter, they will flash three times, pause, then flash once and wave the light back and forth. Like a railroad engineer at a crossing. The password is anaconda."

By nineteen hundred, the ambush was in place. McKenzie looked at the tree line which was heavy and thick. He had gone out earlier and looked at the trails. Both came directly into his area of the perimeter as Fordham had described. He placed the squad between them, more of a listening post than an ambush. He was not going to send them out any further.

The conflict with Captain Haskins had now escalated to a point somewhere close to fighting him every step of the way, a proposition that could only cascade over onto his platoon. This felt like he was being set up. He wanted to draw the line but knew he would be risking relief of command, which might leave the platoon with no officer or worse, a replacement that buys the drill and snaps to without any idea of protecting his men.

The reason some platoon leaders were fragged was a matter of survival. If the platoon leader, the last person between the grunt and a stupid order, decides to do whatever he is told without considering his men or the alternatives, there is no other way in some soldier's mind. Get rid of him and hope for the best from his replacement.

Captain Baskins showed up two hours later. "What's the status of your ambush, One Six?" he said gruffly.

"I put them out about two hours ago," McKenzie said.

"I want to know where they are, One Six."

McKenzie had been eating C-ration crackers and mucky moo when Black Gold Six showed up. He put the meal on the ground and stood up.

"I put them out about thirty meters where I can have direct contact with them in case there is a problem. We have signals and a password to get them back in if need be," McKenzie said.

"That's not what I asked you to do, is it?"

"Well, under the circumstances, we have no radio, Six."

Captain Baskins started walking in a small circle cussing to himself. He came back over to McKenzie.

"I told you perimeter ambush and that means down the trail, not sitting right out in front. It appears you are committed to do whatever the hell you want. I said if you didn't do exactly what I ordered you to do, you would be relieved. When the helicopter picks you up in the morning, don't come back. Just don't come back!" He thrust an index finger at McKenzie's chest.

RELIEVED

McKenzie stood in silence after Captain Baskins turned and walked away. The inevitable had happened and he had been set up. There was no way he was going to operate the way Six wanted him to but he had let his men down. He had tried and now they would have to endure Six on their own until another lieutenant was brought in.

Maybe he could get Black Knight to intervene. Surely the Cave Killer reports and these last series of goof ups in the field would be enough to convince Black Knight he needed to get his company commander in line, not the lieutenants. They were just trying to do their job and protect their men. He would talk to Black Knight when he got back to LZ Nancy.

Word spread quickly. Lawrence was first to say something.

"Don't worry LT. We know you did what you thought was best for us. That's all we could ask for. Don't take any wooden nickels at LZ Nancy. If they want to know what went on out here, you tell them to ask me. I ain't afraid of Six," Lawrence said.

CHAPTER 10 - III CORPS (TAY NINH)
(OCTOBER 29, 1968 - 232 DAYS LEFT IN COUNTRY)

Lieutenant McKenzie had been with Bravo Company from September 21 until the morning of October 29, only thirty-eight days. It seemed like an eternity to him, battling Captain Haskins for the lives and souls of his platoon. He felt lost as the helicopter lifted him away. His orders were to report to Black Knight Six when he arrived but it did not concern him as it had before. He would check in at the infirmary first. His back was extremely painful.

LEAVING BRAVO

The night before was difficult but without unnecessary emotion. Six's rage had appeared sated as he did not insist the ambush move after all. Disappointment over losing their platoon leader was muted.

Sergeant Gibney said, "Its better than having to toss you into a body bag, One Six."

Black Gold Six was due to rotate in December and Fordham philosophized,

"God willing and the creek don't rise, maybe we'll get an early Christmas present like a company commander we can look up to."

"What if you don't?" McKenzie said.

"Hell, LT. I don't think it could be any worse than what we got now. I figure we got fairly good odds at improving our situation," Fordham said.

Gibney agreed, "We kept you alive didn't we? That's sayin something and we didn't have to deal with Parkinson any more. I see the last month as a kind of vacation. You took on Six and it don't get no better'n that. We'll just hunker down and keep on keepin' on. Maybe they'll find you some cush job so you won't have to do any more humpin' in the boonies."

"Right, Sarge. I don't think so. Maybe they'll send me back to Delta Company. I hear their new CO is OK. Charlie Company's also got a new Six and word is, he's a good one. I'm kinda running out of companies. I'll promise you all one thing. If Black Knight has any idea of bringing this down on me, we're gonna have a heart to heart discussion about water buffalos, drunken trips off the LZ, getting lost in the jungle and radios with no batteries," McKenzie said.

That got a good laugh from everyone standing around. Quiet talk extended long into the night and goodbyes were said. McKenzie did not want a big show in the morning. After all, Black Knight could end up sending him back. Sergeant Fordham removed a leather bracelet he made before coming to Vietnam and had worn every day, handing it to McKenzie. He said it was good luck and he wanted to share it.

Just before McKenzie ran toward the waiting log bird, he handed his Swiss Army Knife to Sergeant Fordham. He was the only platoon sergeant he'd been with who was still standing. He looked down as the pilot lifted straight up out of the trees.

Fordham was waving his arm back and forth in a rare show of emotion and Captain Baskins was sitting on his helmet against a tree with his head down, rubbing it.

Cool air pushed against his face like freedom. Vietnam was such a bizarre experience. Down on the ground every dark corner was dangerous, yet up in the air, it was beautiful. He leaned out and looked straight down at the ground whizzing by and almost fell out. It didn't scare him anymore. It was all wrapped tightly into his fate.

LZ NANCY

McKenzie could see LZ Nancy was a busy place. The infirmary orderly told him the entire Division was moving south, somewhere near Saigon. Thirty minutes later with pain pills and muscle relaxers in hand, he went to meet with Black Knight. He found the TOC empty of staff officers. Colonel Fishmuth and his senior officers had flown out to Camp Evans for a command briefing. The battalion sergeant major was cryptic.

"Colonel Fishmuth may not have time to meet with you for a couple of days," he said. "He's got bigger issues but he knows about you coming in. I suggest you check out of Bravo and report to Charlie Company. That's where you're going."

Checking out of Bravo was painless. First Sergeant Balcom was the same, taciturn, sullen NCO as always. McKenzie asked for a copy of Bravo's roster. It was given reluctantly.

"I guess Bravo Company didn't work out too good for you, huh?" Sergeant Balcom said.

"No, Top, it didn't. I guess you know as much about that as I do."

McKenzie sat down and wrote up Gibney, Watson and Mack for their action attacking the bunkers, recommending all three for Bronze Stars with V. He had made several other recommendations over the last month that had not been approved. He wasn't sure if Black Gold was the cause for delay but he would monitor these submissions. Recommendations were usually acted upon quickly and soldiers received their medals in formal ceremonies presented by field grade officers. The higher the medal, the higher the rank of the presenting officer.

The next two days were spent resting his back, getting resupplied, writing letters and consuming as much beer as he could lay his hands on. He found various military newspapers such as the Army Times and Stars and Stripes, lying around. He reluctantly scanned the names of casualties looking for OCS friends.

All was good until the morning of November 1st, when he found an old copy of The Observer, published by MACV. In it was a list of casualties. It was dated August 10, 1968. After breakfast, before the sun managed to rev up, McKenzie sat down to read through his new find.

O'KUSKY

Lieutenant O'Kusky, his friend from Camp Evans was listed in the second row of names. O'Kusky had gone to the First of the Ninth and had died on July, First, only fourteen days after landing in country and only ten days after they said goodbye to each other.

It made his stomach queasy. His mind dragged itself reluctantly back to when he had arrived so long ago. O'Kusky had seemed a little lost and McKenzie recalled wishing that O'Kusky, only twenty years old, would make it. He closed his eyes but had to open them quickly. The vision he saw was Sergeant Smythe dangling at the end of the extraction line.

O'Kusky had been over weight and anxious. Did he make a mistake? Was he put into a bad situation? How could he have died so soon? He was like Private Wright. He'd had no time to learn from his mistakes. He'd been thrown into combat and died. That was it. McKenzie's throat tightened up as tears welled up in his eyes.

He had passed over sometime in the last month to a middle zone where he could be numb. He had not looked at the body of a dead soldier and felt like crying for a long time. People came and went. It had begun with Koop and Kemper. Once a soldier was dead, they ceased to have existed. Only the living held meaning.

He had not cried for Sergeant Smythe. His death had only made him angry because dead soldiers were a tactical problem. They could not be left behind and others risked their lives making sure the body was sent home. Months of training and experience went away with each dead soldier, replaced by someone who knew nothing.

Emotions he had buried deep were suddenly threatening to seep up from his gut like reverse peristalsis as he sat there remembering Wright and O'Kusky and Buggs and Wasserman and even, Sergeant Smythe. Metallic saliva filled his throat as he stared at the name of his friend. Where were Kregor and Kingman? He would have to stop looking for names. He couldn't afford to slip out of the middle zone.

Too late. He saw the one name he feared most. His friend Lt. Rose was also dead. The gentle one. The one that should have been sent to act as press liaison or supply officer but not to the infantry. His eyes filled with tears and he sat there for a long time trying to stop the crying. He reached for his canteen, took a long drink and poured water into his right hand, rubbing it over his face. He would go check in with Charlie Company.

CHARLIE COMPANY

He found First Sergeant Whitlock packing up the company tent. They had talked briefly the first day he arrived.

"Good morning, Lieutenant. You talked with Colonel Fishmuth yet?" Whitlock said.

"No, Top. Nobody's said nothin to me yet. I was wondering why I don't just get on a bird and go out to the field. The Colonel's obviously too busy right now. You got any more information on this move?"

"Yep. Sergeant Major says we're all going to Three Corps between Saigon and the Cambodian border. Division's gonna be located at a place called Phuoc Vinh and the brigades are gonna be spread out between Tay Ninh and Quan Loi. Its gonna happen quick. The First Cav is being sent down to stop Uncle Ho from moving troops out of Cambodia toward Saigon. Ever hear of the Parrot's Beak or the Fishhook along the Cambodian border?"

"Can't say as I have, Top. Why?"

"Cause that's where you're going, sir. Its not like I Corps. Its flat with bamboo which can hide a ton of NVA and VC."

"You're full of cheery information. So, when are we moving?"

"In two days. All companies in First of the Fifth are gonna be pulled out of the field and flown out to Camp Evans. From there, we're all gettin' on C-130s and fly straight in to Tay Ninh. I called Six earlier and he said you might as well stay here and travel down with me. We'll meet up with the company there."

"Wow. This is big. What can I do to help you, Top?"

"Nothin, sir. I got it under control. If I was you, I'd relax and enjoy this break. The whole Division is moving in twelve days total. It might just turn into a huge mess."

III CORPS

With time on his hands, McKenzie found a map of III Corps, glad to have something to do. Phuoc Vinh was about sixty kilometers north of Saigon and Tay Ninh City was a little farther to the Northwest. Tay Ninh Province was huge and sat directly along the border of Cambodia. If there were concentrations of enemy across the border, it did not take a genius to see they would be capable of building up quickly for attacks on American units. The First Air Cavalry Division was being placed directly between the NVA and Saigon. Was this going to be another Khe Sanh or I Drang Valley?

One more day came and went. He was enjoying his stay at LZ Nancy until Black Knight sent word for him to report to his command tent. It was nineteen thirty on November, Second. Most of the day had been spent resting a back that was feeling much better. He had not yet gone to the beer tent.

When McKenzie stepped inside the command center, he could see the desks and radios were gone except for one. Colonel Fishmuth was walking toward the entrance and looked up just as McKenzie appeared.

"Let's step over here, Lieutenant," he said as he walked out and away from the tent up a small hill that overlooked the ammo dump. Below them was a huge mountain of empty artillery canisters. The Colonel turned around.

"I'm going to send you to Charlie Company," he said in a low voice. " It seems you need a little more structure than you were getting at Bravo. Their new CO is West Point and I have confidence in him. I'm gonna consider this a clean slate, Lieutenant McKenzie. You go out to Charlie Company and finish your tour and we'll leave it at that."

"Sir? Do you know what happened between me and Captain Baskins?" McKenzie said.

Colonel Fishmuth shifted his feet slightly and looked up at an approaching Cobra gunship. He watched it fly over the LZ while McKenzie waited. When he looked back his hairless eyebrows and forehead were wrinkled into a frown above dark eyes and his ever twitching nose.

"Lieutenant, I know more than you think I do. As I said, I'm transferring you and we're just gonna leave it at that. That's what you want, isn't it?" His thin lips looked knife sharp.

"Frankly, sir. I was getting my platoon well trained and I hated to leave them this way but I don't see my ever getting along with Black Gold. So, yes, that's probably the best thing unless Delta has an opening."

"No!" Colonel Fishmuth said, shouting into McKenzie's face. "You are going to Charlie Company. Now, I have work to do. Unless you have something else, Lieutenant, you are dismissed."

"No, sir. Thank you sir." McKenzie said. He saluted Black Knight Six who returned it unenthusiastically.

The whole thing felt like a nullity. There were still hot issues that needed to be addressed. McKenzie had no way of knowing whether he could let them go. He was dismayed that Captain Baskins would simply be allowed to continue unchecked and in command of troops. He probably wasn't the worse but he certainly wasn't a credit to the reputation and prestige of the First Cav. McKenzie needed a beer. No, he needed several beers.

McKenzie woke up the next morning around nine nursing a significant hangover and headed over to Charlie Company. The tent had been struck and folded. Conex containers stood open where Top Whitlock was loading the last of his files and equipment.

"Good morning, Top," McKenzie said.

"Oh, there's my new platoon leader. I thought you were gonna miss the boat. We're getting picked up at eleven hundred. You ready to go?"

"Yep. I had my discussion with the Colonel and I guess I'm all yours."

"Great. Meet me down at the helicopter pad fifteen minutes before and we'll catch a ride to Camp Evans," Whitlock said.

LZ Sharon was definitely closing down. Most tents had been struck and a large Chinook was being loaded with containers. Dozens of soldiers sat around on packs or leisurely lay against them, waiting for a ride. Helicopter traffic was heavy.

McKenzie had gained important information in the beer tent from a Division staff officer also waiting to leave. Following Operation Jeb Stuart III, enemy presence in I Corps had been greatly damaged. Saigon was now the big worry and General Abrams, the new MACV commander, was determined to prevent any threat to the capital of Vietnam. Division intelligence reported that four North Vietnamese regiments or larger were congregating along the border of Cambodia. General Abrams had decided to move the First and Twenty-fifth Divisions out and bring the First Air Cavalry in.

"General Abrams told General Forsythe not to worry about secrecy," the officer said. "He wants all the helicopters to keep their First Cav patches where they are so we can show the NVA that the American Army can move a whole division 600 miles in a very, short time," the staff officer explained.

CAMP EVANS

When McKenzie and Top Whitlock landed at Camp Evans, they saw a bewildering number of First Cav troopers lined up along side the airfield, maybe close to a thousand. There were also several companies of ARVN. Charlie Company was down at the far end so McKenzie and Top started to walk in front of the waiting soldiers. They passed Delta, Echo and Bravo companies, all pulled out of the field and waiting. Top moved on as McKenzie stopped to say hello to soldiers he knew in each group. He felt like the battalion good will officer except for the look he got from Black Gold Six.

Lieutenant Parkinson appeared to have adapted well with Echo and Sergeant Fordham said he'd heard they had great clubs in Tay Ninh. He promised to find McKenzie and buy him a beer. Delta Company's new CO was well liked and Lieutenant Ripple, their current One Six, was from Portland, Oregon. Sergeant Doll had gone home and Casey was now the platoon sergeant. McKenzie felt like he knew most of the battalion, except Alpha Company. He would know Charlie Company soon enough.

He immediately liked his new CO. Captain Sheldon stood six feet or more with jet black hair and a hint of New England about him. He was well spoken and affable and moved easily among the soldiers, talking and joking with them. His thin wrists indicated a life of privilege, probably blue blood lineage. He did not seem too concerned with military formality but carried himself with a sense of dignity. He had a bearing that reminded McKenzie of how General Robert E. Lee stood in formal pictures.

"I consider the reasons for your transfer irrelevant to my command," he told McKenzie. "I will judge you on your performance from this day forward."

FIRST PLATOON

The day moved slowly. Staff Sergeant Roy David, another shake-n-bake like Koop, had been running First Platoon for over a month after the previous lieutenant was killed. His accent indicated home was the Bronx, New York and he had a quick mouth. His hair was dark and curly, his skin a reflection of his Italian heritage and he appeared suspicious of McKenzie.

After walking around and talking to members of First Platoon, McKenzie settled down onto the hard tarmac pavement in their midst. As he was pulling out a LRRP meal, two South Vietnamese soldiers approached. The ARVNs had become restless and were wandering around joking with the Americans and practicing their English.

On top of McKenzie's pack was the six inch Buck knife in its black, leather sheath, tied on with a leather string. One of the ARVN stepped over a reclining soldier and reached for it. He was grinning and looking directly at McKenzie as his hand moved slowly toward the knife. McKenzie reached for his M-16, flipped the safety to full automatic, or rock and roll as the soldiers called it, lifted the barrel toward the soldier's face and smiled back.

A sneer came across the man's visage as he withdrew his hand. The other ARVN grabbed his arm and pulled him away but the soldier scowled and never took his eyes off McKenzie as he walked down the flight path.

"Oooh, LT. He didn't like that," one of the men said. "Thought he was gonna lift your knife? Looks like we got us a One Six who's a trigger happy, bad ass boys." Everyone laughed and McKenzie went back to his meal.

The ride to Tay Ninh was hot and uncomfortable. There are no leisure seats in a C-130 so the men sat on the floor along the bulk head where ever they could find room. They had been in the bush for over a month and definitely smelled like it. McKenzie had grown used to smelling clean again. The tropical sun was gonna heat up the inside of that plane and one hundred and two soldiers would sweat and stink and make the inside of that plane extremely pungent.

TAY NINH

McKenzie dropped off to sleep. When the landing woke him, the air was sour and suffocating. He got up stiffly and followed his new RTO into a climate much hotter than I Corps. The large airfield was full of numerous helicopters, some levitated and fluttering back and forth like a swarm of butterflies. The compound, which had previously housed the Twenty Fifth Division, sat shimmering in the distance, like a mirage but the soldiers happily noticed the wooden buildings with metal roofs.

The city of Tay Ninh was spread out to the left and the land in all directions was flat except for one very large mountain to the Southwest.

"Nui Ba Den. They call it the Black Virgin," said Sergeant Smith when he saw McKenzie looking at the mountain. Smith was the escort sent out to lead Charlie Company to their area. "It stands three thousand feet in the air and is made of solid granite with very little tree cover. The Twenty Fifth still has a commo station on top. Everything else is owned by the VC."

Charlie Company followed Sergeant Smith to the southern end of the compound where the men stood silently and marveled at their new homes - wooden hooches containing bunks and dry wooden floors. Sergeant Davis assigned bunks and quickly established a rotation for bunker security. With only three days before the company was expected to move out, no one would have to pull more than one shift. Those not given the first shift were free to head for the clubs or one of two PXs.

McKenzie was famished. He got directions from Sergeant Smith, dropped his gear next to a bunk and headed for the mess hall. What he found was amazing. Tables covered with red plastic table cloths filled a white walled room cooled by a large, humming air conditioner suspended in the far corner.

The yeasty bread and carrot laden beef stew got his attention. He quickly loaded his tray and picked up actual silverware, after holding and looking at each one for a quiet moment. When he turned to look for a place to sit, he almost dropped his tray.

KREGOR

Sitting two tables away was Lieutenant Kregor. McKenzie approached and stopped directly across from his friend. Kregor was examining a hamburger piled with tomatoes and lettuce. Ketchup dripped through his fingers. His uniform was worn and dirty and a dark, green bandana was tied around a sun burnt neck on top of a body that had lost at least 15 pounds since Camp Evans.

"You gonna massage that thing or eat it?" McKenzie said.

Kregor looked up with a scowl as if he'd been interrupted in the middle of performing delicate heart surgery.

"You're shitting me!" he shouted as he put down his hamburger and tried to stand up. His legs caught between the bench and the table causing him to fall backwards. The officer next to him scooted away to keep from getting dumped. McKenzie laughed and sat down his tray as Kregor swung his legs over the bench to the ground and got up.

"Its a wonder you're still in one piece, Kregor," McKenzie said.

Kregor scrambled around the table and grabbed McKenzie in a bear hug, lifting him off the ground. After releasing him, Kregor turned to the other lieutenant and said, "This is one of the first guys I met when I came in country. We went through Camp Evans together. McKenzie, this is Robinson, Second Platoon Leader in my company. By God, you made it, McKenzie."

Kregor was jumping around like a kid at the circus. They stayed away from the topic of combat through lunch. Kregor had not known about O'Kusky until then. The news left him open mouthed. His battalion was being sent up to the Fishhook. McKenzie told him that First of the Fifth was headed for Kontum, a Special Forces Camp below the border. As they left the building, Kregor stopped and McKenzie held out his hand to say goodbye.

"Not so fast, buddy boy," Kregor said. "How about you and me going down to the Philippine International Officer's Club tonight around nineteen hundred? You and me still got a lot to talk about. You know, catch up."

McKenzie agreed but he felt light headed about it. He was glad to see Kregor but afraid to feel good about it. He needed a nap. When he reached the company area, there were distinct signs his soldiers were enjoying their brief vacation. Several were quite drunk and two were sitting on the steps of their hooch with more beer. One had located a guitar and was trying to negotiate a few chords. Wilson, a member of Second Squad, had been in a fight with an Australian soldier and sat nursing a black eye.

McKenzie managed a short nap and then a long shower. He put on clean fatigues dropped on his bunk by someone and headed for the Club which he was told was located outside the US compound. The dirt road was bordered by local shops and restaurants and his decision not to bring his weapon began to make him nervous. In spite of the pit in his stomach, he did not turn around.

Some of the shop owners waved at him to come over. Other American soldiers casually worked their way along the street, including two from his platoon. Numerous Vietnamese males squatted together along side the road or sat in groups of two or three, smoking and talking. Eyes watched and followed him without heads turning, as he made his way down the road. Just like Danang, Tay Ninh City made him uneasy and short of breath. Nui Ba Den blocked out the setting sun.

PHILIPPINE INTERNATIONAL OFFICER' S CLUB

The club was magnificent - a tribute to Philippine engineering. White washed rocks lined the walkway to the front stairs. Inside, he could hear overhead fans whirring as he approached a barrier of multicolored beads separating the entrance to the bar. McKenzie parted the beads and stepped through. The floor was made of stained and polished wood. Pale, yellow, see through curtains hung on the windows. Round tables with red, cushioned chairs were occupied by officers from various countries. Vietnamese waitresses dressed in white, silken Ao Dai, the traditional dress with a split skirt over pants, were floating between the tables, leaving hints of perfume as they walked by.

He found Kregor sitting on a stool, over in the corner, at the far end of the bar. McKenzie thought of Hemingway, who liked to sit with his back to the wall in the Floridita, his favorite bar in Cuba, drinking daiquiris in rapid succession. Kregor was short and stout, the perfect stature for an infantry platoon leader in the jungle.

"So here's to this place," McKenzie said raising his first glass of scotch. "A toast to our mutual survival." He reached out and clinked Kregor's glass.

"I'll say one thing for the Philippinos, they sure know how to fight a war," Kregor said in a rather low key voice. He was usually a quiet person to be around in spite of his enthusiasm at the dining hall.

"So how's it been serving in First of the Seventh, Custer's old outfit? I see some of the officers wearing cavalry hats with yellow cords and the whole bit. They give you one of those yet?" McKenzie said.

"No. Those guys are either pilots or field grade officers. I think I'll keep my steel pot a little longer. You see much action?" Kregor's question was asked seriously and it surprised McKenzie.

"Oh, I don't know. It was a lot busier when I first got up to I Corps. How about you?"

"Man! I haven't seen shit. All the combat I've seen is one VC who ran out in the open and shot at us from a hedge row and disappeared. The rest has been small hit and miss run ins. We get shot at but no one's there. I am so tired of walking in circles, I could puke. At first, I was scared all the time. Then, after a while, it was hard keeping the men on alert. I think they'll be OK if we ever get into a good fight. They say there's a big build up of NVA in Cambodia but I don't know if I'm ready. What if we get hit by a regiment or a battalion?" Kregor had become animated and breathless as he talked rapidly, stringing his sentences together.

McKenzie drained his glass and looked at the bartender, who immediately fixed two new drinks for them. He examined the bartender's multicolored flower shirt while he searched for an answer.

"I don't know. I guess that wouldn't be too good. Why don't we grab a table and get something to eat?" McKenzie said.

Dinner was wonderful. They each had thick steaks covered in a tangy sauce, white rice and a large salad. The waitress brought two more drinks, this time on the rocks. After ice cream and dark, aromatic coffee, McKenzie was forced to finally tell Kregor what he had been through - his combat and his running battles with Black Knight.

He tried to give Kregor an idea of how fearful combat could be. It was not something to look forward to. He didn't want to scare him but he needed to explain about the elephant and how amazing eighteen and nineteen year old soldiers could be. Kregor thoroughly enjoyed the story about McKenzie getting out too far on his first ambush and how Sergeant Doll had jerked him off his feet.

"I don't see how you guys were always running into people and we couldn't find em. We must have been in the wrong area," Kregor said, sounding truly disappointed.

"I don't know but from what I hear, there's gonna be plenty of enemy to go around down here," McKenzie said. "Just keep your head down and trust your men."

The evening sun had dropped low behind the big mountain when they left the club. Shops were still open and American GIs hung out or bargained with Mama Sans as the two walked back. Kregor had brought his weapon. They said goodbye at the gate and promised to meet at the Tan Son Nhut officer's club when their tours ended.

It was the closest thing to real feelings for another person since Koop and Kemper had left. Sergeant Fordham had gotten close. McKenzie did not want to worry about Kregor after O'Kusky had been killed but he knew he was going to. How would Kregor survive after spending four months looking for the war only to be thrust into III Corps with the probability of facing large numbers of NVA? The only thing combat gives is muscle memory. Fear is still there but once a soldier learns to react to it, he does it better than if he had never done it.

DROs

Morning came much too early. He woke to a gentle hand shaking his shoulder. The familiar metallic taste of too much alcohol had taken residence in his mouth as he opened his eyes to see who was shaking him.

"You gonna sleep all day, One Six?" Through the blur, McKenzie could see a face. Gradually, Sergeant Davis came into focus, all dressed, clean and grinning.

"The old man wants to see you, post haste. That was thirty minutes ago. I wasted a bunch of time looking for you in the mess hall, the shower and even the latrine. Where do I find you? Still in bed. Time to get up sleepy head. You must have had a great time last night."

McKenzie rolled over onto his stomach. "Oh, God. I need more sleep. Is Six meeting with all the platoon leaders?"

"Nope. Just you. I'll go tell him you're on the way. I suggest you make that your first priority."

Sergeant Davis kicked one of the bunk's legs, sending shock waves into McKenzie's head. He rolled off the cot and hit the floor on all fours where he stayed until he could determine what his stomach would do. He was hungry but not sick. Good. McKenzie got to his feet, grabbed a razor and headed for the metal sinks sitting just outside his door. He only had time to shave, splash water over his head and get dressed.

First of the Fifth had taken over a row of buildings facing south. Unlike the tents on a fire base, each building was off the ground, surrounded by a double stack of sand bags eight feet or more and covered with a metal roof. Top showed off his new domain proudly to McKenzie the day before. Captain Sheldon was sitting in an actual office going over paperwork.

"Good morning, sir. I hear you want to see me?"

Cool Cousin Six looked up and gave McKenzie the once over.

"Have a seat, Lieutenant. Rough night?" he said.

"Not really, sir. I ran into a platoon leader from the Seventh that I came in country with and we had a few over at the Philippine compound."

"I'd say more than a few. You look a bit stretched around the gills to me. I got bad news for you."

"What's that, sir?"

"Look at these." Captain Sheldon handed a stack of slips to McKenzie. "Your men went out and collected fifteen DROs in just twenty-four hours. Tore up two clubs, hassled an MP and generally raised hell. Each one of these delinquency reports could warrant an Article Fifteen. You decide what you want to do with them but get it under control. Understand?"

"Is First Platoon the only one?" McKenzie said as he thumbed through the slips.

"No! My whole company made themselves well known to the MPs but I've already spoken to Two Six and Three Six. I'm not going to take any action unless you fail to get your guys under control. You're new in this company but you know the drill. I know these guys have been in the bush for the last month, however, we can do a little better than this. Right?"

"Yes, sir," McKenzie said as he read allegations detailing fights, disruptions or just being out of uniform, whatever that meant. Wilson, the man with the black eye, had also pushed an MP and challenged him to a fight. None had been arrested. McKenzie looked up and tore the slips in half.

"Thank you, sir. I'll take care of this. Is that all?"

"No, One Six. Report back here at nineteen hundred hours with your platoon sergeant and we'll go over where we're going in

358

two days. It ain't gonna be pretty so I suggest you make sure all your equipment and supplies are in order. Double up on your ammunition. Good luck rounding up your platoon." Captain Sheldon grinned and returned to his paperwork.

McKenzie walked between the buildings toward the mess. He had to get something on his stomach first. He was amazed how young boys, turned into men by a frenetic and unpredictable war, could abandon all semblance of order in such a short time.

After getting some eggs and coffee down and telling Sergeant Davis to "round em up," McKenzie lay down on his bunk to think about the upcoming mission. He knew very little yet but all the signs told him the rumors about an NVA build up across the border contained more truth than fiction.

What did he know after four months in the field? Was he going to die before his six months were up? Maybe it was time to schedule an early R & R? No. He couldn't do that. Death was no longer a strange idea. Something told him that Charlie Company was going to be his consummation. He had outlasted Colonel Fishmuth so far but he was not satisfied with himself.

CHAPTER 11 - NUI BA DEN
(NOVEMBER 28, 1968 - 202 DAYS LEFT)

Between November, Tenth and the Twenty Eighth, Charlie Company worked the areas around Katum, a Special Forces camp approximately eight kilometers from the Cambodian border, just south of the Fish Hook. McKenzie found that he blended well into the fabric of Charlie Company's, First Platoon and even managed to win over Sergeant Davis. There were skirmishes and ambushes and the rescue of Double Time after they had become surrounded and battered for two days but it appeared the horrific predictions of large enemy forces coming across the border from Cambodia were not yet well founded. McKenzie found a new anger inside that came out swiftly and deadly under fire. It defeated the elephant quickly and moved with him toward the enemy.

On the Twenty Eighth, the company was airlifted back to Tay Ninh to run, what battalion called "mini-cavs" around Nui Ba Den. Intelligence reports speculated there was a build up on the mountain in preparation for a major attack on the base. Charlie company was dropped onto the airfield, told to leave their packs and take only water and ammo. Platoons were then picked up and taken in different directions around the mountain. All completed their first missions without a single contact and were back by eighteen hundred hours where they got a big surprise.

They were hurried off to a comfortable, cool and dry mess hall for a sit down Thanksgiving dinner. Captain Sheldon, the good soldier, stood at the head table and offered his own sort of military blessing, giving thanks for their safety and all sky troopers. He even included the chain of command right up to the Generals and the Commander in Chief.

McKenzie enjoyed the turkey, mashed potatoes and green bean dinner but when the captain was giving thanks, his thoughts had drifted to Kregor and First of the Seventh. There were reports the Seventh had been in heavy contact. Had Kregor seen the combat he was looking for? How did he feel if he had seen it? Was the Seventh getting a hot meal? McKenzie looked around and felt guilty. Tomorrow, he would locate Kregor's company and find out how he was.

He was very full as he walked out of the mess hall. McKenzie let his belt out a little and looked around. He was feeling even more isolated than usual. It would be an imposition to hang around the enlisted men and he still had no desire for officers. Six had said he didn't need to see his platoon leaders until morning.

McKenzie went by and signed for the forty-five-caliber pistol he'd requested. During an ambush two weeks prior, a wounded NVA soldier had rushed him with a knife. Sergeant Davis had shot him but McKenzie decided he needed a pistol. Two things he did not want to experience were hand to hand combat and becoming a POW.

He wandered over to Bravo Company and confirmed that his medal recommendations had been approved and personally awarded by Black Knight the day after Bravo landed in Tay Ninh. That made him feel good. He decided to go find Kregor's company instead of waiting for morning.

Charlie Company, First of the Seventh, was over on the other side of the base, closer to the Black Virgin. The mountain stood off in the distance, looming ever bigger as McKenzie walked toward it. It was a giant hovering over the base, comfortable in its own size. One that appeared to feel it was unnecessary to squash the base because the Americans could not hurt it. Probably why the Viet Cong decided to keg up in its caves. Maybe they got strength from it. He stopped and studied the huge mountain. It was surrounded by nothing but flat rice fields having pushed up long ago like a giant wart on the land, alone and dark. McKenzie turned and walked up the steps to Kregor' company.

Inside, an older NCO sat at a desk listening and talking into the company radio.

"Roger that, Six. I got a log bird scheduled for ten hundred hours tomorrow morning. I'm sending out two replacements and your new One Six," the old soldier said into his radio.

McKenzie sucked in his breath and leaned against the door frame. The white haired sergeant was not aware anyone was behind him until he spun around to stand up.

"Good evening, Lieutenant. Can I help you?" he said in a deep, gravely voice as he walked over to a coffee pot.

"Yea, Top. I was just wondering about a good friend of mine, Lieutenant Kregor? We heard the Seventh got hit hard over the last couple of weeks. Did I hear you say new One Six?"

"Yes, sir, I did. Lieutenant Kregor's in Japan. He was wounded four times, once in the throat. Don't look like he's coming back."

"You gotta be kidding me. Crap," McKenzie said. He turned to leave.

"You want a cup of coffee, sir? Come in and take a load off. How long you know Lieutenant Kregor?"

McKenzie walked to a foot locker and sat down. The First Sergeant poured very black coffee into a beat up beige colored, ceramic, coffee mug and gave it to McKenzie who could feel the emotion he didn't want to feel pushing up from way down deep. He took a slow breath, which came in yups, like a kid who'd been crying.

"We came in country at the same time, Top. I went through orientation with him at Camp Evans. I saw him for the first time since when we landed in Tay Ninh. Damn! I hate this."

"You want a little extra in that coffee, Lieutenant? I think I'll have some myself."

The First Sergeant walked over and opened the bottom drawer of a two drawer Army green file cabinet and pulled out a half bottle of Jack Daniels whiskey. McKenzie noticed the old man's liver spots on his hands as he poured one fingers worth into each cup.

"What happened, Top?" McKenzie said when the sergeant sat down across from him.

"The company was over run by a battalion of NVA. They'd been hit hard for two days. This happened on the third day, right at first light. "The hour of the Pearl," McKenzie thought. He leaned over with his head down and closed his eyes.

"We heard a little in the field, but I didn't know which company it was that got hit."

Top Murphy explained, "There was hand to hand fighting and the CO had to bring air strikes in close. After they were able to pull back into a tight perimeter, Puff came in and hit the bastards hard. Both the other platoon leaders were killed. We had ten friendly KIAs and fifteen WIAs. The NVA lost over a hundred. Everyone said Lieutenant Kregor was amazing, fighting even though he was wounded. The CO recommended him for the Distinguished Service Cross."

McKenzie was listening but the sound came from far away.

"I had to listen to that mess on the radio, sir. It was about the worse thing I've ever had to listen to. If I could have got out there, I think I would have gone. The company's coming in soon if you want to talk to the old man."

By then, both of them were into a second drink of Jack, this time two fingers worth, without the coffee. McKenzie was stunned. Kregor had gone from almost no combat to being over run within two weeks of going back out to the field.

"How bad's his throat, Top?"

"Well, they said he would never be able to talk normal but I seen men recover from all kinds of wounds people said they wouldn't, so I don't know. I got an address if you want to drop him a line, although I can't tell you how long he's gonna be in Japan. He's definitely goin home."

McKenzie stayed for a while and talked. The old First Sergeant wanted to know what unit he was in and how he was doing. Top Murphy had been in the Army twenty-eight years and his CIB, with two stars, had not gone unnoticed by McKenzie. He'd joined the Army when he was twenty-five at the start of WWII and served with Patton in Europe. He'd also served with the Cav in Korea, barely escaping when the Chinese came across the Yalo River in 1950.

He volunteered for Vietnam in 1965 with the stipulation he would be with the First Cav. He spent a year in the field as a platoon sergeant and then a year back in the states before volunteering to come back for a second tour. He had just extended for another year. When McKenzie told him he too had volunteered to come to the Cav, Top Murphy got up and dug out another full bottle of Jack Daniels and poured each a little more.

"Of course, I don't have to hump the boonies any more," he said as he poured. "I damn shore know how to run a company headquarters and how to keep my troopers in supplies. I figure that's the least I can do."

Around twenty-two hundred hours, McKenzie got up to say goodbye. He'd had more than enough to drink and they had talked about everything. Top Murphy, who didn't seem much effected by the liquor, said he had more work to do before morning and so McKenzie left. The old sergeant had listened to him in a way no one else had since he'd been in Vietnam, except maybe the other First Sergeants. It was always the First Sergeants.

He was sick and tired of the fighting and afraid of the growing anger inside him. He wanted out of the field but he didn't want to leave his men. It didn't matter any more whether it was Delta, Echo, Bravo or Charlie Company. The soldiers were all tough and fragile at the same time and he wanted to be with them. With Kregor gone, he was the only infantry lieutenant left from Camp Evans. He wondered where Lieutenant Kingsley was? Before he left, Top Murphy had put his hand on McKenzie's shoulder.

"You know, sir," he said. "No one hates war more than an old career soldier like me and the only reason I'm still here is because there's still wars. That's it. Someone has to be here and if there was never another war, that would be Jim Dandy with me. You finish your tour and go home and have a good life. Maybe that's what you're supposed to do. Just don't forget what you've seen here."

"You know, Top. What bothers me the most is that it seems like the military needs a war every now and then to justify itself. These battalion commanders, who are here now, were most likely commissioned after Korea. If so, they have never had a platoon or a company in combat. I'm afraid they only have this war, right now, to make their whole career on and maybe that gets in their way."

"I can't disagree with you on that, sir but it don't change the fact that you and me still got a job to do. I expect you'll do it. Good luck to ya, son." The old soldier shook McKenzie's hand and watched him leave.

McKenzie wandered through the compound, his thoughts random and disorganized. Sitting on the steps to his hooch, he tried hard to pull his thoughts away from his feelings. Kregor was attacked at first light. That was the moment, when time suspended and held the world and its inhabitants in its fickle grasp. The question was always; what would be revealed in the next instant? Would it be something non-threatening or would it be dangerous and deadly? Was it the war or the military that threatened to create entropy? In McKenzie's world, it was Black Knight.

For the next three days, Charlie Company went out on mini-cavs. On December, First, McKenzie's platoon discovered fifty-one new bunkers in an obvious staging area. Popular wisdom had the enemy out at night and holed up on Nui Ba Den during the day. Cave Killers came in and blew each bunker. After returning to Tay Ninh that day, McKenzie headed for company headquarters. He wanted to find out the next day's assignment before going to talk to Kregor's CO. He found Captain Sheldon sitting on the steps outside.

"Good job, One Six. That was a great find. Maybe the NVA have been set back a couple of months."

"Yes, sir. It was spooky, though. All those bunkers were new. Why do you think we didn't get hit? We were there all day."

"It would have been suicide. We would have spotted them coming off the Black Lady and gun ships would have had their way with them. You're doing exactly what the old man wants, disrupting their plans for an all out attack."

"You mean the one Colonel Fishmuth's been praying for?" McKenzie said.

GOING TO DIVISION

Captain Sheldon gave him a disapproving look. "No," he said. "Anyway, we have perimeter security for the next couple of days and nights and you are going to Phuoc Vinh in the morning."

"I am? Why?"

"We just got a call from Division. You've been selected to fly over to Division and interview for Protocol Officer for Major General Forsythe."

"What the hell's a protocol officer?" McKenzie's voice went higher, as if he was going through puberty.

Captain Sheldon laughed. "As far as I know, its being responsible for running the General's mess, escorting dignitaries, arranging travel and security and setting the General's social calendar." The captain gave him a cheesy grin. McKenzie frowned.

"What are you complaining about? Sounds cushy to me. You should also know that each Brigade is sending one officer, so you're only one in three. I guess its up to you to convince them if you want the job. You leave tomorrow at eleven hundred and if I were you, I'd get a hair cut. Top has some new fatigues and boots for you. We don't want you looking too rough when you go."

"Thank you, sir. I'll take care of that in the morning." McKenzie turned to leave but Captain Sheldon stood up and grabbed him by the arm.

"By the way, I think you should wear these, your orders came through," he said and held out his hand, palm up. Laying inside were two silver bars. McKenzie had become a First Lieutenant on November 22, 1968, one year after being commissioned. He was no longer at the bottom of the totem pole. Captain Sheldon reached up and punched the metal points through his fatigue collar on both sides and fixed brads on the backs.

"Just in time to get out of the field, One Six. Not the way its usually done but better late than never." They shook hands.

McKenzie thanked his company commander and left. He was stunned. Protocol officer at Division? He had no idea what it was Division did in the war. Even when he met General Shadwick at Wonder Beach, it seemed like he was from the Pentagon, not Vietnam. Life at the grunt level was day to day and you dwelt amid whatever orders were given, living only for the moment. Now he was going to Division to interview for a job dealing with generals. At least he would go as a First Lieutenant.

He wanted to get drunk. He felt anxiety about getting the job but at the same time, dreaded facing the moment when he would have to leave combat. He had slowly become addicted to the adrenaline. The higher he got on adrenaline, the better he dealt with the fear. Alcohol, in turn, numbed the memories and quelled the adrenalin.

It wasn't long before Sergeant Davis showed up, shirtless and carrying a beer. McKenzie was half way through his third, sitting on his front steps and pondering his future.

"Hey, One Six, I hear you're leaving us in the morning," Sergeant Davis said. He sat down in the dirt cross legged.

"Jeez, One Five, your intel is pretty damn good. No, I'm not leaving you. I'm flying out to Phuoc Vinh to interview for a job at Division. One overnight and I'll be back. Six says if I get the job it won't start until the end of the month and there's two other officers being interviewed for the same job."

McKenzie retrieved his last two warm beers and gave one to Davis.

"Sarge. You know where we can snag more of these? I wasn't going to drink tonight but that was out the window an hour ago."

BANGALORE TORPEDO

Davis stands up and bends over to pick up his last empty can of Black Label. It's close to twenty-three hundred hours and he's decided to call it a night. A claymore explodes on the company's perimeter and an American machine gun begins to chatter well timed volleys of six to ten bullets at a time. A couple of M-16s open up and they're answered by the crack of AKs. A huge explosion rocks the ground. It's a sound McKenzie's not heard before. "What the hell?"

"Bangalore torpedo!" Davis says as he turns and runs toward his bunker.

McKenzie darts inside, picks up his weapon and a bandolier of magazines. A B-40 rocket explodes on the line and another bunker down the line opens up with small arms fire. "They're working good," McKenzie says to himself. Two flares shoot up in the air and pop open. Two mortar tubes fire from out in the darkness. He hits the ground as a round lands behind and the other slams down to his right. Jesus, this is for real. Maybe this is the one Colonel Fishmuth's been hoping for.

He heads for the bunker closest to where the bangalore torpedo blew. Inside, Collins, a Spec Four machine gunner, is calmly working his gun back and forth while Weston, his ammo bearer, feeds chain linked bullets out of a box. McKenzie taps Collins on the shoulder.

"What the hell's going on, Collins?" he shouts in his ear.

"Gooks in the wire! They set off a trip flare so we blew one of the claymores. Next thing I know, there's a bright flash off to our left and a huge explosion. They been trying to crawl through the hole in the wire and we been knockin' 'em down."

A new flare pops overhead. Coming out of the wire in front is a Viet Cong sapper dressed in loin cloth and carrying a satchel charge. Collins shoots him before he can take another step. Behind are two more. Collins rakes the ground in front of them, then takes them out.

"You got any hand flares?" McKenzie yells at Weston.

"Over there, LT." Weston points to the back corner.

Collins screams for Weston to grab another box of ammo. The volume of firing increases up and down the line. More rockets begin to land and green tracers come through the air like laser beams while red tracers go out. McKenzie snatches a hand full of flares, moves outside and climbs onto the bunker top where he lays out on his stomach, then rolls to his back and hits the bottom of one of the flare tubes. Up it flies, exploding like a 4th of July rocket.

He rolls back. Two black pajama clad VC are trying to cut through a section of wire and three fully uniformed NVA are moving at various locations in the wire. Another claymore detonates and they're gone. Maybe its a platoon sized attack. McKenzie stays on top where he can fire his weapon in any direction. He pulls the forty-five off his hip and lays it beside him.

A Cobra drops down on the left and hovers, firing rockets and mini-guns just beyond the wire. American mortars finally start to fire rounds back into the black night. Bunkers are reinforced by soldiers running down from the barracks. A steady volume of fire grows. McKenzie pops another hand flare and rolls back to fire from his vantage point. A shadow moves on the right side of his bunker. He grabs the pistol and looks over. An NVA soldier is about to go in the back door of the bunker. The elephant lands hard on his sternum threatening to knock the air out of him but his anger pushes it aside. He fires the pistol killing the soldier, then rolls back to his stomach, grabs his M-16 and grins as he fires a full magazine at brown khaki uniforms. An alcoholic buzz smoothes out the anger and calms him.

The fire fight continues for over an hour. There is enemy everywhere in the wire and it feels like a carnival shooting gallery. When there's no more incoming and floating mortar flares reveal no more live enemy in the wire, the land line begins to ring in Collin's bunker. McKenzie jumps off the top of the bunker and walks inside.

"Its the CO," Weston said, handing McKenzie the phone.

~~

Captain Sheldon asks for an assessment. Black Knight is on his way down.

"I think this was only a test, Six, If they'd have got through, they might have done some real damage but its hard to tell what it was," McKenzie said.

He walked back outside just as Sergeant Davis showed up from his right.

"We got a bunch in the wire down where I was, LT. You think that's all?"

"I don't know. Six agrees this was more like a test but he wants a body count ASAP. Any friendlies?"

"Not that I know of, One Six. By the way, the Colonel is coming this way. He was down by Second Squad with his pistol out, stomping around like this was the big one," Davis said. He walked over and examined the dead NVA laying next to the bunker, then over to where the bangalore had gone off. The wire was blown wide open, big enough for a hay truck to drive through. Two helicopters with search lights continued to work the area beyond.

The whole episode seemed horribly useless. What a waste of good soldiers. They just kept coming toward Collin's gun. The bodies, looking bloody and yet waxy gray, lay at odd angles in the wire. McKenzie was hyped on the adrenaline that had washed through him and knew his men would be high for hours. The fear would be buried until the next time they were staring into the darkness alone and then it would sneak back. It always visited during the quiet times. He walked back to Collin's bunker after Davis left.

"You and Weston OK?" he said. The two of them were outside leaning against the front of their bunker, backs against the sandbags, smoking cigarettes.

"Yea, LT. But I didn't like it. That was a little too close," Collins said.

"Lieutenant McKenzie," a familiar voice said behind him. It was Colonel Fishmuth. "Great job. We kicked their ass, didn't we?" he said, turning to the staff lieutenant behind him. "Be sure to get one of the Division photographers down here. I want pictures of all these guys in the wires and this guy next to the bunker. I want a full after action report, Lieutenant. Keep up the good work." The Colonel didn't wait for a response. He walked past McKenzie, trailed by an entourage of battalion officers, his pistol in his right hand.

McKenzie looked back at Collins who was watching the Colonel walk away. " Make sure you have plenty of ammo because I have no idea if this is all for tonight," McKenzie said. "Call and get someone down here to put that wire back together. Count your grenades and flares and let One Five know if you need more. This may only be the first try."

"You're full of good news, LT. I hear you're leavin' us," Weston said.

"Weston, I'm not going anywhere. I'm gonna interview for a new job but even if I get it, I won't leave for another month. You're not getting rid of me that easy."

He was beginning to feel horrible, like when he told his Mom he'd gone into Portland and enlisted. He and Charlie Company had gotten used to each other and First Platoon was working good. They were getting the benefit of everything he had learned, including how to control his nerves when the elephant visited and he had stopped perseverating so much on fighting Black Knight. The question was, had he done enough?

First light jumped out of the East without incident. McKenzie watched the sun climb up the face of Nui Ba Den before he headed for the shower, dressed and got a haircut. He'd changed his mind about seeing Kregor's CO. The First Sergeant said Kregor did good, that was all he needed to know. He had just enough time for some chow.

NEW OFFICERS

Most of the tables in the mess hall were occupied. Colonel Fishmuth was seated near the end of the one closest to the chow line with members of his staff and several new lieutenants. The operations officer was giving a briefing loud enough for McKenzie to hear. He shoveled powdered eggs, French toast and sausage quickly onto his tray and moved to a back table.

"We operate with maximum utilization of our forces - at all times. Large search and destroy operations have been the most effective in both I Corps and III Corps. You will find the support we give in the field is the finest in any AO," the officer told the group.

It seemed a strange place for an orientation. Between bites McKenzie noticed Black Knight looking at him. He gulped down his eggs, sausage and French toast and got up to leave.

"Lieutenant McKenzie, would you step over here for a minute?" Colonel Fishmuth said in his most polite tone.

"Yes, sir. Good morning, sir." McKenzie put his tray down and looked around the group. Of the three new lieutenants, only one was infantry. One was signal and the other had an insignia he did not recognize.

"Lieutenant McKenzie is one of our most experienced platoon leaders. It was his unit that repulsed the attack last night. Maybe you could make yourself available later and give our newest platoon leaders some first hand advice, Lieutenant?"

"I would be glad to, sir but it will have to be after I return from Phuoc Vinh. I'm flying out this morning at eleven hundred. I'll be back sometime tomorrow."

"That would be fine, Lieutenant. Feel free to look him up gentlemen. Have a good trip."

The three new officers stared at McKenzie as if memorizing his face for later. He saluted Colonel Fishmuth and left. Forget about it, he thought. It don't mean nothin.

PHUOC VINH

The day was a blur. He was interviewed first by the departing Protocol Officer and then the Division Chief of Staff. He was picked for the interview, it seems, because he had listed cooking and catering experience on his initial enlistment questionnaire. The truth was he had only cooked for the dormitory food service at college and helped with a couple of banquets, facts he chose not to clarify in the interview. If that was going to get him a prestigious job out of the field, so be it.

The evening was spent at the Division Officer's Club where he ran into his TAC officer from OCS and told him about Black Knight.

"That's one serious pain in the butt, I'd say," Lieutenant Ballin, his TAC officer said. He confirmed that the Army was now offering other branch officers the opportunity to transfer over and serve as platoon leaders because of recent heavy losses. That's who McKenzie saw with Colonel Fishmuth at breakfast. "Its gonna be the blind leading the blind," Ballin said.

Just talking about Colonel Fishmuth raised McKenzie's anxiety level. He would be returning to the field for another month whether he got the job or not, subject to whatever Black Knight came up with. Even worse, his replacement might not be infantry. He exited the club to walk back to his bunk for the night. The image of Colonel Fishmuth walking the perimeter and ordering photographs of dead NVA the night before crept back and then morphed into a picture of Black Knight hung over a strand of concertina wire, a bullet hole in his forehead.

McKenzie walked up a dirt road in the middle of the compound. He was feeling the effects of drinking scotch for several hours. Buildings stood in formation on each side. The evening was cool below a sky displaying a half moon. As he wandered along, he tried to guess who occupied the barracks on each side. Rain had created dry rills in the dirt which required careful attention by someone in his condition. He stepped back and forth across the dirt creases. A shadow moved on his right near the edge of a building. Moon light created angled shadows off the corner of each building. Damn! He had not been paying attention.

McKenzie reached for his forty-five and undid the snap. The shadow moved again. He stepped off the road to his right into a deeper shadow and leaned against a building with his right shoulder. He slowly withdrew the pistol and brought it up to fire. A lighter sparked and lit the face of a young soldier who lazily walked away from the next building and turned up the road, unaware anyone was watching. The flash of the zippo had startled McKenzie. He'd squeezed the trigger but it held firm because he had forgot to release the safety.

His tongue was stuck to the roof of a very, dry mouth. He took a deep breath. Jesus! He almost shot the kid. Probably a REMF his entire tour with little or no thought what an enemy sapper could do. He wondered if there was any real danger between the buildings and considered making a sweep through the compound. These people were not prepared. He was reluctant to holster the pistol once he had removed it. His right thumb snapped the safety off so he could fire if need be. A bead of sweat ran down his face.

He stayed where he was, watching and considering what to do for a long time. Three soldiers walked down the road laughing and talking. He slipped around the building corner and put the pistol away but he did not snap the cover and he did not reset the safety. He saw Colonel Fishmuth's face on one as they passed by. Startled, he quickly pulled the pistol out again and up to a firing position. How easy it would be to kill the man. He turned and walked around the end, then down the other side of the building, behind the walkers. The shot would be easy to make. McKenzie stood in the shadow where the first soldier had come from and watched the three soldiers walk away.

DECEMBER 23, 1968

It finally happened. After a little more than six months in combat as a platoon leader, McKenzie was leaving the field. Somehow he had been chosen to become the next Division Protocol Officer. He would no longer be a grunt. Now that he had field wisdom, that second sense of how to survive all the little moments that came at him every day, he was leaving. It felt like a contradiction.

Field wisdom had come to him in many forms. There were lessons taught by others, some learned by mistakes and some by osmosis. He'd learned to fight when he had to. The killing had become his Rubicon and he wasn't sure if he could get back. Sitting on top of his world was the battalion commander who he considered the biggest threat of all. To just describe him as a loose cannon would be too one dimensional. He was the manifestation of arbitrary authority made available to a malevolent mind. He had been the real danger at first light - every day.

McKenzie felt sorely alone. Only he could protect his men from the enemies around them. Only he could stand in defense of their right to live against the stupefying orders that rained down upon them. He was the only one who had no protector, no fellow knights of the round table. Platoon leaders in Vietnam were rulers of individual islands, capable only of protecting their own shores, not responsible for the other guy's island. That's just the way it was.

Now he was going to learn at Division if Lieutenant
Colonel Fishmuth had been the real enemy. They had been at war
with each other from the beginning and McKenzie realized he
would now have the necessary time to consider if he should exact
revenge for men lost and the unnecessary fear.

He walked around to each squad the night before and tried
to personally talk to each man. They were set up several clicks
from the Cambodian border. It was early morning and the platoon
was spread out along the edge of the landing zone for security. It
was the eyes that betrayed them. Doe eyes full of thoughts too
many to be expressed. He continued to walk among them and wish
them good luck but all he got were grunts or "It don't mean
nothin."

He stood off from the clearing and watched the First Cav
helicopter float in. Next to him stood Staff Sergeant Davis and
Sergeant Collins, the machine gunner he'd promoted to squad
leader. Tears sat unreleased inside the corners of Collin's eyes.
McKenzie saw Sergeant Davis, hard to the end, give Collins a look
of disapproval.

"You guys keep your asses down, you hear me?"
McKenzie's said. His voice cracked. He picked up his pack and
ran for the helicopter, accidentally gulping in dust which
threatened to choke him. He looked at the pilot who was going to
take him away. He looked to his left where the platoon, standing
mute, began to shrink away.

Would he ever be whole again? First Platoon, Charlie
Company had extracted a part of him, as they all had done. It was
theirs and they were not about to return it. Tears escaped from his

eyes and ran through the dust on his cheeks. The door gunner looked away. The helicopter danced at tree level, dove down into a clearing and leaned sideways to pass narrowly between a channel of trees.

When the helicopter set down at Tay Ninh airfield McKenzie headed for company headquarters. He felt spacey. A part of him had not yet grasped that he was permanently out of the field. He felt conspicuous and guilty. He imagined that everyone who saw him would know he had just left his men for a safe job in the rear. Top Whitlock was business as usual.

"Go over to battalion supply. The sergeant there has several sets of new fatigues and a new pair of boots for you." He was polite but it was obvious to McKenzie that Top had already removed him from the roster. The First Sergeant had done it many times and there was no sentimentality from him.

Sergeant Kawinana, a huge, happy Hawaiian, was the supply sergeant. He was the perfect person to process grunts in and out of Vietnam. His Polynesian approach to life was care free, easy to get along with and sensitive.

"You no gonna leave this place lookin' like that, sir. You gonna look good for da General. I got ya two pairs of boots so you can polish 'em up." He smiled a big, white toothy grin and followed it with a belly laugh. "I even heard you like the scotch, so I got ya a bottle."

SPEC FOUR EVANS

"Sarge, I'm beginning to feel good already. Thanks a lot," McKenzie said. "Where do I pick up my pay and orders out of here?"

"That would be Specialist Evans over at Battalion, sir. You take care of yourself wit those Generals."

McKenzie took a shower and changed into his new duds before going in search of Spec. Four Evans. He found him sitting at a metal desk just inside the battalion office with his back to the door and bent over earnestly polishing a pair of airborne boots with a wet cotton ball, circling it around and around over the mirror like surface.

"How you doing, Specialist," McKenzie said. "I need to pick up my orders and pay."

Evens did not indicate he heard what was said. McKenzie could see reflections of the tent and surroundings in the shine of the toe. He waited but Evans just sat there, his back to McKenzie and continued to circle the ball of cotton.

"Specialist, you got about 2 seconds to move before I jerk your insolent ass off that chair."

"Keep your shirt on, sir. I'm comin'," Evens said, letting out a deep breath of air, as if he had a right to be impatient.

McKenzie watched Evans slowly put the boots down one at a time, side by side on the floor, before he turned around. He could feel his face redden as Evans picked up a manila envelope off the file cabinet, walked over and held it out. The tent floor was hot and the humidity hung with a mixed smell of moldy canvas, red clay and Evan's sweat.

McKenzie jerked the envelope away and growled, "If anything's missing, Specialist, I'm gonna come back and choke you until your eye balls fall out."

He was almost run over by a mechanical mule speeding between buildings as he stepped off the stairs. Mortar rounds were piled precariously on the back of the mule and the PFC driving it gave him a "Sorry but I don't really give a shit" look. McKenzie had to laugh. He was definitely going to have to mellow out and planned to start once he got to his hooch and opened the scotch.

MEDAL

He sat down on his bunk and opened the envelope. He hadn't noticed how bulky it was until his fingers bumped into a small, thin box. He pulled it out and when he opened it, he saw a Silver Star laying on a pad of blue silk. Among the papers were the medal citation and orders which described the actions of July, Twenty First, when Delta was ambushed and Orson shot in the mouth. The citation was signed by the Division Chief of Staff at the time, Colonel Sansberry. Captain Moore must have submitted it. McKenzie was stunned. Why hadn't this been presented to him in a medal ceremony?

He sat there for a long time trying to sort his thoughts out, bouncing between anger and bewilderment. The truth was hard to accept. Colonel Fishmuth had chosen not to present it. His antipathy for McKenzie was palpable and the man had violated one of the military's most sacred rules. A medal for valor was always presented in a proper ceremony. No ands, ifs or buts. He poured a double shot of scotch and drank it straight, ruminating.

CHAPTER 12 - PROTOCOL OFFICER
(DECEMBER 24, 1968 - 175 DAYS LEFT)

First Lieutenant McKenzie flew out of Tay Ninh on Christmas Eve. As a child, the night before Christmas was both exciting and scary. Santa was a mysterious phenomenon to a small boy growing up in an old farmhouse, heated by a metal oil stove which occupied the center of a small, living room. The upstairs, where he and his brother slept in the attic, was heated only by ambient heat from the red bricks of the stove's chimney as it climbed to the roof. There was no fire place mantle. Stockings were hung off the edge of an oak dining room table, taped on by their Mom.

Whenever the family traveled to Corvallis for Christmas with his Grammy, however, stockings were properly hung from a beautiful, white brick mantle over a large fire place big enough for Santa and all his gifts. He loved his Grammy who hugged him often with her enveloping large breasts and powdery perfume.

McKenzie's brother, Joe, was currently off shore patrolling the coast of Vietnam in a missile frigate destroyer, the USS Decatur. He'd recently tried to volunteer for river boat duty to get Kenneth out of combat under the brother rule but McKenzie had refused. He had only two months left in the field and his brother would have had to begin a full, in-country tour. It just didn't pencil out. He loved him for the offer and wondered if he could commandeer a helicopter as protocol officer and fly out to the ship. It sounded like something the First Cav could accomplish.

A sudden drop in altitude brought him out of his musings. He looked down. Standing on the landing pad next to a jeep was Blain, the clerk he'd met a month earlier who would be working with him. He was tall and thin with thick glasses and stiff, wavy blond hair.

First Lieutenant McKenzie stepped out of the helicopter, hoisted his NVA pack over one shoulder and waved thanks to the pilot. He'd returned both of his weapons to the battalion armory. The day was beautiful. The tropical sun had not yet enveloped Phuoc Vinh in its heat. An unseen tropical bird cawed off to his left as he walked toward Blain.

"Well, here I am. Ready or not."

Blain threw up a half military salute which McKenzie returned. "Welcome, sir. Lieutenant Eagleton is sure looking forward to seeing you. He's all ready to go home and his plane don't leave for another week."

"Well, he better hang around long enough for me to get my sea legs or I'm gonna be in trouble."

"Don't worry. I'll keep you straight, sir. Tonight, you get to go to the General's mess, so we best get your bunk situation all figured out. I got plans to go to a Christmas party down at Headquarters Company. I'm only good 'til about fourteen hundred."

McKenzie had barely sat down in the passenger's seat when Blain popped the clutch and made the jeep jump. He was being sped toward his new assignment. "Holy crap," he thought to himself. At least the ride was familiar to him from when he had come in for the interview. Dust swirled up behind the jeep as they skidded through the gate.

"Don't bother going to see the LT, sir. He knows I'm gonna get you squared away first. Follow me."

Blain threw McKenzie's pack onto his shoulder and headed for the far end of the command building where the General's mess was. McKenzie followed to a row of barracks with the same thin metal roofs overhead as Tay Ninh. Blain stepped inside the first door of the first barrack to a bunk with a thin mattress sitting alongside the wall. An Army green bookshelf stood at the head of the bunk and a mosquito net hung loosely overhead. That was it. Blain threw the pack onto the bunk and turned around.

HOME SWEET HOME

"This is it. You'll have to fix it up to make it home but its close to the office and the mess. Anything you want me to scrounge for you?"

McKenzie was flabbergasted by the sparseness of his new abode. There were other bunks along both side walls with various forms of home made bunkers but none with the kind of protection from incoming he thought might be necessary if this was home for the next 6 months.

"Who else lives here?"

"Oh, other officers from Headquarters and a couple artillery guys," Blain said.

"Where do the general's aides sleep?"

"They have a separate hooch. They don't hang around much with junior officers, like lieutenants and captains, unless they are part of the general's staff. They mostly hang with the generals."

"Where does Lieutenant Eagleton stay?"

"He got a room to himself when he came in, down at Headquarters."

"Do I get that when he leaves?" McKenzie was starting to get a little irritated by the whole thing.

"No. There's a chemical officer who's already got dibs on it. Its sort of a free for all around here, sir."

"OK, I get it. Can you get me a fan, some sandbags, a pile of sand, eight empty wooden artillery ammo crates and a couple of sheets of landing strip tarmac? I don't intend to sleep with my butt hung out in wooden barracks for the next six months."

"What are you gonna do?" Blain said. He looked a little surprised.

"I'm gonna build me the best damned bunker I can around this cot, Blain. The only thing between that cot there and the next NVA rocket with my name on it is that thin metal roof up there and I didn't survive six months in the field to be killed in my sleep here. Capeesh?"

"Yes, sir. I'll see what I can do. You want enough sand dumped outside your door so you can fill up the ammo boxes too? Forget that. I just had an idea. The General's drivers don't have enough to do and they got jeeps. I'll get them to build you the best bunker you ever saw today when the Generals are out flying around. How does that sound?"

"Great. When was the last time you had incoming?"

"Last week. We had a couple rockets come in down on the South end but you never know. Unless the first one lands in your hip anyway, you're gonna hear em comin'. There's a cement bunker right around the other end of the mess over there. I'll show you where it is on the way back to see Lieutenant Eagleton," Blain said.

CHIEF OF STAFF

When they got to the office, Eagleton told McKenzie the Chief of Staff wanted to see him. Sort of an orientation pep talk, he said. It turned out to be much more than that. Colonel McKinstry was a completely different person from the month before when he'd interviewed McKenzie so seriously. He acted like he'd just given birth to the son he'd always wanted and who he was going to raise to be a fine citizen of the military.

"I chose you, Lieutenant McKenzie, because I saw in you a leader. A person who could step into this job and become a member of our team. At times it will be all on your shoulders to tell generals, senior officers, dignitaries and other VIPs where to go, where to sit, what to do and when to do it. You will have a great deal of power for a First Lieutenant but I think I've got the right man." He was beaming the whole time. It was obvious he was serious.

"I'll try to do for you what my first company commander told me, sir. He said my job was to keep his butt out of trouble and I'll try to do that for you." It was the only thing McKenzie could think to say.

"I never heard it put exactly that way Lieutenant, but you got a deal." He shook McKenzie's hand.

For the rest of the afternoon, McKenzie sat in the protocol office and tried to get a handle on what was happening. Eagleton was a schmoozer, slick on the phone but full of fluff. Blain was the real master mind and McKenzie decided he needed to know everything Blain knew or he wouldn't feel secure in the job.

GENERAL'S MESS

They left the office around sixteen thirty hours to visit the General's mess. Protocol was technically in charge of that area too but the head cook, Staff Sergeant Rossini, was described as a prima donna, more like a temperamental chef than an Army cook.

"If he likes you, your life will be a whole lot easier," Eagleton said.

What McKenzie saw was not your average military kitchen. Everything was spotless, including the floor. Bright pots and pans hung over several large cooking grills, knives were slotted in professional looking wood blocks and everyone was busy. Each cook had a tight, white apron around the waist with a grease towel hung on each side. Several large pots were boiling and salads were being made. A large, Italian looking man with a receding hairline and wavy black hair came around the end of one of the grills and stuck his hand out.

"Welcome to my kitchen, Lieutenant. I'm Sergeant Rossini and I understand you will be replacing Lieutenant Eagleton. If there's anything I can do for you, you need only ask."

It was a polite statement that put McKenzie on guard. The handshake was loose, without genuine meaning. Sergeant Rossini excused himself and went back to his duties.

"Well, that was short and sweet," McKenzie said to Eagleton as they exited through the swinging doors to the eating area where he saw a table full of enlisted men eating dinner.

"These men are the drivers and personal aides to the generals. Sergeant Rossini feeds them early before the Division officers arrive. I'll introduce you," Eagleton said.

"Gentlemen, I want you to meet the new Protocol Officer, Lieutenant McKenzie. He will take over when I leave for the world and I command you to treat him with all the respect you have given me."

It was a strange thing to say and the responses were lazy and almost bizarre. A few looked up but most just kept eating. It reminded McKenzie of the reception he'd received from Delta's First Platoon that first day so long ago at Bien An.

Outside, Eagleton explained that each one had been with an infantry line company before coming to Division. "They were picked because they were either highly decorated, good soldiers, recommended by their company commander, or they had received their third purple heart and it was time to get out of the field. These men are considered special by whichever General they work for. They live a very, cushy life," Eagleton said.

McKenzie returned to his barracks with just enough time to inspect his new bed bunker and change into a clean fatigue jacket before dinner. Blain had somehow corralled those recalcitrant drivers and they had constructed the most beautiful bed bunker he could have imagined.

Ammo boxes full of sand were stacked on each side of the cot with metal sheeting overhead covered by a layer of plump sandbags. A fan stood ready at the foot of the bed, a new mosquito net had been hung overhead and a wooden sign was suspended from the ceiling with the words, "Protocol Bunker" painted in black letters. He laughed out loud. He owed those guys a thank you. No wonder they were a little sullen.

GENERAL'S BAR

McKenzie could hear animated conversation and laughing as he approached the General's Mess. He found Lieutenant Eagleton inside bellied up to the bar talking to a Lieutenant Colonel.

"Good evening, Lieutenant, what can I buy you," Eagleton said without introducing McKenzie to the other officer who turned and walked away. "Ever try a Gin and tonic? Quench your thirst real fast," he said, holding up his own tall glass for inspection.

"Nope but I'm willing," McKenzie said looking around.

"Sergeant Willis, give my replacement a tall gin and tonic, will ya?"

A slender staff sergeant, busy mixing two other drinks, looked up and nodded. A fancy dice table was located perpendicular to the bar. Several officers were taking turns throwing dice out of a leather cup but not really playing. McKenzie counted ten other officers milling around, all majors or above. So far, no one had shown any interest in the new guy.

Camp Gorvad was the official name for this compound. It was considered a secure compound but it was not so far from the jungle that a B-40 rocket couldn't drop through the ceiling and kill a whole lot of command staff in one explosion. He wanted to admonish these guys. Hey, don't you know one grenade could kill you all? Break it up. Spread out.

"A - ten - shun!" someone shouted. Coming through the door was Major General George Forsythe. Behind him strolled Brigadier Generals Firby and Shadwick. Behind them walked a captain and two, first lieutenants - their aides. General Forsythe smiled and said, "At ease." He walked over to McKenzie, who snapped to attention. The General stuck out his hand. He was a short man, only about five foot eight but his bearing was large.

"Lieutenant McKenzie, welcome to Division. Colonel McKinstry briefed me this afternoon on your credentials and your record. Impressive. If you need anything from me, you just let my aide, Captain Short, know what it is and I will see that you get it. Protocol is responsible for how others see us and I expect that you will get full cooperation from my staff." His handshake was firm. He had an easy smile, clear eyes and the confidence of a two star.

"Thank you, sir. I'll do the best I can for you."

"I'm sure you will. Enjoy yourself tonight. Colonel McKinstry will introduce you during dinner and you can tell us a little bit about yourself," the General said. He turned and walking over to the dice table. His aide handed him a drink and shot McKenzie a 'don't get too comfortable' look. Both Generals Firby and Shadwick said hello and shook his hand. General Shadwick remembered him from Wonder Beach. That seemed so long ago.

McKenzie turned to Eagleton. "You forgot to tell me I would have to talk tonight," he said.

"Don't worry," Eagleton said with a smile. "General Forsythe thinks everyone on his staff is family, so just tell them who you are. That's all. Just keep it simple and short."

McKenzie's heart was racing. He began to go over in his mind what he would say. He watched the dice game, which had begun in earnest once the generals arrived. Dinner was announced fifteen minutes later and the tide of officers parted to form a path for the generals to walk into the dining room. Each officer entered in order, according to their rank. McKenzie and Eagleton were last. Everyone remained standing behind their chairs.

The Division Chaplain offered a blessing, followed by the pledge of allegiance and a toast to the Commander in Chief. General Forsythe welcomed everyone, acknowledging it was Christmas Eve and reminded those present of the brave soldiers in the First Air Cavalry who were in danger this evening. With that, he said, "Gentlemen, be seated."

The setting was beyond imagination. Crisp, white linen table cloths were set with fine dinner ware and glass stem ware for water and wine. Each place had a red lettered name card adorned with the Cav's yellow and black horse patch, including one for McKenzie. They were served a small dinner salad and then, steak and lobster, mashed potatoes, fresh rolls and green beans with almonds. The lobster was too rich for McKenzie's stomach which had been limited to C-rations and LRRPs for the last month after Charlie Company left Tay Ninh.

Between the main course and dessert, Colonel McKinstry stood up and said, "Gentlemen, I would like to introduce our new Protocol Officer, First Lieutenant Kenneth McKenzie. Why don't you rise, Lieutenant and tell us a little bit about yourself - where you come from and who you are." All eyes turned in his direction.

McKenzie stood up. "Yes, sir. I have to say first that two nights ago, I was sleeping in the dirt up near the Cambodian border and tonight is a bit overwhelming." There were a few sporadic laughs and a couple hoo-rahs around the table.

"I grew up along the Columbia River in Oregon and attended Boise Junior College in Idaho until I enlisted January 6, 1967. I have a brother serving in the Navy, who, at this very moment, is stationed off the coast on the USS Decatur. I graduated from OCS November 22, 1967 and volunteered to come to Vietnam early on one condition - that I be assigned to the First Air Cavalry Division. I should add that but for a very helpful Spec. Four at Cam Rahn Bay, I might not have gotten here. I look forward to being a part of Division Headquarters and hope that I can live up to this opportunity to be a part of your team."

"Gentlemen," General Forsythe rose to his feet. " A toast to Lieutenant McKenzie, our new Division Protocol Officer."

"Here, here!" the other officers said loudly as they stood and raised their wine glasses to McKenzie who was sure his face was turning red at that moment. He thanked everyone, glad to have it over and amazed at how he had just been greeted. Several officers, who had ignored him before, reached across the table and shook his hand.

General Firby then rose to say goodbye to his aide-de-camp, Lieutenant Grimley, who was going home. Blain had prepared a black lacquered piece of helicopter tail rotor blade he told McKenzie was always presented to departing Division staff members. Glued onto the surface was a brass map of Vietnam, a First Cav patch and a brass square with the recipient's name, rank and dates of service.

Just as General Firby began his speech, a loud concussion shook the walls. Everyone ducked and waited. After a few minutes, General Forsythe rose with his steel pot in place and said with a laugh, "Let's try this one more time." It was not to be. The first explosion was followed by a barrage of incoming mortar rounds and rockets. General Forsythe led a mad dash out the back door to the cement bunker behind headquarters and the rest followed, according to rank.

THE GENERAL'S BUNKER

Rockets and mortars were landing everywhere inside the compound. Artillery batteries returned fire. Off in the distance, several helicopter gun ships fired mini-guns and rockets. The Division officers gathered on either side of the bunker to avoid any down blast which might come from the stairwell. Bad design, McKenzie thought. He had to pee when he came in and it was becoming critical. He waited for someone to say it was time to leave. The shelling appeared to be over.

~~

"How long they gonna wait? Nothing has landed for at least ten minutes," he said to Eagleton.

"Until the General decides its safe."

"If I don't pee, I'm gonna wet my pants. Do you think anyone would care if I make a run for that latrine outside?"

"Go for it." Eagleton chuckles and pats McKenzie on the back.

Conversation is loud as groups of officers pass the time. No one is watching the door. McKenzie eases over, places his right foot on the first step and listens. Still no incoming. Out the door he springs, running up the stairs, across an area of sparse grass to a graveled walkway and into the latrine.

He steps up to the first urinal and lets fly, wondering how many others in the bunker were wishing they could get some relief. Once he starts and the dam has burst, he isn't going to be able to stop. It goes on and on, making him nervous. He reaches down to button up and at the same time, hears the familiar high pitched whine of an incoming B-40 rocket headed in his direction.

He turns and jumps to the ground without touching the stairs and races toward the bunker. The distinctive scream of the rocket sounds right overhead as he dives head first into the opening. An immediate loud explosion and shower of wood and shrapnel hits the steps telling him the latrine has been hit. He lands hard on the bunker's cement stairs and rolls onto the dirt floor. His right arm takes most of the hit. He gets to his feet and finds he is looking directly into General Forsythe's smiling face.

"You're not going to last long around here like that, Lieutenant. Are you hurt?"

"No sir. I had to pee really bad. I'm sorry, sir."

The general laughs with his head back. He puts his arm around McKenzie's shoulders.

"Next time, I prefer to have my protocol officer pee in the corner rather than get killed. That's an order, son. More than a few of us have had to pee in this bunker during an attack. Are we clear?"

"Yes, sir."

General Forsythe declared it was time to leave and walked up the stairs and over to the damaged latrine. He turned around to McKenzie.

"Looks like you moved just right," he said with a smile.

It was almost twenty-three hundred hours when McKenzie finally crawled into his bunkered cot. The command group had gone back to the General's mess and finished the presentation before retreating to the bar for those who needed to calm their nerves. McKenzie had a couple more double gin and tonics. The rocket had hit the very urinal he was standing in front of. He laid his head on the pillow and was instantly asleep.

He woke up right at two thirty, one of the times he liked to walk the perimeter in the field and wandered over to the Division TOC, or tactical operating center, where all the units in the field were constantly being monitored. One radio was on speaker and several officers were standing around it. To his surprise, it was Charlie Company, First of the Fifth, which had linked up earlier in the day with one of Echo's long range patrols after they reported a large unit of NVA moving fast across the border. He saw the faces of his men out there in the field.

The combined units had set up a large scale ambush directly in the enemy's path along side a paved road near the Fishhook and sprung it about sixteen hundred. They were in contact with approximately two companies. Artillery night flares were keeping the area lit up and gun ships were on station but the enemy was probing and trying to find their weak points. Conversation on the radio was frantic as Third Platoon recoiled a succession of counter attacks.

"How are they doing?" McKenzie said to Major Hurst, the Assistant G-3 or operations officer, who wasn't usually in the TOC at this time of night.

"They're holding their own right now but we're keeping an eye on the situation. We've detected more movement across the border and there could be enemy reinforcements moving in. You know these guys?" Major Hurst said.

"That's my old unit," McKenzie's voice weakened when he said it causing the major to look at him again. He could feel the elephant on his chest.

"They sound like a good unit, Lieutenant. They don't seem panicked at all and we've requested Puff but it may not be there for another hour. Right now, the artillery and air support is doing a good job."

Just as the Major finished bringing McKenzie up to date, Black Knight came on the radio telling Captain Sheldon to move

First Platoon onto the road and drive directly into the enemies flank. Major Hurst grabbed a map and looked close.

"How the hell does he know where the enemy is?" he said out loud but to himself. McKenzie's heart was beating so fast he could feel it jump. He wanted to tell the major what a lunatic Fishmuth was. The exchange between Black Knight and Captain Sheldon began to heat up when he said the road wasn't where the most pressure was coming from. Captain Sheldon sounded close to telling Colonel Fishmuth he would not follow orders when Major Hurst reached down and grabbed the handset.

"Black Knight Six, this is Yellow Horse Three One, Over."

"Yellow Horse Three One, this is Black Knight Six, Over."

"Black Knight! We have Puff coming. I would recommend no movement down that road at this time. Over."

A terse, "Roger that, Out," came back.

The radio was silent for a few moments before Captain Sheldon began to communicate again with his platoon leaders. Puff came on station within thirty minutes and did what Puff could do - it put out a devastating curtain of mini-gun fire raining down on the NVA like a violent hail storm in the Midwest. McKenzie grinned. Contact was broken. He left the bunker around four in the morning and fell asleep wishing a rocket had brought down Black Knight's helicopter.

When he checked on Charlie Company in the morning, he learned they had suffered only one KIA and three WIA but counted over 30 enemy dead with multiple blood trails. They had been lucky. McKenzie seethed all day, unable to rid his memory of that voice, that Battalion Commander flying around over a fire fight, trying to interject himself where he couldn't see or assess anything.

He was eager for a drink by the time he went to the General's Mess and pounded down three gin and tonics before dinner. He headed for the officer's club after dinner intent on drowning out the memory, afraid of the thoughts he was having.

Captain Wassen, the Headquarters Company Commander, was sitting next to a window by himself and waived him over. He was an unpretentious man - easy to talk to. McKenzie had met him the day before when he'd wandered down to the Division publication office looking for a few past copies of the Division magazine. McKenzie was venting before long.

"You ever hear of Lieutenant Colonel Fishmuth, the battalion commander for First of the Fifth? Whatever you might have heard, it ain't half of what that idiot does. I spent six months in the field with him and I don't know where he got his training but he couldn't hit his ass with either hand if his life depended on it."

Captain Wassen did not respond. He was sitting with his chair tipped onto the back legs, his boots resting on the table. He was a good listener, the kind that would nod but not say anything.

"You know what that asshole did to me? My captain wrote me up for a Silver Star, which was awarded but never presented to me. I didn't even know about it until I picked up my orders to come here." McKenzie took a long drink of his gin and tonic and examined the glass to see if he needed a refill. Captain Wassen took his feet off the table and leaned forward.

"You got a Silver Star?" he said.

"Yea, for something I did when we got ambushed. What a bunch of shit, right?"

"You don't want it?" he said to McKenzie.

"I didn't say that. I mean Fishmuth disliked me so much, he decided not to award it to me in a proper ceremony. We had many ceremonies where he could have. I read the orders. It was approved last August. This snot nosed Spec. Four stuffed it into my travel envelope when I was transferred here. That's how I found out. Nice huh?"

McKenzie was feeling the effects of this drinking and decided he better leave. He apologized to the captain for spouting off but said he couldn't help it. He was pissed. Captain Wassen laughed and told him to sleep it off. It was just part of the military, he told McKenzie. "Its FUBAR, you know, Fucked Up Beyond All Repair."

The next two weeks flew by in a blur. Eagleton left amid fond wishes for good health and a long life. His goodbye dinner was not as exciting as the last one. Most immediate on the calendar of events was the upcoming Command Briefing at the end of the month. Eagleton had explained that once a month, battalion and brigade commanders were summoned to Division for a command briefing. It was meant to be a "lets get everyone on the same page" meeting and it was filled with protocol.

Eagleton worked hard with McKenzie before he left setting up the lunch and ensuring there were enough vehicles to transport all senior officers who always seemed to fly in at once. "Calls come in on the Division frequency and it's protocol's job to keep ahead of the traffic," he'd said.

"After lunch, the officers walk over to the command bunker and wait. When everyone's in place, all three generals walk in ceremoniously, the officers are called to attention and the briefing begins.

It's up to protocol to sit everyone and signal the aides who notify the generals. There's a certain timing to the whole thing and the Generals," Eagleton said for the third time, "do not like screw ups."

LONG NIGHT

Daily life grew hectic but McKenzie was learning the job. He'd heard that Colonel Fishmuth was finally out of the field and given a rear job somewhere at Brigade. He thought about finding out where.

On the Twenty Second of January, a bright, full moon hung loosely above the pagoda looking Vietnamese school located just outside the compound. McKenzie had just exited the General's mess and stopped to look at it. He remembered those many nights on ambush when the full moon was both a hindrance and a help. Faces of dead soldiers - Buggs, Wright and the rest, flashed before his eyes like an old fashioned Kodak View Master. It was happening more often. He walked back to his barracks feeling light headed and climbed the five stairs.

It had been a sober night for a change. He's had only one scotch early in the evening. He had to be on his best behavior as he was the assigned escort for two Red Cross Donut Dollies invited to the General's Mess once a month. Stagnant air wrapped around him as he sat on the edge of his bunk, removed his fatigue shirt and pants, turned on the fan and slid backwards onto his bed. It was early but maybe it was a good time to write his wife about R & R. He would try to call her from the MARS satellite station later in the week.

A loud concussion woke him from a vivid dream walking along the trail outside LZ Barbara. He'd fallen asleep without writing the letter. He rolled off the cot and dropped onto the floor next to the sand filled ammo boxes to his right. He was intent on going back to sleep but this was not just harassing incoming. Mortar rounds and rockets slammed into the ground all over the compound as if they had been fired simultaneously. A huge explosion to the South shook his building. It sounded like a direct hit on a nearby barrack.

He crawled backward toward the door and looked out in the direction of the blast. Shit! It was the barrack where most of the General's drivers and assistants slept. He pulled on his pants while sitting, slipped on his boots and grabbed a dry tee shirt on his way out the door. McKenzie cleared the stairs and ran toward the barracks.

The rocket had hit the center of the roof sending sheet metal and shrapnel down onto several men and caving in the North wall. He found Waller, General Shadwick's driver first. He was KIA. Adams had been hit in the gut by shrapnel and was crawling on his back toward McKenzie, trailing a smear of red blood. Several others were moaning but he could not see them under the debris. McKenzie rolled Adams over, waded up his tee shirt and pressed it over the gaping wound. He pulled a nearby blanket off a bunk to put under Adams head. Someone behind him shouted.

"How many we got here?"

It was Major Rawlins, the intelligence officer from Second of the Seventh, who had come in from R & R earlier and did not have time to catch a bird out to LZ Brandy where his battalion was. Blain had given him a cot further down toward Headquarters.

~~

"Four, maybe five. I can't tell," McKenzie said. "There's a jeep over at my office and a litter inside the door. If you can stay here and do what you can, I'll go get the jeep so we can move people toward the medical bunker."

"Go, Lieutenant! I'll be here."

McKenzie races across the compound as mortar rounds and rockets continue to land back and forth across the compound. Machine guns fire wobbly strings of tracer laced bullets out from the perimeter. A rocket lands in the area of the General's trailers which are heavily bunkered. McKenzie opens the door to his office, reaches around the corner, grabs the litter, spins around and heads for the jeep, placing the litter on the back seat.

A mortar round slams into the road just beyond the empty guard shack. McKenzie guns the jeep backwards, spinning the wheels and flies across the parking area, hitting a log that makes the jeep co-hop like a skittery horse. Luckily, he has both hands on the thin steering wheel when his butt levitates off the flat plastic driver's seat. He aims for a walk way, straddling it with the wheels and slides to a stop just outside the barrack door. He grabs the litter and runs inside.

Major Rawlins has moved the four wounded closer to the door. Adams is clearly the most serious. Two other soldiers are helping administer first aid. The Major sits holding the shirt compress over Adam's stomach. McKenzie steps around to Adam's feet and they lift him onto the litter. He looks back at the soldiers.

"You guys OK?" he says.

"Yea, LT. You get Adams over to the Doc and we'll hold down the fort."

"We'll be right back," McKenzie says.

Major Rawlins sits backwards in the jeep steadying the litter as McKenzie drives cross country, around several barracks to the back of Division and onto the road. He stops in front of a huge, black bunker with a large red cross on the side, jumps out and grabs the pole ends of the litter on his side. They lift Adams up over the back seat and carry him inside and down a long corridor to a large room. One of the medics turns, almost in slow motion and points to an empty operating table. There are other casualties already in the bunker and the atmosphere is chaotic.

Rawlins leads the way as they run back outside and jump into the jeep. Helicopter gun ships piss red mini-gun tracers to the West but new rockets come in from the South. Mortar crews inside the perimeter pop rounds back and flares drift down in two places. An incoming mortar round lands somewhere behind the jeep as they drive around to the collapsed barrack.

They agree on the way back they should try to get all three of the remaining wounded into the jeep at one time. One is Smith, an aide to General Forsythe. He has lost his left ear and is bleeding badly. The other two are cooks or servers in the General's mess. The smell of thick blood makes McKenzie's nose react. It's the tanginess that always gets to him as if he can smell the iron in a man's blood.

Bork, one of the cooks, sits holding his right arm which has two field bandages above his elbow. Weston, the other cook, has a long, open gash on his right thigh, too big to cover and bright, torn muscle is sticking out around a tied on bandage. There is no morphine and all three are suffering. Smith has begun to cry softly.

They put Weston in the front passenger seat and Major Rawlins sits in back between Smith and Bork, one arm around each, holding them. McKenzie eases the jeep forward trying not to jostle his passengers. A mortar round explodes around the corner of Division. Then another and another. They are being walked in a straight line toward the jeep. McKenzie slams the gear shift back and pops the clutch. Driving backwards, he heads around the side of the mess, to the back of the building where the kitchen is and spins them toward the parking lot. He hits the parking lot log before he can stop and Bork is tossed from the jeep. Rawlins manages to hold on to Smith.

Another mortar round lands across the field close to the Vietnamese school. McKenzie helps Bork back into the jeep. His bandage has come loose and the wound is now full of dirt. He holds it on with his other hand and looks at McKenzie without accusation. Loose tie strings dangle down acting like a wick from which blood drips onto the seat. His arm was broken initially. The lower piece of bone has separated and now sticks upwards, at an angle, out of the bandage. He's in agony but silent.

McKenzie gets the jeep turned around, skirts the log and eases up a small incline to the road. A rocket lands ahead of them about one hundred meters sending small fragments and dirt against the jeep window. He jams down hard on the accelerator, swerving to the left of the impact hole.

After transferring the three soldiers to the care of medics inside the bunker, they return to the barrack area in search of other casualties. They find one other man, two buildings away, unconscious under his bunk pinned under a collapsed wall. Rawlins carries him outside in his arms and holds him on his lap as they return to the medical bunker.

The incoming finally stops. Off in the distance, small arms fire continues near the perimeter and several Cobras hit the tree line to the West. The full moon has moved across a cloudless sky, sending out familiar long shadows like thin fingers on an old woman. McKenzie parks the jeep outside Protocol and offers the major a cup of cold, Jack Daniel coffee.

They sat inside for an hour and talked about the war. Major Rawlins was in for the long haul. He had spent one tour as a company commander with the Ninth Infantry and was about to extend his current tour. Unmarried, the Army was his life.

Battlefield promotions were available and he wanted to command a battalion. It was good he'd had direct combat experience, McKenzie told him.

He asked him if he'd ever heard of Colonel Fishmuth. He hadn't. When the major heard some of the incidents McKenzie related, he did not react. He sat silently sipping his strong coffee. He appeared to be uncomfortable hearing a junior officer criticize a superior but McKenzie felt compelled to talk about it. His thoughts had become more hateful once he knew Black Knight might be where he could get to him. Images of Fishmuth dead or bleeding frequented his dreams. Finally, when Major Rawlins was about to leave, after thanking McKenzie for the libation, he lowered his chin and looked with raised eyebrows.

"Lieutenant, you made it through six months of combat. Were you wounded?"

"No, sir. I was lucky," McKenzie said wondering why he had asked.

"Well, this was good work tonight. I don't know if you intend to stay in the military or not but the chain of command is a jealous mistress. She's fickle and she demands to be followed. Your job is to figure out how to live with her and keep her happy. Combat is confusing. You know that. The job gets done when junior officers follow orders even when they have to be creative about it. Sounds like you did that. Thanks for the coffee."

There was no condemnation of either Fishmuth or McKenzie in what he said. His words did not assuage the anger inside McKenzie but it was a dose of reality from a senior officer. They shook hands and wished each other good luck.

CHAPTER 13 - LT. COLONEL FISHMUTH
(JANUARY 23, 1969 - 145 AND A WAKE UP)

Two other soldiers died the night before. They were killed in their sleep several barracks farther to the South. The mortars and rockets had rained down like a sudden hail storm pushed ahead by a Kansas tornado. They never had a chance. The wounded men McKenzie and Major Rawlins transported all survived.

Blain said one of the dead was supposed to go home in a week. McKenzie sat and listened to Blain tell about the man who was married and had a new baby boy born six months after he'd arrived in Vietnam. Blain folded his arms across his chest to tell the story, then uncrossed them and wiped a tear that had welled up and lay on the crest of his lower right eye lid.

He was headed for Saigon to pick up several more brass plates to put on the iconic plaques for command staff who were ending their tours. He excused himself to pack. McKenzie dropped him off at the helipad an hour later and returned to his office to fine tune his preparation for the upcoming Command Briefing. He was startled from concentration by a deep, command voice coming from the hall doorway.

LIEUTENANT COLONEL MONROE
"You Lieutenant McKenzie?"

A big man with a handle bar mustache wearing a black First Cavalry Stetson hat stood in the doorway. On the hat was a gold braid and tassels which lay on the brim and the silver oak leaf cluster of a lieutenant colonel. McKenzie jumped up.

"Yes, sir. May I help you?"

"I hope so, Lieutenant. I understand you were with Major Rawlins last night?"

"Yes, sir. I was. Is he OK?"

"Of course. I understand you and he were the ones who pulled those kids out of the barracks and drove them through the attack last night to the surgical bunker."

"Yes, sir. Why? Is there something wrong?"

"Hell, no! That was quite a thing you two did, driving through those mortars and rockets to save those kids."

"Thank you, sir. You need a ride? I have a jeep if you need to catch a bird."

"You trying to get rid of me, Lieutenant?" he said followed by a deep laugh, the kind people in charge give when they want their subordinates to know they've made a funny.

The name above his left pocket was Monroe. Major Rawlins had talked about his battalion commander, Colonel Monroe, the night before with great affection. He told stories about the Colonel landing his helicopter more than once to get into the middle of a fire fight and lead his troops with amazing bravery.

His uniform was not the starched, clean uniform of a pretend commander. It was faded and rumpled. He wore a brown shoulder holster with a captured Chinese pistol in it, the red star on the handle. A small baseball grenade hung suspended from his ammo belt. His boots were old and scuffed and his square jaw supported a couple days growth. His head was shaved close on the sides, making his ears look bigger.

"No, sir. What can I do for you, sir?" McKenzie said.

The Colonel, who had not yet moved from the doorway, now casually walked over to a chair next to the desk, took off his hat and set it upside down. The Stetson was brushed clean and well cared for. He motioned for McKenzie to sit down, then stoked his waxy mustache to fine points with both hands.

"I have a proposition, Lieutenant. I think what you and Major Rawlins did last night was beyond the call of duty. Its the kind of thing they give medals for. The problem is, I'm getting everything second hand from the guys in the barracks who came to help and the medics who saw you bring those fellows in aren't much help either except to say that two of them would have died without your quick reactions.

No one, however, knows what the two of you went through except you. So, here's my proposition. I want you to write up Major Rawlins for a bronze star and he's going to write you up for one. How does that sound?"

McKenzie's throat got dry and felt like it was trying to pull itself in tighter. He swallowed but the tightness held and his voice didn't work. He reached for the cold cup of coffee he'd been nursing and held the acrid fluid in his mouth before swallowing.

"Something the matter, Lieutenant?" Colonel Monroe said.

"Sir. I appreciate the thought but I don't think we did anything more than our duty. A soldier comes to the aide of his fellow soldiers. Leave no man behind, right? I wouldn't feel right about trading medal recommendations with Major Rawlins when I saw things done every day in the field by soldiers that took more courage than what we did and they weren't given any medals."

"I understand your feelings but Lieutenant, are you telling me you don't want a medal for what you did?"

"No, sir. I don't. I think I would feel bad if I got one."

"Well, I'll be damned." The Colonel stood up and swooped up his Stetson by the brim and placed it gently on his head with both hands to square it.

"It is my opinion you both deserve a medal and I'm the one who gets to decide. Not you. Good day, Lieutenant."

ANGER

McKenzie stood up and saluted as Colonel Monroe turned and swirled out the door like an Oklahoma dust storm. He sat down feeling as if the room had just had the air sucked out of it. Was he right or wrong to say what he did? He didn't know any more. He didn't seem to be able to keep his mouth shut when he should.

He'd started to gain weight from the alcohol and diet of rich food at the General's mess. His shirts were getting tight but the more he took advantage of the cushy surroundings, the more he suffered and thus, the more he drank. He felt guilty that his men were laying in the dirt, drinking canister water and eating C-rations, hoping the next day would not be their last. He had become a familiar sight at the command bunker, waking up every night around two thirty in the morning.

His dreams were becoming more vivid. They were full of Sergeant Smythe twirling in the air as he was lifted up through the trees or McKenzie hiding behind those Banyan tree flare roots screaming into the radio for his own helicopter to quit firing. At other times, he would see those three NVA faces caught at first light, walking into First Platoon's ambush or relive the killing tail of the crashing log bird as it swung around and decapitated Buggs. There were times he thought sure he could hear Bevans screaming for help. Over and over, the dreams came at him the same way.

Even more often, he saw the bloody hole in the back of White's neck. He needed alcohol so that he could get to sleep. In his dreams, his RTO would show up and shake him for guard duty but when he awoke, it was always another soldier in his barracks shaking him to stop the noise he was making.

His memories were becoming confused. He could remember every minute of the first three months but only sporadic scenes of the last three in the field. His mind had reached a saturation level and there were things he could not recall. He'd kept a journal but when he read through it to see if he was going crazy, he could not bring back some of the memories. He decided it was time to find the MARS station and call his wife to plan for an R & R in Hawaii.

MARS STATION

He went through his check list for the Command Briefing one more time and then notified the duty officer he would be gone for a while and that Blain was in Saigon. He got directions to the

MARS station over by the engineer company. What he saw minutes later was not encouraging.

A long line extended out the door of a Quonset hut, a structure named for the town where they were first made. It was crowned by a blur of antennas. The air inside was bitter with a hot, canvas smell from layers of tent sections on the floor to cover the ubiquitous red dust. He asked a PFC what the procedure was. One phone was specifically designated for officers but there were six others in line ahead of him. He put his name on the sign up sheet and sat down at the end of a row of metal chairs full of waiting officers. At least he was out of the sun.

The whole set up was ingenious. Radio operators would contact a civilian ham radio volunteer in the states and they in turn would place a collect call to a soldier's family or sweetheart and patch the soldier through. Another example of necessity being the motherhood of invention. Each man was limited to a five minute conversation but it was obviously difficult to enforce and the enlisted men running the radios appeared tolerant. McKenzie decided to call his Dad instead.

The operator asked if his Dad would accept the collect call and then pointed to McKenzie who picked up the receiver.

"Hello?" The voice sounded so far away and weak for his Dad.

"Dad? This is Kenneth. Can you hear me OK?"

"Yes, son, I can hear you. Why are you calling? Are you all right?" his Dad said in a voice that was apprehensive.

McKenzie had listened to his Dad's beautiful tenor voice all his life. His Dad would sing at weddings or funerals or in the

Congregational Church on Sunday. He was the Elks Club choir leader and led lunch time songs at the Lions Club. Even when he spoke, the rich timber was there. He couldn't have lost it in the past year.

"Yes, Dad. I just decided to call. How are you?"

"I'm fine. You're not hurt are you?" His Dad's voice still sounded thin and breathy. McKenzie had not meant to scare him but he had.

After he assured his Dad he was not wounded, the strong voice gradually began to assert itself across the miles. There was always a sort of song in the way his Dad talked with clear enunciation and more up and down range than most people. McKenzie listened to his Dad talk about the town, telling him about some of his friends and the football team. It was surprising how clearly he could see it all. Even more surprising how foreign it seemed.

They talked about buying his Dad some camera equipment from the PX where the prices were very good. The operator indicated there was only one minute to go. McKenzie had written his Dad about Colonel Fishmuth. Even though his Dad was a pacifist, raised in a Quaker family, he had been the one person McKenzie shared every detail of combat with in his letters. He couldn't tell his wife and he didn't want to worry his brother, so he'd only told his Dad.

Although he'd probably worried the old man half to death, not once had his Dad offered advice or even acknowledged what he'd been told. He just absorbed it. His return letters were always up beat. Occasionally, he would write that he had seen a TV news report about the First Cav.

"Dad, do you remember what I wrote you about Colonel Fishmuth? I can't let it go. I'm having dreams and I don't know what to do." McKenzie looked up to see if the operator was listening to him. He wasn't.

His Dad was silent. Quakers believed that each man or woman had to decide for themselves what was right and what they believed in. McKenzie heard him take a deep breath and slowly exhale.

"Just remember, son," he said. "Each person is different. You have no idea what pressures the Colonel may have been experiencing and its something you don't need to bring home." That was it. That was all he said.

"Thanks, Dad. I'll be home in June and if I get R & R in Hawaii, I'll call."

"OK, son. Thanks for calling. Anyone you want me to say hello to?"

McKenzie asked him to call his wife and tell her he would try to call within a few days. "And, call Coach Tucker," he said. "Tell him I'm OK."

Numb, he walked out into the bright sunlight. His head felt hollow like an empty coconut, tapped and drained. If he was going on R & R, he would have to get to it. He talked to his wife two days later and confirmed a date in late April when they would meet in Hawaii at Fort DeRussy, situated close to Waikiki Beach. He would be there a week. His R & R was approved but the Chief of Staff reminded him that Blain would be going home in March and a replacement would need to be trained. He wanted no glitches while McKenzie was gone.

BLAIN

The discussion about Blain gave him a case of stomach pains because his sometime errant clerk was overdue. McKenzie decided to go look for him. He called a high school buddy who he'd found out was stationed in Saigon. Ron Hillman was a sort of King Rat, able to get whatever a person needed including transportation. He would know the most likely places GI's hung out. McKenzie gave him the name and address of the shop where Blain had the brass plates made. Ron knew exactly where that was.

McKenzie had not been in a helicopter since December, twenty-fourth. An unexpected shot of panic took his breath away when the Huey lifted off. The door gunner looked down at McKenzie's hands gripping the metal rungs on the seat. A spinning tail rotor blade flashed across his mind and bodies flew off the hillside in all directions. He saw Buggs' head again when he closed his eyes.

The pilot flew along the Saigon River full of cigar shaped boats, black with white tips, that reminded him of frail Marigold seeds, the kind his Mother would plant in her garden to ward off aphids. He was starting to think of home but he was not ready to go yet. He hadn't decided what to do about Colonel Fishmuth.

The helicopter banked right and flew over rows of small metal houses lining dirt streets on the outskirts of Saigon, then past stucco houses with balconies and then larger hotels and finally, the US Embassy, all white and gated, still showing burn scars on the front lawn from when it was attacked during Tet in February, 1968.

The pilot dipped the front end to drop lower, then flared back and settled down at Ton Son Nut Air Base. McKenzie spotted Ron standing next to a deuce and a half truck, his hair longer than regulation and a wide toothy grin below a Fu Manchu mustache. Ron was that way. He was the life of the party in high school and it often appeared rules did not pertain to him.

"Hey, you old son-of-a-bitch, how the hell are you?" he said as McKenzie walked up.

"I'm OK. How the hell do you get away with that hair and mustache?" McKenzie said as he reached out to shake Ron's hand but instead, got a full body hug.

"You forget. I'm not regular GI like you, my man. Do you want me to call you sir?"

"No. I don't want you to call me sir, I just want to go and look for my clerk. I would like to be back in Phuoc Vinh by evening."

"No can do, Kenny, boy. First, I got something to show you and that takes military priority. It sounds like your clerk is shacked up anyway and isn't going to be hard to find. On the other hand, he might already be headed home and you passed each other in the air. Either way, you're gonna spend the night with a buddy aren't you?"

SAIGON ROADS

McKenzie's arguments were in vain and soon Ron had launched the truck onto an oiled dirt road, headed for Saigon.

Local civilians packed the main area of the road with bicycles and mopeds and a few small motorcycles. Everyone seemed to be moving in both directions without any sense of a center line or rules of the road. Ron dove into the maelstrom as if it wasn't there. McKenzie held his breath as people moved out of the way in an uncanny prediction of what Ron was going to do next. Near misses were not just close, they were too close. McKenzie was forced to drop his eyes and not watch.

When Ron started honking his horn. McKenzie looked up. They were entering a traffic circle filled with hundreds of travelers moving in a large circle, like a school of fish. Begrudgingly, bikes and motorcycles got out of the way until, after what seemed like an eternity, the truck emerged on the other side and shot down another oiled road out of Saigon.

Ron laughed fiendishly and pressed harder on the gas. "I'm told the French designed that traffic circle to resemble the one in Paris," he told McKenzie.

Fifteen minutes later they pulled up along side two armored personnel carriers on the other side of the air field where McKenzie had just landed. Sitting inside the first one was Ben Brown, another high school classmate.

For an hour, they drank beer the soldiers had stashed inside their personnel carriers and talked of home. Ben was one of those guys who had an infectious smile and always seemed happy but McKenzie kept thinking; 'Shit! Don't relax. Don't let it penetrate too deeply. Don't go home too early.'

The visit ended when the APC radio reported someone trying to get through the airfield fence down the line and the two vehicles rumbled off with Ben poking his head through the hatch and waving. Dust billowed up from the tracks like smoke from a prairie grass fire as Ben disappeared behind it.

"You wanna go find your man, Kenny?" Ron said.

"Yea. I'd feel a lot better if I had him in tow, even if I decided to stay at your place tonight."

The ride back into Saigon was just as harrowing. It was all a choreographed dance between bicycle riders leaning out of the way at the last minute and mopeds racing across the truck's path as if daring Ron to hit them. Occasionally, they would approach a slow moving Pedi cab and Ron would serve around it, mysteriously clearing others out of his path. By the time they reached Tudo Street, where most GIs hung out, McKenzie was a wreck and eager to stand on solid ground.

TIKI LOUNGE

They had stopped by the brass shop on the way in and picked up the ordered pieces. The owner said Blain had once shown him a picture of a bar girl at the Tiki Lounge. McKenzie was starting to get angry at the thought of Blain not caring about the consequences of his little AWOL. The plaques were due for presentation in two days.

They walked into the Tiki Lounge. It was full of soldiers, some in uniform, others in civilian clothes. A three piece Philippine band was playing rock and roll and bar girls were everywhere, dressed in either tight skirts slit to the hip or go-go shorts. Some wore halter tops squeezed tight to lift their tiny breasts, others wore tight blouses with no bras. Paper Chinese decorations hung from the ceiling where three large fans pushed at the hot air. McKenzie walked among the tables looking at each soldier.

Drunk soldiers looked back and bar girls tried to get his attention. An old Mama San came out of the back room and walked up to him with a big smile full of black teeth from chewing Beetle nut and smelling of cheap perfume.

"You look for girl, GI? I have beau coup girls, all number one. Make you very happy," she said, grabbing his arm.

"No. I'm looking for a soldier named Blain. You know him?", McKenzie said continuing to look around at different tables.

"Yes, Yes, I know him very well. He upstairs with one my best girls. He like her very much. You no bother him!" she said, pushing McKenzie with both hands on his chest.

"Just tell me where he is and I'll go get him," McKenzie said standing firm and looking down into her painted face.

"No! You stay here. I go," she said and stuck a fist up into McKenzie's face before turning around and walking over to the stairway next to the bar. He watched her go up slowly and stop at the top to look back before she disappeared around the corner. McKenzie moved quickly to the stairs. A small Vietnamese man tried to stop him at the bottom but he brushed him aside and bounded two steps at a time up to the hallway. Ron yelled something at McKenzie but it was not clear until a hand grabbed him on the right shoulder.

~~

McKenzie turns around and the small man he had pushed away, is waving a knife in his face and yelling in Vietnamese. McKenzie side kicks the man's feet out from under him and lands with a knee in his chest. The knife slides across the floor. McKenzie pulls out the pistol he'd brought and jams it under the man's chin as he pulls him to his feet.

Behind him, the Mama San screams in Vietnamese and somewhere down the hall he hears Blain's voice. McKenzie walks down the hall pushing the small man in front and looks in the third room on the right where he sees Blain laying naked on a bed covered by a dirty sheet. Next to the bed is an opium pipe surrounded by military pay certificates, some scattered on the floor. A naked girl stands away holding a short towel in front.

"Hey, LT. How ya doing?", Blain says looking through eyes that are half closed and foggy. He tries to raise up on one elbow but falls back.

Mama San comes around McKenzie's right side, looks at the man who's being held by the shirt and then at the gun.

"You go now, please," she says. "I no like trouble. You take Blain." She goes over and pulls Blain to his feet and helps him get dressed. "Pick up all the money and put it in Blain's pocket," McKenzie says. Ron steps into the room.

"We better get the hell out of here before the MPs or worse, the White Mice show up. Come on. Now!", he says, grabbing McKenzie by the arm which is still holding the small man. What he is saying makes sense because the White Mice, if they arrive, are a Vietnamese paramilitary force of questionable authority known to be quite vicious in these kinds of circumstances.

"Mama San, Blain's not coming back, ever. You stay here until we get out the door or there will be real trouble," McKenzie says as he pushes the little man to her and backs out the door, pulling Blain. Ron has the truck started by the time McKenzie gets downstairs and out the door. He opens the passenger door, shoves Blain inside and jumps in. Ron hits the accelerator.

"Jesus, Kenny. Why didn't you tell me you were going in there like Audie Murphy? Man, you been in the jungle too long. You scared the shit out of me. I don't think we made any friends in there."

McKenzie looks at his friend, feeling evil and angry inside. "Hey! I didn't trust that old crow. Last thing I wanted was for them to scoot Blain out the back door. I'm glad I went up there. Look at him."

Blain tried to sit up a little straighter. He looked around with his mouth open, drool running down his chin. He smelled rank. Ron said that was the opium on his breath. After another death defying ride, they pulled up to Ron's apartment house and took Blain upstairs, laying him out on a couch by the air conditioner. He was immediately asleep and began snoring, which McKenzie took as a good sign.

The two old friends from long ago shared coffee while Ron explained how he had managed to develop an intricate system of barter. Technically, his job was clerk for a communications unit but he had no intention of spending a year in Vietnam in uncomfortable surroundings. His company commander was willing to look the other way as long as Ron kept him in good booze. It was a foreign world to a boony rat.

McKenzie told Ron about Colonel Fishmuth and his growing obsession with somehow ending his existence. He said he knew the anger which had exploded at the Tiki Lounge was pent up rage but it had come from deep inside, instant and violent. It had controlled him and he was not sure when it would erupt again or what would trigger it.

"I really don't know what came over me. It felt like someone lit a fuse in my gut and I just exploded," he said.

"Kenny, Kenny, you're losing it, man." Ron said. "We got good times waitin for us back in the world. Don't screw it up now. You're almost home. Leave it alone."

It was good advice and McKenzie mulled it over the next morning as he and Blain flew back to Phuoc Vinh. Blain was shaky. He'd gone to Saigon with over a thousand dollars in military pay and most of it was gone. He had little memory of what had happened. It was a part of Vietnam not visible to the average grunt and McKenzie did not like seeing the crap. It made him feel even more angry. There were evil forces in the world and they were always trying to have their way. Why was it wrong to fight back?

COMMAND BRIEFING

Things gradually returned to normal. The plaque presentations went smoothly and by the next Thursday, the day before the command briefing, Blain was working hard under threat of a court martial if he made one false move. Brigade commanders came in early for dinner with the Generals. Battalion commanders would arrive in the morning. McKenzie walked into his office around twenty one hundred hours after going over seating arrangements in the command bunker. He sat down to look at the full list of incoming officers Blain had picked up from the Division Chief of Staff.

WHAT TO DO

To his surprise, Colonel Fishmuth was among those officers coming in for the briefing. Why? Colonel Fishmuth was no longer a battalion commander and as far as McKenzie knew, he had not been given an important brigade staff job. He wrote out a list of things for Blain to do during the briefing and headed for his bunk. He sat there for a long time cleaning the forty-five caliber pistol he'd taken to Saigon. He intentionally had not returned it to the armory.

It felt like he'd entered a new phase. Thoughts of combat were farther away during the day, pushed there by the endless details of his job. He was no longer willing to get as drunk as he had before. All he wanted at the end of the day was to crawl into his bunkered cot and go to sleep, the cool breeze of the fan blowing protectively over his body.

His fear seemed far away where he couldn't see it. Whenever a mortar round or rocket landed inside the perimeter, he would roll off his bunk onto the floor, his back against the sand filled ammo boxes and go back to sleep. Dreams still filled his nights and hung over him in the early morning of first light but they had transitioned away from combat to violent dreams of revenge.

At two thirty in the morning, he woke as usual. This time he had a craving for C-rations of all things. He knew that Barrett, General Forsythe's new driver, had a penchant for Cs and usually kept a stash near the door. Amazingly, when he found their barrack, Barrett and Wayson, General Shadwick's aide, were still up.

"So, what are you guys doing up?" he said as he stepped into the room.

"Hey, LT. We could ask you the same thing. Can't sleep?" Barrett said.

"Nope. I used to walk the perimeter every night about this time. Old habit. How about sharing some Cs?"

"What's it worth to you, LT?", said Wayson. "This is valuable shit, you know. We had to trade our whiskey to get it."

"Uh, huh, And where do I think you got the whiskey, Wayson? Wouldn't be the General's bar would it? I'll tell you what. You give me a can of ham and eggs and I'll forget the theft."

"LT! You hurt me. However, since you only want ham and eggs, I think we can make a deal. No one else will eat that shit anyway. Have all you want." Wayson tossed McKenzie a can he'd retrieved from under his cot.

"Oh, bullshit. I know, for a fact, you guys sit over here and eat Cs and tell war stories about your great exploits in the jungle all the time. You're just like every other boony rat, glad to be out but you think about going back. Right?"

Barrett leaned back, looking like he'd been punched. He was a good looking kid, handsome with a few freckles, sandy hair and an easy smile. He was the new leader of these guys having earned two Silver Stars and a Bronze Star for valor. He'd been wounded twice walking point. Suddenly, he looked like he needed his Mommy.

"I'll tell you what, LT. I can't sleep. Most nights I'm afraid to close my eyes. I lost some good buddies out there and I see their faces. How the hell am I going to go home and forget this place? I don't like to drink. I wish I did." His eyes were moist.

McKenzie looked at Wayson. "What about you?"

"It don't mean nothin," he said, not looking up.

Wayson had been wounded three times and wore a scar across his right cheek which was still slightly red. Blond, with a thin face and bucked teeth, he did not seem the infantry type.

McKenzie thanked them for the chow and left. He wasn't in any better condition and he sure as hell didn't have any magic words to soothe their inner wounds. He felt exactly like they did. The anger in his chest seemed to grow as he walked the compound for another hour. He needed to do something about Colonel Fishmuth.

COMMAND BUNKER

Battalion commanders with their operations officers and brigade commanders with their S-3s moved into the command bunker and found their places on the stair stepped seating. McKenzie stood by the door giving directions. He watched Fishmuth come in and look for a place to sit. The Sergeant Major stepped over and directed the Colonel down front where he looked a little out of place. Why was the man he despised so much here in this place of respect, where professional, competent officers directed and protected the Division? If he'd been wearing the pistol, McKenzie might have shot the man on the spot.

McKenzie was glaring at Fishmuth, unaware the room had gone quiet, when the Sergeant Major bellowed, "Attention!" The entire bunker of soldiers, full of the most senior officers in the Division, jumped to attention and looked in the direction of the entrance. In came General Forsythe, then Generals Firby and Shadwick. They were straight as pencils yet relaxed as only general officers can be. After all, McKenzie thought, they are in charge, aren't they? Instead of telling the room, "At ease," Major General Forsythe and his Assistant Division Commanders, did a right face and stood at attention in a line before the still standing audience.

Sergeant Major Easterly called out in a loud voice," Lieutenant McKenzie, front and center."

A wave of fright ran up the back of McKenzie's neck making him feel dizzy as he moved quickly to a place in front of the three general officers. Did someone report his angry comments about Colonel Fishmuth to the generals? Did he screw up the briefing preparation? General Forsythe looked past McKenzie to the officers still standing.

"The United States military has a very important tradition," he said in his most commanding voice. "Whenever a soldier is awarded a medal for bravery, that medal will be presented by a superior officer in a ceremony befitting the award."

He gave special emphasis to the word, will. "While serving as a platoon leader, First Lieutenant Kenneth McKenzie was awarded the Silver Star, the Army's third highest medal for bravery. Unfortunately, this medal was not properly presented. That is unacceptable gentlemen and today, we are going to correct that mistake. Sergeant Major, read the citation."

After the citation was read aloud, the Sergeant Major stepped forward with a black box, opened the top and handed a Silver Star to General Forsythe, who pinned it to the flap over McKenzie's left shirt pocket, shook his hand, congratulated him and stepped back, snapping to attention and saluting. McKenzie returned the salute.

Then the Sergeant Major called the name of Major Rawlings, who came forward and after the citations were read, General Forsythe pinned bronze stars with V on both McKenzie and Rawlings, stepped back and saluted. When Major Rawlings did an about face, McKenzie followed. The officers, still standing, began to clap. McKenzie looked at Colonel Fishmuth who's cheeks were deep red. Now he understood why the man was there. The Headquarters company commander must have informed someone about the silver star story and the General had taken direct action.

The briefing concluded two hours later. McKenzie stood by the door and waited for all senior officers to exit. Many stopped to shake his hand and congratulate him. Fishmuth managed to pass behind several officers who were talking to McKenzie but he saw him sneak out with his head down. General Forsythe's new aide, Captain Nevis, told McKenzie he would be expected to wear the medals to dinner that evening. Finally, when the room cleared, McKenzie sat down on the first row bench.

He was stunned. The anger had drained away like the boil on his arm - lanced and ready to heal. He didn't hate Fishmuth any more. The man had managed to climb the ladder to Lieutenant Colonel but had failed to see the wonderful examples of officers around him, failed to understand the bond between infantry officers and soldiers, failed to feel the gravity and honor of his command. His career was probably over. Even with that small amount of satisfaction, McKenzie wished he could see the Colonel's efficiency report. He imagined stinging words that would spell the end to his military career.

Blain came into the bunker and walked over to McKenzie, putting his hand on his bosses shoulder like a big brother.

"I knew about it before hand, sir. I've taken care of everything. All the air transportation is arranged. You go get ready for dinner and relax. I'll clean up here. Congratulations, sir. Its not every day a general pins medals on your chest."

McKenzie looked up at Blain who had that goofy grin he sometimes got when he'd done something good and wanted to be told about it. Sort of like a kid who's always getting into trouble but who decides to clean his room.

"You're a goof, aren't you? Thanks, Blain. That was real nice of you to take care of things. Frankly, I'm still in shock."

GOING HOME

In April, Blain went home and McKenzie arranged to met his wife, Molly in Honolulu for a week of R & R. The morning air was cool and the sky crystalline blue the day he left Phuoc Vinh in a helicopter, headed for Tan Son Nut Air Base. As the pilot lifted off the tarmac, McKenzie felt suddenly disoriented. Being in Vietnam, even after leaving the field, had its own cocoon effect. McKenzie had arrived in country rosy cheeked and young. The war had replaced his name with a number and then dirtied his soul and permanently carved images and emotions into every crevice of his brain. How was he going to explain himself to Molly? They'd only known each other for four months, married for two when he left.

The reality was he didn't want to leave Vietnam. Going back toward what - a vacuous world? There would be no way to explain it all.

The flight to Hawaii was interminable, filled with furtive sleep and dreams of having to protect Molly as they traveled through the back alleys of Honolulu for safety. He landed exhausted.

The plane full of soldiers exit onto an asphalt runway bathed in the early morning sun. McKenzie looks around for signs of trouble.

"C'mon, move it. There's a bus out front headed for Fort DeRussy where you all need to check in," a tan staff sergeant yells. He's dressed in a crisp, starched summer uniform and carrying a clip board.

The line of soldiers, carrying black army satchels and other make do luggage, snake through the airport, the staff sergeant in the lead. They climb into a green bus which looks more like a school bus than a Greyhound. McKenzie takes a seat next to a window. He looks for Hawaii but for the first several miles, there is no Hawaii. New and used car lots, full of shiny cars lit by strings of light bulbs, line both sides of the highway into town. His chest tightens. He realizes this is America. They've taken him back before he was ready. He feels a panic. He has no weapon.

The bus enters Honolulu and pulls into a parking lot next to a brown, flat military building with a sign that reads Fort DeRussy. The staff sergeant stands up next to the driver.

"Now, listen up. Here's what is going to happen. If you have family meeting you here, chances are they're already inside. Remember, you gotta sign in before you leave the building. One last thing. Welcome to Hawaii. Enjoy yourself," he says, smiling for the first time.

McKenzie steps off the bus into a day that has brightened under the sun rising over Waikiki Beach which lies just beyond the building. He can see early morning beach combers walking with heads down. A lone surfer glides toward the beach on a small wave. Up ahead, he can hear relatives greeting soldiers as they enter - screams and laughter and loud voices. He looks for Molly as he walks through the crowd.

He sees her. She's looking back past him toward the door. He walks up next to her and stops. She's more beautiful than he remembered. She turns her face and smiles. "Kenny," she whispers, tears already in her eyes. How will he ever leave her again and go back to Vietnam?

He'd returned from Hawaii in a much better state. Molly had held him when he needed it and they had slowly become reacquainted. He knew his job and he was able to relax without the constant anger fueling his mind and creating dreams of revenge. Until the day he received his medals, he had not known where his anger would take him. More than once he dreamed of Fishmuth crashing in his helicopter while pulling one of his stunts. Once, when it appeared the Colonel had survived the crash, McKenzie saw himself walk over and shoot him in the head. By the 17th of June, the day his plane departed Bien Hoa Air Base for home, he no longer thought about the man he'd put so much energy into hating. He wanted to go home.

After way too many numbing hours and one stop in Guam, one of the stewardesses spoke softly into the plane's intercom, announcing they would be landing in San Francisco in approximately thirty minutes. Next to McKenzie sat Lieutenant Kingman. They had seen each other the night before at the Bien Hoa officer's club and closed the place down, paying the Philippine band to sing 'Hey, Jude' and 'Danny Boy' over and over until they were the only two left. Although McKenzie had tried hard not to drink so much in the past two months, with Kingman there and the two of them finally going home, it seemed they could not drink enough.

Kingman was not the same man McKenzie had met in An Khe. He'd spent part of the year piloting a scout LOH and then managed to get himself transferred to a long range recon unit. The experience had left him prone to blank, silent stares. He had extended and would be going back after a thirty day leave. He would not talk about his year. He wore tattoos of a snake on one arm and a naked woman on the other. He was amazed that McKenzie had applied for an early out and would be returning to college that fall. It was apparent their only bond was being in Vietnam at the same time and surviving, nothing more. On the long flight home, conversation grew thin.

The plane descended through the clouds, coming in low over San Francisco Bay, just clearing the rip rap border before touching down on the runway. Everyone in the plane cheered as the pilot rolled toward the terminal. Military returns were required to exit directly onto the runway and walk across to the terminal. McKenzie walked down the steps, knelt down and kissed the ground. He wasn't the only one. Kingman was gone when he stood up.

He passed through customs and was processed by the military clearing officer before heading for the baggage area. There seemed to be condescension from those in control and he was easily rankled by it. He rode up an escalator and walked down a long corridor of white walls and polished floor. Everything felt bland and abnormally normal. People moved with oblivious lives. No one watched the war on TV monitors. He screamed at them in his head. He felt conspicuous in his summer uniform.

After retrieving his duffel bag, he needed to find the military transportation officer for help in catching a bus to San Diego where his Molly was waiting. He'd told her not to lose time from work, he would be OK. He needed help to locate a bus but after customs had made him feel like a second hand citizen, he wasn't going to take any more crap, from anyone.

He took another escalator down to the transportation level and turned right. He saw a couple walking toward him, both with long hair, barefoot and wearing the same long, tie dyed pull over shirts that looked to him like hippy muumuus. They stopped when they saw him and the boy pulled the girl over against the wall. McKenzie looked around to see if there was something going on behind him. There wasn't. He slowly walked toward the couple. The boy started yelling at McKenzie to get away from them and the girl began to cry. Damn! So this was how it was going to be.

S. Elliott Lawrence is a retired trial attorney who served with the 1st Air Cavalry Division in Vietnam from June, 1968 to June 1969 as an infantry platoon leader and as Division Protocol Officer. His short story, Hat Point Lookout, was published in a collection of short stories and poems published by the Library Association of Eastern Oregon, titled a Sense of Place.

29710537R00248

Made in the USA
San Bernardino, CA
17 March 2019